RANGER'S APPRENTICE

BOOK 9: HALT'S PERIL

RANGER'S APPRENTICE

BOOK 9: HALT'S PERIL

JOHN FLANAGAN

PHILOMEL BOOKS
AN IMPRINT OF PENGUIN GROUP (USA) INC.

First American Edition published 2010 by
PHILOMEL BOOKS
A division of Penguin Young Readers Group. Published by The Penguin Group.
Penguin Group (USA) Inc., 375 Hudson Street, New York, NY 10014, U.S.A.
Penguin Group (Canada), 90 Eglinton Avenue East, Suite 700, Toronto, Ontario M4P 2Y3, Canada
(a division of Pearson Penguin Canada Inc.).
Penguin Books Ltd, 80 Strand, London WC2R 0RL, England.
Penguin Ireland, 25 St. Stephen's Green, Dublin 2, Ireland (a division of Penguin Books Ltd).
Penguin Group (Australia), 250 Camberwell Road, Camberwell, Victoria 3124, Australia
(a division of Pearson Australia Group Pty Ltd).
Penguin Books India Pvt Ltd, 11 Community Centre, Panchsheel Park, New Delhi—110 017, India.
Penguin Group (NZ), 67 Apollo Drive, Rosedale, North Shore 0632, New Zealand
(a division of Pearson New Zealand Ltd).
Penguin Books (South Africa) (Pty) Ltd, 24 Sturdee Avenue, Rosebank, Johannesburg 2196, South Africa.
Penguin Books Ltd, Registered Offices: 80 Strand, London WC2R 0RL, England.

Library of Congress Cataloging-in-Publication Data
Flanagan, John (John Anthony) Halt's peril / John Flanagan.—1st American ed.
p. cm.—(Ranger's apprentice ; bk. 9)
Summary: Tennyson, the false prophet of the Outsider cult,
has escaped and Halt is determined to stop him before he crosses the border into Araluen,
but Genovesan assassins put Will and Halt's extraordinary archery skills to the test.
[1. Fugitives from justice—Fiction. 2. Cults—Fiction. 3. Insurgency—Fiction. 4. Fantasy.] I. Title.
PZ7.F598284Hal 2010   [Fic]—dc22   2009041702
ISBN 978-0-399-25207-5
1   3   5   7   9   10   8   6   4   2

*Dedicated to the memory of Miyuki Sakai-Flanagan,
so that Konan will always remember
what a brave and gentle soul his mother was.*

1

THERE WAS A RAW WIND BLOWING OFF THE SMALL HARBOR.
It carried the salt of the sea with it, and the smell of imminent rain.
The lone rider shrugged. Even though it was late summer, it seemed
to have been raining constantly over the past week. Perhaps in this
country it rained all the time, no matter what the season.

"Summer and winter, nothing but rain," he said quietly to his
horse. Not surprisingly, the horse said nothing.

"Except, of course, when it snows," the rider continued. "Presum-
ably, that's so you can tell it's winter." This time, the horse shook its
shaggy mane and vibrated its ears, the way horses do. The rider
smiled at it. They were old friends.

"You're a horse of few words, Tug," Will said. Then, on reflection,
he decided that most horses probably were. There had been a time,
quite recently, when he had wondered about this habit of his—talking
to his horse. Then, mentioning it to Halt over the campfire one night,
he'd discovered it was a common trait among Rangers.

"Of course we talk to them," the grizzled Ranger had told him.
"Our horses show a lot more common sense than most people. And
besides," he'd added, a note of seriousness creeping into his voice, "we

rely on our horses. We trust them and they trust us. Talking to them strengthens the special bond between us."

Will sniffed the air again. There were other smells apparent now, underlying the salt and the rain: Tar. New rope. Dried seaweed. But strangely, there was one scent missing—one he would have expected in any seaport along the eastern coast of Hibernia.

There was no smell of fish. No smell of drying nets.

"So what do they do here if they don't fish?" he mused. Aside from the slow clop of his hooves on the uneven cobbles, echoing from the buildings that lined the narrow street, the horse made no answer. But Will thought he already knew. It was why he was here, after all. Port Cael was a smugglers' town.

The streets down by the docks were narrow and winding, in contrast to the wide, well-laid-out streets of the rest of the town. There was only an occasional lantern outside a building to light the way. The buildings themselves were mostly two-storied, with loading doors set on the second floors, and lifting gantries so that bales and barrels could be brought up from carts below. Warehouses, Will guessed, with storage room for the goods that shipowners smuggled in and out of the port.

He was nearly down to the docks themselves now, and in the gap that marked the end of the street he could see the outlines of several small ships, moored to the dock and bobbing nervously on the dying efforts of the choppy waves that managed to force their way in through the harbor mouth.

"Should be around here somewhere," he said, and then he saw it: a single-story building at the end of the street, with a low-lying thatched roof sweeping down to just above head height. The walls may have been whitewashed at one time, but now they were a dirty, smudged gray. A fitful yellow light shone through the small windows along the street-side wall, and a sign creaked in the wind over the low doorway. A seabird of some kind, crudely rendered.

"Could be a heron," he said. He looked around curiously. The other buildings were all dark and anonymous. Their business was done for the day, whereas in a tavern like the Heron, it was just getting under way.

He dismounted outside the building, absentmindedly patting Tug's neck as he stood there. The little horse regarded the mean-looking tavern and then rolled an eye at his master.

Are you sure you want to go in there?

For a horse of few words, there were times when Tug could express himself with crystal clarity. Will smiled reassuringly at him.

"I'll be fine. I'm a big boy now, you know."

Tug snorted scornfully. He'd seen the small stable yard beside the inn and knew he'd be left there. He was always ill at ease when he wasn't on hand to keep his master out of trouble. Will led him through the sagging gate into the stable yard. Another horse and a tired old mule were tethered there. Will didn't bother to tether Tug. He knew his horse would stay there until he returned.

"Wait over there. You'll be out of the wind," he said, gesturing toward the far wall. Tug looked at him again, shook his head and ambled to the spot Will had indicated.

Just yell if you need me. I'll come running.

For a moment, Will wondered if he were being too fanciful in attributing that thought to his horse. Then he decided not. For a second or two, he entertained an image of Tug bursting through the narrow door into the tavern, shouldering drinkers aside to come to his master's aid. He grinned at the thought and closed the stable-yard gate, lifting it so that it didn't drag on the rough cobblestones. Then he moved to the tavern entrance.

Will was by no means a tall person, but even he felt it necessary to stoop a little under the low doorway. As he opened the door, he was hit by a wall of sensations. Heat. The smell of sweat. Smoke. Spilled, stale ale.

As the wind rushed in through the open door, the lanterns flickered and the peat fire in the grate on the far wall suddenly flared with renewed life. He hesitated, getting his bearings. The smoke and the flickering light from the fire made it even harder to see inside than it had been outside on the dark street.

"Close the door, fool!" a rough voice bellowed, and he stepped inside, allowing the door to shut behind him. Immediately, the fire and the lantern light steadied. There was a thick pall of smoke from the fire and dozens of pipes. It sat just above head height, trapped by the low thatched roof. Will wondered if it ever had a chance to disperse or whether it just hung there from one day to the next, growing in intensity with each passing evening. Most of the tavern's patrons ignored him, but a few unfriendly faces turned toward him, assessing the newcomer.

They saw a slim, slightly built figure, wrapped in a dull gray and green cloak, face concealed beneath a large hood. As they watched, he pushed the hood back and they saw that his face was surprisingly youthful. Little more than a boy. Then they took stock of the heavy saxe knife at his belt, with a smaller knife mounted above it, and the massive longbow in his left hand. Over his shoulder, they saw the feathered ends of more than a dozen arrows protruding from the quiver at his back.

The stranger might look like a boy, but he carried a man's weapons. And he did so without any self-consciousness or show, as if he was completely familiar with them.

He looked around the room, nodding to those who had turned to study him. But his gaze passed over them quickly, and it was apparent that he posed no risk—and these were men who were well used to gauging potential threats from newcomers. The slight air of tension that had gripped the tavern eased and people went back to their drinking. Will, after a quick inspection of the room, saw no danger to himself and crossed to the rough bar—three heavy, rough-sawn planks laid across two massive casks.

The tavern keeper, a wiry man with a sharp-nosed face, round, prominent ears and a receding hairline that combined to give him a rodentlike look, glanced at him, absentmindedly wiping a tankard with a grubby cloth. Will raised an eyebrow as he looked at it. He'd be willing to bet the cloth was transferring more dirt to the tankard than it was removing.

"Drink?" the tavern keeper asked. He set the tankard down on the bar, as if in preparation for filling it with whatever the stranger might order.

"Not out of that," Will said evenly, jerking a thumb at the tankard. Ratface shrugged, shoved it aside and produced another from a rack above the bar.

"Suit yourself. Ale or ouisgeah?"

Ouisgeah, Will knew, was the strong malt spirit they distilled and drank in Hibernia. In a tavern like this, it might be more suitable for stripping rust than drinking.

"I'd like coffee," he said, noticing the battered pot by the fire at one end of the bar.

"I've got ale or ouisgeah. Take your pick." Ratface was becoming more peremptory. Will gestured toward the coffeepot. The tavern keeper shook his head.

"None made," he said. "I'm not making a new pot just for you."

"But he's drinking coffee," Will said, nodding to one side.

Inevitably the tavern keeper glanced that way, to see whom he was talking about. The moment his eyes left Will, an iron grip seized the front of his shirt collar, twisting it into a knot that choked him and at the same time dragged him forward, off balance, over the bar. The stranger's eyes were suddenly very close. He no longer looked boyish. The eyes were dark brown, almost black in this dim light, and the tavern keeper read danger there. A lot of danger. He heard a soft whisper of steel, and glancing down past the fist that held him so tightly, he glimpsed the heavy, gleaming blade of the saxe knife as the stranger laid it on the bar between them.

He looked around for possible help. But there was nobody else at the bar, and none of the customers at the tables had noticed what was going on.

"Aach . . . mach co'hee," he choked.

The tension on his collar eased and the stranger said softly, "What was that?"

"I'll . . . make . . . coffee," he repeated, gasping for breath.

The stranger smiled. It was a pleasant smile, but the tavern keeper noticed that it never reached those dark eyes.

"That's wonderful. I'll wait here." Will released his grip on the tavern keeper's shirtfront, allowing him to slide back over the bar and regain his balance. He tapped the hilt of the saxe knife. "Don't change your mind, will you?"

There was a large kettle by the fire grate, supported on a swiveling iron arm that moved it in and out of the flames. The tavern keeper busied himself with the coffeepot, measuring grounds into it then pouring the now boiling water over them. The rich smell of coffee filled the air, for a moment supplanting the less pleasant odors that Will had noticed when he entered.

The tavern keeper placed the pot in front of Will, then produced a mug from behind the bar. He swiped at it with his ever-present cloth. Will frowned, wiped it carefully with a corner of his cloak and poured the coffee.

"I'll have sugar if you've got it," he said. "Honey if not."

"I've got sugar." The tavern keeper turned away to get the bowl and a brass spoon. When he turned back to the stranger, he started. There was a heavy gold coin gleaming on the bar between them. It represented more than he would make in an evening's trading, and he hesitated to reach for it. After all, that saxe knife was still on the bar close to the stranger's hand.

"Two penn'orth for the coffee is all," he said carefully.

Will nodded and reached into his purse, selecting two copper coins and dropping them onto the bar. "That's more than fair. You make good coffee," he added inconsequentially.

The tavern keeper nodded and swallowed, still unsure. Cautiously, he swept the two copper coins off the bar, watching carefully for any sign of dissent from the enigmatic stranger. For a moment, he felt vaguely ashamed that he had been overborne by someone so young. But another look at those eyes and the youth's weapons and he dismissed the thought. He was a tavern keeper. His notion of violence amounted to no more than using a cudgel on the heads of customers so affected by alcohol they could barely stand—and that was usually from behind.

He pocketed the coins and glanced hesitantly at the large gold coin, still winking at him in the lantern light. He coughed. The stranger raised an eyebrow.

"Was there something? . . ."

Withdrawing his hands behind his back so that there could be no misunderstanding, no thought that he was trying to appropriate the gold piece, the tavern keeper inclined his head toward it several times.

"The . . . gold. I'm wondering . . . is it . . . for anything at all now?"

The stranger smiled. Again, the smile never reached his eyes.

"Well, yes it is, as a matter of fact. It's for information."

And now the tight feeling in the tavern keeper's stomach seemed to ease right out of him. This was something he understood, particularly in this neighborhood. People often paid for information in Port Cael. And usually, they didn't harm the people who gave it to them.

"Information, is it?" he asked, allowing himself a smile. "Well, this is the place to ask and I'm your man to be asking. What is it you want to know, your honor?"

"I want to know whether the Black O'Malley has been in this evening," the young man said.

And suddenly, that tight feeling was back.

2

"O'Malley, is it? And why are you looking for him?" the tavern keeper asked. Those dark eyes came up to meet his again, boring into them. The message in them was clear. The stranger's hand moved to cover the gold coin. But for the moment he made no move to pick it up and remove it from the bar.

"Well, now," the stranger said quietly, "I was wondering whose gold coin this was. Did you put it here, by any chance?" Before the tavern keeper could reply, he'd continued. "No. I don't recall that happening. As I recall it, I was the one put it here, in return for information. Is that how you see it?"

The tavern keeper cleared his throat nervously. The young man's voice was calm and low-pitched, but no less menacing for the fact.

"Yes. That's right," he replied.

The stranger nodded several times, as if considering his answer. "And correct me if I'm wrong, but usually the one who's paying the piper is the one who calls the tune. Or in this case, asks the questions. Would you see it that way too?"

For a second, Will wondered if he wasn't overdoing the air of quiet menace. Then he discarded the thought. With a person like this, whose life probably centered on informing and double-dealing, he needed to assert a level of authority. And the only form of author-ity this sharp-featured toady would understand would be based on fear. Unless Will managed to dominate him, the tavern keeper was liable to tell him any line of lies that came to mind.

"Yes, sir. That's how I see it."

The "sir" was a good start, Will thought. Respectful, without being too ingratiating. He smiled again.

"So unless you'd like to match my coin with one of your own, let's keep it that I'm asking and you're answering."

His hand slid away from the gold coin once more, leaving it gleaming dully on the rough surface of the bar.

"The Black O'Malley. Is he in tonight?"

Ratface allowed his gaze to slide around the tavern, although he already knew the answer. He cleared his throat again. Strange how the presence of this young man seemed to leave it dry.

"No, sir. Not yet. He's usually in a little later than this."

"Then I'll wait," Will said. He glanced around and noticed a small table set away from the other patrons. It was in a corner, a suit-ably unobtrusive spot, and it would be out of the line of vision of anyone entering the tavern.

"I'll wait there. When O'Malley arrives, you won't say anything to him about me. And you won't look at me. But you'll tug on your ear three times to let me know he's here. Is that clear?"

"Yes, sir. It is."

"Good. Now . . ." He picked up the coin and the saxe knife, and for a moment the tavern keeper thought he was going to reclaim the money. But he held it on edge and sliced carefully through it, cutting it into two half circles. Two thoughts occurred to the tavern keeper. The gold must be awfully pure to cut so easily. And the knife must be frighteningly sharp to go through it with so little effort.

Will slid one half of the gold piece across the bar.

"Here's half now as a gesture of good faith. The other half once you've done as I ask."

The tavern keeper hesitated for a second or so. Then, swallowing nervously, he claimed the mutilated half gold piece.

"Would you be wanting anything to eat while you wait, sir?" he asked.

Will replaced the other half of the gold coin in his belt purse, then rubbed his fingers and thumb together. They were lightly coated with grease from their brief contact with the bar top. He looked once more at the filthy cloth over the tavern keeper's shoulder and shook his head.

"I don't think so."

Will sat, nursing his coffee, as he waited for the man he sought to enter the bar.

When Will had first arrived in Port Cael, he had found a room in an inn some distance from the waterfront, in one of the better-kept areas of the town. The innkeeper was a taciturn man, not given to the sort of gossip that his kind usually indulged in. Gossip was a way of life with innkeepers, Will thought. But this one seemed decidedly atypical. Better section of town or no, he realized, this was still a town that depended largely on smuggling and other forms of illegal trade. People would tend to be close-mouthed around strangers.

Unless a stranger offered gold, as Will did. He'd told the innkeeper that he was looking for a friend: a large man with long gray hair, dressed in a white robe and attended by a group of some twenty followers. There would be two among them who wore purple cloaks and wide-brimmed hats of the same color. Possibly carrying crossbows.

He'd seen the truth in the innkeeper's eyes as he described Tennyson and the remaining Genovesan assassins. Tennyson had been here, all right. His pulse lifted a little at the thought that he might still be here. But the innkeeper's words dashed that hope.

"They were here," he said. "But they're gone."

Apparently, the man had decided that, if Tennyson had already left Port Cael, there was no harm telling this to the young man asking after him. Will had pursed his lips at the news, allowing the gold coin to tumble end over end across the knuckles of his right hand—a trick he'd spent hours perfecting, to pass the time around countless campfires. The metal caught the light and gleamed invitingly as it flipped end over end, first in one direction, then the other, drawing the innkeeper's eyes.

"Gone where?"

The innkeeper looked back to him. Then he jerked his head in the direction of the harbor. "Gone over the sea. Where to, I don't know."

"Any idea who might know?"

The innkeeper had shrugged. "Your best bet would be to ask the Black O'Malley. Happen that he might know. When there's folk looking to leave in a hurry, he's often the one who'll accommodate them."

"A strange name. How did he come by it?"

"There was a sea fight some years ago. His ship was boarded. By . . ." The man had hesitated briefly, then continued, "By pirates. There was a fight and one of them hit him in the face with a flaming torch. The burning pitch of the torch clung to his skin and burned him badly, leaving a black scorch mark on the left side of his face."

Will had nodded thoughtfully. If there had been any pirates involved in the fight, he was willing to bet that they were sailing in O'Malley's company. But that was immaterial.

"And how would I find this O'Malley?" he'd asked.

"Most nights, you'll find him at the Heron tavern, down by the docks." The innkeeper had taken the coin, and as Will turned away, he'd added, "It's a dangerous place. Might not be a good idea to go there alone—you a stranger as you are. I've a couple of large lads do work for me from time to time. Might be they'd be willing to go along with you—for a small fee."

The young man looked back, considered the suggestion and shook his head, smiling slowly.

"I think I can look after myself."

3

It hadn't been any sense of arrogance that led him to refuse the innkeeper's offer. Walking into a place like the Heron with a couple of part-time, and probably second-rate, bullyboys for company would cause nothing but contempt among the genuine hard cases who gathered here. All it would have done was advertise the fact that he was uncertain of himself. Better to be alone and rely on his own skill and wits to see him through.

The tavern had been half full when he'd arrived. It had been too early in the evening for the main trade to begin. But as he waited, it began to fill up. The temperature rose with the growing press of unwashed bodies. So did the sour, stale smell that pervaded the hot, smoke-filled room. The noise level increased as people raised their voices to be heard over the growing clamor.

The situation suited him. The more people present and the noisier it was, the less chance there was of being noticed. With each new set of arrivals, he glanced at the tavern keeper. But each time, the thin-faced man merely shook his head.

It was somewhere between eleven o'clock and midnight when the door was hurled open and three bulky men entered, shoving their way through the throng to the bar, where the tavern keeper immediately began to pump up three large tankards of ale without a word passing between them. As he filled the second and placed it on the counter, he paused and, eyes down, tugged fiercely on his ear three times. Then he continued pulling the final ale.

Even without the signal, Will would have known that this was the man he was looking for. The large black burn mark on the side of his face, stretching from just below the left eye to the jawline, was obvious from across the room. He waited while O'Malley and his two cohorts picked up their tankards and made their way toward a table close to the peat fire. Two men were already seated there, and they looked up anxiously as the smuggler approached.

"Ah now, O'Malley," one of them began in a whining tone, "we've been sitting here since—"

"Out."

O'Malley gestured with his thumb, and the two men, without further demurral, picked up their drinks and rose, leaving the table for the three smugglers. They settled into their seats, glanced around the room and called greetings to several acquaintances. Reactions to the newcomers, Will noted, were more guarded than friendly. O'Malley seemed to instill fear in the other patrons.

O'Malley's gaze touched briefly on the cloaked figure sitting alone in a corner. He studied Will for several seconds, then dismissed him. He inched his chair forward, and he and his companions leaned over the table, speaking in low tones, their heads close together.

Will rose from his seat and moved toward them. Passing the bar, he allowed his hand to trail along the surface, leaving the mutilated half gold coin behind as he did so. The tavern keeper hurried to snatch it up. He made no sign of acknowledgment or thanks, but Will expected none. The tavern keeper wouldn't be eager for anyone to know that he had identified O'Malley to this stranger.

O'Malley became conscious of Will's presence as he approached the table. The smuggler had been muttering something in a low tone to his two companions, and now he stopped, his eyes swiveling sideways to inspect the slim figure standing a meter or so away. There was a long pause.

"Captain O'Malley?" Will asked finally. The man was powerfully built, although not excessively tall. He would have stood a few centimeters taller than Will, but then, most people did.

His shoulders were well muscled and his hands were callused. Together, they showed the signs of a lifetime of hard work, hauling on ropes, heaving cargo aboard, tending a bucking tiller in a gale. His stomach showed signs of a lifetime of hard drinking. He was overweight but still a powerful man and an adversary to be wary of. His black hair hung in ragged curls to his collar, and he had grown a beard, possibly in an unsuccessful attempt to disguise the disfiguring mark on his left cheek. His nose had been broken so many times that it now showed no defining shape at all. It was a lump of smashed cartilage.

His two companions were less interesting specimens. Big bellied, broad shouldered and powerfully built, they were larger and taller than their leader. But he had the unmistakable air of authority about him.

"Captain O'Malley?" Will repeated. He smiled easily. O'Malley frowned in return.

"I don't think so," he said shortly, and turned back to his two companions.

"I do," Will said, still smiling.

O'Malley sat back, looking away for a second or two, then turned his close-set eyes on Will. There was a dangerous light in them.

"Sonny," he said deliberately, the tone condescending and insulting, "why don't you run along now?"

The room around them had gone silent as the drinkers turned to watch this strange confrontation. The young stranger was armed with a powerful longbow, they could all see. But in the confined space of the tavern, it was not the most useful weapon.

"I'm looking for information," Will said. "I'm willing to pay for it."

He touched the purse at his belt and there was a slight musical clinking sound from it. O'Malley's eyes narrowed. This could be interesting.

"Information, is it? Well, perhaps we might talk after all. Carew!" he snapped at a man seated at the next table. "Give the boy your stool here."

The man called Carew hurriedly rose and shoved the stool toward Will. His look of resentment he reserved for the young Ranger. He made sure that no sign of it showed to O'Malley.

Will nodded his thanks, received a scowl in return and pulled the stool up to O'Malley's table.

"So, information, is it?" the smuggler began. "And what might you be wanting to know?"

"You gave passage to a man called Tennyson a few days ago," Will said. "Him and about twenty of his followers."

"Did I now?" O'Malley's shaggy eyebrows came together in a dark frown of anger. "You seem to have a lot of information already, don't you? And who told you that?"

"Nobody in this room," Will said. Then, before O'Malley could query him further, he went on quickly, "I need to know where you took him."

The smuggler's eyebrows rose in simulated surprise.

"Oh, you *need* to know, do you? And what if I don't *need* to tell you? Assuming that I had taken this person anywhere at all—which I didn't."

Will allowed a flash of exasperation to show, then realized that this was a mistake. He composed his features, but he knew O'Malley had noticed it.

"I said, I'm willing to pay for the information," he said, working to keep his voice level.

"And would you be willing to pay another gold coin—like the one I saw you slip to Ryan as you came past the bar?" He glanced angrily at the tavern keeper, who had been an interested observer of their conversation and now shrank back a little. "We'll be having words about that later, Ryan," he added.

Will pursed his lips in surprise. He would have been willing to bet that O'Malley's attention was engaged elsewhere when he placed the half coin on the bar.

"You don't miss much, do you?" He allowed a note of admiration to enter his tone. No harm in a little flattery. But O'Malley wasn't as simple as all that.

"I don't miss *anything*, boy." His angry gaze was back on Will now. *Don't try to butter me up with soft words*, it said.

Will shifted on his stool. He was losing control of this conversation, he thought. Then he amended that. He had never had control of this conversation. O'Malley had steered it from the first word. All Will had done so far was react to him. He tried again.

"Well, yes. I'd be willing to pay gold for the information."

"I've already been paid," O'Malley said. At least there was no pretense now that he hadn't given passage to Tennyson and his followers.

"Then you'll be paid twice. That sounds like good business to me," Will said reasonably.

"It does, does it? Well, let me tell you a little about business. For a start, I'd happily slit your throat for that purse you're carrying. And I have no particular regard for this Tennyson fellow you speak of. If I'd had the chance, I would have killed him and dumped him overboard and no one the wiser. But those purple-cloaked friends of his watched me like a hawk the whole time. I tell you this to point out that trust means nothing to me. Nothing at all."

"Then—," Will began, but the smuggler cut him off with a curt gesture.

"But here's what business is about, boy. I took money from that man to get him out of Clonmel. That's the sort of business I'm in. Now, if I take more money from a second party to tell where I took him, and everyone here sees me do it, how long do you think my business will last? People come to me for one reason: I know how to keep my mouth shut."

He paused. Will sat awkwardly. There was no reasonable answer he could think of.

"I don't believe in honesty," O'Malley continued. "Or trust. Or loyalty. I believe in profit. That's all. And profit means I know how to keep my mouth shut when it's necessary." Without warning, he looked around the tavern. Eyes that had been watching with interest turned quickly away.

"And everyone else in this room had better know the same thing," he said, raising his voice.

Will spread his hands in a gesture of defeat. He could see no way to turn this situation around. Abruptly, he found himself wishing that Halt were here. Halt would know what to do, he thought. And with that thought, he felt thoroughly inadequate.

"Well, then, I'll be on my way." He began to rise.

"Just a minute!" O'Malley's hand slapped down on the table between them. "You haven't paid me."

Will gave a snort of incredulous laughter. "Paid you? You didn't answer my question."

"Yes I did. It just wasn't the answer you were looking for. Now pay me."

Will looked around the room. Everyone present was watching the exchange and most of them were grinning. O'Malley might be feared and disliked here, but Will was a stranger and they were happy to see him bested. He realized that the smuggler had created this confrontation for the purpose of magnifying his own reputation. It wasn't so much the money he was interested in, more the opportunity to show everyone else in the tavern that he was cock of the walk. Trying to hide his fury, he reached into his purse and took out another gold piece. This was getting expensive, he thought, and he'd found out nothing worthwhile. He slid the piece across the table. O'Malley gathered it in, tested it with his teeth and smiled wickedly.

"Good to do business with you, boy. Now get on out of here."

Will knew his face was burning with the suppressed fury inside him. He stood abruptly, overturning the stool behind him. From somewhere in the room, there was a low chuckle. Then he turned and shoved his way through the crowd to the door.

As it banged shut behind him, O'Malley leaned forward to his two followers and said quietly, "Dennis, Nialls. Bring me back that purse."

The two heavily built men rose and followed Will to the door. With a shrewd idea of what they might be about, the tavern customers cleared a path for them. Some watched reluctantly. They'd planned to go after the young man themselves.

Dennis and Nialls stepped out into the clear, cold night, looking up and down the narrow street to see which way the stranger had gone. They hesitated. There were several mean little alleys that led off the street. The youth could be hiding in one of them.

"Let's try—"

Nialls got no further. The air between the two men was split by a vicious hiss as something flashed past Nialls's nose and thudded into the door frame. The two men jerked apart in shock, then stared in disbelief at the gray-shafted arrow, buried quivering in the wood.

From somewhere up the street, a voice carried to them.

"One more step and the next arrow will be through your heart." There was a slight pause, then the voice continued, with obvious venom, "And I'm just angry enough to do it."

"Where is he?" Dennis whispered out of the corner of his mouth.

"Must be in one of the alleys," Nialls answered. The threat of the quivering arrow was unmistakable. But they both knew the danger involved in going back to O'Malley empty-handed.

Without warning, there was another hiss-thud between them. Only this time, Nialls's hand flew to his right ear, where the arrow had nicked him on its way through. Blood ran hotly down his cheek. Suddenly, facing O'Malley seemed like the better alternative.

"Let's get out of here!" he said, and they jostled each other to get back through the door, slamming it behind them.

From an alley farther up the street, a dark figure emerged. Will figured it would be several minutes before anyone chanced coming back again. He ran soft-footed back to the tavern, retrieved his arrows and led Tug from the stable yard. Swinging into the saddle, he galloped away. The little horse's hooves rang on the cobbles, the sound echoing off the buildings lining the street.

Altogether, it had been a very unsatisfying encounter.

4

Halt and Horace crested a small rise and reined in their horses. Less than a kilometer away, Port Cael was spread out before them. White-painted buildings huddled together at the top of a hill, which swept away down to the harbor itself—a man-made breakwater that stretched out into the sea then turned at a right angle to form an L-shaped haven for the small fleet moored inside the walls. From where they sat their horses, the ships could be seen only as a forest of masts, jumbled together and indistinguishable as individual craft.

The houses on the hill were freshly painted and looked neatly kept. Even in the dull sunshine that was breaking through the overcast, they seemed to gleam. Down the hill and closer to the docks, there was a more utilitarian look to the buildings and the predominant color was a dull gray. Typical of any working port, Halt thought. The more genteel people lived on the hill in their spotless homes. The riffraff gathered by the water.

Still, he was willing to bet that the spotless homes on the hill held their share of villains and unscrupulous traders. The people who lived there weren't more honest than the others—just more successful.

"Isn't that someone we know?" asked Horace. He pointed to

where a cloaked figure sat by the side of the road a few hundred meters away, arms wrapped around his knees. Close by him, a small shaggy horse cropped the grass growing at the edge of the drainage ditch that ran beside the road.

"So it is," Halt replied. "And he seems to have brought Will with him."

Horace glanced quickly at his older companion. He felt his spirits lift with the sally. It wasn't much of a joke, but it was the first one Halt had made since they had left his brother's grave at Dun Kilty. The Ranger was never a garrulous companion, but he had been even more taciturn than usual over the past few days. Understandable, thought Horace. After all, he had lost his twin brother. Now the Ranger seemed prepared to slough off his depression. Possibly it had something to do with the prospect of imminent action.

"Looks like he's lost a guinea and found a farthing," Horace said, then added, unnecessarily, "Will, I mean."

Halt turned in his saddle to regard the younger man and raised an eyebrow.

"I may be almost senile in your eyes, Horace, but there's no need to explain the blindingly obvious to me. I'd hardly have thought you were referring to Tug."

"Sorry, Halt." But Horace couldn't prevent a smile touching the corner of his mouth. First a joke and now an acerbic reply. That was better than the morose silence that had enshrouded Halt since his brother's death.

"Let's see what's troubling him," Halt said.

As they drew near, Will stood, brushing himself off. Tug whinnied a greeting to Abelard and Kicker, and the other horses responded in kind.

"Halt, Horace," Will greeted them as they drew rein beside him. "I hoped you'd be along today."

"We got the message you left for us at Fingle Bay," Halt told him, "so we pushed on early this morning."

Fingle Bay had been Tennyson's original destination. It was a prosperous trading and fishing port some kilometers to the south of Port Cael. The majority of shipowners and captains there were honest men. Port Cael was the home of more shady operations, as Tennyson, and then Will, had discovered.

"Had any luck?" Horace asked. While he and Halt had stayed to tidy up things in Dun Kilty, Will had gone ahead to trail Tennyson and discover where he was heading. The young Ranger shrugged now.

"Some," he said. "Good and bad, I'm afraid. Tennyson has fled the country, as you thought, Halt."

Halt nodded. "Where'd he go?"

Will shifted his weight uneasily from one foot to the other. Halt smiled to himself. He knew that his former apprentice hated to fail at any task Halt set him.

"That's the bad news, I'm afraid. I can't find out. I know who took him. It was a smuggler called the Black O'Malley. But he won't tell me anything. I'm sorry, Halt," he added. His old mentor shrugged.

"I'm sure you did all you could. Sailors in a place like this can be notoriously close-mouthed. Perhaps I'll have a talk with him. Where do we find him—this exotically named O'Malley character?"

"There's a tavern by the docks. He's there most evenings."

"Then I'll talk to him tonight," Halt said.

"You can try. But he's a hard case, Halt. I'm not sure you'll get anything out of him. He's not interested in money. I tried that."

"Well, perhaps he'll do it out of the goodness of his heart. I'm sure he'll open up to me," Halt said easily. But Horace noticed a quick gleam in his eye. He was right: the prospect of having something to do had reawakened Halt's spirits. He had a score to settle, and Horace found himself thinking that it didn't bode well for this Black O'Malley character.

Will eyed Halt doubtfully, however. "You think so?"

Halt smiled at him. "People love talking to me," he said. "I'm an excellent conversationalist and I have a sparkling personality. Ask Horace. I've been bending his ear all the way from Dun Kilty, haven't I?"

Horace nodded confirmation. "Talking nonstop all the way, he's been," he said. "Be glad to see him turn all that chatter onto someone else."

Will regarded the two of them balefully. He had hated admitting failure to Halt. Now his two companions seemed to think the whole matter was a joke, and he simply wasn't in the frame of mind to appreciate it. He tried to think of something crushing to say but nothing came to him. Finally, he swung up into Tug's saddle and moved out onto the road with them.

"I've got us rooms at an inn in the upper town. It's quite clean—and reasonably priced," he told them. That caught Horace's attention.

"What's the food like?" he asked.

They stood back a few meters from the end of the alley, concealed in the shadows. From their position, they had a clear view of the entrance to the Heron and could see customers coming and going without being seen themselves. So far, there had been no sign of O'Malley and his two friends.

Will shifted restlessly. It was getting close to midnight.

"They're late—if they're coming," he said softly. "They were here well before this last night."

"Maybe they were early last night," Horace suggested. Halt said nothing.

"Why not wait inside, Halt?" Horace asked. The night was cold and he could feel the damp chill rising through the soles of his boots, into his feet and legs.

"I want to surprise them," Halt said. "If they walk in and see us waiting, the surprise will be lost. If we wait till they're seated, then go in quickly, we'll catch them before they have much of a chance to react. Plus there's always the possibility that if we're waiting for them in there, someone will nip out and tell them."

Horace nodded. It all made sense. He wasn't big on subtlety himself, but he could recognize it in others.

"And Horace," Halt began.

"Yes, Halt?"

"If I give you the signal, I'd like you to take care of this smuggler's two henchmen."

Horace grinned broadly. It didn't sound as if Halt expected him to be subtle about that.

"Fine by me, Halt," he said. Then, as a thought struck him, "What will the signal be?"

Halt glanced at him. "I'll probably say something like, 'Horace.'"

The tall warrior cocked his head to one side.

"Horace . . . what?"

"That's it," Halt told him. "Just 'Horace.'"

Horace thought about it for a few seconds, then nodded, as if seeing the logic.

"Good thinking, Halt. Keep it simple. Sir Rodney says that's the way to do it."

"Anything in particular you want me to do?" Will asked.

"Watch and learn," Halt told him.

Will smiled wryly. He was over his disappointment about his inability to get O'Malley to talk. Now he was strangely eager to see how Halt handled the matter. He had no doubt that Halt would handle it—somehow.

"That never changes, does it?" he said.

Halt glanced at him, sensing the change in his mood, the eagerness that had replaced his disappointment.

"Only a fool thinks he knows everything," he said. "And you're no fool."

Before Will could respond, he gestured toward the narrow street. "I think our friends have arrived."

O'Malley and his two henchmen were making their way up the street from the docks. The three Araluens watched as they entered the tavern, the two bigger men standing aside to let their captain go first. There was a brief hubbub of raised voices as the door opened, spilling light out into the street. Then noise and light were cut off as the door shut behind them.

Horace started forward but Halt laid a restraining hand on his arm.

"Give it a minute or two," he said. "They'll get their drinks and then clear out anyone who might be sitting at their table. Where is it relative to the door, Will?" he asked.

"Inside. Down two steps and half right. About three meters from the door, by the fireplace. Watch your head on the door frame, Horace," he added.

He sensed Horace nodding in the shadows. Halt was standing, eyes closed, measuring off the seconds, picturing the scene inside the tavern. Will fidgeted, wanting to get moving. Halt's low voice came to him.

"Take it easy. There's no rush."

Will took several deep breaths, trying to calm his racing pulse.

"You know what I want you to do?" Halt asked him. He'd briefed the two of them that afternoon in the inn. But it never hurt to make sure.

Will swallowed several times. "I'll stay inside the door and keep an eye on the room."

"And remember, not so close to the door that you'll be knocked over if someone comes in unexpectedly," Halt reminded him. But there was no need for that reminder. Halt had drawn a graphic picture that afternoon of how awkward it might be if Will were suddenly knocked flat by an eager drinker shoving the door open to get in.

"Got it," Will said. His mouth was a little dry.

"Horace, you're clear?"

"Stay with you. Keep standing when you sit. Watch the two bully-boys, and if you say 'Horace,' whack them."

"Very succinct," Halt said. "Couldn't have put it better myself." He waited a few more seconds, then stepped out of the shadows.

They crossed the street and Halt jerked the door open. Will felt the wave of heat and noise and light once again, then stepped inside after Halt and moved to the side. He was conscious of a dull thud as Horace forgot to duck under the doorway.

O'Malley, his back to the fire, looked up at the new arrivals. He recognized Will, and that distracted him for a few seconds so that he was too late to react to Halt, striding quickly across the room to pull out a stool at the table and sit facing him.

"Good evening," said the bearded stranger. "My name is Halt and it's time we had a chat."

5

NIALLS AND DENNIS ROSE TO THEIR FEET INSTANTLY, BUT O'Malley held up a hand to keep them from taking any further action.

"That's all right now, boys. Easy does it."

They didn't resume their seats, but moved to stand behind him, forming a solid wall of muscle and flesh between him and the fireplace. O'Malley, recovering from his initial surprise, studied the man sitting opposite him.

He was small. And there was more gray than black in his hair. Altogether, not someone who would normally cause the smuggler too much concern. But O'Malley had spent years assessing potential enemies, and he knew to look beyond the physical side of things. This man had hard eyes. And an air of confidence about him. He'd just walked into a lion's den, found the head lion and tweaked his tail. And now he sat opposite, cool as a cucumber. Unworried. Unflustered. He was either a fool or a very dangerous man. And he didn't look foolish.

O'Malley glanced quickly up at the man's companion. Tall, broad shouldered and athletic-looking, he thought. But the face was young—almost boyish. And he lacked the smaller man's air of calm certainty. His eyes were moving constantly, between O'Malley and his two cohorts. Judging. Measuring. He dismissed the young man. Nothing to fear there. It was a mistake many had made before him—to their eventual regret.

Now he looked back to the doorway and saw the youth who had approached him the previous night. He was standing away from the door a little, his longbow in his hand, an arrow nocked on the string. But the bow was lowered—at the moment—threatening nobody. That could change in a second, O'Malley thought. Dennis and Nialls had apprised him of the youth's skill with the bow. Nialls's ear was still heavily bandaged where the boy's arrow had all but severed it from his head.

This—he searched for the name the newcomer had given, then remembered it—Halt character had a similar bow. And now O'Malley realized that he was wearing a similar cloak, mottled and hooded. Same weapons, same cloaks. There was something official about them, and O'Malley decided he didn't like that. He had no truck with anyone official.

"King's man, are you?" he said to Halt.

"Not your king." He saw the smuggler's lip curl contemptuously at the words and suppressed a small flame of anger at his late brother for letting the royal office become so downgraded. No sign of the emotion showed in his face or eyes.

"I'm Araluen," he continued.

O'Malley raised his eyebrows. "And I suppose we should all be mightily impressed by that?" he asked sarcastically.

Halt didn't answer for a few seconds. He held the other man's gaze with his own.

"If you choose to be," he said. "It's immaterial to me. I mention it only to assure you that I have no interest in your smuggling activities."

That shot went home. O'Malley was not a man to discuss his work openly. A scowl formed on the Hibernian's face.

"Watch your words! We don't take kindly to people who walk in here accusing us of smuggling and the like."

Halt shrugged, unimpressed. "I didn't say anything about 'the like,'" he rejoined. "I simply said I'm not worried by the fact that you're a smuggler. I just want some information, that's all. Tell me what I want to know and I'll bother you no further."

O'Malley had leaned forward over the table to issue the warning to Halt. Now he sat back angrily.

"If I wouldn't tell the boy," he said, jerking his thumb toward the silent figure by the doorway, "what makes you think I'll tell his grandfather?"

Halt arched an eyebrow at that. "Oh, that's a little harsh. 'Uncle' might be closer to the truth, I think." But now the smuggler had decided enough was enough.

"Get out," O'Malley ordered flatly. "I'm done with you."

Halt shook his head, and those dark eyes bored into O'Malley's.

"Maybe," he said. "But I'm not done with you."

There was a threat and a challenge implicit in the words. And they were delivered in a tone of thinly veiled contempt. It was all too much for O'Malley.

"Nialls. Dennis. Throw this fool out into the street," he said. "And if his little friend by the door raises that bow an inch, cut his throat before you do it."

His two henchmen started around the table toward Halt, Nialls going to his right, Dennis to his left. Halt waited until they were almost upon him, then said one word.

"Horace . . ."

He was interested to see how the young warrior approached the problem. Horace began with a straight right to Dennis's jaw. It was a solid blow but not a knockout punch by any means. It was simply intended to give Horace a little room and time. Dennis staggered back, and before Nialls could react, Horace had pivoted and hit him with a crushing left hook to the jaw. Nialls's eyes glazed and his knees went slack. He dropped like a sack of potatoes, out cold.

But now Dennis was coming back, swinging a wild roundhouse right hand at Horace. The young man ducked under it, hammered two short lefts into the smuggler's ribs and came up with a searing uppercut to the point of Dennis's jaw.

The uppercut had all the power of Horace's legs, upper body, shoulder and arm beneath it. It slammed into Dennis's jaw and sent an instant message flashing to his brain. The light went out behind Dennis's eyes like a candle in a hurricane. His feet were actually lifted several centimeters off the floor by the force of that terrible blow. Then he too simply folded in place and crashed to the rough, sawdust-strewn boards.

The entire sequence took a little less than four seconds. O'Malley goggled in amazement as his two bodyguards were dispatched with such contemptuous ease—and by a young man he had dismissed as no threat. He began to rise. But an iron grip seized his collar, dragging him back down and across the table. At the same time, he felt something sharp—very sharp—against his throat.

"I said, I'm not done with you yet. So sit down."

Halt's voice was low and very compelling. Even more compelling was the razor-sharp saxe knife that was now pressing a little too firmly against the smuggler's throat. O'Malley hadn't seen him unsheathe the weapon. It occurred to him that this graybeard must be capable of moving with alarming speed—just as his young companion had been.

O'Malley looked at those eyes, seeing in the foreground a blurred picture of the murderous steel that rested against his throat.

"Now, I'll let the grandfather remark pass," Halt said. "And I won't even take offense at the fact that you just tried to have your bullyboys assault me. But I will ask you one question and I will ask it once. If you don't answer me, I will kill you. Right here. Right now. Will!" he called in an abrupt aside. "If that big fellow by the sideboard takes another step toward me, put an arrow into him."

"Already saw him, Halt," Will replied. He raised the bow in the general direction Halt had mentioned. The heavily built seaman who had thought he was unobserved suddenly held up both hands. Like most of the others in the room, he had heard of the two arrows that had been shot between Nialls and Dennis the previous evening. Initially, he'd thought it might be worth his while to lend a hand to O'Malley. But it definitely wasn't worth getting himself shot.

Will gestured with the arrow and the man sank down onto a long bench. The gleaming arrowhead was enough to worry him. But of even greater concern was the fact that the bearded man hadn't seemed to glance in his direction once.

"Now," said Halt, "where were we again?"

O'Malley opened his mouth to reply, then shut it again. This was new territory. He was used to setting the agenda, used to having others defer to him. He didn't deceive himself that he was liked by the other men who frequented the Heron. But he knew he was feared, and that was even better. Or so he had thought. Now that the people in the crowded tavern had encountered someone who instilled more fear in them than he did, he was left totally powerless. Had he been liked, maybe someone would have interceded on his behalf. But without Nialls and Dennis, he knew he was on his own.

Halt studied him for a moment, understanding the thought process that was going on in the other man's mind. He saw the flicker of doubt and uncertainty and knew he had a winning position. Everything that Will had told him about his earlier confrontation with the smuggler had led him to believe that O'Malley was not a well-liked figure. Halt had been depending on that, and now he saw that it was true.

"Some days ago, you transported a man called Tennyson and a group of his followers somewhere out of the country. Do you remember that?"

O'Malley gave no sign that he did. His eyes were locked on Halt's. Halt could see the barely suppressed fury there—fury fanned by O'Malley's helplessness in the current situation.

"I hope you do," Halt continued, "because your life may well depend on it. Now remember what I said. I'm going to ask this question once and once only. If you want to continue living, you will tell me what I want to know. Clear?"

Still there was no response from the smuggler. Halt took a deep breath and continued.

"Where did you take Tennyson?"

There was an almost palpable silence as everyone in the room seemed to lean forward expectantly, waiting to see what O'Malley was going to say. The smuggler swallowed several times, the action causing the tip of the saxe knife to dig painfully into the soft flesh of his throat. Then, his mouth dry and his voice almost a croak, he replied.

"You can't kill me."

Halt's left eyebrow shot up at that. A strange half smile twisted his mouth.

"Really?" he said. "And why might that be?"

"Because if you kill me, you'll never find out what you want to know," O'Malley told him.

Halt gave vent to a brief snort of laughter. "You can't be serious."

O'Malley's forehead creased in a frown. He'd played his only card and the stranger was treating it with contempt. He was bluffing,

O'Malley decided, and his confidence, at its lowest ebb, started to grow once more.

"Don't try to bluff," he said. "You want to know where this Tennyson fellow went. And you want to know badly, else you'd never have come back here tonight. So take that knife from my throat and I'll consider telling you. Although it'll cost you." He added the last four words as an afterthought. He had the whip hand, he thought, and he might as well use it.

Halt said nothing for a second or two. Then he leaned across the table. The knifepoint stayed where it was against O'Malley's throat.

"I want you to do something for me, O'Malley. Look into my eyes and tell me if you can see any sign there that I'm incapable of killing you."

O'Malley did as he was told. He had to admit the eyes were a chilling sight to behold. There was no indication of pity or weakness there. This man would be capable of killing him in an instant.

Except for the fact that Halt needed him alive. And that made his victory even sweeter. This gray-bearded wretch probably wanted to kill him right now. But he couldn't.

O'Malley couldn't help a smile forming on his face as he thought about it.

"Sure, I'm convinced you *would*," he said almost breezily. "But you can't, can you?"

It'd never do to gamble with this one, he thought. The bearded face showed no sign of the frustration and uncertainty he must be feeling now that O'Malley had called his bluff.

"Let's just review this, shall we?" Halt said softly. "You say I can't kill you because then I'll never find out what you know. But at the same time, you've told Will over there that you won't divulge that information . . ."

"Ah, well now, that may be open to negotiation," O'Malley began, but Halt cut him off.

"So if I kill you, I'm not losing anything, am I? But it will be some compensation for the trouble you've caused. On the whole, I think I rather want to kill you. You're an annoying person, O'Malley. In fact, now that I think about it, I'm glad you don't want to tell me because then I would feel duty bound to spare your miserable life."

"Now look here . . ." The returning confidence O'Malley had felt had gone again. He'd pushed this man too far, he realized. But now the tip of the heavy knife left his throat and pointed at the tip of his nose.

"No! You listen to me!" Halt said. He spoke quietly but his voice cut like a whip. "Look around this room and tell me if there's anyone here who owes you any sense of loyalty or friendship. Is there anyone here who might protest for one second if I simply cut your throat?"

In spite of himself, O'Malley's eyes wandered quickly to the watchful faces. He saw no sign of help there.

"Now answer me this: once you're dead, are you sure there's not somebody in this room who might know where you took Tennyson, and who might be willing to share that knowledge?"

And that was the point at which O'Malley knew he'd lost. There certainly were people in the room who knew where he had taken the white-robed man. At the time, it had been no big secret. And if he, O'Malley, wasn't around to ensure their silence, they'd fall over themselves telling this grim-faced tormentor what he wanted to know.

"Craiskill River," he said, almost in a whisper.

The knife wavered. "What?" Halt asked him.

O'Malley's shoulders slumped and he lowered his gaze. "Craiskill River. It's in Picta, below the Mull of Linkeith. It's one of our rendezvous points where we deliver cargo."

Halt frowned, disbelieving him for a moment. "Why the devil would Tennyson want to go to Picta?"

O'Malley shrugged. "He didn't want to go there. He wanted to get away from here. That's where I was going, so that's where I took him."

Halt was nodding slowly to himself.

"I could take you there," O'Malley suggested hopefully.

Halt laughed contemptuously. "Oh, I'm sure you could! My friend, I trust you about as far as Horace here could kick you—and I'm tempted to find out how far that is. Now get out of my sight."

He released his grip on the other man's collar and shoved him back. Off balance, O'Malley tried to stand, but Halt stopped him.

"No. One more thing. Empty your purse on the table."

"My purse?"

Halt said nothing, but his eyebrows came together in a dark line. O'Malley noticed that the saxe knife was still in his right hand. He hurried to unfasten his purse and spill its contents onto the tabletop. Halt poked through the coins with a forefinger and selected a gold piece. He held it up.

"This yours, Will?"

"Looks like it, Halt," Will called cheerfully. After having been humiliated by O'Malley, he'd enjoyed this evening's confrontation.

"Take better care of it next time," Halt told him. Then he turned back to O'Malley, his face dark and threatening. "As for you, get out of here."

O'Malley, finally released, rose to his feet. He looked around the room, seeing nothing but contempt in the faces watching him. Then he did as he was told.

6

"Your friend isn't looking too happy." The ship's captain nudged Will with his elbow and gestured with a smirk at the figure huddled in the bow of the *Sparrow*, leaning against the bulwark, the cowl of his cloak drawn up over his head.

It was a raw, overcast day, with the wind gusting at them out of the southeast and a choppy, unpredictable swell surging in from the north. The wind blew the tops off the waves and hurled them back at the ship as it plunged into the troughs, smashing its bow down into the racing gray sea.

"He'll be fine," Will said. But the shipmaster seemed to be uncommonly amused by the thought of someone suffering from seasickness. Perhaps, Will thought, it gave him a sense of superiority.

"Never fails," the skipper continued cheerfully. "These strong, silent types on land always turn into green-faced crybabies once they feel a ship move an inch or two under their feet."

In fact, the *Sparrow* was moving considerably more than that. She was plunging, lurching and rolling against the opposing forces of wind and wave.

"Are those rocks a problem?" Horace asked, pointing to where a line of rocks protruded from the sea as each line of rollers passed over them, seething with foam. They were several hundred meters away on the port side, and the wind was taking the ship down diagonally toward the rocks.

The skipper regarded the line of rocks as they disappeared and then reappeared in time to the movement of the waves.

"That's Palisade Reef," he told them. He squinted a little, measuring distances and angles in his mind, making sure the situation hadn't changed since the last time he'd checked—which had been only a few minutes previously.

"We seem to be getting a little close to it," Horace said. "I've heard that's not a good idea."

"We'll come close, but we'll weather it all right," the captain replied. "Land people like you always get a little edgy at the sight of Palisade Reef."

"I'm not edgy," Horace told him. But the stiff tone of his voice belied his words. "I just wanted to make sure you know what you're doing."

"Well now, my boy, that's why we've got the oars out, you see. The sail is powering us, but the force of the wind is sending us down onto the reef. With the oars out, we're dragging her upwind enough so that we'll reach the back-lift with plenty of room to spare."

"The back-lift?" Will asked. "What might that be?"

"See how the reef line runs into the edge of the Mull?" the captain told him, pointing. Will nodded. He could see the line of troubled water that marked the reef. It did run into the foot of the large headland to the northwest—the Mull of Linkeith.

"And see how the wind is coming from over my shoulder here, and setting us down toward the reef itself?"

Again, Will nodded.

"Well, the oars will keep us far enough to the east to avoid the reef. Then, as we get closer to the Mull, the wind will hit it and be deflected back at us—that's the back-lift. In effect, it'll reverse, and we'll go about so it's actually blowing us clear of the reef. Then we've got a simple run for a few kilometers down the bay to the river mouth. We'll have to row that, because the back-lift will last for only a few hundred meters—enough to get us clear of the reef."

"Interesting," Will said thoughtfully, studying the situation, and assessing distances and angles for himself. Now that it had been pointed out, he could see that the *Sparrow* would pass clear of the end of the reef as they ran in under the Mull. The captain might be lacking in sensitivity, but he seemed to know his business.

"Maybe I should go for'ard and point out the reef to your friend," the captain said, grinning. "That should be good for a laugh. I'll wager he hasn't noticed it yet." He laughed at his own wit. "I'll look worried, like this, shall I?"

He assumed a mock-worried look, puckering his brows and pretending to chew his fingernails. Will regarded him coldly.

"You could do that," he agreed. Then he added, "Tell me, is your first mate a good seaman?"

"Well, of course he is! I wouldn't have him with me, else," the captain replied. "Why do you ask?"

"We may need him to handle the ship when Halt throws you overboard," Will replied mildly. The captain started to laugh, but saw the look on Will's face and stopped uncertainly.

"Halt becomes very bad-tempered when he's seasick," Will told him. "Particularly when people try to make sport of him."

"*Especially* when people try to make sport of him," Horace added.

The captain suddenly didn't look so sure of himself. "I was only joking."

Will shook his head. "So was that Skandian who laughed at him." He glanced at Horace. "Remember what Halt did to him?"

Horace nodded seriously. "It wasn't pretty."

The captain looked from one to the other now. He'd had dealings with Skandians over the years. Most seafarers had. And he'd never met anyone who'd bested one.

"What did he do? Your friend, I mean?" he asked.

"He puked into his helmet," Will said.

"Extensively," Horace added.

The captain's jaw dropped as he tried to picture the scene. Will and Horace didn't bother to explain that Halt was wearing the borrowed helmet at the time, or that he was under the protection of the massive Erak, future Oberjarl of the Skandians.

"And the Skandian? What did he do?"

Will shrugged. "He apologized. What else could he do?"

The captain looked from Will to Halt, and back to Will. The young man's face was serious, with no sign that he was gulling the captain. The captain swallowed several times, then decided that even if he were being deceived, it might be more kind to let Halt suffer his seasickness in peace.

"Sail!"

The cry came from the masthead lookout. Instinctively, all three of them looked up at him. He was pointing behind them, arm outstretched to the southeast. Then they swung to follow that pointing arm. There was a low scud of sea mist farther out to sea, but as they watched, a dark shape began to creep out of it, taking on firmer lines.

"Can you make her out?" the captain yelled.

The lookout shaded his eyes, peering more carefully at the following ship.

"Six oars a side . . . and a square mainsail. She's coming up on us fast. Headreaching on us too!"

The strange ship was running before the wind, and rowing strongly as well. Headreaching meant she was able to aim for a point in advance of the *Sparrow* and reach it before them. There was no way they could avoid her.

"Can you make her out?" the captain repeated. There was a moment's hesitation.

"I think she's the *Claw*. The Black O'Malley's ship!" the lookout called. Will and Horace exchanged a worried glance.

"Then Halt was right," Will said.

The morning after the confrontation with O'Malley in the tavern, Halt had roused his two companions early.

"Get dressed," he told them briefly. "We're heading back to Fingle Bay."

"What about breakfast?" Horace asked grumpily, knowing what the answer was going to be.

"We'll eat on the way."

"I hate it when we eat on the way," Horace grumbled. "It does terrible things to my digestion." Nonetheless, he was an experienced campaigner. He dressed quickly, rerolled his pack and buckled on his sword. Will was ready a few seconds after him. Halt looked them over, checking that they had all their equipment.

"Let's go," he said, and led the way downstairs. He paid the innkeeper for their stay and they made their way to the stables. The horses nickered a greeting as they entered.

"Halt," Will asked, once they were on the road, "why Fingle Bay?"

"We need a ship," Halt told him.

Will glanced over his shoulder at the town they had just left. They were almost at the top of the hill and the forest of masts was clearly visible.

"There are ships here," he pointed out, and Halt looked at him sidelong.

"There are," he agreed. "And O'Malley is here as well. He already knows where we'll be going. I don't want him knowing *when* we go there."

"You think he'd try to stop us, Halt?" Horace asked.

The Ranger nodded. "I'm sure he would. In fact, I'm sure he will. But if he doesn't know when we leave, it may mean we can give him the slip. Besides, the shipmasters in Fingle Bay are a little more honest than that nest of smugglers and thieves back there."

"Only a little?" Will asked, hiding a grin. He knew Halt had a poor opinion of shipmasters in general—probably because of the fact that he hated traveling by sea.

"No shipmaster is too honest," Halt replied dourly.

At Fingle Bay, they'd contracted with the master of the *Sparrow*, a wide-beamed merchantman with enough space for them and their three horses. When the captain heard their destination, he frowned.

"Craiskill River?" he said. "A smuggler's den. Still, it's a good spot for a landing. Probably why the smugglers use it so often. I'll want extra if we're going there."

"Agreed," said Halt. He felt it reasonable to pay the man extra for the risk he was going to take. But not quite as much extra as the captain seemed to think it was worth. Eventually, they settled on a fee and Halt counted it out. Then he added three more gold pieces to the pile on the table in front of them.

The captain cocked an eye at it. "What's this?"

Halt shoved the money toward him. "That's for keeping your mouth shut," he said. "I'd like to leave after dark and I don't want people knowing where we're headed."

The shipmaster shrugged.

"My lips are sealed," he said. Then, turning away, he bellowed a string of curses and instructions at several crew members who were loading barrels into the ship's hold.

Will grinned. "That's a lot of noise for sealed lips," he remarked.

Now here they were, a few kilometers from their destination, and O'Malley had found them.

His ship was faster and handier than theirs. It was designed to outrun King's vessels sent to intercept it. And it carried a larger crew than the *Sparrow*. Will could see their heads lining the bulwarks and the occasional glint of weapons. At the raised stern, he could make out O'Malley himself, straining at the tiller and keeping the *Claw* on course.

"We can't outrun them, can we?"

Will started in surprise at Halt's voice, close behind him. He turned to see that the Ranger had left his post in the bow and was now intent on the ship pursuing them. He was pale, but he seemed in control of himself now.

Will remembered discussing seasickness with Svengal, Erak's first mate, years ago, on the long trip to Hallasholm.

"You need something to take your mind off it," the burly Skandian had told him. "When you've got something else to focus on, you don't have time to be seasick."

It seemed he had been right. Halt's attention was fixed on the smuggler's craft behind them. He seemed to have forgotten his uncertain stomach.

The captain was shaking his head in answer to Halt's question. "No. We can't outrun them. He's faster than us, and he can point up higher into the wind than I can. He'll either drive us down onto the reef or . . ." He stopped, not liking the alternative.

"Or what?" Horace asked. He loosened his sword in its scabbard. He'd seen the armed men aboard the *Claw* as well.

"Or else he'll ram us. The prow of his ship is reinforced. Rumor is he's sunk more than one ship that way." He glared at Halt. "If you'd told me that O'Malley would come after you, I'd never have taken you on board."

The faintest hint of a smile touched Halt's pale face.

"That's why I didn't tell you," he said. "So what do you plan to do?"

The captain shrugged helplessly. "What can I do? I can't outrun him. Can't outfight him. Can't even hand you over to him. He doesn't leave witnesses. We're just going to have to stand here and wait for him to sink us."

Halt raised an eyebrow.

"I think we can do a little better than that," he said. "Just let him get a little closer."

"I can't keep him from getting a little closer." Then he added, "What are you going to do with that?"

Halt was unslinging the longbow that was over his left shoulder. At the same time, he hitched the quiver on his right shoulder up a little and selected a shaft. Will, seeing the movement, unslung his own bow.

"One or two arrows won't stop that ship," the captain told him.

Halt regarded him with some curiosity. "I asked what you had in mind. Apparently you're content to stand here while O'Malley rams us, sinks us and leaves us to drown."

The captain shifted uncomfortably. "We might make it to shore," he said. "I can throw over empty barrels and balks of timber to hang on to. We might be able to make it to the beach."

"More likely we'll be washed onto the reef itself," Halt said. But he wasn't looking at the captain. He'd stepped closer to the rail and had an arrow nocked to the string. His eyes were fixed on the figure at the *Claw's* tiller. O'Malley had his feet braced wide apart as he dragged on the wooden bar, heaving the ship's bow upwind against the thrust on the sail and the pull of the oars. The whole ship was in a delicate state of balance. Wind, oars and tiller created a triangle of conflicting forces that resulted in the ship holding its present headway. Disturb one of those elements, Halt knew, and the result would be some moments of chaos as the remaining forces took charge.

He gauged the distance and the movement of the ship under his feet. Strange: now that he was concentrating on the problem of making an accurate shot, the nausea caused by that movement had receded. He frowned. The *Claw* was lifting and falling too. He'd have to factor that in to the shot. He sensed Will beside him, his own bow ready.

"Good lad," he said. "When I give you the word, we'll both shoot."

"I told you," the captain exclaimed. "A couple of arrows won't stop that ship. We've little enough chance as it is. If you antagonize O'Malley, he'll make sure we're all dead before he leaves."

"The way I see it," Halt said, "he won't be leaving. All right, Will. Now!"

As if they were linked by some invisible force, the two Rangers raised their bows, drew, sighted and shot. The two arrows sailed away within half a second of each other.

7

THE TWO ARROWS, WITH ONE A LITTLE IN THE LEAD, ARCED AWAY into the gray sky. Horace, watching their flight, lost sight of them against the clouds. He was conscious of the fact that Halt and Will had already nocked fresh arrows, ready for the next shot.

Then, eyes intent on the burly figure at the *Claw*'s tiller, he caught a flicker of movement as the two arrows flashed down. He couldn't tell which arrow struck O'Malley. Halt was the better shot, Horace knew, but Will was nearly as skilled.

One arrow thudded, quivering, into the bulwark less than a meter from the helm. The other buried itself painfully in the fleshy part of O'Malley's upper left arm—the side that was facing toward them.

With the noise of wind and sea, Horace couldn't hear the cry of pain from the smuggler. But he saw him stagger, releasing the tiller and clutching his injured left arm.

The effect on the *Claw* was almost instantaneous—and disastrous. Freed of the steadying pressure of the rudder, holding her across the wind, she suddenly flew up ahead of the wind, her square sail bulging and ropes snapping like overtuned harp strings with the increase in pressure as the force came from dead astern. The lurching of the ship threw O'Malley to the deck. At the same time, several oarsmen completely missed their stroke and tumbled backward on the rowing benches. One oar came unshipped. Several others tangled with their neighbors. The result was chaos.

The precise balance of forces that Halt had observed was totally disrupted. The *Claw* swung wildly downwind, already passing astern of the *Sparrow*, rushing madly toward the boiling waters of Palisade Reef.

One of the crew was lurching across the plunging deck, heading for the tiller, which was smashing back and forth, out of control.

"Stop him, Will," Halt said briefly. They crossed to the opposite side of the deck, where they had a clearer view of the out-of-control smuggler ship. Again they shot. This time, both arrows found their mark and the man pitched forward, rolling into the scuppers as the ship heeled.

The *Sparrow*'s captain watched, openmouthed.

"Nobody can shoot like that," he said softly. Horace, beside him, allowed himself a humorless smile.

"These two can," he said.

On board the *Claw*, the stricken crew realized that it was too late to save their ship from driving onto the reef. They began to scramble toward the raised stern, trying instinctively to avoid the point of first impact. Their ship, rolling wildly, struck the first of the rocks, hidden below the seething water. There was a grating crash and the ship shuddered, her movement checked for a moment. The mast bowed forward under the sudden impact, then snapped off clean, a meter above the deck. It came crashing down across the ship in a tangle of rope and canvas and splintered wood, crushing and trapping a few who had been caught beneath it. The extra weight to one side heeled the ship downwind, and that seemed to release it momentarily from the grip of the first rock. It surged upward, staggered farther into the tangle of the reef and crashed hard against another black, jagged mass rising from the sea. A wave broke over the trapped hull and several of the men on board were swept away. Halt and Will had lowered their bows. The bearded Ranger turned now to the captain.

"We should do something to help them," he said.

The captain shook his head fearfully. "I can't take my ship down into that!" he protested.

"I'm not suggesting you do. But we could toss some barrels overboard to float down to them. It might give them a chance." Halt glanced coldly back toward the wrecked ship. "Which is more than they would have given us."

At a word from the captain, some of the *Sparrow's* crewmen left the oars and began to heave empty casks over the rail, and he moved to help them. Soon a line of bobbing, floating barrels was drifting down toward the sinking ship.

The captain turned to Halt, fear in his eyes.

"I need my men back on the oars now," he said, "or we'll join them on the reef."

Halt nodded. "We've done all we can for them. Let's get out of here."

The sailors scrambled back to their benches and began to heave on the oars again. Slowly, the *Sparrow* began to drag herself away from the dreadful reef. But it was a close-run thing. One of the jagged rocks passed a few meters by their bow and was actually hidden by the port bulwark as they surged past it, emerging a few minutes later in their wake. Horace shuddered at the sight of it. Then he felt a strange sensation as the wind on his right cheek faltered and died, to be replaced by a gust from the left, then another, then a steady breeze. They'd reached the back-lift!

"Go about!" the captain was yelling, and the crew left the oars and rushed to the halyards. The big square sail began to swing ponderously, then filled with a loud crack on the opposite tack. As if she were aware of the danger she had just faced, the *Sparrow* surged gratefully away from the reef.

They beached the ship on the southern bank of the wide river mouth, running her prow into the sand so that she gradually eased to a halt. As the crew rigged a sling to the mast to haul the three horses overboard, the captain confronted Halt.

"You should have told me," he said accusingly. "You should have told me O'Malley was an enemy."

Surprisingly, Halt merely nodded.

"You're right," he said. "But I knew you'd never take us if I did, and I needed to get here."

The captain shook his head and began to say something further. Then he hesitated, remembering the uncanny skill of the two bowmen when they had sent their arrows streaking across the water at the smuggler's ship. Perhaps it might not do to show too much indignation with such men, he thought. Halt saw the struggle on his face and touched his arm gently. He understood the man's feelings, and he had to admit to himself that he had used him and his crew and had put them all in danger.

"I'd pay you more," he said apologetically, "but I need all the gold I have left." He thought for a moment, then said, "Bring me a pen and paper."

The skipper hesitated for a moment, then, as Halt urged him with a nod of his head, disappeared into the low cabin at the stern. It was several minutes before he emerged, with a ragged-edged sheet of vellum and a writing quill and inkhorn. He had no idea what Halt intended, and his expression said as much.

Halt spread the paper on the flat surface of the capstan top and dipped the quill in ink.

"What's your name?" he said. The question took the captain by surprise.

"Keelty. Ardel Keelty."

Halt thought for a second or two, then wrote quickly. He covered the vellum with half a dozen lines, leaned back to read what he had written, his head at a slight angle, then nodded, satisfied. He signed the sheet with a flourish and waved it in the air to allow the ink to dry. He handed it to the captain, who looked at it and shrugged.

"I'm no great hand at reading," he said.

Halt nodded. He took the paper back and read it aloud.

"Captain Keelty and the crew of the ship *Sparrow* have been instrumental in the taking and sinking of the notorious pirate and smuggling ship *Claw* off the coast of Picta. I request that these men be given a suitable reward from the royal coffers. Signed, Halt, Araluen Rangers." He looked up and added, "It's addressed to King Sean. Present it to him and he'll make it worth your while."

The captain snorted derisively as Halt handed him the sheet again. "King Sean? Never heard of him. Ferris is the King of Clonmel."

"Ferris is dead," Horace put in. He wanted to spare Halt the anguish of discussing his brother's death. "We're following the men who killed him. His nephew Sean has taken the throne."

The captain turned to Horace. He was mildly surprised at the news of the King's death. Fingle Bay was a long way from the capital, after all. He looked skeptically at the words Halt had written.

"So if he has," he said, "why should this new king take any notice of you?"

"Because he's my nephew," Halt told him. His dark eyes burned into Keelty's and the captain knew, instinctively, that he was telling the truth. Then a further thought struck him.

"But you said . . . he was Ferris's nephew?" he said. "So that means you're . . ." He stopped, not sure if his line of thinking was correct, not sure if he was missing something.

"It means I'm keen to get off this rolling tub of bilgewater and be on my way," Halt said briskly. He glanced around and saw that Will had brought their packs and saddles up from the small sleeping berth they had shared. He nodded his thanks and moved to the bow. The sailors had placed a ladder so that the three passengers could negotiate the two-meter drop to the sand more easily. Halt swung a leg over the bulwark and looked back at Keelty, standing with the sheet of paper fluttering in the wind.

"Don't lose that," he admonished him.

Keelty, his mouth open as he tried to put all the factors together, nodded absently. "I won't."

Halt looked at his two companions. "Let's go," he said, and ran lightly down the ladder to the sand. He was grateful to have the feeling of solid ground under his feet once more.

8

THEY PUSHED INLAND, FOLLOWING A ROUGH TRAIL THAT WOUND erratically through the dotted clumps of low-lying scrub and long grass that covered the ground. The wind was a constant force about them, keening in off the sea, bending the grass before it. Will glanced around. No trees in sight. For a moment, the sound of the wind soughing through the grass took him back to the terrifying night he had spent on the Solitary Plain, in his first year as an apprentice, when he and Gilan and Halt were hunting the Kalkara.

He mentally corrected himself. When the Kalkara were hunting them.

"Be nice to see a tree," Horace said, echoing Will's earlier thought.

Halt looked around at him. "They won't grow here. The wind brings in the salt from the sea and it kills them. We'll need to get farther inland to see trees."

Which raised a point that had been bothering Will. "Halt, where are we going? Do you have any idea?"

Halt shrugged. "We know Tennyson landed at Craiskill River. And this is the only path from the landing site. So reason says he must have gone this way."

"What happens when we hit another path?" Will asked. Halt gave him the ghost of a smile.

"Then we'll have to do some alternative reasoning."

"Can't you find their tracks or something?" Horace asked. "I thought you Rangers were supposed to be good at that."

"We're good," Halt told him comfortably. "But we're not infallible." The minute the words left his mouth, he regretted them. He saw the look of mock surprise on Horace's face.

"Well," said the young warrior, "that's the first time I've ever heard you admit that." He grinned easily at Halt, who scowled in response.

"I preferred you when you were young and had a modicum of respect for your elders," Halt said.

In truth, there were signs that people had passed along this track, but Halt and Will had no way of knowing whether they had been left by Tennyson's party or by other people. This was, after all, a path leading from a popular smugglers' rendezvous. It stood to reason that the Scotti used it constantly, bringing goods to trade with the smugglers and taking back the casks of spirits and bales of wool they brought ashore.

So they rode on, content for the moment to follow the trail, and with no real alternative to make them choose another direction.

They had started in the late afternoon, and night was nearly upon them when they found a fork in the trail. One branch continued in the general direction they had been taking—eastward. The other forked off to the south. Both branches seemed to be equally well used.

"We'll decide which way to go tomorrow," Halt said. He led them off the track, through the high grass and scrub. They found a more or less suitable campsite behind a clump of scrub and blackberry bush, which grew to a little more than head height. They led the three horses in a series of circles for a few minutes to trample down the long

grass, then unsaddled and watered the horses and settled down themselves, leaving the animals to crop the grass around them. Kicker was
attuned to travel with the two Ranger horses by now and Horace had
no need to hobble him. He'd stay close by his two companions.

He listened to the grinding, chomping sound of the three horses
as they ate and looked around, a frown on his face. "Don't know
where I'll find firewood."

Halt regarded him with a slight smile. "No point in looking," he
said. "There's none around and we can't have a fire anyway. Once it's
dark, even a small fire will be visible for miles and we never know
who's watching."

Horace sighed. Cold food again. And nothing but cold water to
wash it down. He was nearly as fond of coffee as the two Rangers.

"Let me know when we start having fun," he said.

There was a fine rain in the night and they woke under damp blankets. Halt rose, stretched and groaned as his aching muscles nagged
at him.

"I really am getting too old for this," he said. He looked around
the low horizon, bounded by scrubby heather and long grass, and
saw no sign of anyone watching them. He gestured toward the blackberry bush and said to Will, "I think we can risk a fire this morning.
See if you can cut some dry branches from inside that thicket."

Will nodded. He'd be grateful for a hot drink to start the day. He
crawled into the tangled blackberry bush and swore quietly when a
bramble stuck him.

"Watch the brambles," Halt said.

"Thank you for stating the obvious," Will told him. But he got
to work with his saxe knife and cut a bundle of the thin dry stalks.
Halt was right. The thick tangle had kept the rain from penetrating,
and Will backed out of the tunnel he had cut with a substantial

bundle of sticks. None of them would burn for long, but they'd give off little smoke.

"Should be enough to boil the coffeepot," he said. Halt nodded. They'd eat a cold breakfast again—hard bread and dried fruit and meat. But it would be more palatable with a hot, sweet mug of coffee to wash it down.

A little later, they sat, savoring their second cups.

"Halt," Will said, "can I ask you something?"

He saw his old mentor's mouth begin to frame the perennial answer to that question and hurried on before Halt could speak.

"Yes, I know. I just did. But I want to ask you something else, all right?"

A little miffed that Will had forestalled his stock answer, Halt gestured for him to go ahead.

"Where do you think Tennyson is heading?"

"I'd say," the Ranger answered after a few seconds' deliberation, "that he'll be heading south now that he has the chance. Back into Araluen."

"How do you know that?" Horace asked. He was always impressed at the two Rangers' ability to read a situation and come up with the correct answer to a problem. Sometimes, he thought, they almost seemed to have divine guidance.

"I'm guessing," Halt told him.

Horace was a little disappointed. He'd expected a detailed analysis of the situation. A faint smile showed on Halt's face. He was well aware that Horace occasionally entertained exaggerated ideas of Ranger skills and abilities.

"Sometimes that's all you can do," Halt said, a note of apology in his voice. Then he decided it might be a good idea to explain his train of thinking. He reached behind him to his saddlebag and took out a leather map case. He spread a map of the northern half of the border country between Araluen and Picta out before him. The two young men positioned themselves on either side of him.

"I figure we're about here," he said, tapping his forefinger on a spot several centimeters in from the coast. Will and Horace could see the Mull of Linkeith marked, and the Craiskill River, which meandered back to the northeast, angling away from the relatively direct eastern path they had been following. Horace leaned forward, peering more closely.

"Where's the path we're on?" he asked. Halt regarded him patiently.

"We don't mark every little footpath and game trail on these maps, you know," he said. Horace stuck out his bottom lip and shrugged. The action said that he thought such things should be marked. Halt decided to ignore him.

"Tennyson probably wants to head south," he said. "And this fork in the trail has been the first opportunity he's had to do it."

Will scratched his head thoughtfully. "Why south? You said that last night. What makes you so sure?"

"I'm not sure," Halt told him. "But it's a reasonable assumption."

Horace snorted disparagingly. "Fancy word for a guess."

Halt glared at him but Horace made sure he wasn't making eye contact with the Ranger. Halt shook his head and continued.

"We know Tennyson didn't particularly *want* to come to Picta," he said. "O'Malley told us that, remember?"

Understanding was beginning to dawn on Horace's face. His faith in Ranger infallibility was slowly being restored.

"That's right," he said. "He said Tennyson just wanted to get out of Hibernia."

"Exactly. And Picta was the place O'Malley was going. So he dropped Tennyson off at the Craiskill River. Now, I'd be willing to bet that the Outsiders don't have any influence in Picta so far . . ."

"What makes you say that?" Will wanted to know.

"The Scotti aren't particularly tolerant of new religions," Halt told him. "And the local brand of intolerance is a little more violent than it is in Araluen. Try to start a new religion in this country and they'll string you up by your thumbs—particularly if you ask them for gold as the price of conversion."

"Not a bad policy really," Horace said.

Halt regarded him levelly. "Exactly. However, it's reasonable to assume that there are pockets of influence dotted around the remote parts of Araluen. I'd be surprised if Selsey was the only place they've infiltrated."

Selsey was the isolated west coast fishing village where Halt had first discovered the Outsiders' activity.

"And even if that's not the case, he really has no other choice, does he?" Will said. "He can't stay in Hibernia because he knows we were after him there. He can't stay in Picta—"

"Or they'll string him up by the thumbs," Horace put in, grinning. He liked the mental image of the overweight, self-important Tennyson dangling by his digits.

"So Araluen is the logical choice," Halt finished. He tapped the map again, indicating a location south of the position he had originally pointed to. "And this is the closest path through the mountains back into Araluen: One Raven Pass."

The border between Araluen and Picta was delineated by a range of rugged mountains. They weren't particularly high, but they were steep and forbidding, and the easiest ways through them were a series of mountain passes.

"One Raven Pass?" Horace repeated. "Why One Raven?"

"One raven is sorrow," Will said absently, repeating the old proverb.

Halt nodded. "That's right. The pass is the site of an old battle many years ago. A Scotti army was ambushed in the pass and wiped out to a man. Legend has it that since then, no birdlife will live there. Except for a solitary raven, who appears every year on the anniversary of the battle and whose cries sound like Scotti widows weeping for their men."

"How many years ago did this happen?" Horace asked. Halt shrugged as he rolled up the map and replaced it in his map case.

"Oh, three or four hundred years back, I suppose," he said carelessly.

"And how many years does a raven live?" Horace asked, a small frown furrowing the skin between his eyes. Halt rolled his eyes to heaven, seeing what was coming.

Will tried to step in. "Horace . . ."

Horace held up a hand to forestall him.

"I mean, it's not as if it's breeding there and this is its great-great-great-great-grandson raven, is it?" he said. "After all, it's one raven, and one raven can hardly have great-great-great-grandsons on its own, can it?"

"It's a *legend*, Horace," Halt said deliberately. "It's not meant to be taken literally."

"Still," said Horace doggedly, "why not call it something sensible? Like Battle Pass? Or Ambush Pass?"

Halt regarded him. He loved Horace like a younger brother. Even like a second son, after Will. He admired his skill with a sword and his courage in battle. But sometimes, just sometimes, he felt an overwhelming desire to ram the young warrior's head against a convenient tree.

"You have no sense of drama or symbolism, do you?" he asked.

"Huh?" replied Horace, not quite understanding. Halt looked around for a convenient tree. Luckily for Horace, there were none in sight.

9

TENNYSON, SELF-STYLED PROPHET OF THE GOD ALSEIASS, scowled at the platter that had been placed in front of him. The meager contents—a small piece of stringy salted beef and a few withered carrots and turnips—did nothing to lighten his mood. Tennyson was a man who enjoyed his creature comforts. But now he was cold and uncomfortable. And, worst of all, hungry.

He thought bitterly of the Hibernian smuggler who had put him and his party ashore on the wild west coast of Picta. He had demanded an exorbitant fee from the Outsiders and, after a great amount of haggling, had grudgingly agreed to provide them with provisions for their overland journey south. When the time had come for them to disembark, they had been virtually manhandled off the ship like so much unwanted ballast, and half a dozen sacks had been tossed onto the beach after them.

By the time Tennyson had discovered that at least a third of the food provided in the sacks was spoiled and inedible, the smuggler's ship was already well offshore, swooping over the rolling waves like a gull. He raged impotently on the beach, picturing the smuggler laughing to himself as he counted the gold coins he had extorted from them.

At first, Tennyson was tempted to claim the largest share of the small store of food for himself, but caution prevailed. His hold over his followers was tenuous. None of them were abject believers in Alseiass. These were the hard core of his group, his fellow criminals, who knew that the Outsiders cult was nothing more than an opportunity to extort money from simple country folk. They saw Tennyson as their leader only because he was skilled in persuading gullible farmers and villagers to part with their money. But at the moment, there were no farmers or villagers nearby and they felt no sense of deference to the bulky gray-haired man in the flowing white robe. He might be their leader, but right now he wasn't returning any profit to them, so he didn't deserve any more than the rest of them.

The truth was, he needed them as much as they needed him. Things were different when they were surrounded by several hundred converts, eager to pander to Tennyson's every whim. When that was the case, they all lived high off the hog, and none higher than he. But now? Now he would have to share with the rest.

He heard footsteps approaching and looked up, the sour expression still on his face. Bacari, the senior of the two Genovesan assassins still remaining in his employ, stopped a few paces away. He smiled sarcastically at the platter of food on Tennyson's knee.

"Not exactly a feast, Your Holiness."

Tennyson's brow darkened in anger. He needed the Genovesans but he didn't like them. They were arrogant and self-centered. When he ordered them to carry out a task, they did so with an air of reluctance, as if they were doing him a favor. He'd paid them well to protect him, and he expected that they might show him a little deference. But that was a concept that seemed beyond them.

"Did you find anything?" he asked.

The assassin shrugged. "There's a small farm about three kilometers away. There are animals there, so we'll have meat at least."

Tennyson had sent the two Genovesans to scout out the surrounding area. What little food they had remaining was almost inedible, and they were going to have to find more. Now, at the mention of fresh meat, his spirits lifted.

"Vegetables? Flour? Grain?" he asked. Bacari shrugged again. It was an infuriating movement, Tennyson thought. It conveyed a world of disdain for the person being addressed.

"Possibly," Bacari said. "It seems like a prosperous little place."

Tennyson's eyes narrowed. Prosperous might equate with well populated. "How many people?"

Bacari made a dismissive gesture. "Two people so far as I could see," he said. "We can handle them easily."

"Excellent!" Tennyson rose to his feet with renewed enthusiasm. He looked at the distasteful contents of the platter and hurled them into the heather beside the track. "Rolf!" he called to his chief henchman. "Get everyone ready to move! The Genovesans have found us some food."

The band began preparing to move out. The mention of food had heartened all of them. The surly looks and angry muttering that had become the norm for the past few days were gone. Amazing what the prospect of a full belly would do for people's spirits, Tennyson thought.

It was a well-kept thatched cottage with a barn beside it. Smoke rose in a lazy curl from the chimney. A cultivated field showed the green tops of vegetables growing—kale or cabbage, Tennyson surmised. As they approached, a man emerged from the barn, leading a black cow behind him on a rope. He was clad in the typical attire of the region—a long plaid covering his upper body and a heavy kilt wrapped around his waist. He didn't notice them at first, but when he did, he stopped in his tracks, the cow dropping its head to graze the long grass.

Tennyson raised his hand in a sign of peace and continued toward the Scotti farmer. Rolf and his other followers spread out in a line on either side of him. Bacari and Marisi, the second Genovesan, stayed close by him, a pace behind him. Both had their crossbows unslung and held unobtrusively close to their sides.

The farmer turned and called back to the house. A few seconds later, a woman appeared at the door and moved to join her husband, standing ready to defend their home against these strangers.

"We come in peace," Tennyson called. "We mean you no harm."

The farmer replied in his native tongue. Tennyson had no idea what the words were, but the meaning was clear—stay away. The man stooped and drew something from the leather-bound legging on his right leg. He straightened and they could see a long, black-bladed dirk in his hand. Tennyson smiled reassuringly and continued to move forward.

"We need food," he said. "We'll pay you well for it."

He had no intention of paying and no idea if the farmer could understand the common tongue he spoke in. Probably not, this far away from civilization. The important thing was the soothing and placating tone.

But the farmer wasn't convinced. He turned and shoved the cow violently, attempting to herd it back to the shelter of the barn. The black animal raised its head in alarm and began to wheel heavily away.

"Kill him," Tennyson said quietly.

Almost immediately, he heard the *slap-whiz* of the two crossbows, and two bolts streaked across the field to bury themselves in the man's back. He threw up his hands, gave a choked cry and fell facedown in the grass. His wife uttered a scream and dropped to her knees beside him, speaking to him, trying to rouse him. But Tennyson knew from the way the man had fallen that he was dead when he hit the ground. It took a minute or so for the woman to come to the same realization. When she did, she rose to her feet, screamed what was obviously a curse at them and turned to run. She had gone three paces when Bacari, who had reloaded, shot again and sent her sprawling facedown, a few meters from her husband.

The cow, unnerved by the shouting and the metallic smell of blood, stood uncertainly, swaying its head, offering a halfhearted threat to the approaching strangers.

Nolan, a burly man who was one of Tennyson's inner circle, moved forward and seized the cow's halter, bringing it under control. The cow looked at him curiously, and then Nolan slashed his knife across its throat. The cow staggered a few paces before its legs gave way and it collapsed into the grass.

The Outsiders stood around the animal in a circle, regarding it with satisfaction. There would be enough meat there to keep them fed for some time.

"Clean it and joint it," Tennyson told Nolan. Before joining Tennyson's band, the big man had worked as a butcher. He nodded contentedly.

"Give me a hand," he ordered three of the men around him. He'd need them to hold the carcass steady while he skinned and butchered it. Tennyson left him to the task and strode into the farmhouse. The doorway was low and he had to bow his head to enter. A quick search revealed a supply of potatoes, turnips and onions. His men gathered them up while he sent another two to pick some of the cabbages growing in the cultivated field. He looked around the neat little house. He was tempted to spend the night here under a roof for a change. But he had no idea if the farmer might have friends living nearby. It would be safer to gather up the food and keep moving.

Another of his followers met him as he emerged from the house.

"There are two more beasts in the barn," he said. "Do we want them?"

Tennyson considered the question. They had plenty of meat now, as well as the potatoes and onions from the house. If they were to carry anything more, it would only slow them down. He glanced across to where Nolan was already working on the carcass.

"No," he said. "Burn the barn when we leave. And the house." There was no real reason to burn them, he thought. But then, there was no reason not to either. And the act of wanton destruction would go a long way toward restoring his good spirits.

The Outsider nodded. Then he hesitated, not sure what Tennyson intended.

"And the cows?" he asked. Tennyson shrugged. If he couldn't use them, he didn't see any sense in leaving them for anyone else.

"Burn them in it."

10

THE PATH LED HALT, WILL AND HORACE A LITTLE EAST OF south, and the coastline was angling out to the west. So as they traveled, they moved farther and farther away from the sea. The constant salt-laden wind died away and they began to see trees again.

The land itself was wild and hilly, covered for the main part in gorse and heather. It lacked the gentle green beauty of the southern parts of Araluen that Will and Horace were accustomed to. But it had its own form of beauty—wild and rugged and unkempt. Even the trees, as they began to appear with greater frequency, seemed to stand as if challenging the elements to do their worst, their roots wide-set in the sandy ground, their branches thick and braced like brawny arms.

They had traveled perhaps a kilometer when Halt gave a low grunt. He swung down from the saddle and stepped off the trail to examine something. Will and Horace, riding single file behind him, dismounted and moved to peer over his shoulder. He was studying a small tuft of cloth, caught on a branch of tough heather that grew beside the trail.

"What do you make of that, Will?"

"Cloth," Will said. Then, as Halt looked piercingly at him, he realized that he had stated the obvious and his mentor wanted more from him. He reached out and touched the small fragment, feeling it, rolling it gently between his forefinger and thumb. It was a smooth linen weave, perhaps from a shirt, he thought.

"It's nothing like the rough plaid the Scotti wear," he said thoughtfully. Now he realized why they wove that thick, rough cloth. The heather and gorse of their homeland would rip anything lighter to shreds within a few weeks.

"Good work," Halt said approvingly.

Horace smiled as he watched his two friends, crouched by the side of the track. In some ways, he knew, Halt would never stop teaching the younger Ranger. Will would always be his apprentice. And as he had the thought, he realized that Will, without thinking about it, would probably always want it that way.

"So what else occurs to you?" Halt asked.

Will looked around, studying the sandy path they had been traveling, seeing traces there that people had passed this way within the previous few days. But the rain and wind had made it almost impossible to deduce whether they had all traveled together or were in several separate parties.

"I'm wondering why the owner wasn't walking on the path itself. Why would he be shoving his way through the bushes when there's a clear path?"

Halt said nothing. But his body language, as he leaned toward Will and nodded encouragingly, told the young Ranger that he was on the right track. He looked at the path again, at the jumble of footprints, one over the other.

"The path is narrow," he said finally. "No room for more than two abreast. The person wearing this"—he indicated the small piece of material—"was jostled off the path by the numbers. Maybe he stopped for a moment and was bumped aside."

"So we're following a large group of travelers. I'd say there are more than a dozen of them," Halt said.

"Tennyson had about twenty people with him," Will said.

Halt nodded. "Exactly. And I'd guess we're a day or two behind them."

They stood erect. Horace shook his head in admiration.

"You mean you can figure out all that just from one little scrap of cloth?"

Halt regarded him sardonically. He was still bristling a little from Horace saying, "Fancy word for a guess" the previous day. Halt didn't forget criticism.

"No," he said. "We're guessing. We just wanted to make it sound scientific."

Halt paused for a few seconds, as if inviting Horace to make some kind of reply, but wisely, Horace chose not to. Finally, the Ranger gestured to the path ahead of them.

"Let's get moving," he said.

The wind had blown away the rain clouds of the previous night and the sky above them was a brilliant blue, even though the air temperature was cold and crisp. The heather that surrounded them varied in color from deep brown to dull purple. Under the bright sunlight it seemed to shimmer with color. Will spotted the next fragment of cloth almost by chance. It was nothing more than a thread, really, snagged on another branch—this time, one growing close to the path. And it would have been easy to miss in the purple heather because it blended in.

It too was purple.

Will signaled Horace, who was riding behind him, to rein in. Then he leaned down from the saddle and plucked the thread from the bush.

"Halt," he called.

The bearded Ranger checked Abelard and swiveled in the saddle. He squinted at the purple thread on Will's forefinger, then smiled slowly. "And who do we know who wears purple?"

"The Genovesans," Will replied.

Halt took a deep breath. "So it looks like we're on the right track."

That was confirmed for them a few kilometers later. They smelled it first. The wind was too strong for the smoke to hang in the sky. It was blown away almost instantly. But the stench of burned, charred wood and thatch—and something else—carried to them.

"Smoke," Will said, reining in and turning his face to the wind to try to catch the scent more clearly. There was a faint trace of something else—something he'd smelled before, when he had been following the trail of one of Tennyson's raiding parties, far away to the south in Hibernia. It was the smell of burned flesh.

Then Halt and Horace caught the scent too. Will exchanged a glance with his teacher and knew he'd recognized that ominous smell as well.

"Come on," said Halt, and he urged Abelard into a canter, even though he knew they were already too late.

The crofter's cottage had stood in cleared ground, a few hundred meters from the path.

Now it was a pile of blackened ruins, still smoking a day after it had been consumed by fire. One section of the thatched roof remained partly intact. But its support structure had collapsed and it lay at an angle, propped up by the charred remnants of one wall.

"Thatch must have been damp," Halt said. "It didn't burn completely."

They'd reined in a few meters short of the cottage. There was nobody left alive here. The bodies of a man and a woman sprawled facedown in the long grass.

There had been a second building beyond the cottage—a barn, Will guessed. It too had been burned to ashes. There was nothing left of its walls, although, as with the cottage, some sections of the damp thatch had survived, only to collapse into the ruins. Tug side-stepped nervously as Will urged him toward the barn. The smell of burned flesh was much stronger here, and the horse objected to it. Among the ashes, Will could see two large, charred bodies. Cattle, he thought.

"Easy, boy," Will told Tug. The little horse tossed his head un-comfortably, as if apologizing for his nervous reaction. Then he steadied. Will swung himself down from the saddle and heard a low warning rumble in Tug's chest.

"It's all right," he told the horse. "Whoever did this is long gone."

And it soon became apparent who was responsible. Will knelt beside the body of the crofter and gently moved the man's tangled plaid to one side, from where it had bunched up as he had fallen. Concealed by the folds of rough wool, he found the implements that had killed him: two crossbow bolts, barely a centimeter apart, buried deep in the man's back. There was little blood. At least one of the bolts must have hit the man's heart, killing him almost instantly. That was something to be grateful for, at least, Will thought. He looked up. Halt and Horace were still sitting on their horses, watch-ing him.

"Crossbow," he said.

"Not a Scotti weapon," Halt observed.

Will shook his head. "No. I've seen bolts like this before. They're Genovesan. Tennyson has been here."

Horace looked around the tragic little scene. His expression was a mixture of sadness and disgust. Picta and the Scotti might nomi-nally be enemies of Araluen, but these people weren't soldiers or raiders. They were simple country folk, going about their day-to-day business, working hard and scraping a meager living from this tough northern land.

"Why?" he said. "Why kill them?"

In his young life, Horace had seen his share of battles and knew there was no glamour in war. But at least in war, soldiers knew their fate was in their own hands. They could kill or be killed. They had a chance to defend themselves. This was the pitiless slaughter of innocent, unarmed civilians.

Halt indicated another corpse, farther away and half concealed in the long grass. There was a small cloud of flies buzzing about and a crow hopped on top of it, ripping at the carcass with its dagger of a beak. It was all that was left of another of the crofter's cattle. But this one had been killed and butchered for its meat.

"They wanted food," he said. "So they took it. When the crofter objected, they killed him and his wife and burned their house and barn."

"But why? They could have overpowered him, surely. Why kill him?"

Halt shrugged. "They've still got a way to go to the border," he said. "I guess they didn't want to leave anyone behind who could raise the alarm against them." He looked around now, but saw no sign of other habitation. "I'll bet there are half a dozen other little crofts like this within a few kilometers. Chances are there's a hamlet or village as well. Tennyson wouldn't want to take the risk that these people might gather a party and come after him."

"He's a murdering swine," Horace said quietly as he listened to Halt's reasoning. The bearded Ranger gave a slight snort of disgust.

"Are you only now beginning to figure that out?"

11

Halt glanced warily around the horizon. "We should get out of here," he said, but Horace was already swinging down from his saddle.

"We can't leave them like this, Halt," he said quietly. "It's just not right."

He began to unstrap the short shovel that was part of his camping equipment. Halt leaned forward in the saddle.

"Horace, do you want to be here if some of these Scottis' friends turn up?" he asked. "Because I don't think they'll be too willing to listen to explanations."

But Horace was already surveying the ground, looking for a soft spot to begin digging.

"We should bury them, Halt. We can't just leave them here to rot. If they have any friends nearby, they'll appreciate the fact that we took the trouble."

"I think you're assuming far too much reasoning power from the Scotti," Halt told him. But he could see that he wouldn't change Horace's mind. Will had dismounted and had his own shovel as well. He looked up at Halt.

"Halt, if we don't bury them, they'll attract more crows and ra-vens. And that might attract their friends' attention," he reasoned.

"What about that?" Halt asked, indicating the butchered carcass. Will shrugged.

"We can drag it into the middle of the barn's ashes," he said. "Cover it with sections of the thatch."

Halt sighed, giving up the argument. In a way, he thought, Horace was right. It was the decent thing to do—and that was what set them apart from people like Tennyson. And besides, Will's argu-ment made sense. Maybe, Halt thought, he had become a little too cold-blooded and pragmatic in his old age. He swung down from the saddle, took his own shovel and began digging.

"I'm too set in my ways to start doing the right thing," he com-plained. "You're a bad influence, Horace."

They covered the two bodies with the thick plaids they had been wearing and laid them side by side in the shallow grave. While Will and Horace filled it in, Halt hitched a rope to Abelard's saddle and dragged the carcass into the blackened remains of the barn. Then he heaved several sections of the half-burned thatch over the body. The other two beasts were so badly burned that there was nothing left to attract scavengers.

Once their task was complete, the three Araluens mounted their waiting horses. "Let's pick up the pace," Halt said, swinging Abelard's head to the south again. "We've got a lot of time to make up."

They held the horses to a steady lope throughout the rest of the afternoon. Tug and Abelard, of course, could maintain a pace like that for days if necessary. Kicker didn't have quite the same endur-ance, but his longer stride meant he was making the same progress for a lot less effort. The clear skies of the morning had gone as the wind shifted and brought banks of cloud rolling in from the west. Halt sniffed the air.

"Could rain tonight," he said. "Be good to be into the pass by then."

"Why's that?" Will wanted to know.

"Caves," Halt told him succinctly. "The walls of the pass are lined with them, and I'd rather spend the night in a nice, warm, dry cave than sleeping out in this Pictish rain again."

They reached One Raven Pass with the last light of day. At first, Will and Horace could see no sign of it. Then they realized that a few meters after the entrance, the pass took an abrupt ninety-degree turn to the left, so that the rock wall opposite seemed to fill the opening. They rode in cautiously, their hoofbeats echoing from the rock walls that soared above them. For the first fifty meters or so, the path was narrow, a winding track between the high mountains. Then gradually it opened out, until the floor of the pass was thirty or forty meters wide. The ground was still rising and the surface was rough. Inside the pass, the shadows were deep and the going was treacherous. Kicker stumbled several times and Halt held up his hand.

"We might camp for the night," he said. "The horses could break a leg in these conditions and then we'd be in real trouble."

Will was peering around the heavily shadowed walls. "Don't see any of those warm, dry caves you mentioned," he said.

Halt clicked his tongue in annoyance. "The notes on the map say they should be here." Then he pointed. "That overhang will have to do us."

A large, flat spur of rock jutted out from the wall of the pass, providing an area of shelter underneath. There was plenty of headroom. In the absence of a cave, it would serve the purpose, Will thought.

"At least it'll keep the rain off," he said.

They set up camp. Will and Horace had carried a supply of fire-

wood from the previous campsite, and Halt decided they could risk
a fire. They were cold and low-spirited, he realized, and all too ready
to snap at one another. A fire, some hot food and coffee would go a
long way toward restoring their spirits. There was a slight risk that
it might be seen, he thought, but the twists and turns of the pass
should conceal it pretty effectively. Besides, so far they'd seen no sign
that anyone was following them. And moving in the dark over the
uneven, rock-strewn, sloping ground of the pass would be risky for
any pursuer. Doing so quietly would be well nigh impossible. All in
all, he thought, the potential gains outweighed the dangers.

They settled into their blankets and cloaks early, covering the fire
with sand before they did so. It was one matter to heat food and
water for a few minutes, another altogether to leave the fire burning
to signal their presence while they slept. Horace offered to take the
first watch, and Will and Halt accepted gratefully.

Horace's hand on his shoulder roused Will from a deep, dreamless
sleep. For a second, he wondered where he was, and why there was a
pebble pressing painfully into his hip through his blankets. Then he
remembered.

"Is it my watch?" he mumbled. But Horace crouched over him,
his finger to his lips for silence.

"Listen," he whispered. He turned away to face down the pass.
Will, sniffing and yawning, sat up in his blankets, propped on one
elbow.

A long, rasping cry echoed down the pass, bouncing from one
wall to the other and back again so that the echoes continued long
after the original noise had ceased. Will felt his skin rise in goose
bumps at the sound. It was a sound of sorrow, a wavering, croaking
cry of pain.

"What the devil is that?" he whispered.

Horace shook his head. Then he leaned forward again to listen, his head cocked slightly to one side.

"It's the third time I've heard it," he said. "The first two were so quiet I wasn't really sure I heard them. But now it's closer."

The cry came again, but this time from a different direction. The first had been from down the pass, Will thought. This one was definitely behind them, issuing from somewhere back the way they had come.

Suddenly, he recognized the sound.

"It's a raven," he said. "The raven of One Raven Pass."

"But that one was from up there," Horace began, pointing back along the pass, then turning uncertainly toward the direction from which they'd heard the first cry. "There must be two of them."

"Or one of them flying around," Will put in.

"You think so?" Horace asked. He would face any enemy unflinchingly. But to sit here in this shadowy cleft in the mountains listening to that mournful sound set his nerves on edge.

A long-suffering voice came from the pile of blankets that covered Halt. "I've heard ravens do tend to fly around," he said. "Now will you two kindly shut up and let me sleep?"

"Sorry, Halt," Horace said, abashed. He patted Will on the shoulder. "You go back to sleep too. I've got another hour to go."

Will settled down again. The croaking call came again, from a third direction.

"Yes," said Horace to himself. "It's definitely one raven, flying to different positions. Definitely. That's what it is, all right."

"I'm not going to warn you again," came Halt's muffled voice. Horace opened his mouth to apologize, thought better of it and remained silent.

. . .

The raven continued its mournful croaking throughout the night. Will took over the watch from Horace, then handed over to Halt a few hours before dawn. As light began to touch the higher edges of the rock walls around them, the raven gradually became silent.

"Now that he's gone," Horace said as he extinguished the breakfast cooking fire, "I almost miss him."

"That's not how you felt last night," Will said, grinning. He made his eyes wide and staring and waved his hands in mock fright. "Ooooh, Will! Help! There's a big bad raven come to carry me away."

Horace shook his head, somewhat shamefaced. "Well, I suppose I was a little startled," he said. "But it took me by surprise, that's all."

"I'm glad I was here to protect you," Will said, with a slightly superior tone.

Halt, watching them as he rolled his pack, thought his former apprentice was pushing it too far. "You know," he said quietly, "just after you first heard the raven, Will, I actually heard a strange crackling noise as well."

Will regarded him curiously. "You did? I didn't notice it. What do you think it was?"

"I couldn't be sure," the Ranger said thoughtfully, "but I suspect it was the sound of your hair standing on end in fright."

Horace gave a short bark of laughter and Halt allowed him one of his brief smiles. Will turned to roll his own pack, feeling his cheeks redden.

"Oh yes. Very amusing, Halt. Very amusing," he said. But he did wonder how the bearded Ranger had known that his hair had done just that.

They continued along the pass, still moving slightly uphill. After a while, the path became level and then sloped gradually down again. An hour or so after they had left the campsite, Halt pointed out a small, flat-topped cairn of rocks set by the eastern wall of the pass.

"That's what our friend the raven was crying about," he said.

They rode closer to study the pile, which resembled a small, rough altar. The stones were very old and their edges worn smooth. On the rock wall beside them, there were faint carvings visible, weathered by years of wind and rain.

"It's a memorial to the men who died here," Halt told them.

Will leaned forward a little to study the carvings. "What do they say?"

Halt shrugged. "They're pretty hard to make out, worn as they are. And I can't read Scotti runes anyway. I suspect they tell the story of the battle." He indicated the steep walls. At this point, the pass had narrowed again so that it was barely twenty meters wide. "There are ledges up there where the enemy stationed their archers," he said. "They fired down into the ranks of the Scotti as they were packed together down here. They fired arrows, rolled rocks, threw spears. The Scotti soldiers got in their own way trying to retreat. When they were hopelessly tangled together and confused, the enemy cavalry came around the next bend there and hit them."

His two young companions followed his account of the ancient battle, looking from one point to another as he described it. Young as they were, they were both experienced in battle, and they could picture the terrible slaughter that must have taken place in this crowded, shadowy cleft in the rocks.

"Who were they, Halt?" Horace asked. He kept his voice lowered in an unconscious mark of respect for the warriors who had died here. Halt looked at him, not understanding the question, so he elaborated.

"Who were the enemy?"

"We were," Halt told him. "The Araluens. This antagonism between the two nations isn't something recent, you know. It goes back for centuries. That's why I'm keen to get out of Picta and back onto Araluen soil."

It was an obvious hint, and the two young men urged their horses after him as he rode south, heading for the exit from the pass. Horace glanced back at the small memorial once or twice, but soon a twist in the pass hid it from sight.

An hour later, they found the second set of tracks.

12

HALT AND WILL, INTENT ON THE TRACKS LEFT BY TENNYSON and his followers, noticed the different set almost simultaneously.

"Halt . . . ," Will said. But his old mentor was already nodding.

"I see them." He reined in Abelard. Will and Horace stopped as well, and the two Rangers dismounted to study this evidence of new-comers. Horace, aware of a certain tension in the air, surreptitiously loosened his sword in its scabbard. He was bursting to question the Rangers, but he knew any such distraction would be unwelcome. They'd tell him when they'd assessed the situation.

Will glanced back down the trail. There was a small subsidiary defile leading in from the left-hand side of the pass a few meters back—a narrow gap in the rocks that joined the major route into Araluen. They had ridden past it, almost without noticing. They had seen plenty of narrow tracks leading off the main path. Most of them petered out after twenty to thirty meters, ending in blind walls of rock.

This one was different. The tracks had come from it.

Will ran lightly back and disappeared into the cleft. He was gone for some minutes and then, to Horace's intense relief, he reappeared. The tall young warrior was uncomfortable when his friend vanished suddenly like that. So was Tug, he realized. The little horse had shifted nervously and stamped his hoof when his master seemed to vanish into the rock.

"That's where they came from," Will said thoughtfully, jerking his thumb back at the gap in the wall. "The trail in there goes back quite a way. I went forty or fifty meters in and it didn't seem to end. And it widened out quite a bit."

Halt scratched his beard thoughtfully. "There are dozens of subsidiary trails leading into the main pass," he said. "This is obviously one of them." He looked down at the scuffed ground before him, twisting his mouth thoughtfully to one side. Horace decided that his companions had had long enough to assess the situation.

"Who are they?" he asked.

Halt didn't answer immediately. He looked at Will. "What would you say?"

The days were long past when Will would blurt out an unconsidered answer to such a question from Halt. Better to be accurate than fast, he had learned. He went down on one knee, touching one of the tracks with his forefinger, tracing its outline in the sand. He looked left and right, studying the faint outlines of other footprints.

"The footprints are all big," he said. "And quite deep on this hard surface. So whoever they are, they're heavily built."

"So?" Halt prompted.

"So they're all men. There are no smaller prints that I can see. No women or children with them. I'd say they're a war party."

"Following Tennyson?" Horace asked, his mind going back to the pathetic scene at the crofter's cottage.

Will chewed his lip thoughtfully. He looked at Halt but the older Ranger gestured for him to continue his line of reasoning.

"Maybe," he said. "They came through several hours after

Tennyson did. You can see where their tracks overlay his party's. And they're fresher. I'd say these were made early this morning."

"Well, let's hope they catch him," Horace said. To his way of thinking, if a vengeful Scotti war party wiped out Tennyson and his Outsiders, that would be a neat solution to the whole situation.

"Maybe," Will repeated. "But . . . if they're chasing Tennyson, why did they come into the main trail here from the east?" He indicated the side trail again. "Anyone following Tennyson after what he and his men did would be more likely to come straight down the pass behind us—from the north."

"Maybe it's a shortcut," Horace suggested, but Will shook his head.

"If you could see the way it snakes and twists in there, you'd know it's no kind of a shortcut. I'd say it originates from somewhere else entirely. Somewhere farther to the east." He looked at Halt for confirmation and the bearded Ranger nodded.

"I tend to agree," he said. "I think it's just coincidence that we've run across them. Odds are, they have no idea that Tennyson and his thugs are ahead of them."

"Couldn't they see the tracks?" Horace asked, waving his hand vaguely at the sandy, rock-strewn surface of the path. Halt allowed himself a brief smile.

"Could you?" he asked.

Horace had to admit that if the two Rangers weren't there to point out the faint scuffs and imprints in the sand, he probably wouldn't. He shook his head.

"The Scotti are no great shakes at tracking," Halt told him. He gestured for Will to remount and swung up into Abelard's saddle.

"So if they're not after Tennyson, what are they doing here?" Horace asked.

"My guess is, they're planning a cattle raid in Araluen. There are several small villages close to the border, and they may be heading for one of them."

"And if they are?" Will asked.

Halt fixed his unblinking gaze on him. "If they are, we'll have to discourage them. Which could be a nuisance."

The intentions of the Scotti party became clearer shortly after they emerged from One Raven Pass into Araluen itself. Tennyson's party veered slightly to the east, but basically continued to follow a southerly route. The Scotti raiders swung almost immediately to head west of southwest, heading almost ninety degrees away from the Outsiders.

Halt sighed heavily when he interpreted the signs on the ground. He looked to the southeast, hesitating, then reluctantly turned Abelard's head to follow the raiders.

"We can't leave them to their own devices," he said. "We'll have to take care of them and then come back to pick up Tennyson's trail again."

"Can't the locals take care of themselves?" Will asked. He was reluctant to leave the pursuit of Tennyson and his followers just because a few cattle might be stolen. Halt shook his head wearily.

"This is a fairly large party, Will. Maybe fifteen or sixteen armed men. They'll pick out a small farm with only two or three men to defend it. They'll kill the men, burn the buildings and crops and take the cattle. And they'll probably take the women as slaves too, if they're in the mood."

"And if they're not?" Horace asked.

"They'll kill them," Halt said coldly. "Do you want to let that happen?"

Both young men shook their heads. They could see the scene at the crofter's cottage all too vividly once more.

"Let's get after them," Will said, his face grim.

Mounted as they were, they were gaining ground rapidly on the Scotti raiders. The countryside on this side of the border changed dramatically, and they were moving through heavily wooded land now. Halt called Will alongside him.

"Go ahead and scout the way," he said. "I don't want to catch up with them without knowing it."

Will nodded his understanding and urged Tug forward. The horse and rider disappeared into the mist that filtered between the trees. Halt had no qualms about Will's ability to track the Scotti without being seen or heard. Both he and Tug were trained for the task. Horace wasn't so sure.

"Maybe we should have gone with him," he said, a few minutes after his friend was lost to sight.

"Three of us would make four times the noise he will," Halt said.

Horace frowned, not quite understanding the equation. "Wouldn't three of us make three times the noise?"

Halt shook his head. "Will and Tug will make hardly any noise. Neither will Abelard and I. But as for you and that moving earthquake you call a horse . . ." He gestured at Kicker and left the rest unsaid.

Horace was suitably offended at this slur on his faithful horse. He was very fond of Kicker.

"That's a little harsh, Halt!" he protested. "In any case, it's not Kicker's fault. He's not trained to move quietly . . ." He trailed off, realizing that he'd just reinforced the very point Halt was making. The Ranger caught his eye and inclined his head meaningfully. Sometimes, Horace thought, a simple look or a tilt of the head could convey more sarcasm than a torrent of words.

Halt, understanding the concern for Will that lay behind

Horace's suggestion, decided he should reassure him. But not for a few minutes. He was enjoying pulling the warrior's leg again. It was like old times. Then he scowled. He was getting sentimental.

"Will knows what he's doing," he told Horace. "Don't worry about him."

An hour later, Abelard suddenly raised his head and snorted. Then, a few seconds after that, Will and Tug slipped out of the mist once more, cantering toward them. Ranger horses were amazingly light-footed, Horace thought. Tug's hooves made only the slightest of noises on the soft ground.

Will reined in beside Halt.

"They've stopped and camped in the woods about two kilometers away," he said. "They've eaten and most of them are sleeping now—aside from the pickets."

Halt nodded thoughtfully. He glanced at the sun.

"They've been traveling hard all day," he said. "They're probably going to rest up for an hour or two before they attack. Did you see any sign of a farm farther on?"

Will shook his head. "I didn't go past them, Halt. I thought I'd better let you know what was happening first," he said apologetically. Halt made a small hand gesture, dismissing the need for apology.

"No matter," he said. "There'll be a farm close by. That's what they'll be heading for. They'll attack in late afternoon, when the sun's almost down."

"How can you be sure?" Horace asked. Halt turned to look at him.

"Standard procedure," he said. "There'll be enough light to attack, but the farmers won't be able to see them clearly. So they'll be surprised and confused. And once the cattle are run off, darkness will cover the Scotti's tracks from any pursuit. They'll have the whole night to make their getaway."

"That makes sense," Horace observed.

"They've got it down to a fine art, believe me," Halt told him. "They've been practicing for hundreds of years."

"So what will we do, Halt?" Will asked.

The gray-bearded Ranger considered his answer for a few moments, then said, speaking almost to himself, "Can't pick them off from a distance in this wooded country, the way we did at Craikennis." In Hibernia, he and Will had decimated an attack with their rapid, long-range shooting. "And the last thing I want is to get tied down in a defensive fight with them." He looked up at Will. "How many did you count?"

"Seventeen," the young Ranger replied promptly. It was one of the questions he knew Halt would want answered.

Halt stroked his beard thoughtfully. "Seventeen. And chances are there'll be only three or four able-bodied men at the farm."

"If we get inside the farm buildings, the three of us could hold them off easily enough," Horace suggested.

Halt glanced at him, conceding the point. "That's true, Horace. But if they're stubborn, and the Scotti tend to be that way, we could be tied up for a day or more. And all that time, Tennyson will be slipping farther away. No," he said, coming to a decision. "I don't want to just hold them off. I want to send them packing."

The two young men watched him expectantly, waiting to hear what he had in mind. After a short silence, he spoke.

"Let's bypass the Scotti camp and get in front of them. I want to see where they're heading. Can you lead us past them, Will?"

Will nodded and turned Tug around, heading into the trees again.

"Just a moment." Halt turned in the saddle and rummaged in his saddlebags for a few moments, producing a folded garment in brown and gray. He passed it across to Horace. "You might as well put this on. It'll help conceal you."

Horace took the garment and shook it out, revealing a camouflage cloak similar to those worn by the Rangers.

"It might be a tight fit. It's a spare one of mine," Halt explained.

Horace swung the cloak around him delightedly. Even though it was made for Halt's smaller frame, the Ranger cloaks were of such a capacious design that it fitted him reasonably well. It would be far too short, of course, but on horseback that didn't matter too much.

"I've always wanted one of these," Horace said, grinning at the cloak. He pulled the deep cowl up over his head, hiding his face in its shadows, and gathered the gray-brown folds around him.

"Can you still see me?" he asked.

13

THEY SWUNG IN A WIDE ARC TO SKIRT AROUND THE SCOTTI CAMP. Then, when Will judged they were well clear of it, they returned to their original path. The trees began to thin out for the last few hundred meters, until they rode into a small cleared field. There was a farmhouse and a larger barn on the far side, nestled into a thicker grove of trees. Smoke rose in a thin wisp from the farmhouse chimney.

Between the house and the barn was a fenced-off enclosure where they could see dark brown shapes moving slowly.

"That's what they came for," Halt said. "Cattle. There must be twenty or more in that paddock."

Horace sniffed the pleasant smell of wood smoke from the chimney. "Hope they're cooking something," he said. "I'm starved."

"Who said that?" Will asked, feigning surprise and looking around in all directions. Then he pretended to relax. "Oh, it's only you, Horace. I didn't see you there in that cloak."

Horace favored him with a long-suffering look. "Will, if it wasn't funny the first half-dozen times you said it, why do you think it would be funny now?"

And to Will's chagrin, Halt gave a short bark of laughter at

Horace's question. Then he was all business again. "Where is everybody?"

At this time of day—in the mid afternoon—they would expect to see people working around the farmyard. But there was nobody in sight.

"Maybe they're napping," Horace suggested. Halt glanced sidelong at him.

"Farmers don't nap," he said. "Knights nap."

"That's where we get the expression 'a good knight's sleep,'" Will said, smiling at his own wit. Halt turned a baleful eye on him.

"Horace is right. You're not funny. Come on."

He led the way across the small field. Horace noted that both his companions now had their longbows unslung and resting across their saddlebows. And the flaps in their cloaks that protected their quivers from damp weather were folded back. He touched his right hand to his sword hilt. For a moment, he considered unslinging his round shield from where it hung behind him, on the left side of the saddle. Then he reconsidered. They were nearly at the house now.

The thatched roof slanted down to form a shallow porch along the side of the house that faced them. Halt drew rein and leaned down in the saddle to peer under the edge of the roof.

"Hello the house," he called experimentally. But there was no reply.

He looked around at his companions and signaled for them to dismount. Normally, a rider arriving at a farmhouse wouldn't do this without invitation, but it seemed there would be none forthcoming.

Horace and Will followed him as he walked to the door. He rapped with his knuckles on the painted wood and it swung half open under the impact, the leather hinges creaking.

"Anyone home?" he called.

"Apparently not," Will said after a few seconds' silence.

"Nobody home and the door unlatched," Halt said. "How curious."

He led the way into the little farmhouse. They found themselves standing in a small kitchen–cum–living room. It was furnished with a wooden table and several rough-carved wooden chairs—obviously homemade. A cooking pot hung on a swiveling arm beside the fire-place. The fire was still burning, although it was almost down to coals. It had been some time since fresh wood had been added to it.

Two other rooms led off from the large central room, and a short ladder on one side led to a loft set under the thatch. Will mounted the ladder and peered around while Horace checked the other rooms.

"Nothing," Will reported.

Horace nodded agreement. "Nothing anywhere. Where could they have gone?"

It was obvious from the condition of the room, the fire and a few eating and drinking implements on the table that the house had been inhabited quite recently. There was no sign of a fight or a struggle. The floor had been swept and the broom replaced beside the door. Halt ran a finger over a shelf beside the fireplace, where cooking implements were stored. He inspected his fingertip for signs of dust and found none.

"They've gone," Halt said. "They must have got wind that the Scotti are coming and run off."

"And left everything here?" Horace questioned, sweeping an arm around the room.

Halt shrugged. "There actually isn't much. And if you'll notice, there are no cloaks or coats beside the door—just a set of empty pegs where they might have hung."

He indicated a row of hanging pegs set into the wall beside the door—the spot where someone entering the room would hang an outer garment. Or, Will realized, where they would don it as they were leaving.

"But why leave the cattle behind for the Scotti?" Horace asked.

"They couldn't take them along, could they?" Halt replied. He crossed to the door and went outside again. Horace and Will followed as he made his way to the fenced cattle yard.

"They tried to drive them off," he said, indicating the yard gate, where it stood wide open. "But there's feed in the troughs there, and water. I guess once the people were gone, the cattle simply wandered back."

The cattle looked up at him peacefully. Most of them were busy chewing, and they seemed completely unalarmed by the sight of a stranger. They were stocky and solid, with shaggy coats to protect them from the northern winter months. And above all, they were placid beasts.

"Maybe they hoped that if the Scotti got the cattle, they wouldn't bother to burn the house and barn," Will suggested.

Halt raised an eyebrow. "Maybe. But they'd bother, all right. Burning a house and barn is part of the fun for a Scotti."

"So what should we do?" Horace asked. "Simply fade away? After all, the farmer and his family will be safe from the raiders now."

"True," Halt said. "But with the cattle gone and their home and barn and crops burned, they'll probably starve in the winter."

"So what do you suggest we do, Halt?" Will asked.

Halt hesitated. He seemed to be considering a plan of action. Then he said, "I think we should give them the cattle."

Will regarded his mentor as if he had taken leave of his senses.

"If we're going to do that, why did we bother detouring here in the first place?" he asked. "We might as well have continued on after Tennyson." But then he noticed Halt was smiling grimly.

"When I say *give them the cattle*, I don't mean as a gift. Let's give them the cattle right in their faces."

Understanding began to dawn on Will and Horace. Will was about to say something further when Halt stopped him and gestured to the far side of the clearing.

"Get back over there and keep watch. I want to know when they're coming. When they're clear of the thick trees, we'll stampede the cattle at them."

Will nodded, a grin forming on his face at the thought of the surprise that was in store for the raiding Scotti. He swung up into Tug's saddle and galloped away across the field, riding on until he was some thirty or forty meters inside the tree line. The trees here were more widely spaced than in the forest proper, he noted. And the trunks were narrower and lighter. It was probably an area that had been progressively thinned out over the years, providing the homestead with building materials and firewood. The widely spaced saplings would provide little shelter for the Scotti against a herd of charging cattle.

He found a leafy bush growing between two saplings, positioned Tug behind it and dismounted. He glanced back quickly at the farmhouse, where he could see the distant figures of his two friends standing by the cattle yard. It occurred to him that he had no idea how to stampede a herd of cattle. But he was confident that Halt would know. There was nothing that Halt didn't know, after all.

"How do you stampede cattle?" Horace asked.

"You startle them. You alarm them. We'll get them running, then mount up and drive them at the Scotti when they hit open ground," Halt told him. He was walking among the herd, who watched him incuriously. He shoved at one of them. It was like shoving the side of a house, he thought. He waved his arms experimentally.

"Shoo!" he said. The cow broke wind noisily but made no other movement.

"You certainly scared that out of him," Horace said, grinning.

Halt glared at him. "Perhaps if you whipped off your cloak, they might be startled by your sudden appearance," he suggested acidly.

Horace's grin broadened. He was, in fact, taking off his cloak, but its removal seemed to have no effect on the herd. One or two of them rolled an eye at him. Several others broke wind.

"They do a lot of that, don't they?" he remarked. "Maybe if we got them all pointed the same way, they could blow the Scotti back down the pass."

Halt made an impatient gesture. "Get on with it. You were raised on a farm, after all."

Horace shook his head. "I wasn't raised on a farm. I was raised in the Ward at Redmont," he said. "You were a Hibernian prince. Didn't you have herds of cattle?"

"We did. But we also had great oafs like you to take care of them." He frowned thoughtfully. "The bull is the key. If we can get the bull running, the cows will follow him."

Horace looked around the small herd. "Which one's the bull?"

Halt's eyebrows both went up—a rare expression of astonishment from the Ranger.

"You really did grow up in the Ward, didn't you?" Then he pointed. "That one would appear to be the bull."

Horace looked at the animal he was indicating. His eyes widened a little.

"He certainly would," he agreed. "So what do we do with him?"

"Startle him. Annoy him. Frighten him," Halt said.

Horace looked doubtful. "I'm not completely sure I want to do that."

Halt snorted in disgust. "Don't be such a ninny!" he said. "After all, what can he do to you?"

Horace regarded the bull suspiciously. He wasn't as big as some bulls he had seen in the meadows around Redmont. But he was solidly built and well muscled. And, unlike the cows, he wasn't regarding the two strangers with a placid, docile gaze. Horace thought he could see a light of challenge in those little eyes.

"You mean aside from gore me?" he asked, but Halt waved the protest aside dismissively.

"With those little horns? They're barely bumps on his forehead."

In fact, the horns, while not being the wide-spreading ones that some northern cattle possessed, were substantial. The ends were rounded and blunt rather than pointed. But they still looked capable of inflicting damage.

"Come on!" Halt urged him. "All you have to do is roll up your cloak and whack him over the face with it. That'll get him upset."

"I already said, I don't *want* to get him upset," Horace protested.

"For pity's sake! You're the famous Oakleaf Warrior! You're the slayer of the evil Morgarath! The victor of a dozen duels!" Halt told him.

"None of which were against bulls," Horace reminded him. He definitely didn't like the look in that bull's eyes, he thought.

"What north country bull is going to stand and face you?" Halt said. "Hit him with your cloak and he'll run away. And the cows will go with him."

But before Horace could reply, they heard a piercing whistle. Looking across the cleared field, they could see Will running toward them, with Tug trotting behind him. Farther back among the thinly spaced trees, they could see signs of movement.

The Scotti were coming.

14

Halt sprang into Abelard's saddle as Horace still hesitated, uncertain what to do.

"Get on with it!" Halt yelled. "They're coming!"

At the same moment, Will arrived back at the cattle yard.

"They're coming, Halt!" he said unnecessarily. There was a note of tension in his voice so that it was pitched a little higher than normal.

"Get mounted. Once they're running, we'll keep driving them," Halt told him. Then he turned back to Horace. "Get them moving, Horace!"

Horace was finally galvanized into action. He stepped forward and swung the folded cloak, smacking it right between the bull's horns and across his face.

Then everything seemed to happen in a rush.

The bull squealed with rage, blinked three or four times, then lowered his head and charged, stiff legged, at his tormentor. He butted Horace in the midriff and, jerking his head upright, sent the unfortunate warrior sailing several meters, to land heavily on his back with a dull thud and an "Ooooof!" of escaping breath.

For a second, it seemed the bull might follow up its advantage.

But then Kicker intervened. Trained for years to protect his master against attack in combat, the massive battlehorse interposed himself between Horace and the bull. The bull squealed a challenge, pawing the ground in front of him, tearing up the grass and dirt and tossing his head in fury.

It was too much for Kicker. In the Araluen animal world there was a certain order of precedence, and a carefully bred and trained battlehorse ranked far above a shaggy country bull of indeterminate lineage. The mighty horse reared onto his hind legs and danced forward, shrilling a challenge, his forehooves slashing the air in front of him.

Those iron-shod hooves flashed past the bull's face. The bull realized he was overmatched and bellowed with frustration. He turned away, taking a few uncertain paces as he prepared to retreat.

But he had defied Kicker, challenged him even, and in the horse's mind, that insult must be erased. He dashed forward and gnashed his big blunt teeth at the bull, catching him on the rump and removing a painful piece of flesh and hide.

The bull howled in pain and outrage and fear. He kicked his hind legs up in a vain attempt to catch his attacker. But Kicker was trained in a hard school and he had already pulled back. As the bull's rear hooves hit the ground again, Kicker pirouetted and lashed out in his own turn, slamming his rear hooves into the bull's already damaged backside.

That was the final straw. Fear, pain and now the thundering impact of a double kick. The bull bellowed and took off, running across the field. Alarmed by his cries, the herd went with him, their panicked mooing and the dull thunder of their hooves filling the air.

"Come on!" Halt yelled. He urged Abelard forward after the racing cattle, whipping at the rearmost with his bow. Will followed suit, riding to the other side of the herd to keep them bunched.

The first of the Scotti had emerged from the thinning trees into the open ground of the field when the stampede broke. They saw the tightly packed knot of racing cattle coming at them, hesitated, turned to retreat and blundered into the men behind them. A few, quicker thinking than the others, tried to run to the sides to escape the charge. Halt saw them and reined Abelard in, rising in his stirrups as he nocked an arrow and sent it hissing through the air, following it quickly with three more.

Two of the raiders went down in the long grass. On the far side of the herd, Will had seen Halt's action and followed suit. The Scotti quickly realized the danger of running to the side. Threatened by the hail of arrows, they bunched together uncertainly. A few seconds later, the crazed cattle smashed into them.

The impact of blunt horns, sharp cloven hooves and hard-muscled bodies sent the Scotti raiders spinning and falling like nine-pins. As they went down, the cattle in the rear ranks continued to charge over them, injuring those who had already fallen even more severely.

When the stampede passed, at least half of the raiding party were lying, seriously wounded, on the field. The remainder had managed to escape to the point where the trees grew more densely.

The cattle, reaching the thicker trees, swung off to the right and thundered away, bellowing still. Halt reined in, an arrow ready on his bowstring, with Abelard half turned to the raiders who watched him from the trees. Around him, a few survivors were slowly picking themselves up to hobble or crawl back to join their companions. Virtually none of the raiding party had escaped injury of some kind. Three of them lay still and unmoving, struck down by the Rangers' arrows.

"Get back to Picta!" Halt called to them. "Half your men are dead or badly injured. Once the local people know about it, they'll hunt you down. Now get out of here."

The leader of the raiding party lay dead in the grass, trampled by half a dozen of the cattle after he'd been thrown from his feet. His second in command regarded the grim figure facing him on the shaggy horse. As he watched, the second gray-cloaked horseman rode up beside his companion, his longbow threatening them as well.

The Scotti knew that the success of a raid like this depended on speed and surprise. Strike swiftly. Burn and kill and run off the cattle. Then get back across the border before the enemy could organize themselves. Before they even knew there was a raiding party in the area.

Speed and surprise were gone now. And once the local Araluens knew of their presence, his men would be easy targets as they limped and staggered, nursing their injuries and carrying their wounded, back to One Raven Pass. The thought of abandoning his wounded countrymen never occurred to the new leader. That wasn't the Scotti way.

In addition, he'd seen the accuracy and speed of the two cloaked archers who faced him now. If they started shooting again, he could lose another half dozen men in a matter of seconds. Shaking his head in frustration and despair, he signaled to his men and they turned and made their painful way back toward the north.

Will let go a deep breath and relaxed in his saddle.

"Good thinking, Halt," he said. "That certainly worked like a charm."

Halt shrugged diffidently.

"Oh, it's nothing if you know how," he said. "Looks as if we have company," he added, nodding toward the farmhouse where Horace stood, leaning painfully against Kicker's side, his hands holding his bruised ribs.

Behind the farmhouse, several figures were visible among the densely growing trees. As Halt and Will watched, they made their tentative way back toward the farm buildings.

"They must have been hiding in the woods watching," Will said.

Halt nodded grimly. "Yes. Nice of them to lend us a hand, wasn't it?" He touched Abelard with his heel and began to canter slowly back to the cattle yard. Tug, sensing the motion as his companion tensed his muscles, followed a few paces behind.

Horace nodded a greeting as they dismounted.

Will frowned a little. His friend was still holding his ribs and seemed to be having trouble breathing without pain. "Are you all right?"

Horace waved his concern aside, but winced as he did so. "Bruises," he said. "That's all. That little bull certainly knew how to use his head."

The farm people had reached them now and Halt greeted them.

"Your farm's safe," he said. "They won't be back for a while." He couldn't keep a small note of satisfaction from creeping into his voice.

There were five people. An older man and woman, in their fifties, Will judged. Then a young couple in their thirties and a boy who looked to be about ten. Grandparents, parents and son, he thought. Three generations.

The older man spoke now.

"Cattle are all run off. You ran them off." He said it accusingly. Will raised his eyebrows.

"That's true," Halt said reasonably. "But you'll be able to get them back. They'll stop running soon."

"Take days to round them up, it will," said the farmer lugubriously.

Halt drew a deep breath. Will had known him for years. He knew Halt was making an enormous effort to keep his temper in check.

"Probably," he agreed. "But at least you won't have to rebuild your farmhouse in the meantime."

"Hmmmmphhh," the farmer snorted. "That's as well. We'll be days rounding up the cows again. All over the forest, they'll be."

"That's better than lining a Scotti belly," Halt said. His restraint was becoming thinner and thinner.

"And who'll milk them when they're in the forest, eh?" It was the younger man. In spite of his comparative youth, he seemed equally as doleful as his older companion. "Need milking every day, they do, else they'll go dry."

"Of course, that might happen," Halt said. "But better dry cows than no cows at all, surely."

"That's a matter for opinion," said Grandpa. "Mind you, if we had the help of some men with horses to find them, we'd get it done quicker, like."

"Men with horses?" Halt said. "You mean us?" He turned to Will and Horace in disbelief. "He does. He means us."

The farmer was nodding. "Aye. After all, you were t' ones who ran 'em off in the first place. Weren't for you, they'd be back here."

"If it weren't for us," Halt told him, "they'd be halfway to Picta by now!"

He glanced up at Will and Horace and realized they were both hiding grins. Far too obviously, in fact. It seemed to him that they were being so obvious about hiding their grins precisely so he would realize that they *were* hiding them.

"I don't believe this," he said to them. "I don't exactly expect gratitude. But to be blamed for this man's troubles is a little much." Then he thought about what he had said. "No. Change that. I *do* expect gratitude, blast it." He turned back to the farmer.

"Sir," he said stiffly, "it's because of our efforts that you still have your farmhouse, your barn and your cattle yard. It's thanks to us that your cows are safe, even if they are a little scattered. In the course of saving your property, my companion here suffered a cowardly attack from your vicious little bull. Now you can have the graciousness to say thank you. Or I'll ask my friends to set fire to your farmhouse before we go on our way."

The farmer regarded him stubbornly.

"Just two words," Halt said. "Thank you."

"Well then . . ." The farmer hesitated, swaying ponderously from side to side. He reminded Horace of the bull. "Thank you . . . I suppose."

"It's our pleasure." Halt spat the words at him, then swung Abelard's head to the west. "Horace, Will, let's go."

They were halfway across the field when they heard the farmer add, "But I don't see why you had to run off t' cattle."

Will grinned at the erect figure of the Ranger riding beside him. Halt was all too obviously pretending that he hadn't heard the farmer's parting words.

"Halt?" he said. "You wouldn't really have burned down the house, would you?"

Halt turned a baleful gaze on him.

"Don't bet on it."

15

HALT HAD HOPED TO PICK UP TENNYSON'S TRAIL AGAIN BEFORE nightfall, but the short northern day defeated him. As the sun finally sank below the trees and shadows flooded out across the country-side, he reined in and gestured to an open patch of ground beside the track they had been following to the east.

"We'll camp here," he said. "No point blundering around in the dark. We'll get an early start and cast around for their tracks."

"Can we risk a fire, Halt?" Horace asked.

The Ranger nodded. "I don't see why not. They're a long way ahead of us now. And even if they do see a fire, there's no reason for them to suspect that someone's following them."

After they'd attended to their horses, Horace built a fireplace and scouted around the campsite for wood. In the meantime, Will busied himself skinning and cleaning two rabbits that he'd shot during the late afternoon. The bunnies were plump and in good condition, and his mouth watered at the prospect of a savory stew. He jointed the rabbits, keeping the meaty legs and thighs and discarding some of the bonier rib sections. Too much trouble to pick over, he decided. Then he opened the saddlebag where they kept their supply of fresh food. Often, when they were on the trail, Rangers made do with dried meat and fruit and hard bread. When they had the chance to eat more comfortably, they made sure they were ready for it. He briefly considered spitting the rabbits over the open fire and roasting them but discarded the idea. He felt like something more rewarding.

He sliced onions thinly and chopped several potatoes into small pieces. Taking a metal pot from the small array of cooking gear, he placed it in the edge of the fire Horace had started, setting it on glowing embers. When he judged that the iron of the pot was heated, he poured in a little oil, then dropped the onions in a few seconds later.

They began to sizzle and brown and filled the air with a delicious scent. He added a clove of garlic, smashing it to a paste with the end of the stick he was using to stir the pot. More delicious aromas rose. He sprinkled in a handful of spices and seasonings that were his own special mix, and the cooking smells grew richer and richer. Then the joints of rabbit went in and he moved them around to brown and become coated with the onion and spice mixture.

By now, Halt and Horace had moved to sit on either side of the fireplace, watching him hungrily as he worked. The rich smell of cooking meat, onions, garlic and spices filled the air and set their stomachs rumbling. It had been a long, hard day, after all.

"This is why I like traveling with Rangers," Horace said after a few minutes. "When you get the chance, you manage to eat well."

"Very few Rangers eat this well," Halt told him. "Will has quite a knack with rabbit stew."

Will added water to the pot, and as it began to simmer, he slowly dropped the potato chunks in as well. When the rich-looking liquid began to bubble again, he stirred it and glanced at Halt. The older Ranger nodded and reached into his own saddlebag, from which he produced a flask of red wine. Will added a generous glug of it to the stew.

He sniffed the fragrant steam rising from the pot and nodded, satisfied with the result. "May need a little of this later, to top it up," he said, setting the flask of wine to one side.

"Use all you want," Halt said. "That's what it's for."

Halt, like most Rangers, drank wine only sparingly.

Two hours later, the stew was ready and they ate it with relish. The fragrant, rich meat literally fell off the bones as they ate. Halt had mixed flour and water and salt together into a flat circle and placed it in the hot ashes to one side of the fire. When Will served out the stew, he produced an ash-covered loaf, and dusted it off to reveal a golden outer crust. He broke pieces off and passed them to his companions. It was perfect for sopping up the savory juices of the stew.

After they had eaten, they gathered together, huddling over Halt's map.

"Tennyson and his people were heading this way," Halt said, tracing a path south of southeast. "We're currently heading due east to the point where we left them to go after the Scotti. I think we should try to make up lost ground and assume they'll continue the way they've been going. If we cut the corner and head this way"—he indicated a southeasterly direction that would intersect the Outsiders' trail at an angle—"we should cross their trail tomorrow around the middle of the day."

"Unless they change direction," Will said.

"That's a risk, of course, but I don't see why they should. They have no idea we're tailing them. There's no reason why they shouldn't head directly for their destination. But if they have, we'll just have to go back to the point where we first left their trail and track them from there."

"If we're wrong, we'll lose the best part of two days," Will warned him.

Halt nodded. "And if we're right, we'll pick up the best part of a day."

Horace listened absently to the discussion. He was happy to go along with whatever his friends decided. And he knew that, these days, Halt was willing to listen to Will's views on the matter. The days were long past when Halt made all the decisions without consultation. Will had earned Halt's respect and Horace knew he valued the younger Ranger's opinion.

Horace glanced idly at the map. One place-name struck him. He leaned forward and tapped his forefinger on the parchment.

"Macindaw," he said. "I thought the countryside looked familiar. That's to the east of us. If we do as you say, we'll be passing pretty close to it."

"Be fun to drop in and see how they're doing," Will said.

Halt grunted. "We don't have time for social calls."

Will grinned easily. "I didn't think we did. I just said it'd be fun . . . if we did have the time."

Halt grunted again and began to roll up the map. Will knew his former teacher's moods by now. He knew that this sudden gruffness was a sign that the older Ranger knew he was taking a calculated risk in heading southeast. He'd never show that he was worried he might be making a mistake. But after years spent together, Will could usually read his thoughts correctly. He smiled to himself. When he was younger, he would never have dreamed that Halt could have doubts. Halt always seemed infallible. Now he knew that the older Ranger had an even greater mental strength—the ability to decide on a course of action and adhere to it, without letting doubt or uncertainty divert him from it.

"We'll get them, Halt. Don't worry," he said.

Halt smiled grimly. "I'm sure I'll sleep better for that reassurance," he replied.

+   +   +

They broke camp early. Breakfast was coffee and the remainder of the bread toasted over the fire's coals and smeared with honey. After kicking dirt over the fire, they mounted and rode out.

The hours passed. The sun went directly overhead and then began to slide down to the west. An hour after noon, they crossed a track heading roughly to the south. As far as Horace was concerned, it seemed no different from three or four others they had crossed that day, but Will suddenly swung down from the saddle. He went down on one knee and studied the ground in front of him.

"Halt!" he called, and the older Ranger joined him. There were definite signs that a party of travelers had passed this way. Will touched one footprint, clearer than the rest. It was off to the side of the track in a fortuitously damp section of ground. The footprint had been left by a heavy boot, with its sole bearing a triangular patch along the outer edge.

"Seen that before?" Will asked.

Halt leaned back, releasing a sigh of relief. "Indeed I have. Up in One Raven Pass. This is Tennyson's party, all right."

Now that his action was proved to be correct, he was free of the doubt and worry that had plagued him all morning. It had been a risk to take the shortcut. If they had had to return to the point where they first left Tennyson's track, anything could have happened—a storm or heavy rain might have washed out the tracks, leaving them floundering, with no idea which direction Tennyson had taken.

"By the look of these tracks, they're less than two days ahead of us," he said with great satisfaction.

Will had moved a few meters away, studying the tracks. "They've picked up some horses," he said abruptly.

Halt looked at him quickly, then moved to join him. There were clear traces of several sets of hoofprints in the soft earth and grass, a little way off the trail.

"So they have," he agreed. "God knows what poor farm they raided to get them. There are only three or four, so most of the party will still be on foot. We could be up to them by tomorrow."

"Halt," said Horace, "I've been thinking . . ."

Halt and Will exchanged an amused glance. "Always a dangerous pastime," they chorused. For many years, it had been Halt's unfailing response when Will had made the same statement. Horace waited patiently while they had their moment of fun, then continued.

"Yes, yes. I know. But seriously, as we said last night, Macindaw isn't so far away from here . . ."

"And?" Halt asked, seeing how Horace had left the statement hanging.

"Well, there's a garrison there and it might not be a bad idea for one of us to go fetch some reinforcements. It wouldn't hurt to have a dozen knights and men-at-arms to back us up when we run into Tennyson."

But Halt was already shaking his head.

"Two problems, Horace. It'd take too long for one of us to get there, explain it all and mobilize a force. And even if we could do it quickly, I don't think we'd want a bunch of knights blundering around the countryside, crashing through the bracken, making noise and getting noticed." He realized that statement had been a little tactless. "No offense, Horace. Present company excepted, of course."

"Oh, of course," Horace replied stiffly. He couldn't really dispute Halt's statement. Knights did tend to blunder around the country- side making noise and getting noticed. But that didn't mean he had to like it.

Halt continued. "The best thing we have going for us is the element of surprise. Tennyson doesn't know we're coming. And that's worth at least a dozen knights and men-at-arms. No. We'll continue as we are for the moment."

Horace nodded grudging agreement. When they caught up with the Outsiders, they'd have a stiff fight on their hands. Will and Halt would have their hands full dealing with the two Genovesan assassins. He would have liked to have even three or four armed knights behind him to take on the rest of the false prophet's followers.

But in the time he'd spent with Halt and Will, he'd learned repeatedly how valuable an ally surprise could be in a fight. Reluctantly, he decided that what Halt said made good sense.

The two Rangers remounted and they set off again, following the trail with renewed purpose. The knowledge that they had narrowed the gap between them and Tennyson to less than a day urged them on. They scanned the horizon before them with extra caution, looking for the first sign that they had caught up with Tennyson.

Will spotted him first.

"Halt!" he said. He had the good sense not to point in the direction he was looking. He knew Halt would follow his gaze and that if he were to point, he would alert his quarry to the fact that he had been seen.

"On the skyline," he said quietly. "To the right of that forked tree. Don't do that, Horace!"

He had seen his friend's hand begin to move and instinctively knew Horace was planning to shade his eyes as he gazed at the figure. Horace changed the gesture at the last minute and pretended to scratch the back of his neck. At the same time, Halt dismounted and inspected Abelard's left front hoof. That way, whoever it was wouldn't think they had stopped because he had been spotted.

"Can't see anything," Halt told him. "What is it?"

"A rider. Watching us," Will told him. Halt glanced sideways at the hill without moving his head. He could vaguely make out what might have been the shape of a man and a horse. He was grateful for Will's keen young eyes.

Will reached down and unslung his water canteen from the pommel of his saddle. But he managed to do it without losing sight of the figure. He raised the water bottle to his lips, still watching. Then there was a brief flash of movement and the rider wheeled his horse and disappeared from the skyline.

"All right," he said. "You can relax. He's gone."

Halt released Abelard's hoof and remounted. His stiff muscles and joints seemed to groan as he did so.

"You recognize him?" he asked.

Will shook his head. "Too far to make out details. Except . . ."

"Except what?" Halt asked.

"When he turned away, I thought I caught a flash of purple."

Purple, Horace thought. So maybe, he said to himself, we might have just lost the element of surprise.

16

Conditions had improved in the Outsiders' camp since the raid on the Scotti farm. As the band moved south through Araluen, Tennyson had continued to send parties out to raid isolated farms that they passed. They brought back not just food, but also equipment to make their camp more comfortable—canvas, timber and rope to make tents, and furs and blankets to keep out the chill of the cold northern nights.

In the last raid, they had also chanced upon four horses. They were sorry animals, but at least now Tennyson and the two Genovesans could ride instead of walk. The fourth horse he needed for another purpose. Now, as he sat in the relative comfort of his tent, he explained it to the young man he had chosen to be its rider.

"Dirkin, I want you to ride on ahead," he said. "Take one of the horses and make your way to this village."

He indicated a spot on a roughly drawn map of the northeast.

"Willey's Flat," the young man said, reading the name of the spot Tennyson had indicated.

"Exactly. It's just beyond this range of cliffs, a little to the south of them. Look for a man named Barrett."

"Who is he?" the messenger asked. Normally, Tennyson didn't encourage his followers to question orders, but on this occasion it would help if the young man knew why he needed to make contact with Barrett.

"He's the leader of a local chapter of our people. He's been recruiting converts in this area for the last few months. I want you to tell him to gather however many followers he's managed to convert and we'll rendezvous at a campsite near the cliffs."

Always planning to gain a foothold in Araluen once more, Tennyson had sent two groups of followers to establish the cult in remote areas, well away from the eyes of officialdom. One had been at Selsey, the fishing village on the west coast. The second had been here, in the wild northeastern part of the kingdom. The last message he'd had from Barrett had indicated that he'd managed to convert, or rather recruit, around a hundred followers to the religion. It wasn't a lot, but Barrett wasn't an inspiring figure. And one hundred followers was a start, at least. They'd provide the gold and jewelry Tennyson would need to start up again.

The young man looked with interest at the map.

"I thought we were the only group," he said. Tennyson's brows came together angrily.

"Then you thought wrong," he told him. "A wise man always has something in reserve in case things don't go according to plan. Now get going."

Dirkin shrugged the implied rebuke aside and stood to leave. "But it'll probably take a few days for this Barrett character to get the people assembled."

"Which is why I'm sending you on ahead," Tennyson told him, a sarcastic note creeping into his voice. "But if you plan to stand around talking about it, I might have to find someone else for the job."

Dirkin heard the tone and capitulated. Truth be told, he'd be happy to ride on ahead. He stuffed the map inside the breast of his jacket and turned toward the entrance of the tent.

"I'm on my way," he said. Tennyson's angry grunt was the only response.

Dirkin headed for the entrance and was forced to step back as another figure entered hurriedly, bumping into him. An angry complaint rose to the young man's lips, but he bit it off as he recognized the newcomer. It was one of the Genovesan assassins Tennyson had retained as bodyguards. They were not people to insult or annoy, Dirkin knew. Hastily, he mumbled an apology and scuttled around the purple-cloaked figure, leaving the tent as quickly as he could.

Marisi curled his lip in contempt as he glanced after the young man. He was well aware that many of the foreigners avoided him and his compatriot. Tennyson glanced up at him now, frowning slightly. Since they had acquired the horses, the two Genovesans had begun to check their trail every few days to be sure nobody was following them. It was a routine measure that Tennyson had insisted on, and so far, there had been nothing to report. But now that Marisi was here, Tennyson suspected there was bad news. Bacari, the senior of the two, reported only when the news was good.

"What is it?" Tennyson demanded.

"We're being followed," Marisi replied.

Tennyson slammed his fist down on the small folding table they'd stolen from a farmhouse some days ago.

"I knew things were going too smoothly. How many of them are there?"

"Three," the Genovesan told him, and Tennyson's spirits rose a little. Three people following them was nothing to be concerned about. But the assassin's next words changed his mind.

"They're the three from Hibernia. The two cloaked archers and the knight."

Tennyson came out of his chair with the shock of the news. It tumbled over backward onto the grass, but he didn't notice.

"Them?" he shouted. "What are they doing here? How the devil did they get here?"

The Genovesan shrugged. How they got here was immaterial. They were here and they were following the small band of Outsiders. And they were dangerous. That much he already knew. He waited for the self-styled prophet to continue.

Tennyson's mind raced. The smuggler! He must have told them. Of course, they would have bribed him and he would have taken their money and betrayed the Outsiders.

He began to pace up and down the restricted space inside the makeshift tent. This was bad news. He needed to gather the faithful at Willey's Flat. He needed the gold and jewelry he'd get there. And he'd be delayed while they came in from their outlying farms. He couldn't take the risk that the three Araluens might catch up with him.

"How far back are they?" he asked. He should have asked that immediately, he thought.

"Not far. A day, at most."

Tennyson considered the answer and then came to a decision. A day was not enough of a lead. Particularly when he was held down to walking pace. He looked up at the assassin.

"You'll have to get rid of them," he said abruptly.

Marisi's eyebrows went up in surprise. "Get rid of them," he repeated.

Tennyson leaned across the little table, his fists planted on the rough wood.

"That's right! That's what you people do, isn't it? Get rid of them. You and your friend. Kill them. Use those crossbows you're so proud of and make sure they stop following us."

Those cowled archers and their muscular friend had been nothing but trouble for him. Now, the more he thought about it, the more
he wanted to know they were dead.

Marisi had been considering his order. He nodded thoughtfully.
"There's a good spot where we can ambush them. We'll have to go
back and lay a trail for them to follow. But of course . . ." He paused
meaningfully.

For a few seconds Tennyson didn't register the fact, but then he
snarled, "Of course what?"

"They're dangerous enemies, and our contract said nothing
about 'getting rid of' people like them."

The implication was obvious. Tennyson breathed heavily, con-
trolling his rising anger. He needed these two men, no matter how
much they infuriated him.

"I'll pay you extra," he said, his teeth gritted.

Marisi smiled and held out a hand. "Now? You'll pay now?"

But Tennyson shook his head violently. He wasn't going to capit-
ulate quite so far as that.

"When you've done the job," he said. "I'll pay you then. Not
before."

Marisi shrugged again. He hadn't really expected the heavyset
preacher to agree to pay in advance, but it had been worth a try.

"You'll pay later," he said. "We'll arrange a fee. But . . . if you pay
later, you pay more."

Tennyson swept that fact aside carelessly with one hand. "That's
fine. Tell Bacari to come and see me and we'll agree on a payment."
He paused and then added, for emphasis, "Later."

After all, he thought, with any luck, they'll all kill each other and
save me the extra payment.

17

"We'll have to assume he saw us," Halt said as they rode on. They had been riding single file, but now Horace and Will pushed their horses up beside Halt so they could confer more easily.

"But did he recognize us?" Will said. "After all, we're a long way away and we could just be three riders."

Halt turned slightly in the saddle to look at his former pupil. What Will said was correct. Yet Halt hadn't lived as long as he had by taking chances and assuming that his enemies might make mistakes.

"If he saw us, we also have to assume that he recognized us."

"After all," Horace chipped in, "when you two aren't skulking in the bushes, you're pretty recognizable. There aren't a lot of people riding around the countryside carrying great big longbows and wearing cowled cloaks."

"Thank you for pointing that out," Halt said dryly. "But in fact, you're right. And the Genovesans are no fools. Now Tennyson will know we're behind him."

He paused, scratching his beard thoughtfully as he pondered the situation.

"The question is," he said, more to himself than to the others, "what to do next."

"Should we drop back a little?" Will suggested. "If we drop out of sight, Tennyson might assume that the Genovesan was mistaken and we just happened to be three riders with no interest in him."

"No. I don't think so. That's hoping for too much. And if we drop back, we give him more time to give us the slip. I think we should do the opposite. Push up on him."

"He'll know we're here," Horace said.

Halt nodded at him. "He knows we're here anyway. So let's push him. Let's make him feel crowded. That way he'll have to keep moving, and a moving target is easier to see than a concealed one." He came to a decision and added, in a positive tone, "We'll put pressure on him. People under pressure make mistakes, and that could work for us."

"Of course . . . ," Horace began, then hesitated. Halt gestured for him to go ahead. "Well, I was thinking, we'll be under pressure too, won't we? What if *we* make the mistake?"

Halt regarded him for several seconds without speaking. Then he turned to Will. "He's a regular ray of sunshine, isn't he?"

They continued in silence for a few minutes. They were working their way up a long uphill slope to the point where they had seen the Genovesan on the skyline. They still had about a hundred meters to go to reach the crest when Halt held up his hand to signal the others to stop.

"On the other hand," he said in a quiet voice, "Horace has a good point. The Genovesans are assassins and one of their favorite techniques is ambush. It occurs to me that it might not be a good idea to go romping over that next crest assuming that there's nothing to be concerned about."

"You think he's waiting for us?" Will said, his eyes scanning the crest.

"I think he could be. So from now on, we don't go over any crests without scouting the land ahead of us."

He made a move to swing down from the saddle, but Will forestalled him, dropping lightly to the trail.

"I'll do it," he said.

Halt made as if to argue, then closed his mouth. His natural preference was always to keep Will out of harm's way, but he realized that he had to let the young man take his share of the danger.

"Don't take any chances," he said. Tug echoed the thought with a low rumble from his barrel of a chest. Will grinned at them both.

"Don't be such a pair of old grannies," he said. Then he slipped off into the shoulder-high gorse that lined the track. Bent double, he suddenly disappeared from sight. Horace made a slight sound of surprise.

Halt looked at him. "What is it?"

Horace gestured at the rolling clumps of coarse bush that covered the hillside. There was no sign of Will, no sign of anything moving in the bushes, other than the wind.

"It doesn't matter how often I see him do that, it still spooks me every time. It's uncanny."

"Yes," said Halt, his eyes scanning the hillside above them. "I suppose it would. He's very good at it. Of course," he added modestly, "I taught him all he knows. I'm regarded as the expert on unseen movement in the Ranger Corps."

Horace frowned. "I thought Gilan was the real expert," he said. "Will once told me he learned all the finer points from Gilan."

"Oh really?" Halt said with a hint of frost in his voice. "And just who do you think taught Gilan?"

That hadn't occurred to Horace. Not for the first time, he found himself wishing that his tongue wouldn't run so many meters in advance of his brain.

"Oh . . . yes. You did, I suppose," he said, and Halt bowed slightly in the saddle.

"Exactly," Halt said with great dignity.

"So can you see where he is at the moment?" Horace asked curiously. He wondered if it worked that way. If you taught someone how to move without being seen and you knew all their tricks, could you see them? Or were they invisible even to the person who taught them?

"Naturally," Halt replied. "He's up there."

Horace followed the direction of his pointing finger and saw Will standing erect at the crest of the hill. A few seconds later, they heard his signal whistle and he waved for them to come forward.

"Well, now you can see him," said Horace. "I can see him now! But could you see him before he stood up?"

"Of course I could, Horace. How could you doubt me?" Halt said. Then he urged Abelard forward, gesturing for Tug to follow. His face was hidden from Horace as he went ahead, so the young warrior never saw the smile that creased it.

"He seems to have kept on moving," Will said as they drew level with him. "Although he could be anywhere out there."

Below them, the land gradually sloped away, covered by the same thick gorse and bracken. Will was right. A crossbowman could be concealed anywhere in that tangle. Halt scanned the area thoughtfully.

"This is going to slow us down," he said.

"Which is the whole idea," Will said.

"Precisely." Halt let go a sigh of exasperation.

"I suppose this puts an end to the idea of putting pressure on him," Horace said. Halt regarded him coldly for a few seconds. The Ranger's good humor seemed to desert him when his plans were thwarted, Horace thought. He also thought it might be a good idea to say nothing further for a while. Halt, satisfied that his unspoken message had registered, turned back to Will as he came to a decision.

"Very well. You scout ahead, Will. I'll give you fifty meters and then we'll come up to you. You know the drill: Look. Shout. Shoot."

Will nodded. He signaled for Tug to stay where he was and half ran down the trail, his eyes on the ground, scanning the tracks left there. Halt edged Abelard around so he was on an angle on the trail, leaving Halt room to shoot, and nocked an arrow to his bowstring. His eyes scanned the ground on either side of the track as Will proceeded.

"All right if I ask you something, Halt?" Horace said tentatively. He wasn't sure if he should intrude on the Ranger's concentration with a question. But Halt simply nodded without taking his attention off the rolling bushes.

"Look. Shout. Shoot. What's that?" Horace asked.

Halt began to answer. If Horace was going to be working with them in the future, it would be just as well to explain their methods to him whenever he asked. "It's the way we . . ."

Then, catching sight of a small movement in the bushes to Will's right, he stopped talking and raised himself slightly in the stirrups, his bow coming up to the aiming position, the arrow beginning to slide back to full draw.

A small bird fluttered out of the bush that he had been watching, flew a few meters, and then settled fussily on another branch, burying its beak inside the petals of a flower.

Halt relaxed, letting the arrow down again. Horace noticed that Will had caught sight of the movement too. He'd dropped to a crouch. Now, warily, he rose again, and glanced back up to where Halt and Horace were watching. Halt waved him ahead. He nodded and began to move again, searching the ground as he did so.

"Sorry, Horace," Halt said. "You wanted to know about 'Look. Shout. Shoot.' It's the way we approach a situation like this. Will is looking for their tracks, and for any sign that someone might have left the trail and moved out to the side to wait in ambush. While he's doing that, his attention is distracted. So I keep watch on either side of the track, just in case someone has left the path farther along and doubled back behind him. If I see a crossbowman rise up out of the bushes, I shout and Will drops to the ground instantly. At the same time, I shoot the crossbowman. Look. Shout. Shoot."

"He looks. You shout and shoot," Horace said.

"Exactly. And we do it in fifty-meter increments, because if there is an ambush, my arrow will hit the ambusher all the more quickly. The problem's going to be when we reach those trees ahead of us."

Horace looked up. The undulating gorse-covered terrain continued for another two or three kilometers. But then he could see the dark line of a thick forest.

"I guess you can't see for fifty meters in there," he said.

Halt nodded. "That's right. We'll have to do it in twenty-meter rushes once we get there. Come on," he added. "Will's calling us forward."

They rode down the slope to where Will was waiting for them. He grinned up at Halt as the two riders reined in. Tug nuzzled him and made grumbling noises. He was never happy when Will went on without him.

"Worrywart," Will told him, patting his soft nose. But Halt looked approvingly at the little horse.

"Take him with you this time," he said. "Should have thought of it before. He'll sense someone in the bushes quicker than we will."

Will looked a little concerned at the idea. "I don't want to risk Tug getting hit by one of those crossbow bolts."

Halt smiled at him. "Now who's the worrywart?"

Will shrugged. "All the same," he said, "I'd be more comfortable if he were back with you if someone starts shooting."

"And I'll be more comfortable if he is with you," Halt told him. Then he patted the longbow where it lay across his knees. "Don't worry. The only one who's going to start any shooting is me."

18

As Halt had predicted, their progress became even slower when they reached the dense wood they had sighted on the horizon. Here, the trees grew in thick, unordered confusion on either side of the narrow path. As Horace walked through them, the changing angles from which he viewed the moss-covered ranks of tree trunks seemed to create a sensation of movement in the shadows, so that he was constantly stopping to look again, making sure that he hadn't just seen something moving.

They were assisted by the two Ranger horses, of course. Tug and Abelard were both trained to warn their masters if they sensed the presence of strangers. But even their abilities depended on the direction of the wind. If someone were downwind, his scent wouldn't be carried to them.

They proceeded in a series of short rushes. First Will would go forward ten to twenty meters while Halt stood, bow ready, until Will gained the cover of a tree trunk. Then Will would scan the forest while Halt moved forward and went past him to another point twenty meters farther along. Then they would repeat the process, leapfrogging each other, one watching while the other went forward.

Frequently, they stopped to let the horses test the air for any out-of-place sounds or scents from the trees around them.

Horace brought up the rear. He had his shield slung over his back for protection. If he needed it in a hurry, he could quickly shrug it around onto his left arm. His sword was drawn. When he had first drawn the weapon, he had felt a little self-conscious—concerned that it might make him appear nervous. But Halt had nodded approvingly when he caught the gleam of the sharp blade in the dull light under the trees.

"Nothing more useless than a sword you've left in its scabbard," he had said.

Halt had also instructed him to turn suddenly from time to time and scan the path behind them, making sure there was no one about to strike at them from behind.

"Don't do it at regular intervals," Halt had told him as they were about to enter the dim green world of the forest. "Anybody trailing us will recognize a regular pattern and they'll match it and move more freely. Mix things up. Keep changing it."

So now, from time to time, Horace would turn to scan the path, turn back, and then whip around again immediately. Halt had told him that this was the best way to catch a pursuer unaware.

But each time he did it, there was nobody there.

That did nothing to lessen the tension. He was only too aware that, at any moment, he could turn like this and there *might* be someone moving on the track behind them. He realized that his hand on the sword grip was damp with tension, and he wiped it carefully on his jacket. In a battle, Horace would face any enemy, and any number of enemies, without flinching. It was the uncertainty of this situation that unsettled him—the knowledge that, no matter how many times there had been nothing behind them, this could be the time when it all went wrong.

He also felt extremely vulnerable in the company of Will and Halt. He watched them as they ghosted between the trees, their cloaks helping them blend into the gray and green shades of the forest so that at times he had trouble seeing them clearly.

He was wearing the cloak that Halt had given him, of course. But he knew that the skill of concealment depended on more than just the camouflage patterns on the cloak. It was a result of years of practice, of learning how to use the smallest amount of cover available. How to move swiftly without breaking twigs or rustling dead leaves underfoot. Knowing when to move and when to stand utterly still, even though your nerves shrieked at you to dive into cover. Compared with the two almost silent shadows who accompanied him, he felt like a huge, blundering draft horse, lurching and crashing through the trees and undergrowth. The grim thought occurred to him that any ambusher with half a brain would look for the easiest, most visible target for his first shot.

And that would be him.

Unconsciously, he wiped his damp hand on his jacket again.

Up ahead, as Halt moved forward past him, Will glanced quickly back at his best friend, bringing up the rear. It was just an extra precaution, making sure that nobody was stalking Horace. The man in the center of the line, whether it was Halt or Will, had the responsibility for checking front, back and sides as they progressed. He was impressed by Horace's calmness. The young warrior hadn't been trained for this sort of shadowy, nerve-stretching maneuvering. Yet he seemed to be cool and unflustered. Will, on the other hand, was surprised that neither of his friends could hear his heart hammering inside his rib cage. The tension beneath the trees was almost palpable. The expectation that a crossbow bolt could come ripping out of the shadowy forest, the concern that any slight inattention on his part could cost the lives of his friends, was close to unbearable. He shook his head angrily. That sort of thinking would lead to exactly the inattention he was worried about.

Clear your head. Clear your mind of all distractions, Halt had told him hundreds of times during the years they had trained together. *Become part of the situation. Don't think. Feel and sense what is around you.*

He took a deep breath and settled himself, emptying his mind of doubts and worries, focusing his attention and subconscious on his surroundings. After a few seconds, he began to hear the small sounds of the forest more clearly. A bird flashing from one tree to another. A squirrel chattering. A branch falling. Tug and Abelard stepped quietly beside him, their ears twitching as they listened for potential danger. Ahead of him, he could hear Halt's soft footfalls as he slipped forward; behind, the louder sounds made by Horace and Kicker, no matter how much the tall youth tried to move quietly.

This was the state of attention he needed. He had to hear the total spectrum of sound in the forest so that anything abnormal, any irregularity, would register immediately. For instance, if there was a shrill warning note in the squirrel's chattering call, it would indicate the presence of something, or someone, unwelcome in its territory.

Most other small animals would respond to that sort of territorial declaration by moving back, he knew. A predator mightn't. A human predator definitely wouldn't.

Halt had stopped, stepping into the cover of an ancient, lichen-covered elm. Will surveyed the ground before him, picking his path so that he wouldn't move in a straight, predictable line, and then slid out from behind the tree that sheltered him and ghosted forward yet again.

Tug and Abelard paced soft-footed behind him.

Eventually, the dim light began to grow brighter and the trees became more widely spaced. With each forward rush, Will and Halt could cover more territory until they had almost reached the edge of the forest. Will began to move forward, toward the open, grass-covered heath, but Halt held up a hand and stopped him.

"Look first," he said softly. "This could be just the place where they'd lie in wait, knowing we're lax once we're out of the forest."

Will's mouth went dry as he realized that Halt was right. The sense of relief that he'd felt, the sudden lessening of tension, had almost led him into what could have been a fatal mistake. He crouched beside Halt and together they studied the terrain ahead of them. Horace waited patiently, a few meters behind them, with the horses.

"See anything?" Halt asked quietly.

Will shook his head, his eyes still moving.

"Neither do I," Halt agreed. "But that doesn't mean they're not there." He glanced up at the tree they sheltered behind. It was one of the taller trees, longer established than its neighbors.

"Slip up the tree and take a look," he said, then added, "Stay on this side of the trunk while you do it."

Will grinned at him. "I wasn't born yesterday."

Halt raised an eyebrow. "Maybe not. But you could have died today if I'd let you go blundering out into the open a few minutes ago."

There was no answer to that. Will looked up into the tree, selected the handholds and footholds he would use, and swarmed up into the branches. He'd always been an excellent climber, and it took only a few seconds for him to be ten meters above the forest floor. From this vantage point, he had a clear view of the land that lay before them.

"No sign," he called softly.

Halt grunted. "Can you find a good shooting position up there?"

Will glanced around. A few meters above him was a wide branch that would give him a good position, with a clear view of the land ahead. He saw the sense of Halt's question. From an elevated position, he would see any ambusher's movement before they were in a position to shoot.

"Give me a moment." He went higher up the tree. Halt watched him, smiling at the ease with which he could climb. It's because he's not nervous, he realized. He feels at home up there and isn't afraid of falling.

"Ready," Will called softly. He had an arrow ready on the string, and his eyes scanned from side to side.

Halt rose from his kneeling position beside the tree and moved out into the open ground before them. He could make out the tracks of the Outsiders once more—a heel print here, a patch of broken, flattened grass stems there—so faint that only an experienced tracker would see them.

He moved out ten meters. Then twenty. Then fifty. Unconsciously, he had moved in a crouch, his every muscle ready to dive into cover or loose a return shot at a moment's notice. Gradually, as he moved farther he realized that the danger was past. He stood more erect; then, stopping, he signaled for Will and Horace to join him.

The grass here was only knee high. It provided nothing like the cover the shoulder-high gorse had. Anybody waiting in ambush here would be in more danger than their intended victims, Halt thought. They'd have to lie facedown to conceal themselves, so that they'd waste precious seconds rising to see their quarry and get ready for a shot. The Genovesans were too skilled to put themselves at such a disadvantage.

They mounted and rode on, more relaxed now but still scanning the ground carefully and still turning from time to time to check their rear. The grassland continued for several kilometers. Then they reached a ridge and looked down into a wide valley below them.

"Now *that's* where we're going to have to be careful," Halt said.

19

THE FLAT PLAIN AHEAD OF THEM STRETCHED FOR KILOMETERS. In the distance, they could see the steely glint of a river as it twisted its way through the countryside, always searching for the lowest-lying point.

Immediately before them, at the base of the ridge upon which they found themselves, the grass sloped gradually down. Then the land changed dramatically.

Gaunt, bare tree trunks rose from the flat ground, massed together in irregular ranks. Their bare limbs reached to the sky, jagged and uneven, devoid of any covering of leaves, twisted into weird shapes, as if in agony and supplication. There were thousands of them. Possibly tens of thousands, in close-packed ranks. And all of them dead, gray and bare.

To Will's eye, used to the soft green tones in the forests around Castle Redmont and Seacliff, the sight was unutterably sad and desolate. The wind sighed through the dead branches and trunks, whispering a forlorn sound that was only just audible. Without a cloak of leaves, and with their inner layers long devoid of sap, the branches didn't sway gracefully. They remained stark and stiff, their sharp, ugly lines unwavering as they resisted the gentle force of the breeze.

Will guessed that in a strong wind the dead limbs would crack and split by the dozen, falling to the ground below like so many warped, gray spears.

"What is it, Halt?" he asked. He spoke in almost a whisper. It seemed more suitable somehow, in the proximity of so many dead trees.

"It's a drowned forest," Halt told them.

Horace leaned forward, crossing both hands on the pommel of his saddle as he surveyed the scene of utter desolation that stretched before them.

"How does a forest drown?" he asked. Like Will, he kept his voice low, as if not wishing to disturb the tragic scene. The gray, gaunt shapes stretching out below them seemed to demand such a measure of respect. Halt pointed to the distant glitter of the river, visible beyond the thousands of trees and a low ridge.

"I'd say that river must have flooded," he said. "It would have been fifty, sixty years ago, in a particularly wet season. The floodwaters spread over the low ground, and basically, the trees drowned. They're not capable of living when their root systems are underwater, so gradually, they died off."

"But I've seen floods before," Horace said. "A river floods. The waters rise. Then they recede and everything pretty much goes back to normal."

Halt was studying the lay of the land now, and he nodded acknowledgment of Horace's statement.

"Normally, you'd expect it to happen that way," he said. "And over a short period of time, the trees will survive. But look more closely. The river is contained by that low ridge beyond the forest. Once the waters rose over that ridge and flooded down to where the forest stood, there was no way it could recede again once the rain stopped. And I suspect that the rain kept on going for some time. The flood-water was trapped there among the trees. That's what killed them."

Halt had been looking for the trail down the slope as they were speaking. Now he saw it and urged Abelard toward it. The others followed behind him. As they reached the flat ground below their earlier vantage point, they realized what a formidable barrier the drowned forest was. The gray trunks were all the same shade, and their twisted, irregular shapes made it difficult to distinguish one from another. They merged together in a gray wall. It was almost impossible to discern detail or perspective.

"Now, this is what I'd call a good ambush site," Halt said. Then, a few seconds later, he swung down from his saddle and walked for-ward several paces, studying the ground. He beckoned the others to join him.

"Will," he said, "you saw the tracks Tennyson and his party left in the grassland once we got out of the forest?"

Will nodded and Halt gestured at the ground around him. "Take a good look at these and see if you can find any difference."

There was a thread of wool hanging from a low bush in the grass. Farther along, something gleamed on the ground. Will went to it and picked it up. It was a horn button. A little farther along, he saw a distinct, perfectly formed heel print in a soft patch of ground. The grass itself was heavily trampled and beaten down.

"So, what do you think?" Halt asked.

There was definitely something wrong, Will thought, and Halt's question seemed to confirm that the older Ranger felt the same way. Mentally, he pictured the tracks they had seen at the top of the rise behind them. Vague impressions in the dirt, occasional bruised blades of grass, almost invisible to a follower. Now here, conveniently, there were threads, buttons, and a deep footprint—just the sort of thing that Tennyson's party had seemed to be avoiding only a few hundred meters away. And the line of visual clues pointed in one clear direction—into the dead forest.

"It all seems a little . . . obvious," he said at length. And the moment he said it, he realized that was what had been bothering him about these tracks. Suddenly, after leaving a trail that could be followed only by highly trained trackers, the party ahead of them were leaving tracks that even Horace could follow.

"Exactly," Halt said, staring into the gray depths of the dead forest. "It's all very convenient, isn't it?"

"They wanted us to find the tracks," Will said. It was a statement of fact, not a question, and Halt nodded slowly.

"They want us to follow," Horace said, surprising himself slightly. Halt gave him a grin.

"Well thought out, Horace. That cloak must be making you think like a Ranger." He gestured toward the forest ahead of them. "They wanted to make sure that we knew they'd gone this way. And there's only one reason for them to have done that."

"They're waiting for us somewhere in there," Will said. Like Halt, he was gazing steadily into the gray wasteland that faced them, frowning slightly as he tried to discern some sign of movement, some out-of-place item, among the long-dead trees. He had to blink several times. The tree trunks merged together in his vision and seemed to blur into one mass.

"It's what I'd do," Halt said quietly. Then, with just a hint of contempt, he added, "Although I hope I'd be a little more subtle about it. Those signs there are almost an insult to my intelligence."

"They're not to know that, of course," Horace put in. "None of them will have had much to do with Rangers before."

Halt nodded. "The Genovesans have no idea that we know the first thing about tracking. They may suspect it. But they're not taking chances with this"—he indicated the footprint, the thread and the horn button—"this spoon-feeding."

"So, what do we do now?" Horace asked.

"What we do now," Halt replied, "is have you take the horses back a few hundred meters and wait. Will and I will flush these Genovesans out."

Horace stepped forward to remonstrate with the Ranger, his hands outstretched.

"Oh, come on, Halt! You can trust me!"

But Halt was already shaking his head, and he laid a hand on Horace's forearm to reassure him.

"Horace, I trust you every bit as much as I trust Will. But this is not the sort of fight you're trained for. And you're not armed for it either," he added.

Without his realizing it, Horace's hand dropped to the hilt of his sword, sheathed at his side, in an instinctive gesture.

"I'm armed, all right!" he insisted. "Just let me get to close quarters and I'll show these assassins how well armed I am! I think I'd like to have the murderer who killed Ferris at the point of my sword."

Halt didn't release the young man's arm. He shook it gently to make his point.

"That's why I want you to wait back a little. This won't be a close-quarter fight. These men kill from a distance. Will and I have our bows, so we'll be fighting them on even terms. But you won't get near them. They'll put enough crossbow bolts into you to make you look like a porcupine before you get within twenty meters of them."

"But . . . ," Horace began.

"Think about it, Horace. You won't be able to help if it comes to a fight. They'll be too far away. You'll just provide them with an extra target. And if Will and I have to keep an eye on you, we won't be able to concentrate on finding them and killing them before they kill us. Now please, take the horses back out of bow shot and let us do what we've been trained to do."

The struggle was all too evident on the young warrior's face. It went against the grain for him to retire and leave his friends to do the difficult and dangerous task that lay before them.

Yet deep in his heart, he knew Halt was right. He could be of no help in the coming engagement. He would, in fact, be a hindrance or, worse still, a distraction for his friends.

"All right," he said reluctantly. "I guess what you say makes sense. But I don't like it."

Will grinned at him. "I don't like it either," he said. "I'd much rather stay back with you and the horses. But Halt hasn't given me the choice."

Horace smiled at his old friend. He could see the light of determination in Will's eyes. It was time for them to take the fight to the Genovesans, and Horace knew that, in spite of his protests to the contrary, Will was ready to do just that.

Feeling worse than useless, Horace reached for Tug's bridle. "Come on, boy."

For a moment, the little horse resisted, turning an inquiring eye on his master and giving vent to a troubled neigh.

"Go along, Tug," Will said, accompanying the order with a hand signal. The little horse trotted reluctantly after Horace and Kicker.

"Abelard, follow," Halt said. His horse tossed its head rebelliously but turned to follow the other two horses back from the rows of twisted gray tree trunks.

Horace turned and called softly back to his friends. "If you need me, just call and I'll . . ."

His voice trailed off. There was no sign of the two Rangers. They had simply disappeared into the drowned forest. Horace felt a thrill of nervousness go up his spine. He glanced at Tug.

"Gives me the creeps when they do that," he said. Tug shook his head violently, vibrating his shaggy mane in agreement. "Still," said Horace, "I'm glad they're on our side."

Tug regarded him out of one eye, his head cocked to the side. *That's what I was trying to tell you,* he seemed to be saying.

20

Will and Halt, separated by about five meters so they wouldn't offer a grouped target to the Genovesans, slipped silently into the dead forest. Their eyes darted from side to side, quartering, seeking, going back again as the two Rangers ghosted from one piece of cover to the next, searching for that one sight of movement or flash of color that would give them a warning.

Will searched from left to center then back again. Halt went from right to center then reversed his scan. Between them, they covered the entire 180 degrees from their extreme left and right to their front.

Every so often, without creating any predictable pattern, one or the other would spin suddenly to check their rear.

They had progressed some forty meters into the forest when Halt found a larger-than-normal piece of cover. A tree had grown with multiple trunks, and now it provided enough protection for the two of them. There were also two other features in the topography close to the tree that had taken his attention. Checking their back trail and finding it clear, he gestured for Will to join him. He watched approvingly as his former apprentice slid between the trees, taking full advantage of every piece of cover. He seemed to be a blur, never clearly visible, even to Halt's trained eyes.

They crouched together behind the spreading trunks. Now that they were within the forest, Will realized that the trees had a sound of their own. Normally, in a densely packed forest, he would expect to hear the gentle soughing of the wind through the leaves, the call of birds and the movement of small animals. Here, there were no leaves, no birds or animals. But, despite what he had thought earlier, the trunks and limbs moved slightly, groaning and creaking in protest as their dry joints were forced to give by the ever-present breeze. Sometimes one bare limb rubbed against a close neighbor with a cracking, shrieking noise. It was as if the forest were groaning in its death agony.

"Ugly sound, isn't it?" Halt asked.

"Gets on my nerves," Will admitted. "What do we do now?"

Halt nodded to the narrow path that lay through the trunks in front of them. It wound and twisted from side to side as it found its way around the massive gray trunks. But it always returned to its original direction, which was southeast.

"I see they're still leaving a clear trail for us to follow," he said.

Will glanced in the direction he indicated. He could see a small fragment of cloth trapped on the sharp end of a broken branch.

"I see they're not being any more subtle about it," he answered. Both of them kept their voices low, only just above a whisper. They had no idea how close the enemy might be.

"No indeed," Halt agreed. "I've seen plenty of footprints along the way too. You'd swear they were made by a giant, from the depth of them."

Will reached down and felt the ground with two fingers. The grass was short here among the dead trees, and the ground beneath it was dry and hard. "Not as if it's soft ground either."

"No. This ground dried out many, many years ago. They're doing it intentionally again. Letting us know exactly which way they've gone."

"And which way they want us to follow," Will said.

A faint smile creased Halt's face. "That too."

"But we're not going to do that?" Will said. It seemed logical to him. If your enemy wanted you to do something, it only made sense to do something else entirely.

"We're not," Halt agreed. "I am."

Will opened his mouth to protest, but Halt held up a hand to forestall him.

"If we seem to be doing what they want, they may grow over-confident. And that can only be good for us." As he spoke, his eyes were scanning the forest unceasingly, searching for any trace of move-ment, any sign that the Genovesans might be close.

"True," Will admitted. "But I—"

Once again, Halt's upraised hand stopped him in midsentence.

"Will, we could be in here for days searching for them if we don't do something to make them show their hand. And all the while, Tennyson is getting farther and farther away. We've got to take a risk. After all, we're only assuming they're here in the first place. What if they've second-guessed us—left all these convenient signs so we'd think they're trying to lure us in, and then hightailed it out of here, leaving us creeping around trying to find them—and wasting hours of daylight doing it?"

Will frowned. That hadn't occurred to him. But it was possible.

"Do you think they've done that?" he asked.

Halt shook his head, slowly and deliberately. "No. I think they're here. I can sense them. But it is a possibility."

Behind them, a branch moved with a louder-than-normal,

drawn-out groan of tortured wood. Will spun around, his bow coming up as he did so. Once again, he felt that tight knot in the pit of his stomach as he wondered where the enemy was, when they might show their hand. Halt leaned a little closer, his voice even quieter than before.

"I'm going to wait an hour or so. We've got a good position here and we're covered pretty well from all sides. Let's see what they do now they know we're here."

"Do you think they'll move?" Will asked.

"No. They're too well trained for that. But it's worth a try. In an hour, the sun will be lower and the shadows deeper and longer in here. That'll work for us."

"Them too," Will suggested, but Halt shook his head.

"They're good," he said. "But they're not trained for this the way we are. They're more used to working in cities, blending into crowds. Plus our cloaks give us a big advantage in here. The colors match the surroundings a lot better than that dull purple they wear. So we wait for an hour and see what happens."

"Then what?"

"Then I'll move on again, following that very obvious trail they're leaving." Halt saw Will's quick intake of breath and knew the young Ranger was about to protest. He gave him no opportunity. "I'll be careful, Will, don't worry. I have done this sort of thing before, you know," he added mildly. And he was rewarded by a reluctant smile from his apprentice.

"Did I say something amusing?" he asked.

Will shook his head, seemed to ponder whether he should say anything, and then decided to go ahead.

"Well, it's just that . . . before we left Redmont, Lady Pauline spoke to me. About you."

Halt's eyebrow shot up. "And exactly what did she have to say about me?"

"Well . . ." Will shrugged uncomfortably. He wished now he'd decided against bringing this up. "She asked me to look after you."

Halt nodded several times, digesting this piece of information before he spoke again. "Touching to see she has so much faith in you." He paused. "And so little in me."

Will thought it might be best if he said nothing further. But Halt wasn't going to let the matter drop.

"I assume this instruction was accompanied by some sort of statement along the lines of 'He isn't getting any younger, you know'?"

Will hesitated just a second too long. "No. Of course not."

Halt snorted disdainfully. "The woman seems to think I'm senile." But in spite of himself, he smiled fondly as he thought about his tall, graceful wife. Then he recovered himself and came back to business.

"All right. Let's get down to it. The reason I'm going to go ahead is that I need your movement skills. You're smaller and nimbler than I am, so you've got a better chance of remaining unseen. I'll break cover and move out after them. You wait here for five minutes and then circle out to the left there. They should be watching me by then, and if you're as good as you say you are, they won't notice you."

He indicated a shallow indentation in the ground, leading to the left. After about ten meters, a tree had fallen across it and its massive gray trunk lay at a slight angle to the indentation. These were the two items he'd noticed as he took cover behind the large tree. He'd been looking for something of the kind since they'd entered the forest.

"Belly-crawl along that little gully there, as far as the fallen trunk. Then stay behind that and keep going. That should get you at least thirty meters away from here without them seeing you go. With any luck, they should think you're still in here, ready to give me support if I need it. But all the while, you'll be circling out to flank them."

"Even though we don't know where they are?" Will asked. But he was beginning to see the good sense behind Halt's plan.

Halt studied the forest in front of them once more, the corners of his eyes crinkled with concentration.

"They won't be far from the track," he said. "These trees will see to that. It's too hard to shoot accurately through this tangle at any range greater than about fifty meters. More like thirty, really. If you work your way out a hundred meters to the left, then begin to move parallel to me, you should stay well outside them. And you'll be placed to come up behind them."

Will was nodding as he took in the details. It sounded like a good plan. But there was one potential snag.

"I still don't like the fact that you're going to draw their attention," he said.

Halt shrugged. "Can't see any other way to do it. But believe me, I'm not going to be walking along pointing to my chest and saying, 'Just put a bolt here, please.' I'll be dodging from cover to cover. And the longer shadows will help. You just make sure that if they do try to shoot, you're ready to beat them to it. I'm sure I'll be trying to."

Will took several deep breaths. In his mind's eye, he could see the situation developing, with him slipping out to flank the Genovesans as Halt moved through the trees. It was a simple enough plan, and that was a good thing. Simple plans usually worked better than complex ones that relied on a sequence of events falling into place. The fewer things there were to go wrong, he'd learned, the better.

He imagined one of the assassins rising from cover. Odds were, he thought, they'd have hidden behind a fallen tree trunk. Their crossbows would be better suited to shoot from low-lying cover like that. Unlike a man armed with a longbow, they wouldn't have to rise to their feet to shoot. And they'd expose less of themselves than if they had to step from behind a standing tree to make their shot.

Halt could see his young friend's mind working and let him think it through. He was in no hurry to move. The shadows weren't long enough for his liking yet, and he could see that Will was assimilating the plan of action, setting it in his mind to make sure there was no misunderstanding. After a minute or two, he spoke again.

"We've got several things going for us, Will. One, these assassins won't be familiar with Ranger training or our skill levels. If they don't see you leave cover behind this tree, they'll assume you're still here—and that will give you an edge.

"Two, they're using crossbows. It'll be relatively short range, so we won't have any particular edge in accuracy. But on the other hand, they won't outrange us."

The most powerful crossbows could outrange a longbow. But firing a short bolt or quarrel rather than a longer, more stable arrow, they became less accurate the longer the shot traveled. In the restricted space inside the trees, they'd be on even footing.

"They're not using full-power crossbows in any event," Will said. A really powerful crossbow had massive limbs and cord. It was recocked and loaded by use of a two-handed crank set into the butt. And it could take several minutes to ratchet the string back for each shot. The Genovesans used a quicker, less powerful version, with a stirrup at the front of the bow. The bowman placed his foot in the stirrup to hold the bow steady, then, using a two-handed tool that hooked onto the string, he would pull it back to the cocked position, using both hands and all the muscles of his back. The range was reduced but so was the loading time—to around twenty or thirty seconds. And the bowman had to stand erect during the procedure. They could release their first shots from behind low cover, he realized. But when reloading they'd be vulnerable to the Rangers' return shots.

"They'll have to show themselves after the first shot," he said.

Halt pursed his lips. "They may have more than one bow each," he reminded Will. "So don't take chances. But either way, we'll shoot faster than they will."

It would take around twenty seconds for the crossbowmen to reload. Then they'd have to aim and shoot again. Will could nock, draw, aim and shoot in less than five seconds. Halt was a little faster. By the time a Genovesan was ready with his second shot, the two Rangers could have more than a dozen arrows in the air, all heading for him. The Genovesans had the advantage of shooting from ambush. But if they missed with their first shots, the odds suddenly swung in the Rangers' favor.

Halt studied the forest around them for the tenth time. Moving his head slightly as he faced west, he could see the glare of the sun between the trunks. The shadows were longer now, and visibility among the trees was becoming more and more uncertain. If he left it much longer, they'd be caught inside the trees in the gathering darkness. It was time to move.

"All right," he said. "Remember: five minutes, then slip out through that gully."

Will grinned sardonically. It was more of a dent in the ground than a gully, he thought. But Halt didn't see the reaction. Again, he was studying the forest to the front and sides of their position. He rose from his kneeling position into a half crouch.

"Let's invite these fellows to dance," he said, and slipped silently out onto the path, a green and gray blur that quickly melded into the shadows of the forest.

21

HALT'S EYES WERE SLITS OF CONCENTRATION AS HE MOVED forward between the trees, following the narrow, indistinct path. He scanned constantly, noting, with a sardonic smile, the occasional clues that had been left behind by the men he was following—a scrap of cloth snagged on a branch here, an all-too-obvious footprint there. He maintained the pretense of searching for these signs and following the tracks they had left. It wouldn't do to let his quarry know he was on to their little game, he thought.

The ground was littered with deadfalls—branches and twigs that the wind had snapped off from the trees high above and dropped to the forest floor. They formed an almost continuous carpet beneath his feet, and, skilled as he was at moving silently, even Halt couldn't avoid some noise as they cracked and snapped under his soft tread. He could do it if he moved slowly, testing the ground with each foot before he put weight on it. But moving slowly was too dangerous an option. He needed speed. By moving quickly, he became an indistinct, gray-toned blur sliding among the bare trunks—and that would make him a more difficult target. Besides, there wasn't much point in moving silently if he wanted the Genovesans to know he was here.

He slipped into the cover of a thick gray trunk and crouched, scanning the forest ahead. Long years of training made sure that his head barely moved as he did so. It was his eyes that darted from side to side, seeking, testing, consciously changing their depth of focus to search from close in to farther out. His face remained in the shadow thrown by the deep cowl. The Genovesans, if they were watching, would have seen him dart behind the tree. But now they would have lost sight of him as he blended in, and so long as he didn't move, they would be uncertain if he were still there or not.

All of which meant they would be looking for him, and not Will. He felt a grim sense of satisfaction knowing that Will was backing him up. By now, Halt thought, his young student would have begun to move, snaking away from the three-trunk tree they had sheltered behind, crawling low-bellied along the shallow gully to the shelter of the fallen trunk.

He couldn't think of anyone he would rather have with him. Gilan, perhaps. His unseen movement skills were second to none in the Corps. Or Crowley, of course, his oldest comrade.

But, skilled as they both were, he knew Will would always be his first choice. Crowley was experienced and calm under pressure. But he couldn't match Will in unseen movement. Gilan might move more stealthily than Will, but there was very little to choose between them. And Will had an advantage that Gilan didn't. His mind moved a little more quickly, and he was inclined to see the unconventional alternative faster than Gilan. If the unexpected occurred, he knew Will could act on his own initiative and come up with the right solution. That wasn't to denigrate Gilan at all. He would think through a situation and probably come to the same conclusion as Will. But with Will, it was an instinctive ability.

There was one other point, and it was a very important one in the current situation. Halt knew, although Will probably didn't, that Will was a better shot than either Crowley or Gilan.

In fact, he thought, that might prove to be the most important point of all.

He waited a few more seconds, letting his breathing and his heart rate settle. In spite of what he had said to Will—that he had done this sort of thing before—he didn't like the idea of intentionally drawing the enemy's notice. Moving as he was through the trees, the skin on his back crawled with the expectation that any second, a bolt might slam into it. The very idea of moving so that his enemy could see him went against all his deeply ingrained training. Halt preferred to move without anyone ever seeing him or being aware that he was there.

He knew that in these conditions, and with his cloak, he was presenting a very poor target. But the Genovesans were skilled marksmen. They were more than capable of hitting a poor target. That's why they were so highly paid by those who hired them, after all.

"You're wasting time," he muttered. "You just don't want to go back out there again, do you?"

And the answer, of course, was no. He didn't. But there was no alternative. He surveyed the path once more, picked out his route for the next five or ten meters, then glided quickly out from behind cover and went forward into the gray maze of dead trees.

Belly to the ground, using elbows, ankles and knees to propel himself forward and never rising higher than a completely prone position, Will slid out from behind the multiple-trunk dead tree. It was a technique called the snake crawl, and he'd practiced it for hours on end as an apprentice, sliding through low cover, trying to remain unseen by the keen gaze of his teacher. Time and again he would feel he was getting the technique right, only to have his ego dashed by a sarcastic voice: *Is that a bony backside I see sticking up out of the grass by that black rock? I think it is. Perhaps I should put an arrow in it if its owner doesn't GET IT DOWN!*

Today, of course, there was more at risk than a sarcastic ribbing from his teacher. Today, Halt's life, and his own, were dependent on his being able to keep that errant behind down, close to the ground with the rest of his body. He crawled slowly, moving the loose branches and twigs out of his path as he went. Unlike Halt, he couldn't afford to make the slightest noise. True, the forest was maintaining its litany of groans and scrapes and creaks. But the sharp sound of a snapping twig would tell a keen listener that someone was on the move out here.

Flat to the ground as he was, he found his vision focused on the short blades of grass only a few centimeters away from the tip of his nose. His world became this tiny space of dirt and grass and gray branches. He watched a small brown beetle hurry past only centimeters from his face, ignoring him completely. A file of ants marched steadfastly over his left hand, refusing to be diverted from their purpose. He let them go and then edged forward slowly, carefully brushing a branch to one side. It made a small noise, magnified by his raw nerves, and he paused for a moment. Then he told himself that nobody could have heard that slight scrape over the background noises of the forest, and he continued. The shelter of the fallen tree trunk was only a few meters away by now. Once he was behind that he could afford to move more swiftly—and more comfortably.

But for now, he resisted the urge to hurry into the cover of the trunk. Doing that could well undo all the work he'd put in so far. A sudden movement could draw attention. Instead, he concentrated on the old technique he'd taught himself as an apprentice, trying to sense that his body was actually *forcing itself* into the ground beneath him, becoming conscious of its weight pressing into the rough grass and dirt and sticks.

He felt completely vulnerable because, for once, he was effectively unarmed. In order to crawl completely prone, he'd had to unstring his bow, pushing it through two small retaining loops on his cloak, made for that purpose. Trying to crawl with a strung bow in these conditions was risking that a branch or twig or even a clump of grass could become snagged in the angle where the bowstring met the notched end of the bow. Now it was held firmly in a straight line along his back, a straight piece of yew wood that would slide smoothly past snags and obstructions.

For the same reason, he'd hitched his belt around so that the buckle and his double knife scabbard were placed in the small of his back, beneath the cloak. Again, it made for smoother, quieter progress. But it also meant that if he were discovered, he would waste precious seconds trying to draw either of his knives.

It went totally against the grain to move in the presence of enemies while he was disarmed this way. He particularly regretted the need for the bow to be unstrung. As the old Ranger saying went, "An unstrung bow is a stick." It had been a joke when he'd first heard it, five years ago. Now there was nothing amusing about it at all.

At last, he made it into the shelter provided by the horizontal tree trunk. He allowed himself a small sigh of relief. There had been no cries of alarm, no sudden, searing agony as a crossbow bolt buried itself into his back. He felt the tension along his back ease a little. Without realizing it, his muscles and flesh had been bunched instinctively, in a vain attempt to lessen the pain of such a wound.

Rising slightly from his totally prone position—although not too much—he began to make faster progress. When he was farther away from the track, he rose carefully to his feet, slid behind the largest tree he could find, and restrung his bow. He felt another lessening of tension. Now he wasn't the one at risk anymore. The Genovesans were.

Halt was down on one knee, pretending to study another intentional sign left by the Genovesans. In fact, though his head was lowered, his eyes were raised as he searched the tangle of gray trunks and dim shadows ahead of him.

Briefly, among the trees to his left, he saw a slight movement, and perhaps a hint of dull purple in the shadows. He remained unmoving. Crouched as he was, he made a poor target for the crossbowman, if indeed he was out there. Odds were, the assassin would wait until he rose to his feet and gave him a larger target.

He glanced left. The trees he had been passing for the last few meters had been narrow—a new grove when they were wiped out by the flood. Some were little more than saplings, and none of them provided the sort of substantial cover he would prefer. He smiled grimly. Which, of course, was why the Genovesans had chosen this spot to leave another clue. They would know that a person following them would stop and kneel to study it, then rise to his feet once more.

And in that totally vulnerable moment, he would be a perfect target for them. Halt's eyes sought that source of movement and color again, but he saw nothing. That made sense. Once he stopped, the crossbowman would have brought his weapon up to the aiming point. That was the small flash of movement he'd noticed. Now, he'd be stock-still again, crossbow trained on the spot where he'd expect Halt to rise to his feet. Halt tensed his muscles, preparing to move.

He glanced to his left and saw one tree that was marginally thicker than its neighbors, although not thick enough to fully conceal him. Nevertheless, he thought, it would have to do. He hoped

Will had got into position by now. He'd glanced far left a few times—not enough to make the Genovesans aware of it—and had seen no sign of him.

Which could mean he was out there. On the other hand, it could mean he had been delayed by some unforeseen event. He might be nowhere in sight. Then Halt felt a sense of certainty. This was Will he was thinking about. He'd be there.

Without warning, he launched himself sideways off his bent right knee, rolling smoothly into the partial shelter of the tree he had picked out. And waited, nerves tense and screaming.

Nothing.

No dull smack of a crossbow string being released. No vicious, triple-barbed bolt whirring overhead to thud into the trees behind him. Nothing. Just the eerie groaning of the dead trees as they moved and twisted and rubbed against each other. That told him something. The Genovesans weren't going to be tricked into a rushed shot by his sudden, unexpected movement. Their discipline was too good to allow that.

Alternatively, he thought, he might have imagined that small movement in the trees. There might be nobody there at all.

Yet somehow, he knew that they were there, waiting. Some sixth sense told him this was the time and the place. The combination of factors—the obvious clue on the trail, the thinning trees—told him that they were just a few meters away, waiting for him to make his next move. He lay prone behind the tree. For the moment, he was concealed. But as soon as he started to rise to his feet, he'd be visible. He glanced around. He could crawl to a larger tree, but the nearest was some distance away. And the thinner growth of trees here meant he'd be badly exposed if he tried to move.

Which was, he told himself for the second time, precisely why the Genovesans had picked this spot. Because now he was certain he had seen that movement. It was a perfect ambush site. And he was in a helpless position. He was relatively safe for the moment and would remain that way so long as he hugged the ground. But he couldn't see. He knew if he raised his head to study the situation, he'd be inviting a crossbow bolt between the eyes. He was stranded here and, effectively, blinded. All the advantages lay with the Genovesans. They had seen where he had gone. His sudden movement, rolling to the side, must have told them that he knew they were there. All they had to do was wait for him to move and they had him cold.

No matter how he thought it through, the situation got no better. If he remained here, sooner or later one of the assassins would move to flank him while the other kept his crossbow trained on the spot where he lay concealed. He thought with grim humor of the discussion he'd had with Will only an hour or so earlier.

After the first shot, all the advantages will be with us.

Except for one awkward detail. After the first shot, he'd probably be dead.

He closed his eyes and concentrated fiercely. He had one chance, and that depended on Will being in position behind the Genovesans. Then he felt a fierce certainty flooding through him again. Will would be there because Halt needed him to be there. Will would be there because he was Will—and he had never let Halt down.

Halt opened his eyes. Still lying flat, he eased an arrow from his quiver and nocked it to the string of his bow. Then he gathered his feet and legs beneath him and crouched. He considered his next move. All his instincts screamed at him to rise slowly to his feet, to postpone the moment when the Genovesan pulled his trigger. But he discarded the thought. A slow movement would simply give the Genovesan more time to align his sights.

A sudden movement might startle him and cause him to rush his shot. It wasn't likely, he admitted to himself. But it was possible. And that made it the better choice.

"I hope you're there, Will," he muttered to himself. Then he lunged to his feet, bow up, arrow drawing back, searching desperately for some sign, some flicker of movement in the trees.

22

THE FOREST HAD SEEMED A LIFELESS EXPANSE, BUT, AS HALT had discovered, some undergrowth had recently established itself among the gray trunks. As Will crept quietly out of the solid shelter afforded by the fallen tree, he encountered another variety.

A trailing tendril of stay-with-me vine had wound its way up one of the former forest giants, spiraled along a dead, snapped-off branch, then allowed its end to drop off into clear air. He brushed against it as he passed the tree that was its host.

Instantly, four of the hooked thorns fastened themselves into the tough material of his cloak, holding it and him firmly in place. He cursed under his breath. He didn't have the time to deal with this delay but he had no choice. He reached behind him and grabbed a handful of the cloak. Gently at first, then with increasing pressure, he tried to pull the garment free from the tenacious vine.

At first, he thought he was succeeding, as he felt a slight give. But this was just the elastic vine itself, stretching as he pulled. Then it reached the end of its stretch and he was held firm. In fact, he realized angrily, he was now more firmly snagged than before. His movement had made the thorns bite more deeply. Worse still, the vine held him trapped in a half-standing position.

There was nothing for it. He would have to take off the cloak and cut the vine away. Held from behind as he was, he couldn't reach the infuriating creeper. That meant he had to remove his quiver, which he wore over the cloak, then the cloak itself.

All of which meant extra movement, which could well give him away to the Genovesan assassins as they lay in ambush somewhere out there. Again, he cursed silently. Then slowly, with infinite care, he slid the strap of the quiver over his head and put it to one side. Unfastening the clasp that held the cloak in place at his throat, he eased the garment from his shoulders.

Hurry, he thought. Halt is depending on you getting into position!

But he resisted the panicked impulse and moved with infinite patience, knowing that a hasty movement might betray him. He had the cloak off and drew his saxe knife. The vine had snagged high on the cloak, between his shoulder blades. He sliced through it easily with the razor-sharp blade, then slowly, the cloak bunched in his hands, he sank to the ground.

Still maintaining the same painfully measured movements, he re-donned the cloak. For a moment he considered leaving it behind, but the extra concealment it afforded decided him against such a course. He passed the quiver strap over his head and settled the arrows on his shoulder, adjusting the flap on his cloak that covered the distinctive feathers of the fletching. He strung his bow and was ready to move again. He took a quick look back through the forest, the way he had come. There was no sign of movement, no sign that he had been noticed. Still, he thought, the first indication of that was likely to be a crossbow bolt.

He had to assume that he had remained unseen, so he moved on, crouching low to the ground and sliding quietly from one piece of cover to the next. Several times he detoured to avoid more hanging tendrils of the innocent-looking stay-with-me vine. He'd learned that lesson the hard way.

When he judged that he had come nearly seventy meters to the left, he swung right a little to parallel the path Halt was following. Any farther out and he'd be too far away if anything happened. The dense wall of dead trees would block his view completely. And gradually, as he moved forward, he began to angle back in toward the path being taken by his mentor.

He was standing now, trading concealment for extra speed, hoping to make up the time he had lost with the vine. But this far out, he could afford the risk, he thought. Unless he and Halt had it all completely wrong, the assassins would be somewhere to his right, hopefully on the same side of the path and looking away from him. Noise was his main enemy now, and he placed his feet with extreme care on the litter of dead sticks that covered the ground, inching and easing his soft boots between the sticks to keep from snapping them.

Fifty meters to his right, he noticed a patch of forest where the trees were more widely spaced and the trunks were noticeably thinner than the majority of trees in the forest. He slipped to a new vantage point and studied the lay of the land from behind the bole of a tree.

Nothing moved. But his senses told him this would be the place. He eased away from the tree, slipped forward another five meters, then went behind another tree, his eyes never leaving that area where the trees thinned.

He had actually raised his right foot to step out from behind cover when he spotted a brief flicker of movement and froze instantly. He waited, foot partially raised, eyes boring into the gray ranks of trees, waiting to see if the movement might be repeated.

Then he saw them. And once he'd picked them out, he wondered how he'd ever missed seeing them in the first place—although he had to admit that the dull purple cloaks blended well into the shadows of the forest.

He smiled. It was the movement that had betrayed them. *Move and you're almost certain to be seen,* Halt had told him over and over as they had practiced.

"You were right, Halt," he said silently to himself.

As he had expected, the two crossbowmen were crouched behind a fallen tree trunk. They had added a haphazard pile of fallen branches to it, creating a higher barrier, but one that would still go relatively unnoticed. Both men had their crossbows leveled across the top of this makeshift parapet. They were half turned away from him. The fallen tree ran at an angle to his position, and their attention was fixed on a point in the forest some thirty meters from where they crouched.

He followed the line of their gaze as best he could but could see nothing. Odds were, that was where they had sighted Halt, and now he had gone to ground.

He heard a small sound, then—a shuffling sound, of a body moving quickly over the ground, accompanied by the loud snapping of several branches. It seemed to come from the point they were watching, and one of them actually rose a little higher behind the barrier, his crossbow ready and seeking a target.

The trees formed a thick screen between him and the Genovesans. He was farther away from them than he'd like to be. If he had to shoot, his arrow could be deflected by any one of a dozen trees or branches. He estimated that he was sixty meters out, and he really needed to get closer to be sure of his shot.

Whatever it was that he'd heard moving a few seconds ago, and he assumed it was Halt moving into cover, had attracted their full attention. There was no risk they'd see him if he moved, unless he was stupid enough to step on a dry branch. He flicked the cover flap away from his quiver and drew an arrow, nocking it onto the bowstring. Then he stepped, light-footed as a fox, out from behind the tree that sheltered him and began to close in on the two crossbowmen.

Five meters. Ten. Another five. Still they concentrated on the trees to his right. If they hadn't been watching so intently, they might have seen him in their peripheral vision. He was approaching them on an angle, just behind their right side. But he could tell by their body language that they were completely focused away from him. They were like two hunting dogs, bodies almost quivering with excitement and tension as they caught the first scent of their quarry.

Another step. Feel the bent branch under the ball of your foot, gently work the toe *under* the branch, check that your foot is on flat ground now, then let your weight go forward onto the ball of that foot. Then start the whole process over again with the other foot. He was into a more comfortable range now. The trees formed less of a screen between him and the two Genovesans. In another few paces he'd be . . .

Halt stood up.

There was no warning. One moment, the forest seemed empty. Then, with a rustle of undergrowth, the gray-bearded Ranger seemed to rise out of the ground, his bow already trained, an arrow on the string and drawn back.

Will heard a short cry of surprise from one of the crossbowmen, saw Halt shift his aim slightly as the sound revealed the man's position. Both crossbows came up fractionally and Will drew and shot at the man closest to him. As he did so, he heard the deep-throated thrum of Halt's bow, closely followed by the dull slap of the crossbow string smacking into the stop.

The first bolt missed. It was fired by the Genovesan Will had picked as a target, and in the second before he squeezed the cross-bow's trigger, Will's arrow slammed into his side. He lurched side-ways, jolting against his companion and throwing him off his aim. Then Halt's arrow slashed into his chest and he jerked the trigger with dead fingers as he toppled backward. A branch jutting out from the trunk caught him and held him sprawled half erect across it.

Will cursed as he realized they had made a dangerous mistake. He and Halt had wasted both their shots on the same man, leaving the other crossbowman uninjured and partly obscured by his fallen comrade. Will saw the crossbow swing toward him now. He snapped off a shot, knew he had missed and pivoted back into cover, behind the tree next to him. He heard Halt shoot again, heard his arrow glance off an intervening tree. Then a bolt gouged a long furrow out of the hardwood that sheltered Will, spinning harmlessly away to clatter among the deadfalls.

Two crossbows. Two shots, he thought exultantly. Now they had him!

He stepped clear of the tree, continuing the pivoting movement so that he emerged on the side opposite to the one where he had gone into cover, and his mouth went dry as he saw the Genovesan aiming another crossbow toward Halt, heard the dull smack of the cord again. Halt had warned him that they might have more than one bow apiece, and he'd been right.

Then Will's heart froze at the most chilling sound he had heard in his young life: Halt's brief cry of pain, followed by the sound of his bow dropping.

23

"HALT!" HE SCREAMED, ALL THOUGHT OF THE GENOVESAN forgotten for a moment. He searched vainly, looking to where Halt had risen into view. But there was no sign of him now. He was down, Will thought dully. He had been hit and he was down.

He heard a sudden movement, swung back and saw the Genovesan disappearing through the screen of tightly packed tree trunks. He was no more than a blur of movement, a brief glimpse of the purple cloak. Will shot three arrows after him, heard them all strike against the intervening trunks and branches. Then he heard the dull hammer of a horse's hooves. The assassins had obviously left their horses tethered back among the trees, and there would be no chance of catching the survivor now.

There was no need for silence or stealth any longer. He rushed to the spot where he had last seen Halt, snapping branches and twigs underfoot, shoving through tendrils of the stay-with-me vines as they swung into his face and snatched at his cloak to impede him.

His heart pounded as he saw the Ranger doubled over, turned away from him. Wet, red blood stained his cloak. There seemed to be a lot of it.

"Halt!" he cried, his voice breaking with fear. "Are you all right?"

For a second, there was no reply and Will felt a dreadful darkness steal into his heart. Then it was instantly dispelled as the bearded Ranger rolled over to face him, his right hand clenched over his left forearm, partially stemming the flow of blood. Halt grimaced in pain.

"I'm all right," he said through gritted teeth. "That bolt only scraped my arm. But it hurts like the very devil."

Will went down on one knee beside his master and eased Halt's hand away from the wound.

"Let me see," he said. He moved Halt's hand, tentatively at first, afraid that he'd see the jetting, pulsing spurt of blood that would tell him a major artery had been severed. He gave a sigh of relief when he saw there was just a steady welling of blood. Then, reassured, he took his saxe knife and cut the Ranger's sleeve away from the area. He studied it for a moment, then reached into the wound pack that every Ranger carried on his belt and took out a clean piece of linen, wiping the blood away so he could see the extent of the damage.

"He nearly missed you," he said. "A centimeter to the left and he would have missed you completely."

There was a shallow score across the skin of the forearm—about four centimeters long but not deep enough to cut muscles or tendons. Will unstoppered Halt's canteen and flooded the wound with water, wiping with the cloth again and clearing the blood away momentarily. It quickly welled back again and he shrugged. At least the wound was clean. He applied some salve, took a field dressing from his pack and wound it around Halt's forearm.

"You ruined my jacket," Halt said accusingly, looking at the neatly slit sleeve that now dangled down either side of his arm. Will grinned at him. The grumpy, complaining tone of voice did more than anything else to reassure him that the Ranger was only slightly wounded.

"You can sew it up tonight," he told him.

Halt snorted indignantly. "I'm wounded. You can sew it for me." Then he added, in a more serious tone, "I take it the second one got away. I heard a horse."

Will took his right arm and helped him to his feet, although really there was no need to. Halt was only superficially injured, after all. But the older Ranger recognized that Will's mother-henning was a reaction to the worry he'd felt when his teacher had been hit, so he accepted his ministrations without resisting. By the same token, he allowed Will to retrieve his fallen longbow and hand it to him.

"Yes," Will said, in answer to the question. "Seems they'd tethered their horses a little farther back in the trees. I shot at him, but I missed. I'm sorry, Halt."

He was remorseful, feeling that he'd let his mentor down. Halt patted him gently on the shoulder.

"Can't be helped," he said. "This forest makes accuracy almost impossible. Too many branches and trees in the way."

"We made a mistake," Will said, and when Halt raised an eyebrow in an unspoken question, he continued, "We both shot at the same man. That left the other man clear to shoot at you."

"That couldn't be foreseen. I've told you over and over, something always goes wrong in a fight. There's always something you can't plan for."

"I suppose so. It's just . . ." Will stopped, unable to articulate his thoughts. He sensed that somehow, he could have done better, could have saved Halt from the pain of this wound—and the fact that he had come so close to death. Halt put a hand on his shoulder and shook him gently.

"Don't worry about it. Look at the result. One of them is dead and all we have to show for it is a scratch on my arm. I'd say that's a pretty fair outcome, especially when you consider that they started with all the advantages. Wouldn't you?"

Will said nothing. He was picturing Halt lying on the forest floor with a crossbow bolt buried in his chest, eyes staring sightlessly up into the stark branches overhead. Halt shook him again, a little more vigorously than before.

"Well, wouldn't you?" he repeated, and Will slowly allowed a tired grin to show on his features.

"I suppose so," he agreed.

Halt nodded in satisfaction, although secretly he wished they had managed to kill or capture the second Genovesan as well. Their task would certainly be a lot easier if that had been the case. "All right, let's get back and find Horace. He's probably going crazy, wondering what's become of us."

Horace was, in fact, on tenterhooks. He had set up a small campsite, but then was too wound up to sit and relax in it. He had paced anxiously up and down, waiting for some sign of his friends, and had actually worn a furrow in the knee-high grass. The three horses were less concerned, idly cropping grass around them.

Naturally the Rangers caught sight of Horace before he saw them. Even approaching a friendly camp, they tended to move unobtrusively, allowing themselves to blend into the background. Will whistled shrilly. Tug's head shot up instantly, ears pricked, and he whinnied in reply. Horace saw them then, and ran through the grass to meet them. He stopped a few meters short of them, seeing Halt's torn sleeve and the bandage around his arm.

"Are you all . . . ?"

Halt held up a hand to reassure him. "I'm fine. Nothing but a scratch."

"Literally," Will added. Now that he was over the initial shock and fear he'd felt when he'd seen his mentor wounded, he could afford to joke about it. Halt looked sidelong at him.

"That's a little harsh," he said. "It's actually very painful."

"What happened?" Horace interrupted, sensing they might launch into one of those interminable exchanges of banter that Rangers seemed so fond of. "Did you get them?"

"One of them," Will replied, the smile on his face fading quickly. "The other one got away."

"Only one?" Horace said before he could stop himself. He wasn't used to partial success from the Rangers. Then he noticed their expressions and realized that his exclamation might have been a little tactless.

"I mean," he amended hastily, "that's excellent. Well done." He paused awkwardly, waiting for a sarcastic reply. He was faintly surprised when none came.

The truth was, of course, that both Halt and Will agreed with the sentiment he'd expressed. Both of them wished they had managed a more complete result. And although neither would voice the thought aloud, they both felt they had left the job half done.

Horace regarded them for a second or two, puzzled at their non-reaction, and then gestured for them to come into the campsite, where he had a small fire burning and the ever-present coffeepot sitting ready by its side.

"Sit down," he told them. "I'll make coffee and you can tell me what happened."

They briefly recounted the events among the drowned trees. Neither of them mentioned the moments of dry-mouthed fear as they faced up to an invisible enemy, knowing that the first sign they might have of him was the sudden flash of a crossbow bolt coming

at them. Similarly, Will omitted the desperate moments he had spent
freeing himself from the stay-with-me vine's thorns. A few more seconds' delay there, he realized, and he might not have arrived in time
to save Halt from that first crossbow bolt. He pushed the thought
aside. That was the sort of detail that didn't need pondering.

"So what do we do now?" Horace asked as they sat cross-legged
around the small fire, sipping their coffee. "Do you think the survivor
will be likely to set up another ambush?"

Will and Horace both looked at Halt as he considered the
question.

"I doubt it," he said at length. "The Genovesans are mercenaries.
They fight for money, not for any cause or out of any sense of com-
mitment. And our friend knows that now the odds are stacked
against him. If he waits for us again, he might get one of us. But the
chances are that the other one will get him. That's not good business.
It might suit Tennyson's purpose, but I doubt he'll be able to convince our purple friend that he should give his life for the Outsiders'
cause."

He glanced toward the west. Already the sun had dipped well
below the tops of the dead trees. Nightfall would be upon them
soon.

"We'll camp here for the night," he declared.

"And tomorrow?" Will asked him.

Halt turned and reached behind him for his saddlebag. He
winced in discomfort as he stretched his left arm toward them. The
wound had dried and stiffened, and the movement set the blood
welling again inside the bandage. Horace rose quickly to his feet and
fetched the saddlebag for him.

"Thanks, Horace," he said. He took his map from the saddlebag
and spread it out before him.

"Pity that map doesn't indicate the dead forest," Will said. Halt nodded agreement.

"It will after this," he said. "It's actually shown here as Ethelsten Forest. Doesn't mention that it's all dead trees. But it does show something that is important to us."

Will edged around to see the map more clearly, and Horace knelt on one knee behind Halt, gazing over his shoulder.

"I don't *think* our friend will lie in wait for us again, but I could be wrong. And *I was wrong* have been the last words of too many careless travelers. So I'm not about to blindly follow him through that forest again. We'll go in farther along—say, down here about a kilometer or so to the west of where we are now—and make our way through from there."

"How will we pick up their tracks again?" Will asked. "They could have gone in any direction once they were through the forest."

"Could have," Halt said. "But any direction they go, they're hemmed in by the river that caused all this trouble." He indicated the gray trunks, now ghostly in the evening shadows. "No matter where they're heading, they'll have to cross it. And there's only one ford within fifteen kilometers. That's where they'll have headed."

"True," said Horace with a grin. "Somehow I can't see Tennyson being too keen to swim across a deep river and get himself all soaking wet."

"He is a man who enjoys his comforts, isn't he?" Halt agreed dryly. "But that's another reason for us to move west a little before we head into the forest again. Aside from avoiding any further traps set by that purple assassin, it'll bring us out close by the ford."

"Where we should pick up their tracks again," Will said with a sense of satisfaction.

"With any luck," Halt agreed. He rolled up the map and replaced it in his saddlebag. "And I think it's time a little luck went our way for a change. The other side seems to be getting the lion's share."

"Except for the one who's still in the forest," Will said.

Halt nodded. "Yes. Except for him. I suppose I'm being ungrateful. We've had our share of good luck today."

Which was ironic, in light of what was to happen the following morning.

24

THE DAY STARTED NORMALLY ENOUGH. THE THREE TRAVELERS rose early. It was going to be a long day in the saddle, so they ate a substantial breakfast, then broke camp and rode west through the grassland along the forest's fringe. After several kilometers, Halt spotted a narrow path between the trees, swung Abelard's head south and led the way into the forest.

Will and Halt were familiar with the sepulchral feeling of the gray, lifeless shapes massed around them. Horace, on the other hand, was a little overawed by his surroundings. His eyes darted continuously from side to side, trying to pierce the blur of dead trunks.

"How did you manage to see anyone in this mess?" he asked. The two Rangers grinned at him.

"It wasn't easy," Will said. The monotone coloring of the trees tended to destroy any sense of perspective, as he had noted the day before.

"Gilan did well to get the first one," Halt said absently.

Will looked at him with a slight frown. "Gilan?"

Halt looked at him curiously. "What about him?" he asked, his face blank.

"You said, 'Gilan did well to get the first one,'" Horace explained. Now it was Halt's turn to frown.

"No, I didn't," he said. Then he added, "Did I?"

The expressions on the faces of his two companions told him that he had said Gilan. He shook his head and gave a short laugh.

"I meant Will," he said. "Sorry, Will. You know I'm always confusing the two of you."

"No matter," said Will. But as they rode on, he felt a worm of worry in his mind. He had never before known Halt to confuse him with Gilan. He glanced quickly at Horace, but the tall warrior seemed satisfied with the explanation, so he let it pass.

There was little opportunity to discuss it as they traversed the forest. Halt spread them out in single file at five-meter intervals, just in case the surviving Genovesan had decided to set another trap and had discovered the path they were taking. This time, feeling sympathy for Horace, Will acted as the rear guard, regularly checking the trail behind them for any sign of pursuit.

All three of them heaved silent sighs of relief when they finally emerged from the drowned forest. Ahead of them lay grasslands, and once they topped the low ridge on the far side of the forest, the tree-covered banks of the river wound before them.

"I'm glad to be out of those trees," Horace said.

Halt smiled at him. "Yes. I couldn't help thinking the Genovesans might have something cooked up for us."

Again, Will frowned. "*Genovesans?* How many do you think there are?"

Halt looked at him, momentarily confused.

"Two," he said. Then he shook his head. "No. One, of course. You got one of them, didn't you?"

"We both got him," Will reminded him. Halt looked blank for a moment and then nodded, as if remembering.

"Of course." He paused, frowned again and asked, "Did I say two?"

"Yes," Will said. Halt gave a short bark of laughter and shook his head, as if to clear it.

"Must be getting absentminded," he said cheerfully.

Will was beginning to sense that something was very wrong. Halt wasn't usually so affable. And he definitely wasn't absentminded. He spoke tentatively now, not wanting to offend his teacher.

"Halt? Are you sure you're all right?"

"Of course I am," Halt said with a trace of his usual asperity. "Now let's find that ford, shall we?"

He touched his heels to Abelard and surged ahead of them, cutting off further conversation on the matter. As he rode, Will noticed that he was rubbing his injured left arm.

"Is your arm all right?" he called.

Halt immediately stopped rubbing it. "It's fine," he replied shortly. Behind him, riding side by side, Will and Horace exchanged slightly puzzled looks. Then Horace shrugged. It wasn't the first time that Halt's behavior or demeanor had ever puzzled him. He was used to the older Ranger's unpredictable moods. Will was less inclined to dismiss the matter, but he hesitated to say anything to Horace about his growing concern—partly because he wasn't completely sure what he was concerned about.

They came to the ford, a place where the river widened, so that the fast-flowing water slowed somewhat, and shallowed as it spread out to fill the wider space between the banks. Halt rode forward until Abelard was fetlock-deep in the water. He leaned out to the side, staring down into the clear water below him and ahead of him.

"Clean sandy bottom by the look of it," he said. "Seems to stay shallow enough." He urged Abelard forward, walking him out to the center of the river. The water rose slowly past the little horse's knees as he moved forward, then stayed at a constant depth.

"Come ahead," he called to Will and Horace, and they splashed through the water after him. As they came level with him, they slowed and he proceeded, checking the bottom carefully as he went. They let him go a few paces, then followed, maintaining their distance behind him in case of an unexpected deep hole in the riverbed. But there was none and the water level began to fall again as they passed the midpoint. A few minutes later, they splashed up onto the far bank.

"Well, well. What do we see here?" Halt asked. He was pointing to the riverbank where it sloped gently up from the water. The ground was muddy and had been heavily traveled only recently. There were multiple tracks leading away from the bank.

Will dismounted and knelt to study the tracks. He found several familiar signs among them, noting that the bulk of their quarry was still on foot.

"It's them all right," he said, looking up at Halt. The gray-bearded Ranger nodded and swept his gaze around the horizon before them.

"Still heading south?" he said.

"Still heading south."

Halt pondered the information for a few seconds and then scratched his bearded chin. "Maybe we should camp here for the night."

Will looked sharply at him, not sure if he'd heard him correctly.

"Camp?" he said, his voice rising in pitch. "Halt, it's barely noon! We've hours of daylight left!"

The Ranger seemed to absorb this information. Then he nodded assent.

"Right. We'll push on then. Lead the way."

Halt seemed remote, Will thought as he swung up into Tug's saddle. He nodded from time to time, as if he were going over information in his mind. And as he nodded, he muttered to himself, but in a low tone so that Will couldn't make out the words. The small thread of worry Will had felt earlier in the day was now a broad ribbon of concern. There was definitely something wrong with his old mentor. In all the years they had been together, Will had never seen him so . . . he searched for the right word and found it eventually . . . *disconnected* from the world around him.

They emerged from the band of trees that lined the banks of the river. Now they were traveling in more open country—grassland interspersed with clumps of trees and low-lying bushes.

They had left the coarse heather and gorse of the border country behind them, and the land was more lush and gentle. In the distance, Will could see a dim line that marked a range of hills. He estimated that they were at least a day's travel away, possibly more. The clear air made distances deceptive.

"Looks like they're heading for those hills," he said.

"That'd make sense," Halt replied. "The map says there are caves all through them. And the Outsiders just love to hide away in dark places. I think we'll go into combat formation," he added.

Will glanced at him, but the suggestion made sense. The countryside here was open and the going was easy. There was no reason to bunch up together on the trail. Combat formation meant they would ride on a wide front, with some thirty meters between them. That made them a more difficult target and allowed each of them to provide cover and support for his companions if necessary.

Will edged Tug out to the left while Horace went right. Halt stayed in the center and they rode quietly, in a long extended line, for about an hour. Then Halt whistled and placed his clenched fist on top of his head, the field signal for "join me."

Mystified, because he had seen nothing to indicate a reason to move closer again, Will trotted Tug through the long grass to where Halt sat waiting on Abelard. Horace joined them a few moments later and Will waited until he was with them before he queried Halt.

"What is it?"

Halt looked a little puzzled. "What's what?"

Alarm bells began to jangle even louder than before in Will's brain at the reply. He spoke carefully and patiently.

"Halt, you put us into combat formation an hour or so ago. Now you're calling us in. What happened to make you change your mind?"

"Oh, that!" A look of comprehension dawned on Halt's face as he realized the reason for Will's question. "I just thought we might ride together for a while. I was feeling . . . lonely, I suppose."

"Lonely?" It was Horace who said it, his voice shrill with disbelief. "Halt, what are you . . . ?"

Will made a quick hand gesture to Horace and the young warrior left the question unfinished.

Will nudged Tug closer to Abelard and leaned toward Halt, peering closely at his face and eyes. He seemed a little pale, he thought. He couldn't see the eyes clearly. The shadow of the cowl of Halt's cloak hid them.

Abelard moved nervously, taking little steps in place. He uttered a deep rumble in his chest. It wasn't because of the proximity of Will and Tug, the young Ranger knew. Abelard was completely at home with both of them. He realized that the horse sensed something was wrong with Halt as well and was unsettled by the fact.

"Halt, look at me, please. Let me see your eyes," he said.

Halt glared at him and urged Abelard a few paces away.

"My eyes? There's nothing wrong with my eyes! And don't crowd in on me like that! You're bothering Abelard!" Unconsciously, he rubbed his injured forearm.

"How's the arm?" Will asked, keeping his voice calm and unconcerned.

"It's fine!" Halt flared angrily at him, and again Abelard shifted his feet nervously.

"It's just that you were rubbing it," Will said in a placating tone. But Halt's temper was fully aroused by now.

"Yes. I was. Because it hurts. Let yourself get shot by a crossbow one of these days and you'll know about that! Now are we going to dillydally here all day talking about my eyes and my arm and worrying my horse? Be still, Abelard!" he snapped.

Will's jaw dropped. He had never, ever, in the time he had spent with Halt, heard the Ranger raise his voice to Abelard. Rangers just didn't do that with their horses.

"Halt," he began, but Halt interrupted him.

"Because while we waste time here, Farrell and his henchmen are getting farther and farther away!"

"Farrell?" This time it was Horace's turn to be totally concerned. "Halt, we're after Tennyson, not Farrell. Farrell was the Outsider leader at Selsey village!"

He was right. Farrell had led a band of Outsiders in an attempted raid on a small isolated fishing village on the west coast of Araluen. It was this event that first alerted Halt to the Outsiders' wider plans in Hibernia. Halt glared now at Horace.

"I know that!" he snapped. "Do you think I don't know that? Do you think I'm mad?"

There was a pause. Neither Will nor Horace knew what to say next. Halt swung his furious glare from one to the other, challenging them.

"Well? Do you?" he repeated. Then, when neither of them said anything, he shook Abelard's reins roughly and set him to a slow canter.

Heading west.

"Will, what's happening?" Horace asked as Halt rode off in the wrong direction.

"I don't know. But it's all bad, I can tell you that," Will replied. He urged Tug after Abelard, calling after his mentor.

"Halt! Come back!"

Horace followed uncertainly. The bearded Ranger didn't bother to turn in the saddle to reply to Will. But they heard him calling.

"Come on, if you're coming! We're wasting time and those Temujai can't be far behind us now!"

"Temujai?" Horace said to Will. "The Temujai are thousands of kilometers away!"

Will shook his head sadly, urging Tug to increase his pace.

"Not in his mind," he said grimly. He understood now. Something had caused Halt to lose all sense of the situation and time. He was seeing enemies and events from the past. From a few months back and from years before that, all hopelessly jumbled in his mind.

"Halt! Wait for me!" he called.

Then, suddenly, he set Tug to a full gallop as his mentor threw up his arms, let out a strangled cry and fell crashing to the ground beside a thoroughly alarmed Abelard.

And lay there, unmoving.

25

"HALT!"

The anguished cry was torn from Will as he urged Tug to an even greater speed. Reaching the still figure lying in the long grass, he threw himself from the saddle and knelt beside him. Abelard stepped nervously beside his master, his head down, trying to nudge Halt with his muzzle, looking for some sign of life. The little horse nickered constantly, but there was a whine of anxiety in the sound—a note that Will had never heard before.

"Still, Abelard," he said quietly. He gestured with the back of his hand to wave the horse away. "Get back, boy."

The horse wasn't doing Halt any good, and his stepping and nudging could only get in the way. Reluctantly, Abelard paced back a few steps. Although he would normally respond only to Halt, he was intelligent enough to recognize that his master was incapacitated and that Will was next in the chain of command. Reassured by the calm tone of Will's voice, he stopped making the small, distracted noises and stood still. His ears were pricked upright, however, and his eyes never strayed from Halt.

Halt was lying facedown, and Will gently rolled him over. He moved the cowl back from Halt's face. His eyes were shut and his face was deathly pale. He didn't seem to be breathing, and for a moment Will felt a surge of horror rush through him.

Halt dead? It couldn't be! It was impossible. He could not imagine a world without Halt in it.

Then the still figure gave a shuddering sigh and began to breathe again, and Will felt relief flood through his system. Horace arrived, swinging down from the saddle and dropping to his knees on the other side of the fallen Ranger. The concern was obvious on his face.

"He's not . . ." He hesitated.

Will shook his head. "He's alive. But he's unconscious."

Halt gave vent to another shuddering breath that seemed to shake his entire body. Then his breathing settled a little. But he was breathing raggedly, and taking only shallow breaths. That was why, Will realized, he was being racked by those great shuddering sobs every so often. He needed the extra oxygen in his lungs.

Quickly, he stood and removed his cloak, folding it to form a makeshift cushion.

"Lift his head," he told Horace. The tall warrior gently raised Halt's head clear of the grass and Will slid the folded cloak under it. Horace studied the still form of the Ranger, his sense of helplessness showing on his young face.

"Will," he said, "what do we do? What's happened to him?"

Will shook his head, leaned forward and gently raised one of Halt's eyelids with his thumb. There was no reaction from the unconscious Ranger. But as Will studied his eye, he noticed that the pupil remained dilated, even though the day was relatively bright. He knew that it was an automatic reaction for the pupil to close down when exposed to sudden bright light. Apparently, Halt's system wasn't reacting normally to stimuli.

"What is it?" Horace asked. He hoped that the fact that Will had done something, anything, was an indication that he had some idea of what the problem might be.

"I don't know," he muttered.

He allowed the eye to close again. He put one finger on Halt's throat, feeling for the pulse in the large artery there. It was fluttery and uneven, but at least it was there. He sat back on his haunches, pondering the situation. All Rangers were trained to administer basic medical treatment in the event of a colleague being wounded. But this was beyond bandaging and stitching. This wasn't a wound he could isolate and . . .

A wound! The moment he had the thought, he was reminded of Halt's constant rubbing and scratching at the minor wound to his forearm. He gripped the sleeve of Halt's jacket, along the line that he had stitched up only the night before, and ripped the stitching apart, letting the sleeve fall back away from his arm.

The bandage was still in place. A slight stain showed on it where blood had seeped through the material before the bleeding stopped. He leaned forward and sniffed lightly at the wound, and then recoiled hurriedly with an exclamation of disgust.

"What is it?" Horace asked quickly.

"His arm. It smells foul. I think that might be where the trouble lies." Mentally, he berated himself. He should have thought of that sooner. Then he dismissed his moment of self-criticism. The wound had seemed like a minor one. There had been no reason to suspect any connection between it and Halt's current behavior. He drew his throwing knife and slid the razor-sharp edge under the end of the bandage. Abelard rumbled a warning.

"It's all right, Abelard," he said without lifting his eyes from his task. "Settle, boy. Settle."

Tug moved to stand close to his companion, brushing against Abelard and offering comfort and support. He nickered gently, as if to reassure Abelard that Will had the situation well in hand. Will wished that he felt the same confidence.

He slit the bandage and lifted it away from Halt's arm. The cut ends opened easily, but where the bandage lay over the wound, it seemed to have stuck. That puzzled him a little. He didn't think there would have been enough blood from the wound to have dried and stuck the bandage in place like this. He was loath to simply rip the bandage away. He didn't know how much extra damage that might do.

He put a hand out to Horace.

"Get me a canteen," he said, and the tall youth hurried to fetch the canteen that was tied to the saddlebow on Kicker. Abelard was closer, but in his current state of nervousness, Horace wasn't sure how he would react if he was approached. He handed the canteen to Will, who began to pour water carefully over the bandage, letting it soak through and loosen whatever it was that was causing it to stick to the wound.

After a minute or so, he tugged gently at the edge and felt it give a little. Halt stirred, moaning quietly. Abelard whinnied.

"Easy," Will said gently. "Easy there." He wasn't sure whether his words were addressed to Halt or Abelard. He decided he was talking to both. Horace knelt again, eyes wide and fascinated as he watched his friend gradually work the bandage loose from the crusted, dried matter that surrounded the wound.

It took several minutes' soaking and gently easing the cloth away, but eventually it fell clear and they could see what they were faced with.

"Oh my god," said Horace quietly. The horror in his voice was obvious. Will made an inarticulate sound in his throat and, for a moment, turned his eyes away from the terrible sight of Halt's arm.

The graze itself, which he might have expected to have dried and scabbed over by now, was still weeping. The flesh around it was coated with a discolored mass of oozing, vile fluid. The rotting smell that Will had noticed earlier was now all too evident. Both young men instinctively recoiled from it. But perhaps worst of all was the flesh on the rest of the arm. It was swollen to almost twice its normal size. No wonder Halt had been rubbing and scratching at it for the past day, Will thought. And the entire forearm was discolored. A sickly yellow around the wound gradually gave way to a dark blue tone, shot with bands of livid red. He touched Halt's arm gently with one forefinger. The skin was hot to the touch.

"How did this happen? You cleaned and dressed the wound almost immediately!" Horace said in a shocked, low voice. Both he and Will had seen their share of battles and wounds in the past few years. Neither of them had ever seen anything like this. Neither of them had seen such a level of infection, which this surely was, develop in a clean wound in such a short time.

Will's face was grim as he studied it. Halt stirred fretfully, groaning and trying to reach with his other hand for the dreadful discolored arm. Will stopped him gently, forcing Halt's free hand back down by his side.

"There must have been something on the crossbow bolt," he said finally, and Horace looked at him, not comprehending.

"Something?"

"Poison," Will said briefly. The sense of hopelessness and uncertainty began to well up in his chest again. He had no idea what to do here, no idea how to treat this terrible injury. No idea how to counteract the poison—for that was almost certainly what it was.

Then he felt the hopelessness being submerged by a sense of panic. Halt could lose his arm. Worse, he could die here, miles from anywhere. And all because Will, his trusted protégé, the famous Will Treaty, renowned throughout the Kingdom of Araluen for his fast thinking and decisive action, didn't have the first inkling of what to do. He reached out uncertainly to touch that damaged arm and realized his hand was shaking. Shaking in fear and panic and from a sense of utter uselessness.

He had to do something. Try something. But what? Again he faced the inevitable answer. He didn't know what to do. Halt could be dying and he didn't know how to help him.

"Do you have any idea what it is? The poison, I mean?" Horace asked. His horrified gaze was fixed on Halt's arm. Horace was a warrior who faced his enemies in fair combat. The very idea of poison was anathema to him.

"No! I don't have the faintest idea what it is!" Will shouted at him. "What do I know about poisons? I'm a Ranger, not a healer!" The panic was threatening to take charge of him now and his eyes were blurring with tears. He started to reach out for Halt again, paused uncertainly, then drew back his hand. What was the point of touching him? Of poking and prying at him? He needed care and expert treatment.

Perhaps stirred by the sound of Will's voice, Halt tossed slightly and muttered something incomprehensible.

"Maybe we could clean the wound?" Horace suggested. It seemed logical that Halt might feel better if that oozing liquid was cleared away. And clean water might soothe the swollen, feverish, discolored flesh as well.

With a giant effort, Will gained control of himself. Horace, as he so often did, had cut through to the heart of the matter. When all else fails, fall back on basic principles. Basic treatment for a wound was to clean it. To wipe away as much corruption and poison as possible. That much he could do for Halt, he thought. And now that he had a clear course of action, he felt the clutching, debilitating panic receding. He held out his hand and looked at it. The shaking had stopped.

"Thanks, Horace. Good thinking." He looked up at his big friend and gave him a sad smile. "Would you mind getting a fire going? I'll need some boiling water to sterilize the bandages and clean his arm up."

Horace nodded and rose to his feet. "I might as well set up the campsite," he said. "I guess we'll be staying here for a while."

"I guess so," Will said. As Horace moved away and began to gather stones for a fireplace, Will became conscious of another pair of eyes watching him. He looked up and there was Abelard, his head moving slightly from side to side. He uttered a subdued whinny as Will looked at him.

"Don't fret," Will told him. "He'll be all right."

He tried to put as much conviction as he could into the words. He wished he could believe them himself.

Once the fire was lit and water boiled, Will set about the task of cleaning Halt's wound. He soaked pads of linen in the boiling water, then, after letting them cool a little, used them to wipe away the pus and crusted matter around the edge of the wound. As he worked, swabbing as gently as he could, he was rewarded by the sight of clean blood again seeping from the lacerated flesh. He thought that might be a good thing. He remembered hearing somewhere that fresh blood tended to clean out a wound. At least there was no new pus or discoloration forming.

He dabbed it gently with clean linen until the faint flow of blood stopped. Then he applied some of the painkilling salve that all Rangers carried in their wound kits. It was highly effective, he knew, but he was always a little uncomfortable using it. It was derived from the drug warmweed, and the faintly pungent aroma it gave off brought back unpleasant memories for him.

At least, now that the wound was clean, the smell of corruption they had noticed before seemed to have abated. That too might be a good sign, he thought.

He decided not to rebandage the arm. Keeping it bandaged may have contained the poison and magnified its effects. Instead, he soaked a pad of linen in boiling water, then, allowing it to cool a little, draped it in place. If need be, he would secure it with a loose bandage.

He had soaked more cloth in cool water, and now he placed this over the swollen flesh farther up the arm that had been so hot to his touch earlier. He thought that the swelling seemed to have gone down a little. He arranged the cooling cloths on Halt's arm and shrugged.

"That's all I can do for the present, I'm afraid," he said.

"You seem to have done a lot," Halt replied. His voice was weak, but his eyes were open and there was a little color back in his cheeks. Whether it was the effect of the cleaning, the warmweed salve or just coincidence, he had regained consciousness.

This time Will couldn't stop the tears as they flooded out of his eyes and ran freely down his cheeks.

Halt was alive. And he seemed to be improving.

26

WHEN HORACE HAD THE CAMPSITE SET UP, THEY SPREAD OUT Halt's bedroll and lifted him gently onto it.

At first, he protested, waving them away and attempting to rise to his feet. But his strength failed him before he had even managed to sit up, and Will saw a quick flash of fear in his eyes as he sank back again.

"Maybe you'd better carry me," he said, and they did so. Horace arranged one of their tents as a lean-to shelter to shield Halt from the sun. Will looked around, studying the sky and the weather.

"Looks like it'll stay fine tonight," he said. "We'll keep him in the open. Fresh air might be good for him."

He was guessing, he knew. But he was convinced that the interior of a stuffy little one-man tent would not be the place for Halt over the next few hours. He was conscious that the slight smell of corruption was still present around the wound, even though it was nowhere near as strong as before. It might well become suffocating if Halt were confined inside a tent.

Almost as soon as they moved Halt, he lost consciousness again. He muttered and tossed in his sleep. But at least now his breathing seemed more regular. Will sat hunched beside him, watching like a hawk.

At one stage, Horace laid a hand on his shoulder. "I'll watch him for a while. You need to rest."

But Will shook his head. "I'm fine. I'll watch him."

Horace nodded. He understood how his friend felt. "Let me know if you need a break." Will grunted in reply, so Horace busied himself making a thin broth from their provisions. He thought they could feed it to Halt when he woke again. Broth was good for injured men. He kept it simmering in the edge of the fire and made a simple meal for Will and himself, using flat bread and some cold beef and pickles that they had been carrying. He took a plate to Will, who was still sitting, staring at his teacher. The young Ranger took the plate and glanced up.

"Thanks, Horace," he said briefly. Then his eyes went back to Halt and he began eating the food mechanically.

Around sunset, Halt's eyes opened again. For a moment or two, he looked around, puzzled, as he tried to remember what had happened, why he was lying here with Will huddled in his cloak beside him and dozing. Then it came back to him. He glanced down at the loosely bandaged arm. He could see the swollen, discolored flesh and feel the throbbing heat that shot through it. A cold hand clutched his heart as he realized what had happened to him.

He made a small sound in his throat, and Will's head shot up as he instantly came awake.

"Halt!" he said, relief evident in his voice. The older Ranger made a small gesture with his right hand. A short distance away, Abelard's ears pricked up and he whinnied briefly, moving closer to the recumbent figure. The small horse hadn't moved more than a few meters from his master's side in the past three hours.

Halt grinned weakly up at him.

"Hello, old friend," he said. "Been worried about me, have you?"

Abelard moved forward and leaned his head down to nuzzle Halt's cheek. Halt said a few words to him, speaking in Gallic, as he often did when he was talking privately to Abelard. Watching the simple interaction between them that said so much about the bond they shared, Will's eyes filled with tears once more. But this time, they were tears of relief.

Finally, Halt gestured with his uninjured arm, gently shooing Abelard away.

"Off you go, boy. Will and I need to talk a little."

The horse backed away a few paces. But his ears were still up and he was still alert to any move or noise that Halt might make. Will edged closer and seized Halt's uninjured hand. The return grip was surprisingly weak and he felt a thrill of alarm. Then he dismissed it. Halt had been close to death. He would take some time to recover.

"You're all right now," he said.

Halt glanced around, trying to see more of the campsite. "Is Horace here?"

Will shook his head. "He's out setting snares. There's a pond nearby where he thinks ducks might settle at dusk, so he's gone to try his luck. We're getting short on fresh food." He dismissed the unimportant matter of Horace and their provisions with a quick gesture. "My god, Halt, it's good to see you awake again! We thought we'd lost you for a while. But now you're on the mend."

He caught the quick flash of apprehension in Halt's eyes, instantly masked, and suddenly a horrible doubt struck him.

"Halt? You are all right, aren't you? Of course you are! You're awake and talking. Maybe a little weak but you'll get your strength back, and before you know it we'll be . . ."

He stopped, aware that he was babbling, aware that he was talking to convince himself, not the bearded Ranger who lay before him. There was a long silence between them.

"Tell me."

Halt hesitated, then glanced down at his injured arm. He drew a deep breath before he spoke.

"You understand that the bolt was poisoned, don't you?"

Will nodded disconsolately. "I guessed as much. I should have thought of it earlier."

Halt shook his head gently. "But I should have considered it. Those blasted Genovesans know all about poisons. I should have realized that it wouldn't be beyond them to dip their crossbow bolts in it."

He paused. "I vaguely remember going a little crazy. Did I think the Temujai were after us?"

Will nodded. "That's when we really got worried. Then you galloped off in the wrong direction and fell off your horse. You were unconscious when I reached you. I thought you were dead at first."

"I wasn't breathing?" Halt asked.

"No. Then you gave a sort of huge sigh and started breathing again. That's when we thought to look at your arm. It occurred to me only then that it had been bothering you all day."

He briefly described the condition the arm had been in and, at Halt's urging, what actions he had taken. His teacher nodded thoughtfully as he described how he had cleaned the wound again and applied the warmweed-derived salve to it.

"Yes," he said, "that might have slowed it down a little. Warmweed tends to have a few other properties besides reducing pain. I've heard that some people have used it for treating snakebites—which is a pretty similar thing to this when you think about it."

"And it worked?" Will asked. He didn't like the way Halt paused before he answered.

"Up to a point. It slowed the effect of the venom. But the victim still needed treatment. The trouble is, with this sort of poison, I don't know what the correct treatment might be."

"But Halt, you're improving! You're so much better than you were this afternoon! I can see you're recovering . . ."

He stopped as Halt laid a hand on his arm. "That's often the way with these poisons. The victim seems to recover, then he has a relapse. And each time, after each bout of consciousness, he's a little worse than before. And gradually . . ." He stopped and made an uncertain gesture in the air.

Will felt he was staring into a deep, black hole before him. The realization of what Halt was saying constricted his throat so that he could barely talk.

"Halt?" he choked. "Are you saying you're . . . ?"

He couldn't finish the sentence. Halt said it for him.

"Dying? I'm afraid it's a distinct possibility, Will. I'll have bouts of consciousness like this. Then I'll pass out again. Each time, I'll take a little longer to recover and I'll be weaker than the time before."

"But Halt!" The tears gushed from Will's eyes, blinding him. "You can't die! You mustn't! How could I manage without . . ." Suddenly he was beyond speech and his body was racked with great sobs. The tears coursed down his face unheeded. He hunched forward on his knees, rocking back and forth and making a terrible keening sound in the back of his throat.

"Will?" Halt's voice was weak, and it didn't penetrate Will's grief. The older Ranger took several deep breaths and gathered his strength.

"Will!"

This time the familiar bark of authority was there and it cut through to Will's consciousness. He stopped rocking and looked up, wiping his eyes and streaming nose with the hem of his cloak. Halt smiled at him, a tired, crooked little smile.

"I promise I'm trying my best *not* to die. But you have to be prepared for it. The next twelve hours or so will be the critical period, I'd say. If I feel stronger tomorrow morning, who knows? I might have beaten it. Dealing with poison isn't an exact science. Some people are affected worse than others. But I'll need all my strength to fight it and I'll need you to be strong for me."

Red-eyed and ashamed of himself, Will nodded. His back straightened. Weeping and wailing would do nothing to help Halt.

"I'm sorry," he said. "I won't let that happen again. Is there anything I can do for you?"

Halt looked down at his injured arm. "Maybe change that dressing in another hour or so. And use a little more salve. How long since you put it on?"

Will considered the question. He knew that the salve couldn't be used too often. "Four, maybe five hours."

Halt nodded. "Fine. Give it an hour, then put some more on. Not sure if it'll help, but it can't hurt. Maybe a little water now if you've got some?"

"Of course," Will said. He unstoppered his canteen and propped Halt up so that he could drink slowly. The bearded Ranger was experienced enough to know that he shouldn't gulp the water greedily.

He sighed as the water trickled through his parched mouth and throat.

"Oh, that's so good," he said. "People always underestimate water."

Will glanced quickly at the campfire, where the coffeepot sat in the embers to one side.

"I can get you some coffee if you like. Or soup?" he suggested. But

Halt shook his head, lying back against the saddle, padded with his own folded cloak that was serving as his pillow.

"No. No. Water's fine. Maybe some soup later." His voice was sounding tired, as if the effort of their conversation had exhausted him. His eyes slid shut and he said something. But he spoke so softly that Will had to lean forward and ask him to repeat himself.

"Where's Horace?" he asked, his eyes still shut.

"He's setting the snares. I told . . ."

He was going to say "I told you that," but he realized that Halt's mind had begun to wander again, just as he had forecast.

"Yes. Yes. Of course. You told me. He's a good boy. So's Will, of course. Both good boys."

Will said nothing. He simply gripped Halt's free hand a little tighter, not trusting his voice if he were to try to speak.

"Can't let him face Deparnieux, of course. Thinks everybody fights by the rules, young Horace does . . ."

Again, Will squeezed Halt's hand, just to let him know that he wasn't alone. He hoped the contact would register with Halt's wandering mind. Deparnieux had been the evil Gallic warlord who held Halt and Horace captive years ago, when they were searching for Will and Evanlyn.

The poison had taken his mind again and he was no longer living in the present. His words died away to a mutter and he drifted into sleep. Will sat and watched over him. The breathing was deep and even. Perhaps he would recover. Perhaps a good night's rest was all he needed. Will would re-dress the wound in an hour. The warmweed salve would work its magic. In the morning, Halt would be on the road to recovery.

Horace, returning shortly after dark with a brace of ducks, found Will crouched beside his teacher. He took in the tear-stained face and the red eyes and gently led him away to the fire. He gave him coffee and flat bread and made him drink some of the beef broth he had prepared for Halt.

When Will had recovered his composure a little, he told Horace all that Halt had said about the poison and the possible outcome they faced. Horace, determined to keep a positive frame of mind, assessed Halt's condition while Will cleaned and re-dressed the wound.

"But he said he *could* get better?" he insisted.

"That's right," Will said, replacing the linen bandage over the wound. There seemed to be no improvement. But it hadn't deteriorated any further either. "He said the next twelve hours would be critical."

"He's sleeping peacefully now," Horace noted. "None of that tossing and turning. I think he's getting better. I definitely think he's getting better."

Will, his jaw set in a determined line, nodded several times. Then he replied forcefully, "You're right. All he needs is a good night's rest. In the morning, he'll be fine."

They took turns watching over the stricken Ranger through the night. He slept peacefully, without any sign of distress. Around three in the morning, he woke briefly and talked calmly and lucidly with Horace, who was on watch. Then he fell asleep again and it seemed that he was winning the battle against the poison.

In the morning, they couldn't wake him.

27

"HALT! HALT! WAKE UP!" HORACE'S SHOUT ROUSED WILL FROM a deep sleep. For a second, he was confused, wondering what was happening and where he was. Then he remembered the events of the previous day and threw back his blankets, coming quickly to his feet.

Horace was crouched over Halt, who lay on his back as they had placed him. As Will reached his side, Horace looked up at him, fear in his eyes, then turned back to shout again.

"Halt! Wake up!"

Abelard, who had remained close by his master during the night, sensed the air of concern and neighed nervously, pawing the ground. Halt tossed restlessly on the thin bedroll, trying to throw off the blanket that covered him. His eyes remained shut, but he was muttering to himself. As they watched, he cried out, as if in pain.

Horace spread his hands in a helpless gesture.

"He seemed fine," he said, his voice breaking with emotion. "I was talking to him a few hours ago and he seemed fine. Then he went back to sleep. Just a few minutes ago, he started tossing and fretting like this and I tried to wake him, but . . . he won't wake up."

Will leaned forward, closer to the bearded Ranger, and put his hand on his shoulder.

"Halt?" he said tentatively. He shook him gently, trying to rouse him. Halt reacted to the touch, but not the way Will hoped he would. He jerked and shouted something inarticulate and tried to throw Will's hand away from his shoulder with his uninjured hand. He remained unconscious, however.

Will tried again, shaking him a little harder this time.

"Halt! Wake up! Please!" Again, Halt reacted against the touch of Will's hand.

"Do you think you should be shaking him like that?" Horace asked anxiously.

"I don't know!" Will's angry reply was evidence of the helplessness he was feeling. "Can you think of something better to do?"

Horace said nothing. But it was obvious to Will that shaking Halt wasn't achieving anything—it was only distressing him more. He relinquished his grip on the older Ranger's shoulder. Instead, he laid his palm gently on his forehead. The skin was hot beneath his touch and felt strangely dry.

"He's feverish," he said. All their hopes that Halt would improve after a night's rest were suddenly dashed. He had deteriorated badly in the last few hours.

Still keeping his touch as gentle as he could, Will removed the linen bandage covering Halt's forearm. He bent closer, sniffing at the wound. The smell of corruption was faintly noticeable, but it seemed no worse. The discoloration was still evident as well. But, like the odor, it hadn't worsened during the night. If anything, the swelling might have come down a little. He touched one fingertip to the swollen skin. Yesterday, it had been hot to his touch. Today, its temperature felt relatively normal.

"Still hot?" Horace asked.

He shook his head, a little puzzled. "No. It feels all right," he said. "But his forehead is burning up. I don't understand."

He sat back to consider the situation. He wished desperately that he knew more about healing.

"Unless," he said slowly, "it means that the poison has moved on from his arm and is in his system now . . . working its way through him." He looked up and met Horace's worried gaze, then shook his head helplessly. "I just don't know, Horace. I just don't know enough about all this."

He busied himself soaking more linen strips in a bowl of cool water and laying them over Halt's forehead, trying to cool him down. He had some dried willow bark in his medical pack, which he knew would reduce the fever. But the problem would be getting Halt to take it. The Ranger was still tossing and groaning, but his jaw was now clenched tight.

Horace stood and went to Halt's saddlebags, which were a few meters away. He unstrapped the lid of one and rummaged inside, finally producing Halt's map of the area. He studied it for a few minutes, then walked back to sink down beside Will, who was busy ministering to Halt.

"What are you looking for?" Will asked him, intent on his task. Horace chewed his lip as he studied the map.

"A town. Even a large village. There must be somewhere near here where we could find an apothecary or a healer of some kind."

He tapped the map with one forefinger. "I figure we're probably somewhere about . . . here," he said. "Give or take a few kilometers. How about this? Maddler's Drift? It couldn't be more than half a day's ride away."

"Are you proposing we take Halt there?" Will asked.

Horace sucked his cheeks in thoughtfully. "Moving Halt might not be a good idea. Might be better to see if there's anyone there who could help. The local healer. Go there and bring him back." He looked up at Will and saw the doubtful expression on his face. "I'll go if you like," he offered.

But Will was slowly shaking his head. "If either of us goes, it should be me," he said. "I can move a lot faster than you can."

"Yes. I know," Horace conceded. "But I thought you might not want to leave him. So I just . . ."

"I know, Horace. And I appreciate it. But think it through. It's only a hamlet. Odds are there's no healer there. And if there is, do you think a country healer will have the faintest idea how to cure this?" He jerked a thumb at Halt, who was groaning, muttering and grinding his teeth.

Horace let out a deep sigh. "It might be worth a try." But his voice confirmed that he didn't believe his own words.

Will laid a hand on his forearm. "Let's face it. Even a good country healer is not much more than an herbalist. And the bad ones are little more than charlatans and witch doctors. I don't want someone chanting and waving colored smoke over Halt while he's dying."

The word was finally out in the open before he could stop himself. Dying. Halt was dying. The hoped-for recovery in what Halt himself had said was a vital twelve-hour period simply hadn't happened.

Horace was stricken as he heard Will say the word. He had spent hours refusing to confront it. Refusing to even consider it.

"Halt can't die. He can't! He's . . ." He paused, not sure what he was going to say, then finished weakly, "He's Halt."

He let the map drop from his fingers and turned away, not wanting Will to see the tears that had sprung to his eyes. Halt was . . . indomitable. He was indestructible. He had always been part of Horace's world, for as long as the young man could remember. Even before he had got to know the grim-faced Ranger and learned that his forbidding appearance masked a warm and quietly humorous nature, he had been conscious of him as an ever-present feature of life at Castle Redmont.

He was a larger-than-life presence, a mysterious figure about whom fantastic tales were told and wild rumors flew. He had survived a score of battles. He had faced warlords and fearsome monsters and triumphed every time. He couldn't die because of a slight scratch on his arm. He couldn't! It just didn't seem possible.

Like Will, Horace had been orphaned when he was young, and in recent years he had grown to look upon Halt as a special person in his life. He knew that Will regarded Halt as a father figure and that Halt returned the feeling. The close personal relationship between master and apprentice was obvious to anyone who knew them.

Horace didn't presume to have the same closeness they enjoyed. Theirs was a unique relationship. But Halt had come to assume a role in Horace's life similar to a much-loved and vastly respected uncle. He turned back, no longer concerned if Will saw the tears on his face. Halt deserved those tears, he thought. They were nothing to be ashamed of.

Will leaned back on his haunches. He couldn't think of anything more he could do for Halt. The cool cloths on his forehead seemed to be easing him a little. The groaning had died away and he could no longer see the muscles at the side of Halt's jaw clenched tight. Perhaps if Halt relaxed further, he might be able to coax him to take a few sips of willow bark infusion to bring down his fever. And he could put more salve on the wound, although he sensed that the wound itself was no longer the problem. It had been the source, but now the poison had moved on.

The breeze caught the map Horace had dropped and it began to flutter away. Absentmindedly, Will caught it and began to fold it. When he looked down, a word seemed to leap off the page.

Macindaw.

Castle Macindaw. Scene of his battle with the Scotti invaders. And close by Macindaw, clearly marked on the map, stood Grimsdell Wood, home to Malcolm, once thought to be the reincarnation of Malkallam the Sorcerer, but now known to a select few as the most skilled and knowledgeable healer in all of Araluen.

"Horace?" he said, staring fixedly at the map.

They were old friends. They had been through a great deal together, and Horace knew Will sufficiently well to sense the change in his friend's voice. The hopelessness had gone. Even with that one word, Horace knew that Will had the germ of an idea. He dropped beside his friend and looked over his shoulder, studying the section of the map that was open before him. He too saw the name.

"Macindaw," he breathed. "Malcolm. Of course!"

"A few days ago, you said we'd pass close by if we took that detour," Will pointed out. "Where do you think we are now?"

Horace took the map and unfolded it to open the next section. He found the reference points he'd used before—the river, the drowned forest.

"Around here," he said, indicating a position on the map. "We've come a good way south of the spot where I said it."

"True. But we've also come a good way east. And Macindaw was to the east of us when you pointed it out. What we've lost by coming south, we've picked up by coming east."

Horace pursed his lips uncertainly. "Not quite," he said. "But we're probably only a day and a half away. Maybe two days."

"I'll do it in one," Will said. Horace raised his eyebrows in disbelief.

"One day? I know Tug can go all day and all night. But even for him, that's stretching it. And you'd still have to make the return journey."

"I won't be riding Tug all the way," Will told him. "I'll take Abelard too. I can switch between them to rest them."

Horace felt a surge of hope. Will could make it to Macindaw in that time if he rode both horses, he realized. Of course, the return journey, with Malcolm, would be slower.

"Then take Kicker as well," he said. He saw Will open his mouth to dismiss the suggestion and hurried on to explain his idea. "Don't ride him on the way to Macindaw. Save his strength for the return journey. That way, you'll always have one horse resting while you and Malcolm ride the other two."

Will nodded slowly. Horace's suggestion made good sense. He would be returning with Malcolm, and that would mean the healer would have to ride Abelard. But with Kicker along as well, they'd always have a relatively fresh horse. And neither he nor the slightly built healer would weigh anything like Horace in full armor.

"Good idea," he said finally. He studied the map again and came to a decision. "I can save time if I cut across country here." He indicated a spot where the trail made a wide detour around an expanse of rising ground.

Horace nodded agreement, then, noticing something marked on the map at that point, leaned forward to read the notation.

"Barrows?" he said. "What are barrows?"

"They're ancient burial mounds," Will said. "You find them from time to time in sparsely populated areas like this. Nobody knows who's buried in them. They're assumed to be some ancient race that died out long ago."

"And why does the path curve around them the way it does?" Horace asked, although he thought he already knew the answer.

Will shrugged, trying to look unconcerned.

"Oh . . . it's just that some folk think they're haunted."

28

HORACE WATCHED AS WILL PREPARED FOR THE JOURNEY TO Macindaw. He stripped the three horses of all extraneous weight, dumping camping gear, provision packs and saddlebags in a neat pile by the campfire.

Abelard and Tug carried spare arrow cases for Halt and Will, and he left these behind. Chances were he wouldn't need to fight and the two dozen arrows in his quiver would be enough in case he ran into unexpected trouble. Kicker was usually loaded with Horace's shield and the heavy mail coat, helmet and chain-mail hood that he wore when going into battle. These he left behind as well. The horses were left relatively unburdened, with just their saddles and bridles.

He'd be riding Tug for the first leg of the trip, so he loosened the girths on Abelard's and Kicker's saddles. They might as well be as comfortable as possible, he thought. Abelard nickered gratitude. Kicker, as was the custom with his breed, accepted the gesture stolidly.

He selected a small rucksack from his kit, emptied out the spare clothes it contained and crammed it with basic traveling rations: a loaf of flat bread, along with dried fruit and several strips of smoked beef. The last-mentioned was hard to chew, but he knew from past experience that it had the nourishment he'd need to restore his strength. Plus it allowed him to eat in the saddle without the need for a stop.

"I'll take all three of our canteens," he said to Horace as he was cramming the rations into the rucksack. "You've got the pond close by and I don't want to have to search for water while I'm traveling." Satisfied that he had enough food, he tied the small sack to Tug's saddlebow, where he could reach it easily as he rode.

Horace nodded agreement and collected the three canteens. He shook them experimentally.

"They could all use some topping up," he said. "And you may as well start out with fresh water." After a few hours, as they both knew only too well, the water would take on the leathery taste of the canteens.

Will smiled his gratitude. "Thanks," he said. "I'll have a bite to eat while you're doing it. Might as well set off with a good meal under my belt."

Once Will had finished eating and making the last of his preparations, he ran through a mental checklist and nodded to himself. He had everything he needed. The horses were fed and watered and ready to travel. What little equipment he was taking was securely fastened to their saddles.

Horace returned with the three canteens. He fastened one each to Kicker's and Abelard's saddles, tying them down securely with restraining thongs so they wouldn't bounce and jolt with the horses' movement. As he turned away from Abelard, the third canteen knocked against the stirrup iron with a hollow sound.

Will frowned, puzzled. "That sounds empty."

Horace smiled and walked to the campfire.

"It is at the moment. The other two are for the horses. This one is for you." He picked up the coffeepot and carefully poured the fragrant liquid into the narrow neck of the canteen. His eyes were intent on the task as he continued, "You might as well have some coffee. I assume you won't be stopping to make camp anywhere?"

Will shook his head. "I'll stop for a few minutes' sleep when I need it. But I won't be camping, just rolling up in my cloak."

"Thought so." Horace finished filling the canteen and pushed the stopper home. "So you might as well have some coffee. It'll stay warm for a while, and even cold coffee is better than leathery water." He smiled as he said it and Will grinned back.

"Good thinking, Horace."

Horace looked pleased. He wished he could do more for his friend, but this small, thoughtful gesture of support spoke volumes about their friendship.

"Plus it'll give you the sort of pick-me-up you might need along the way."

Their smiles faded as they thought about the journey that faced Will. The land itself was wild, and who knew what dangers he might encounter. In isolated parts of the Kingdom like this, locals tended to resent strangers, and it was possible that bandits were operating between here and Macindaw. Once he got close to the castle, of course, there was a distinct chance that he might run into Scotti raiding parties, like the one they had foiled several days back. And Will would be concentrating on speed, not stealth.

"I wish I was coming with you," Horace said quietly. The concern was obvious in his eyes. Will slapped his shoulder and grinned.

"You'd only slow me down, blundering along behind me." Unintentionally, he used the words Halt had used several days previously. They both realized it and their smiles faded once more as they turned to look at the still figure lying under the lean-to. There was silence between them.

"I'm glad you'll be here to watch over him," Will finally said. "It makes it easier for me to go."

Horace nodded several times, not trusting himself to speak. Abruptly, Will turned and walked to where Halt lay, going down on one knee and taking the Ranger's right hand in both of his.

"I'll be back, Halt. I promise you. I'll be back within three days. You just make sure you're here waiting for me, do you hear?"

Halt stirred and muttered, then settled again. It was possible that the sound of Will's voice had penetrated through the fog of poison that held him captive. Will hoped so. He shook his head sadly. It pierced his heart to see Halt, normally so strong, so capable, so indefatigable, reduced to this muttering, tossing shadow of himself. He touched the Ranger's brow. His temperature seemed to have come down. He was warm but not burning with fever as he had been. Will stood and, after one last sad look, turned to Horace.

"Keep an eye on that fever. If he gets hot again, use the cool wet cloths on his forehead. And clean the wound out every four hours or so. Use the salve every second time."

He doubted that treating the wound would serve any purpose now. The sickness had gone deeper into Halt's system. But at least Horace would feel he was doing something positive, and Will knew how important that was.

He gripped Horace's right hand, then the two of them moved closer and embraced.

"I'll take care of him, Will. I'll guard him with my life," Horace said.

Will nodded, his face buried against his larger friend's shoulder.

"I know you will. And keep watch at night. You never know, that Genovesan killer might decide to come back."

He stepped back from the embrace. Horace smiled but it was a smile without any humor in it.

"You know, I almost hope he does," he said.

They walked together to where the horses waited. Abelard shifted nervously, rolling his eyes and rumbling deep in his chest. Will stepped up to him, placed his hands on either side of his muzzle as he'd seen Halt do, and blew gently into his nostrils to get the horse's attention.

"I know you're worried," he said softly. "But you have to come with me. Understand? You're coming with me and we'll get help for him."

The little horse shook his head and mane in that sudden, vibrating manner so common to Ranger horses. He stopped the nervous pacing and whinnying and stood ready.

Horace shook his head in amazement. "You know, I'd swear he understood what you said," he remarked.

Will patted Abelard's soft nose and smiled at him fondly.

"He did," he replied. Then he swung into Tug's saddle and took Kicker's lead rein as Horace passed it up to him. Abelard, of course, would follow without needing to be led.

"Take care, Will," Horace said, and Will nodded.

"Three days," he said. "Look for me then. And keep your eyes open while I'm gone."

He touched his heel to Tug's side and the little horse swung away, Kicker following easily on the lead rein. It seemed that after spending so much time in the company of the two Ranger horses, he was content to stay with them without further urging. Abelard looked once more at the figure lying beneath the blankets, tossed his head in farewell and wheeled, trotting to catch up to the other horses.

For a long while, Horace stood watching them as they trotted away then increased their speed to a slow lope. Finally, they passed over the ridge and were lost to his sight.

+ + +

Will was tempted to clap his heels into Tug's side and urge him on to a full gallop. But he knew that in the long run, they'd make better time by maintaining a slower pace. He held the little horse to a steady lope, a gait the Ranger horses could maintain hour after hour. Abelard matched the pace, and Kicker, free of his normal load and with a longer stride than either of the other horses, kept pace with them easily. The big battlehorse almost appeared to be enjoying himself, running free and unloaded.

Will reached the river and turned eastward, following the bank and looking for another crossing. There was a horse ford marked on the map to the east—too deep for foot traffic, which was why Tennyson and his group had been unable to use it. But the horses should manage it easily enough. It had the added advantage that it would put him across the river at a point clear of the drowned forest. He had no wish to reenter that gray wasteland in a hurry.

Three hours' steady riding took him to the ford. He urged Tug forward into the water. Abelard followed readily, although Kicker balked at first as he saw the water rising past Tug's shoulders, almost to his withers. Then the battlehorse seemed to realize that he was several hands higher than his smaller companion and came forward with a rush, throwing spray in the air as he plunged forward in a series of surging leaps, threatening to crash into Tug and unseat Will.

"Settle down, Kicker!" Will ordered him. Once again, he had the sensation that Kicker was having fun. That was something that didn't happen often in a battlehorse's life. But Kicker calmed down and moved more smoothly through the river until the three of them, streaming water, lurched up onto the far bank.

Will paused for a few minutes. He let the three horses drink, but not so much that they'd be heavy and overfull when they moved off.

Abelard and Tug, naturally, stopped as soon as he gave them a word command. Kicker, thirstily sucking huge drafts of the cool river water, had to be led away. He shook his mane and glared at Will for a second or two. The young Ranger regarded him evenly.

"Kicker! Do as you're told!"

He said it firmly. He didn't shout, but there was an unmistakable tone of command in his voice that left the big horse in no doubt as to who was in charge here. Kicker looked back reluctantly at the river, but let himself be led away. As he did so, Will rubbed his muzzle gently.

"Good boy," he said softly. "We'll make a Ranger horse of you yet."

A few paces away, Tug whinnied derisively.

You do amuse me at times.

29

He had been riding Tug for several hours, and now that they were across the river it seemed a good time to switch horses. He loosened Tug's saddle girth. The little horse looked slightly insulted.

I can keep going, you know.

"I know you can," Will told him gently. "But I'll be relying on you later, when we're all bone tired."

Tug shook his mane. He agreed. But he didn't have to like it. Even though Abelard was his friend, he would prefer to carry Will himself. He knew, even if Will didn't, that he could do it day after day, hour after hour, without wearing himself out.

Will tightened Abelard's girth. Unlike some horses, Ranger horses would never fill their lungs with a deep breath to expand their bodies while a strap was being tightened, only to release the breath, and loosen the strap, as soon as it was buckled. He tugged the saddle experimentally, and began to raise his left foot to the stirrup when he realized that Abelard had turned his head to look expectantly at him.

"Of course," he said softly. "Excuse my bad manners." He looked the horse steadily in the eye and said the words Halt had told him so many years ago, outside Old Bob's cottage in the woods.

"*Permettez moi?*" He hoped he had the accent right. His Gallic wasn't the best. But Abelard tossed his head encouragingly a few times and Will put his foot in the stirrup and swung up astride Halt's horse. For a second he waited, wondering if he had said the password correctly, wondering if Abelard was simply waiting for him to relax so he could toss him high in the air to have him come crashing down on the grass. Strangely, in all the years he and Halt had been together, he had never had occasion to ride Abelard before this. Given that the little horse had known him for years and recognized him as a friend of Halt's, he doubted that he would throw him off. But training was training.

After a few seconds, he realized that there was going to be no violent corkscrewing explosion of horseflesh under him. Abelard was waiting patiently for the signal to proceed. Will twitched Kicker's lead rein to get his attention, then touched his heels to Abelard's barrel of a body and they moved off, building gradually to the familiar lope.

They rode clear of the fertile flats that bounded the river. The trees began to thin out so that they were occasional clumps and outcrops set among the grassy downs. There was a faint path, sometimes difficult to see, but there were few obstructions and the horses were all sure-footed, even Kicker. They made good time as the sun sank inexorably closer to the western horizon, firing the low clouds' undersides with a rich orange and purple glare. From time to time, as they crested a hill, he could see glimpses of the gray, stark expanse of the drowned forest off to the east. But they became fewer and fewer as he made progress.

When darkness fell, he spelled the horses again, letting them drink sparingly from the small folding leather bucket that he carried for the purpose. He took a large swig of the coffee, now with almost no trace of heat left in it. But the taste and the sweetness revived him. The moon was due to rise in an hour and he decided to wait for it. He was traveling unfamiliar ground, and sure-footed as they might be, he didn't want to risk one of the horses stumbling or falling. He'd switch back to Tug when they set out again. It was time to do so anyway, and although Tug and Abelard were very similar, Abelard's gait was slightly different—a little stiffer and more abrupt. In time, he knew, he would become accustomed to it. But if they were traveling by night, he'd prefer to lead the way on Tug.

After a time, the moon soared up over the eastern horizon, huge and silent and watchful while it was low down, seeming to shrink as it reached higher into the night sky. He put an arm around Abelard's neck, letting the horse nuzzle against him.

"Thanks, Abelard," he said, then, on an impulse, "*Merci bien, mon ami.* You've done well."

The little horse rumbled acknowledgment and butted against him several times. Kicker, grazing nearby, looked up as Will retrieved his lead rope from the tree where it was tied and moved to mount Tug.

Once again in the familiar saddle—even Halt's saddle felt slightly different from his own—he looked around at the other two horses, patiently waiting his command.

"All right, boys," he said. "Let's get going."

He was tired. Inestimably tired. And his body ached in a hundred different muscles. He had changed back to Abelard, then to Tug once more, and even the familiar saddle created its own form of torture for his aching legs and back and behind. He estimated that it was after midnight, so he had been riding, with a few brief stops, for well over twelve hours. And while he was riding, he was also concentrating fiercely. Concentrating on the course they were following, steering by the stars. Watching the ground ahead of them, alert for any obstacles or dangers.

The effort that went into this sort of concentration was almost as exhausting as the physical exertion.

The moon had set hours ago but he continued by starlight. The trees were becoming fewer and farther between, and he was climbing gradually to a plateau. The terrain now was a series of bare knolls, covered only by long windswept grass. Soon, he decided, he would have to stop for a brief rest. Once again, it would be the lesser of two undesirable alternatives. If he kept riding too long, his attention would wander and sheer fatigue might lead him into a mistake—a wrong direction, or a poor choice of path. In the back of his mind, he nursed the fear that one of the horses might stumble or fall and injure himself because of some mistake made by Will—a mistake he might not have made if he had all his wits about him.

Once, they startled a large animal close to the faint trail they were following. There was a brief snarl of surprise and it bounded away, disappearing into the long grass before he could get a good look at it. The horses started nervously. Kicker neighed in alarm and pulled at the lead rope, nearly jerking the exhausted young Ranger from the saddle. He had no idea what the animal might have been. A wolf, perhaps, or a large hunting cat. He had heard that there was a species of lynx in this part of the country that could grow as large as a small bear.

Or it could have been a bear.

Whatever it was, if they chanced upon another one, he needed to remain alert. He realized with a guilty start that he had actually been dozing in the saddle when they had blundered upon it. Almost certainly, Tug and Abelard would have given him warnings. But he had been too exhausted to notice them.

He reined Tug in. It was time to stop and have a substantial rest. To close his eyes and sleep, if only for half an hour, and let his body be revitalized. Half an hour's proper sleep would do it, and as he had the thought, the idea of stretching flat out, rolling himself in his warm cloak and letting his eyes close and stay closed was too much to resist.

He glanced around the surrounding countryside. The terrain had been rising for some time now and they were close to the top of a large, bare hill. In the distance, he made out several irregular shapes in the dim starlight, and for a moment he frowned, wondering what they were.

Then he realized. They were the barrows. The ancient burial mounds of long-dead warriors.

He recalled his flippant remark to Horace: *Some folk think they're haunted.* It had tripped off the tongue so easily in the daylight, scores of kilometers away. Now, here on this bare hill, with only the dim light of the stars, the whole idea seemed more forbidding, the barrows themselves more ominous.

"Great place you picked for a rest," he muttered to himself, and groaning with the effort, he swung down from Tug's back. His knees gave slightly as he touched the ground, and he staggered a pace or two. Then he fastened Kicker's lead rope to Tug's saddlebow, loosened the little horse's girth and looked for a clear space in the grass. Ghosts or no ghosts, he had to sleep.

The ground was hard and the cold struck through his cloak. But from the moment he first stretched out and groaned softly with pleasure, it felt as comfortable as the softest goose-down mattress. He closed his eyes. He would wake in half an hour, he knew. If by any chance he didn't, Tug would wake him. But that was half an hour away.

For now, he could sleep.

◆   ◆   ◆

He woke.

Instinctively, he knew that he hadn't been asleep for the full thirty minutes he had allotted to himself. Something had woken him. Something foreign.

Something hostile.

There had been no noise, he realized, as he tracked his thoughts back a few seconds. No sound had intruded into his consciousness to arouse him. It was something else. Something he could *feel* rather than see or hear. A presence. Something, or someone, was close by.

There was no outward sign that he was awake. His eyes were slit so that he could see but not apparently open. His breathing maintained the same steady rhythm that it had fallen into a few seconds after he had stretched out.

He took stock of the situation, reminding himself of where everything lay around him. The hilt of his saxe knife dug into his right side, where he had laid the double scabbard as he settled in to sleep. The fingers of his left hand touched the smooth surface of his bow, wrapped with him inside the cloak to protect the string from the dampness of the night air.

If someone was close by, the saxe would be the better choice, he thought. He could spring to his feet and have it drawn and ready in a matter of seconds. The bow would be more cumbersome. He searched his senses, trying to determine a direction. Something had disturbed him. He was sure of that. Now he tried to sense where it lay. He gave himself over to pure instinct.

Where is it? Which direction?

He forced all conscious thought from his mind, letting it become a blank, removing all extraneous distractions the same way he did in the instant before releasing an arrow. His senses told him *left*. He slid his eyes sideways, without moving his head. But he still had them slitted, feigning sleep, and he could see nothing.

He tossed and muttered, as if still asleep, and managed to turn his head to the left. Then he allowed his breathing to settle again into the deep even rhythms of sleep.

Something was there. He couldn't see it clearly but it was there. A huge, indistinct shape. Perhaps a man. But larger than any man he'd ever seen. He had a vague impression of armor. Ancient armor, with high-rising shoulder guards and a helmet decorated with huge, angular wings.

Somehow, it looked familiar. He tried to remember where he had seen this figure before, but his memory retreated down an unlit corridor as soon as he made the attempt. He concentrated on continuing to breathe deeply and evenly. The temptation was to catch his breath as he considered the situation.

He prepared himself, forcing oxygen into his limbs, ensuring that his mind was sharp and uncluttered, focused on what he was about to do. He rehearsed his actions in his mind. Right hand on the saxe knife. Draw it from the scabbard as he leapt to his feet, using his left hand to thrust up from the ground. Use his legs to spring up and to one side, in case the strange figure was prepared to strike at him. The sideways movement would force him to reconsider his stroke and the delay would help Will survive the first vital few seconds.

He prepared his muscles. His hand closed silently around the saxe knife hilt.

And then he was up. In one smooth, uncoiling movement, without any warning or visible preparation, he was on his feet and dancing to his right to avoid a possible sword or ax strike. The saxe gleamed in his hand as he flicked it to release it from its scabbard. He took up a combat crouch, the saxe held out low before him, tip slightly raised, his knees tensed and ready to spring either way, the rest of his muscles loose and ready for instant movement, either attack or defense.

There was nothing. No giant indistinct warrior in ancient armor. No enemy ready to attack.

There was just the starlit night and the gentle soughing of wind through the long grass. Slowly, he relaxed, rising from his crouch and lowering the point of the saxe so that it lay alongside his thigh.

Then he remembered why the shape had seemed familiar. The Night Warrior, the terrifying illusion that Malcolm had created in Grimsdell Wood, had looked like that. With that realization, he allowed the last of the tension to flow out of his body. He dropped the saxe point down into the soft ground and slumped wearily.

Had he dreamed it? Had his imagination, fed by the thought of the barrows and the legends of ancient ghosts, simply created the situation? He frowned, thinking. He was sure that he had been fully awake just before he leapt to his feet. But had he? Or had he been in that deceptive state of half sleep, half wakefulness that so often took an exhausted mind and body? And had an old memory stirred within him?

He shook his head. He didn't know. He couldn't tell when he had woken fully. He walked to the horses. They definitely seemed alarmed. But then, they would. After all, he had just leapt to his feet unexpectedly, waving his saxe knife around like a lunatic. He approached Tug and Abelard now. Both of them stood tensed, ears pricked, alert and nervous. Tug shifted his weight from one foot to another. Kicker had relaxed again, but Kicker wasn't trained to the fine edge of awareness that the Ranger horses were.

Tug made that familiar low rumbling noise in his chest. Often that was a sign of danger. Or that he was uncertain. Will stroked his nose, speaking gently to him.

"What is it, boy? Do you feel something?"

Undoubtedly, the little horse did. But whether it was some presence close by or he was simply reacting to Will's sense of alarm, Will couldn't tell. Gradually, as Tug settled down and his eyes stopped flicking from one point to another in the surrounding night, Will decided that it was the latter. Tug and Abelard were nervous and alert simply because they could detect the same sense of alarm in him. After all, they had made no warning sound as he lay, feigning sleep. Gradually, Will's own racing pulse settled and he came to accept that there had been nothing. It had all been the result of imagination, combined with exhaustion. The fact that the intruder had appeared to look like the Night Warrior finally convinced him that it had come from within his own mind, and he felt slightly foolish.

He retrieved his saxe knife, replaced it in the scabbard and buckled the scabbard around his waist. Then he donned his cloak, shaking some of the damp from it first, slung his quiver over his shoulder and picked up his bow.

"Imagination or not," he said softly, "I'm not staying here a second longer."

He tightened the girth on Abelard's saddle and mounted. Then, leading Kicker and with Tug trotting beside him, he rode quickly away from his temporary resting place. The hairs on the back of his neck prickled slightly but he didn't look back.

Behind him, in the darkness, the ancient, invisible presence that inhabited the hill slipped silently back to its resting place, satisfied that another interloper had moved on.

30

Back at the camp, the hours passed slowly for Horace. Most of the time, Halt lay still. From time to time he would rouse himself to toss and turn, muttering a few words, none of which made much sense.

Occasionally, Horace would hear Will's name mentioned, and once, his own. But most of the time, Halt's mind seemed to be in a place a long way away and a long time ago. He mentioned names and places Horace had never heard before.

Whenever Halt began these muttered outbursts, Horace would hurry to kneel beside him. He kept a supply of cloths soaking in a bowl of cool water, because he noticed that Halt's tossing and turning usually coincided with an increase in his temperature. It was never as dry and burning as it had been on the first day, but he was obviously uncomfortable, and Horace would mop his face and brow with the damp, cool cloths, crooning a wordless tune of comfort as he did so. It seemed to settle the Ranger down, and after a few minutes of these ministrations, he would fall into a deep, untroubled sleep once more.

Infrequently, he would wake and become lucid. Usually, he knew who and where he was and what had happened to him. On these occasions, Horace took the opportunity to coax him to eat a little. He made more of the beef broth, using some of their smoked, jerked beef, soaking it and simmering it. It was quite tasty and he hoped it had some nourishment in it. Halt needed nourishment, he felt. He was looking weaker and weaker every time he awoke. His voice was no more than a thin croak.

Once, he was awake and conscious for more than an hour and Horace's hopes soared. He used the time to get Halt to give him instructions on how to make the campfire bread. It was simple enough: flour, water and salt, molded into a shape and then left buried under the embers for an hour or so. Unfortunately, by the time it was ready to eat, Halt had slipped away again. Horace disconsolately chewed the warm bread by himself. It was doughy and thick, but he told himself it was delicious.

He cleaned his armor and sharpened his weapons. They were already razor-sharp, but he knew that rust could quickly form if he didn't give them constant attention. And he practiced his weapon drills as well, working for several hours until his shirt was damp with perspiration. All the time, his ears were alert for the slightest sound from the stricken Ranger, only a few meters away.

He wondered where Will was, and how far he had gone.

He looked at the map and tried to project Will's path and progress on it. But it was a vain attempt. There were too many uncertainties. Trails could be blocked or obliterated. Fords could have deepened or rivers could have flooded because of rain kilometers away. A dozen different things could force a traveler to make a detour in unknown country. Will had said he would be back in three days. That meant he planned to reach Macindaw, and Grimsdell Wood, where Malcolm had his cottage, in just over one day. The return journey would take longer. Malcolm couldn't be expected to ride nonstop without adequate rest as Will could do. Will had allowed two days' solid traveling, with a full night's rest period in between. It would be tough on the elderly healer, but it would be manageable.

Horace realized that his stock of firewood was getting low. At least replenishing it would give him something to do. He checked on Halt, watching the Ranger sleep for several minutes before deciding that he wasn't about to stir. Then he took the ax and a canvas log carrier and headed for a small grove of trees two or three hundred meters away. There were plenty of deadfalls there that would supply him with dry, ready-to-burn firewood.

He gathered sufficient kindling and then looked for heavier pieces, cutting them into manageable lengths with quick blows of the ax. Every so often, he would pause and turn to look back at the campsite. He could make out the figure lying near the smoldering fire. Chances were, of course, that if Halt were to cry out, he wouldn't hear him at this distance. It was hard enough to hear him from across the campfire.

Satisfied that he had enough small pieces for cooking and a supply of heavier, longer-burning logs to last through the dark hours, he loaded the wood into the log carrier. With the ax over his shoulder and the log holder in the other hand, he trudged back to the camp.

Halt was still sleeping, and so far as Horace could tell, he hadn't moved in the half hour that the tall warrior had been absent. In the back of his mind, Horace had nursed a vain hope that he would return and find Halt wide awake and recovered—or at least, on the road to recovery. The sight of the silent, unmoving shape filled him with sadness.

Moodily, he sat on his haunches and fed a few of the smaller branches into the embers, fanning them so that tiny flames began to lick from the coals and eventually caught onto the wood. The cof-

feepot was standing upside down where he'd left it after throwing
away the dregs from the last pot he'd made earlier in the day. He
filled the coffeepot and set it to boil and then selected their store of
coffee from the ration pack.

He hefted the little calico sack experimentally. It was nearly half
empty, and he had no idea where they would be able to replenish it
in this wilderness.

"Better go easy," he said aloud. He'd taken to talking to himself
since Will had left. After all, there was no one around to hear him.
"Can't have Will arriving back and no coffee to give him."

When the water began to bubble and steam, he measured a little
less than the usual amount into the palm of his hand and threw it
carefully into the boiling water.

Then he edged the pot away from the flames a little so that it
settled down as the coffee began to steep. The delicious, unmistakable aroma rose from the pot, despite the tightly closed lid.

Later, he wondered if it was that familiar smell that roused Halt.
It certainly seemed so, judging by his first words.

"I'll have a cup of that when it's ready."

Horace swung around, startled by the sound of Halt's voice.
Halt sounded stronger and more positive than he had the last time
he had spoken. Horace moved closer to him, seizing his right hand.

"Halt! You're awake! How are you feeling?"

Halt didn't answer immediately. He peered at the figure leaning
over him and tried to raise his head a little but then let it drop back,
defeated.

"Who's that?" he said. "Can't see too clearly for some reason. Must
have taken a knock on the head, did I?"

"It's me, Halt. And no, you were . . ." Before Horace could continue to explain what had happened, Halt began talking again, and

the young warrior's heart sank as he realized that, despite the apparent strength in Halt's voice, he was even more far gone now than he had been before.

"That Thorgan, wasn't it? Him with his club. I never saw him coming till he was on me."

Horace actually recoiled a little in shock. Thorgan? He'd heard the name. He'd heard it when he was a little boy in the Ward at Redmont. It was a famous tale of courage and loyalty throughout Araluen and one that had helped cement the remarkable legend of the Ranger Corps.

Thorgan the Smasher had been an infamous brigand who had terrified the northeastern region of Araluen many years ago. His crew of cutthroats robbed and murdered travelers and even raided small villages, burning, robbing and terrorizing wherever they went. Thorgan himself carried an immense war club, from which he derived his nickname.

Halt and Crowley, having just revitalized and re-formed the Ranger Corps, had vowed to stamp out Thorgan's band and to bring Thorgan before King Duncan's court of law. But in a running battle in a forest, Crowley had been ambushed by three of Thorgan's men and was fighting desperately for his life. Halt went to his aid, shooting two of the bandits and cutting the third down with his saxe knife. But in saving Crowley, he failed to see Thorgan concealed in the trees until it was almost too late. The huge bandit leapt out, swinging a terrible blow with the massive club. Halt just managed to evade its full force, slipping catlike to one side at the very last moment. Still, it caught him a glancing blow on the head and he only just managed to drive his saxe knife deep into Thorgan's body before falling unconscious across Crowley. Even in that movement, he was trying to protect his friend.

The two friends were found some hours later by a patrol of

Duncan's cavalry. They were huddled together, both unconscious. Close by, the body of Thorgan was leaning against the bole of a tree, a surprised expression on his face and the hilt of Halt's saxe knife protruding from his ribs.

That was the event, from so long ago, that was now foremost in Halt's wandering mind. His next words confirmed Horace's suspicion.

"Are you all right, Crowley? Thought I was too late getting to you, old friend. Hope you didn't think I'd let you down."

Crowley? Horace realized, with a sick feeling in the pit of his stomach, that Halt had mistaken him for the Ranger Commandant. There seemed to be no point in trying to convince him otherwise. Either he would realize his mistake or not. Horace squeezed his hand.

"You'd never let me down, Halt. I know that."

Halt smiled and closed his eyes briefly. Then he opened them once more and there was a strange calm in them.

"Don't know if I'm going to make it this time, Crowley," he said in a matter-of-fact voice. Horace felt his heart lurch with sadness— more at the tone of acceptance than the words themselves.

"You'll make it, Halt. Of course you'll make it! We need you. I need you."

But Halt smiled again, a sad little smile that said he didn't believe the words he was hearing.

"Been a long road, hasn't it? You've been a good friend."

"Halt . . . ," Horace began, but Halt raised a hand to stop him.

"No. Might not have too long, Crowley. Got to say a few things . . ." He paused, breathing deeply, gathering his strength. For a terrible moment, Horace thought he had drifted away. But then he rallied.

"The boy, Crowley. Look after him, won't you?"

Instinctively, Horace knew he was talking about Will. Halt's sense of time and events seemed hopelessly jumbled, hopelessly out of kilter. But he was searching Horace's face now, obviously seeing only a blur and waiting for a reply.

"Crowley? You still there?"

"I'm here, Halt," Horace said. He swallowed past a huge lump in his throat, desperately forcing the hot, stinging tears back as they threatened to force their way out through his eyes.

"I'm here. And I'll watch out for him, never fear." He felt a twinge of guilt at the deception but deemed it for the best. Halt had become troubled as he'd thought "Crowley" hadn't heard his request. He relaxed a little when Horace answered him.

"Thought maybe you'd gone," Halt said. Then, with a trace of his sardonic grin, he added, "Thought maybe I'd gone." Then the grin faded as he remembered what he had been saying. "He could be the greatest of us all, you know."

Horace bowed his head but he knew he had to answer. He had to keep Halt talking. If he was talking, he was alive. That was all Horace knew.

"He had a great teacher, Halt," Horace said, his voice breaking.

Halt waved a weary hand in dismissal. "Didn't need to teach him. Just needed to point the way." There was a long pause, then he added, "Horace too. Another good one there. Watch over him. He and Will together . . . They could be the future of this Kingdom."

This time Horace couldn't talk. He felt a numbing wave of sadness, but at the same time, a glow of pride was in his heart—pride that Halt would talk about him in such terms. Unable to speak, he squeezed the Ranger's hand once more. Halt made another effort to raise his head and managed to get it a few centimeters off his pillow.

"One more thing . . . Tell Pauline . . ." He hesitated and Horace was about to prompt him when he managed to continue. "Oh . . . never mind. She knows there's never been anyone else for me."

That last effort seemed to exhaust him and his eyes slowly closed. Horace opened his mouth to scream his grief, but he realized that the gray-bearded Ranger's chest was still rising and falling. The movement was slow. But he was still breathing. Still alive.

And Horace bowed his head and wept. Maybe from fear. Maybe from anguish. Maybe from relief that his friend continued to live.

Maybe from all three.

31

EXHAUSTED, SLUMPED IN THE SADDLE, WILL REINED ABELARD in to a stop. The ride through the night since they had left the barrows was a blur in his mind: a constant sequence of holding to the steady, disciplined lope for two hours, then dismounting and walking for a quarter of an hour, then mounting the spare horse and setting off once again at the same steady lope. He had stopped twice for short rests, with no further interruption to his sleep. The rests had revived him a little. But they also served to let the aches and stiffness in his muscles really set in. Each time he restarted, he suffered several minutes of agony until his senses became dulled to the discomfort.

Now, he was almost at the end of his journey. Or at least, the first part of it. To his left, he could see the solid bulk of Castle Macindaw. To his right lay the dark mass that delineated the beginning of Grimsdell Wood.

For a moment he was tempted to ride to the castle. He would be welcomed there, he knew. There would be hot food, a hot bath and a soft bed. He looked at Abelard. The little horse stood, head down and weary. Tug, who hadn't been carrying Will's weight for the past two hours, looked a little better but still tired. Even Kicker, who had carried no load so far, would be leg weary. If he went to the castle, the horses would be cared for, fed and watered and stabled in comfort.

He could possibly send a messenger to Malcolm while he regained his strength and energy. Surely Orman, the castle lord, must have some way of contacting the eccentric old healer, he thought. Just a few hours. Surely it wouldn't do any harm.

The temptation swayed him—literally. He realized he was actually swaying in the saddle as it became harder and harder to hold open his eyes. Any moment, he'd crash to the ground and lie there on the grass, and he knew if that happened, he might not have the strength, mental or physical, to rise again.

He shook himself, tossing his head violently, blinking his eyes rapidly, to beat back the drowsiness that threatened to engulf him.

"No!" he said suddenly, and Abelard's head raised, ears pricked, at the sudden sound of his voice. The horse wasn't as tired as he seemed, Will realized. He was simply conserving his strength against the need for further effort.

Will knew, in his heart, that if he were to go to Macindaw, he would be severely delayed. He would have to explain the situation, answering a hundred questions, and then persuade Orman to send a messenger into the woods.

Assuming that such a messenger could find Malcolm's cottage— and there was no certainty of that—he would then have to convince Malcolm of the urgency of the situation. And that urgency would be reduced by the mere fact that Will had not come himself. Delay would mount upon delay, and then it would be dark and too late to set out. It could cost him hours, and he knew Halt didn't have that time. Halt could die because his apprentice had decided that a few hours on a feather mattress were more important than his closest friend's life.

It would be quicker if he went to Malcolm himself to explain the situation. And if the healer showed any reluctance or hesitation about dropping whatever he might be doing and riding for two days to assist someone he'd never met, Will would simply grab him by the scruff of the neck and drag him along.

The decision made, he sat a little straighter in the saddle and turned Abelard's head toward Grimsdell Wood.

It was some time since he had last been here, but gradually it came back to him and he began to recognize landmarks.

He dismounted stiffly, groaning at the pain the movement caused him. He loosened Abelard's girth and patted him on the neck.

"Good boy," he said. "You've done well."

There was plenty of grass in the clearing. He tethered Kicker to a young sapling. The lead rein would give the big horse room to move and graze if he chose to. Abelard, of course, required no tether. Will simply held up a hand, palm outward, then pointed to the ground.

"Stay here," he said quietly. The horse tossed his head in acknowledgment.

He'd decided to ride Tug into the almost senseless tangle of Grimsdell Wood. He wasn't completely sure that he would be able to find Malcolm's cottage. The trails he had followed previously might well be overgrown by now. New trails might have been formed. He thought he knew the way, but it would help to have Tug's extra senses along as well. Briefly, he thought of the dog, Shadow, and wished grimly that she was with him. She would find the cottage without hesitation.

He tightened Tug's saddle straps and mounted, groaning again as the stiff muscles were stretched and racked by the movement. He hesitated, looking at the wall of trees around them. Then he thought he could make out the faintest trace of a trail. It seemed vaguely familiar. He was sure that was the way he and Alyss had gone last time.

"Let's go," he said to Tug, and they rode into Grimsdell Wood.

The path was obviously a trail left by small animals, who stood closer to the ground than Tug. Consequently, about a meter and a half from the ground, it was obstructed by overhanging branches, vines and creepers that all conspired to delay Will's progress, forcing him to duck under them or cut them aside. He saw several clumps of the ubiquitous stay-with-me vines and avoided them carefully.

The canopy of the trees overhead grew so close together that there was no sight of the sun, and few of its rays penetrated to the forest floor. He rode in a dark, half-shadowed world and, with no idea where the sun might lie, quickly lost all sense of direction. He thought bitterly of his seeker needle, miles away in the pack he had left behind at the campsite. In his hurry to find help for his stricken master, he had forgotten how treacherous Grimsdell Wood could be and had blindly assumed that he would be able to find his way through it once more.

He sensed that Tug was feeling the same confusion— undoubtedly because of the fact that he couldn't see the sun and had no way of judging his own direction. The trail they followed wound and twisted and doubled back so that after a few minutes, there was no way of knowing exactly where they were heading. All they could do was keep going.

"At least we don't have to contend with Malcolm's bugaboos this time," he told Tug.

The first time he had entered this wood, Malcolm had lined the way with frightening signs and sounds and flashing lights that ap-peared then disappeared. There was no evidence of them now.

Gently, he reined Tug in as they reached a slightly wider part of the trail. He sat still for a moment, considering their position. After a few seconds, he was forced to accept the truth. They were lost. At least, he was.

"Do you have any idea where we are?" he asked Tug. The horse tossed his head and neighed sharply. It was an uncertain sound. For once, Tug's almost supernatural senses were defeated.

"We can't be too far away," Will said hopefully—although, in truth, they could have been traveling entirely in the wrong direction for the past hour. He had seen nothing familiar. He paused, scanning the trees that grew close around them. He shoved back his cowl and listened, alert for any sound that might give him an idea of his position.

And heard frogs.

Several frogs, croaking.

"Listen!" he said urgently to Tug, and pointed in the direction from which he had heard the insistent sound. Tug's ears went up and his head swung to follow the sound. He heard them too.

"Find them," Will ordered, and with a definite task in mind, Tug set off into the trees, brushing aside several saplings, forcing his way through some low undergrowth until he emerged on another path. It was just ten meters from the one they had been following and appeared to be much more traveled. After a few meters, it diverged, angling away toward the sound of those frogs.

With growing certainty, Tug surged forward, and then, without warning, the trees opened out and they emerged on the edge of a wide, black body of water.

"Grimsdell mere," Will said triumphantly. From here, he knew, they were barely ten minutes away from Healer's Clearing. But ten minutes in which direction? The black mere itself was familiar, but the part of the bank where they had emerged wasn't. Once it was lost to sight, they could go blundering about the wood and lose themselves again within a few minutes.

Tug turned his head to look at him. *There are the frogs. I did my bit.*

Will patted his neck gratefully. "Well done. Now it's time for me to do something."

An idea came to him, and placing his fingers in either side of his mouth, he let go a shrill, piercing whistle. Tug started at the unexpected sound.

"Sorry," Will told him. "Here goes again."

Again, he whistled, long and loud and shrill. The sound seemed to be swallowed up by the dark mass of the wood around them. He waited, counting the seconds till a minute had passed, then whistled once more.

He repeated the action another four times, allowing a minute to pass between each whistle. And each time, he scanned the trees around them, hoping that his idea would work.

He was placing his fingers for a seventh whistle when he heard a rustling sound in the undergrowth close by. Tug rumbled a warning, which quickly turned to a sound of greeting. Then a black and white shape emerged, body low to the ground, heavy, white-tipped tail sweeping slowly from side to side in welcome.

Will dismounted painfully and moved to greet her, fondling the soft fur of her head, rubbing under her chin in the way dogs love to be patted. She raised her head to his touch, her eyes, one brown, the other a surprising manic blue, half closed in pleasure.

"Hello, Shadow," he said. "You have no idea how delighted I am to see you."

32

From the crest of a ridge overlooking the small camp, Bacari watched.

He wondered why the young archer had ridden away. Maybe he'd given up the chase? Then he shook his head. That didn't seem to fit with what he had seen of these three so far. More likely he'd gone in search of a local apothecary or healer.

The bearded one would be in bad shape by now, he knew. Bacari had heard him cry out and heard the clatter of his bow as he'd dropped it. That told him that his bolt had at least wounded his enemy.

And a simple flesh wound was as good as a killing shot with the poison he had used on the bolt. He was surprised that the bearded stranger had survived as long as he had. He must be in excellent physical condition to resist the effects of the poison for so long. The Genovesan smiled grimly to himself. The young man's quest for a healer would be in vain. No country potion merchant would have the faintest idea how to counteract that poison. In fact, he thought, very few healers in large towns would know either.

It was all to the good, he thought. The campsite where Tennyson had arranged to meet with his local followers was barely four hours' ride away. If their pursuers had continued to follow them, they would have caught up in another half day's march. And with Marisi killed in the encounter in the dead forest, the odds were tilting in their pursuers' favor. Bacari didn't relish another straight-out confrontation with the two younger riders, even if the older one was out of the way.

For a few seconds, he considered working his way into crossbow range and taking a shot at the young warrior. But he quickly abandoned the idea. He'd be crossing open ground, where he might easily be seen. If he missed his shot, he'd have to face the swordsman, and he'd seen ample evidence of his skill in Hibernia. In addition, he had no way of knowing when the younger archer might return. No, he decided. Leave them be. They represented no immediate danger, and his own priorities were changing.

It was time to report back to Tennyson, he thought. He'd already decided that his time with the self-styled prophet might be coming to an end. But before he left, he had to discover where Tennyson kept the gold and precious stones that he'd brought from Hibernia. So for the time being, he'd play the part of the faithful bodyguard.

By the time he reached the sprawling campsite, he could see that the numbers had already grown. There must have been more than fifty new arrivals. He rode slowly through the camp to Tennyson's tent. He smiled as he saw that the simple canvas enclosure had been replaced with a more substantial pavilion. The newly arrived converts had obviously brought the materials with them.

One of the white robes stood guard outside the pavilion. As Bacari dismounted and walked stiffly toward the entrance, the guard began to draw himself up, as if he were going to bar the way. Bacari smiled at him, but there was something in the smile that told the man he was not a good person to cross. Hastily, the guard stepped back and beckoned him to enter.

Tennyson was seated at a folding table, writing on a large piece of parchment. He looked up in annoyance as Bacari entered unannounced.

"Don't you ever knock?" Tennyson asked sourly.

The Genovesan made a pretense of looking around for something in the canvas walls to knock on. With bad grace, Tennyson waved him to a folding canvas chair on the opposite side of the table.

"So, what do you have to report?" the prophet said, finishing the last few words on the parchment.

"They've stopped," Bacari said. The burly man dropped his quill pen and looked up.

"Stopped? Where?"

"About four, maybe five hours' ride away. The older one is sick. He'll die soon."

"You're sure of that?" Tennyson put in.

"Yes. The poison is in him. He's been wrapped in his blankets for almost two days now. I haven't seen him move. There's no way he will survive. Nobody does."

Tennyson nodded several times. A cruel smile formed on his lips. "Good," he said. "I hope he dies in pain."

"He will," Bacari assured him.

"What about the others? The two young ones?"

Bacari frowned as he answered. "One has gone. The other stayed with the graybeard."

"What do you mean, 'gone'?" Tennyson asked.

"Gone means gone," Bacari said insolently. "He rode away. The other one stayed behind. He seems to be tending the bearded one."

Tennyson rose and began pacing the tent, his mind sorting through this strange turn of events. He turned back to the Genovesan. "Did he take anything with him?"

Bacari made a small gesture with his hands—it seemed to indicate that the information was unimportant.

"Not that I could see. Aside from the two other horses." He noticed that Tennyson's face was beginning to flush with rage as he heard this piece of news.

"He took all the horses?"

Bacari shrugged and nodded. He didn't say anything.

"Did it occur to you," Tennyson said, his voice heavy with sarcasm, "that he obviously plans to bring someone back? That's why he took extra horses."

"He may be planning to bring back a healer. I thought of that. But if he is, so what? It will be no use. The bearded one has no chance. And besides, the nearest large settlement where he might hope to find a healer is Collings Vale—and that's more than a day's ride away. That means they won't be moving for at least three days—more if they wait to see if their friend can be cured."

Tennyson pondered this, his anger slowly subsiding. But the Genovesan's arrogant manner was still a thorn in his side.

"True enough. You're sure there's no cure for this poison of yours?"

"There's a cure. But they won't find it. However, the longer the bearded one survives, the better it is for us."

"Just how do you figure that?" Tennyson asked.

"They won't travel any farther while he's sick. So if they find a healer and he delays the inevitable, then that's all the better. At least so far as we're concerned," he added with a cruel grin. "Postponing things won't do the bearded one much good."

Tennyson thought about what the Genovesan had said and nodded several times. Finally he came a decision. "I think you're right," he said. "But I want you to get back there and keep an eye on things, just in case."

The assassin bridled with anger. "To what purpose?" he demanded. "I've just ridden four hours. I tell you they're not going anywhere. I'm not going to spend a night out in the wet grass just because you're jumping at shadows! If you want to watch over them tonight, you go and do it."

Tennyson glared at him. Sooner or later, he had known it would come to this with the Genovesans. They were too proud, too arrogant. And too sure of themselves.

"Keep a respectful tongue in your head when you talk to me, *Signor* Bacari," he warned. The Genovesan let go a short bark of contemptuous laughter.

"Or what? I don't fear you, fat man. I don't fear any of your men or your false god. The only person in this camp who is to be feared is me. Understand?"

Tennyson forced down the rage that was welling up in him. The Genovesan was correct, he realized. But that didn't mean that, as soon as the chance arose, Tennyson wasn't going to kill him. For the moment, however, he would maintain an outward appearance of agreement.

"You're right," he said. "You must be tired and cold. Get some food and rest."

Bacari nodded, satisfied that his point had been made. Now he could afford to compromise, for the sake of good relations—and until he found where Tennyson had stashed his gold.

"I will sleep tonight," he said haughtily. "Tomorrow, before dawn, I will ride back to check on them."

"Of course," Tennyson said in a silky tone. He wondered if Bacari knew how much he hated him at this moment—but took care not to let any hint of that fact enter his manner or tone of voice. "That's an excellent compromise. After all, for the moment, they're not going anywhere, as you say."

Bacari nodded, satisfied. But he couldn't resist one last barbed statement.

"That's right," he said. "It is as *I* say."

And he turned and swept out of the tent, his purple cloak swirling round him. Tennyson stared after him for several minutes, his fists clenching and unclenching in rage.

"One day, my friend," he said in a whisper, "your turn will come. And it will be long and slow and painful. I promise you that."

33

Someone was watching them. Horace didn't know how he knew. He simply knew. Some sixth sense, the same extra sense that had kept him alive in a dozen combats, told him that someone was watching. He thought he'd detected a presence on the previous day, when Will had left. Today, he was sure of it.

He continued to move around the campsite, attending to the chores that needed his attention. He cleaned his breakfast utensils and the frying pan he'd used, scouring them with sand and then rinsing them clean in a bucket of clear water from the pond. Halt was still asleep and seemed to be resting easily. Horace thought he preferred Halt that way, compared with the way he had been—mistaking Horace for Crowley and talking about a long-ago battle with bandits. There had been something decidedly unnerving about that. It forced him to acknowledge the fact that Halt was seriously ill, even close to death. The sight of him resting peacefully was more encouraging. He could believe—or at least he could hope—that the Ranger was actually recovering from the effects of the poison. Logically, he knew that it was only a matter of time before Halt woke again and rambled on about events long past. But hope doesn't always follow logic, and he clung to it desperately.

Besides, there was the small matter of someone watching them. That would need to be addressed before too long. He assessed the situation. He knew it would be a mistake to let the watcher know that he had been detected. But here in the open, there was no way he could scan the surrounding countryside to search for some sign of the observer without alerting him.

The odds were that the unknown watcher was somewhere on the ridge to the southeast—the direction in which Tennyson and his group had been traveling. That, after all, was the direction of greatest danger. Of course, it could be someone who had no connection to their present situation—a random traveler who had crossed their trail. Or perhaps a robber, awaiting his chance to steal into the camp, assessing his chances against the strangers, measuring their strengths and weaknesses.

But the greater likelihood was that they were being observed by one of Tennyson's followers. And if that were so, it would most likely be the surviving Genovesan. For a moment, his flesh crawled at the thought of a crossbowman lying hidden somewhere out there. Then he relaxed. The low ridge was more than three hundred meters away and Will had told him that the Genovesans were armed with relatively low-powered crossbows. Maximum accurate range couldn't be more than one hundred and fifty meters.

But still, the thought that he was being watched rankled him. It was like an itch that he couldn't reach to scratch. He glanced casually around the surrounding terrain. The nearest cover where he could scan the horizon without being seen was by the pond, some fifty meters away. It was in a depression in the ground, and there were several trees and bushes growing beside the water. From there, he could easily find a concealed observation point. The only problem was, he had already fetched fresh water for the camp. It had been his first task of the morning, before he became aware of the eyes upon him. The watcher might not have been there at that time. But if he had, he would wonder why Horace was fetching water again so soon. And if he started to wonder, he'd likely grow suspicious.

Then he'd either move off or move against them, and Horace wasn't ready for either of those alternatives. He wanted to know who was out there. And why. He wished Will was back. But the earliest he could expect him would be the next day—assuming he'd been able to maintain the pace he had planned on.

An idea struck him. He moved to the fire and selected a few medium-sized branches from the pile of firewood. Adding them to the fire, he turned away and kicked against the full bucket of water. It lurched sideways and he stooped quickly, as if trying to prevent it tipping. In reality, he finished the job, shoving the bucket over onto its side, spilling the water.

Some of the water ran into the freshly replenished fire, creating a plume of steam and smoke that would be easily visible to the observer. Just to make sure he got the full picture, Horace aimed a kick at the bucket, sending it spinning away, and yelled in a loud voice.

He was rather proud of that bit of byplay. He recalled a conversation at Castle Araluen some months before, with a member of a touring acting company. The actor had advised Horace to take a seat a little way down the hall for their performance, not right at the front.

"We have to play to the back of the house," he had explained, "so our expressions and gestures are somewhat larger than life. Sit too close and it becomes unrealistic."

At the time, Horace had thought he was simply creating an excuse for what seemed to be excessive overacting. But now he saw the sense of it.

I certainly played to the back of the house then, he thought with grim satisfaction.

Halt had stirred and murmured briefly when Horace swore and kicked at the offending bucket. Horace checked on him now, reassuring himself that the Ranger had settled. He winced as he moved. His toe was bruised from the solid contact with the bucket, and he knew it would ache for a day or two. He shrugged philosophically. Sometimes, an actor had to suffer for his art.

He moved to retrieve the bucket, then, walking through the camp, bent quickly to his pack and picked up his sword and scabbard, holding them close against his side, out of sight. With any luck, the distant observer wouldn't have seen what he'd picked up.

Trying to look casual, he strolled across the grass to the pond. He walked down the shallow incline to the bank, dropping below ground level as he did so. As soon as the horizon was concealed from his sight—and, by the same token, he was concealed from anyone watching from there—he went into a crouch and placed the bucket on the ground. Staying in the crouch, he moved quickly to the cover of the trees and bushes, where he dropped belly down on the ground.

Pushing himself along on elbows and knees, he squirmed carefully through the undergrowth until he could see the distant ridge.

He began to scan it carefully, dividing it into sectors and searching methodically back and forth, keeping his eyes moving so they wouldn't become fixed to one point. It took a couple of minutes, but finally he saw a quick movement. He caught it with his peripheral vision, then swung his eyes and focused on it. The watcher had edged forward. Perhaps, after Horace had dropped from sight, he was trying to find a better vantage point to catch sight of the young warrior again.

Now his head and shoulders were visible above the ridgeline. If he hadn't seen that small movement, chances are Horace would never have noticed. But now he could see the shape clearly. And he fancied he could also see a faint tinge of dull purple.

"So you've come back, have you?" he muttered. He glanced around, searching the surrounding countryside, looking for a way he could approach the assassin without being seen.

"I need a gully or a stretch of dead ground somewhere," he said to himself. But he could see no such feature in the land between him and the ridge. Ruefully, he decided that if he were a Ranger, he would have the skill to ghost forward unseen and unheard through the long grass. But even though Halt had given him a camouflage cloak, he knew the task was beyond him. And the thought of approaching an expert crossbowman across open ground was not an inviting one.

Besides, it would take too long. The Genovesan would be expecting him to reappear in the next few minutes, heading back to the campsite with a replenished water bucket. If he became suspicious, who knew what his next action might be? No, Horace decided, since he couldn't get close to the man, it was best to pretend he hadn't spotted him. It would be a sleepless night tonight, he thought.

He retrieved the bucket and, at the last moment, remembered to refill it. His mind was so preoccupied with the problem of the watching Genovesan that he had nearly forgotten that small detail. If he'd had to make a return trip, that would really have roused the observer's suspicion, he thought.

When he arrived back at the camp, the problem of the hidden watcher was pushed from his mind for a few minutes. He was delighted and surprised to find Halt awake and lucid.

As they talked, it became apparent that Halt knew where they were and what had happened. He no longer mistook Horace for Crowley, and his mind was well and truly back in the present.

His throat was dry, however, and Horace fetched him a cup of coffee. He could see the color flowing back into Halt's face as he drank the reviving beverage. After a few appreciative sips, Halt looked around the neat campsite.

"Where's Will? I assume he's gone on after Tennyson?"

Horace shook his head. "He's gone to fetch Malcolm," he replied, and as Halt momentarily puzzled over the name, he added, "The healer."

That brought a frown of disapproval to Halt's face and he shook his head.

"He shouldn't have done that. He should have left me to my own devices and followed the Outsiders. They'll be miles away by now! How long did you say I've been unconscious?"

"Tomorrow will be the third day," Horace said, and the frown on Halt's face deepened.

"That's too big a lead to give them. They could give you the slip. He shouldn't have wasted time going after Malcolm."

Horace noted the phrase *they could give you the slip*. Obviously, Halt had ruled himself out of further action against the Outsiders. He hesitated, wondering whether to tell him about the Genovesan who had been keeping watch on them. If the Genovesan was reporting back to Tennyson, the Outsiders couldn't be too far away, he thought. But he decided, on balance, that it might be better not to trouble Halt with the news that they were being observed. Instead, he replied, "Would you have done that in his place? Would you have left him and gone on?"

"Of course I would!" Halt replied immediately. But something in his voice rang false and Horace looked at him, raising one eyebrow. He'd waited a long time for an opportunity to use that expression of disbelief on Halt.

After a pause, the Ranger's anger subsided.

"All right. Perhaps I wouldn't," he admitted. Then he glared at Horace. "And stop raising that eyebrow at me. You can't even do it properly. Your other eyebrow moves with it!"

"Yes, Halt," said Horace, in a mock-subservient tone. He felt an indescribable tide of relief sweeping over him now that Halt seemed to be getting back to normal. Perhaps they wouldn't need Malcolm after all, he thought.

He fixed Halt a light meal of broth and bread. At first, he tried to feed the gray-bearded Ranger. Halt's indignant refusal lightened his spirits even more.

"I'm not an invalid! Give me that spoon!" the Ranger said, and Horace turned away to hide his grin. That was more like the lovable Halt of old, he thought.

Late in the afternoon, with Halt sleeping calmly, he became aware of a strange sensation. Or, more correctly, a lack of sensation. Since the morning, he had felt the constant scrutiny of the Genovesan's eyes. Now, suddenly, the feeling was gone.

With apparent casualness, he scanned the horizon around the camp. He knew where the Genovesan had lain up during the day. Several times, without appearing to look, he had seen a brief flicker of movement from the ridge as the man changed position or eased his cramped muscles.

"You'd never make a Ranger," he muttered. Time and again he'd seen Halt and Will's uncanny ability to maintain a position without moving for hours on end. "Then again," he'd continued, grinning, "neither would I." He knew he didn't have the patience or the self-discipline that the Rangers seemed to possess in large amounts.

As the shadows began to lengthen and the sun dropped inexorably toward the horizon, he came to a decision. It would be logical for him to make a quick patrol of the area before dark. Such a move shouldn't rouse the Genovesan's suspicions, if he were still there.

Accordingly, Horace donned his mail shirt and helmet, buckled on his sword and picked up his shield and set out from the camp. He started toward a point on the ridge some two hundred meters to the left of the Genovesan's last position. From there, he would patrol in an arc along the ridge, checking the land to the south.

He felt a little more secure now that he had the shield on his left arm. It would stop a crossbow bolt easily, and he had confidence in his own reactions. If the Genovesan were still in position, and if he rose to shoot, Horace would have ample time to take the bolt on his shield. And then, with the crossbow unloaded, he might just get within sword's length of the treacherous assassin. He'd quite enjoy that.

He trudged up to the ridgeline, made a show of scanning the ground out to his left, then turned right and began to work his way along the ridge. He reached the spot where he had seen movement and looked carefully around. The grass had been depressed by the shape of something, or someone, lying there for an extended period. It was an ideal observation point. The ridge here was a little higher and gave a wider view of the land before it. He glanced back at the camp, seeing the smudge of smoke from the fire, blowing sideways and lying low to the ground in the freshening evening breeze, and the still form, wrapped in blankets, sleeping beside it.

On an impulse, he strode down the far side of the ridge and scanned left and right. It took only a few minutes to find what he had been looking for. There was a pile of fresh horse dung in the grass, and evidence of where a picket stake had been driven into the ground then removed. The Genovesan had tethered his horse here—back from the ridge and hidden from the campsite, but close enough to make a hurried escape if he needed to do so.

"He was here all right," he said. "And now he's gone. Question is, will he come back? And if so, when?"

He trudged back to the camp, turning the problem over in his mind. As darkness fell, he prepared a meal. He shook Halt gently and was surprised and relieved when the Ranger's eyes opened al-most immediately.

"Dinner," Horace told him.

Halt gave a small snort. "About time. Service around here is very slow."

But he accepted the plate of food eagerly and ate quickly. After he had satisfied his immediate hunger, he held up a piece of the bread that Horace had cooked in the coals.

"Did you make this?" he asked.

Horace, with some pleasure in his new skill, assured him that he had. It didn't take long for Halt to burst his bubble.

"What is it?" he asked.

Horace eyed him for a long second. "I think I preferred you when you were sick."

Later, when Halt was sleeping again, Horace banked the fire, then slowly withdrew from the uneven, flickering circle of light that it threw. There was a fallen tree some fifteen meters away and he sat with his back against it, a blanket wrapped around his shoulders and his drawn sword resting ready across his knees. He spent a sleepless night, watching for an enemy who never appeared.

In the morning the Genovesan was back.

34

THE TWO HORSEMEN, LEADING A THIRD, LARGER HORSE BEHIND them, appeared over the horizon from the north.

Horace felt an overwhelming sense of relief as they drew closer and he could make them out more clearly. There was little likelihood that any other two horsemen might be approaching, of course, but the whole time he had been alone, he had worried over the possibility that Will had arrived at Healer's Clearing to find that Malcolm had been called away to another part of the fief, or was incapacitated in some way. Or had simply refused to come.

"I should have known better," he told himself as he began to walk out from the campsite to greet them. They saw him coming and lifted the horses from a slow trot to a canter. The horses, like their riders, looked travel-stained and weary. But Tug still had the energy to raise his head and send a nicker of greeting to Horace. It was as if he were reminding Kicker of his duties as the big battlehorse looked up at the sound, recognized his master and whinnied briefly.

They slowed as they came level with him, and he held up his hand in greeting, engulfing the birdlike healer's thin hand in his own as he gripped it.

"It's good to see you," he said. "Thanks for coming, Malcolm."

Malcolm reclaimed his hand, wincing slightly at the pressure of Horace's grip.

"How could I refuse? Do you always try to crush your friends' hands in that massive paw of yours?"

"Sorry. Just relief at seeing you, I suppose." Horace grinned.

"How's Halt?" Will asked anxiously. It was the question that had been plaguing him the whole time he had been away. Horace's easy manner was reassuring. Will knew he wouldn't be so cheerful if Halt had deteriorated further. But he needed to hear it said.

"As a matter of fact, I think he's improving," Horace told them. He saw Will's shoulders lift in relief. But he was puzzled by Malcolm's reaction. The healer frowned slightly.

"Improving?" he asked quickly. "In what way?"

"Well, two days ago he was rambling and raving. Had no idea where he was, what was happening. He thought it was sometime twenty years ago. And he thought I was someone else as well."

Malcolm nodded. "I see. And what makes you think he's getting better?"

Horace made a vague gesture with his hands. "Well, yesterday, he came out of it. He woke up and was totally aware of where he was, what had happened and who I was." He grinned at Will. "He was annoyed at you for going to fetch a healer. Said you should have kept on after Tennyson and left him."

Will snorted. "I'm sure that's just what he'd do if I were poisoned."

Horace grinned. "I said much the same thing to him. He wiffled and waffled a bit, but he admitted I was right. Then he complained about my cooking."

"Sounds as if he is on the mend," Will agreed. They had reached the campsite and Malcolm dismounted from Abelard. He wasn't a skilled rider, and he accomplished the feat by swinging one foot over the pommel and sliding down on the wrong side. Horace caught him as he stumbled, his stiff legs giving way under him.

"Thanks," said the healer. "I'd better take a look at him straight away. Has he been asleep long?"

Horace thought before he answered. "A couple of hours. He woke this morning. Then went back to sleep. Then he woke again around noon. He's sleeping much more peacefully," he added. He wondered why there was a vague expression of concern on Malcolm's face. Maybe he was annoyed that he'd traveled so far and so fast only to find he wasn't needed after all, he thought. He dismissed the matter and turned to Will.

"Why don't you take a break?" he said. "I'll look after the horses."

But Will had been trained in a strict school. He always felt vaguely delinquent if he allowed someone else to look after his horse.

"I'll do Tug," he said. "You can do the others."

They led the horses a little way from the fireplace and gave them water from the bucket Horace had refilled only a short while ago. Then they unsaddled the horses and began to rub them down. Kicker seemed inordinately pleased to see his master. In fact, he had had the easiest time of all three horses on the journey. Malcolm had looked at him in horror when he first saw him.

"You expect me to ride on that?" he had asked. "He's the size of a house!"

Consequently, he had spent most of the journey on Abelard's back. The sturdy little horse barely noticed his weight. Malcolm was small and thin, to the point of being scrawny.

"Anything happen while I was gone?" Will asked. "Aside from Halt improving?"

"Actually, yes," Horace told him. He looked quickly around to where Malcolm was crouched beside Halt, leaning over him and ministering to him. He decided that he was out of earshot, although why that mattered he wasn't totally sure. In a low voice, he quickly told Will about the watcher on the southern ridge.

Will, experienced in such matters, didn't make the novice's mistake of looking toward the ridge. He kept his eyes down.

"You're sure it's the Genovesan?"

Horace hesitated. "No. I'm not sure. I *think* it's him. I'm sure it's someone. I found the spot where he was hiding."

"And you say he left at nightfall?" Will continued. This was becoming more and more difficult to fathom.

"That's right. And came back this morning," Horace told him. Will pursed his lips, finished rubbing Tug down and patted him absently on the neck several times.

"Show me where," he said.

Horace was no novice either. The tall warrior moved around to pick up a dry cloth, then faced toward Will, his back to the southern ridgeline.

"Should be just over my right shoulder," he said. And Will, pretending to look at him as they talked, let his eyes scan past Horace's shoulder, probing the horizon. Horace, watching his face, saw his eyes stop moving and the skin around them tighten suddenly.

"I see him," Will said. "Just his head and shoulders. Now he's ducked down. If he hadn't done that, I mightn't have spotted him."

"He's getting cocky," Horace told him. "He's not trying too hard to hide himself. And he moves a lot, as well."

"Hmm," Will said. "What the devil is he up to? Why hasn't he just ridden away?"

"I've been thinking about that," Horace said. "Maybe Tennyson has been delayed, and our friend here is making sure we don't follow on too soon."

"Delayed by what?" Will asked, and Horace shrugged.

"Could be he's sick or injured. Maybe he's waiting for someone. I don't know. But he must be holed up somewhere close at hand, because his spy up there heads off at night and then is back here by daylight."

"He's waiting to see what we'll do," Will said as it became clear to him. "He knows Halt is poisoned. He heard him cry out when the bolt hit him. So he assumes he's going to die. He can't know who Malcolm is, or how skilled he is."

Funny, he thought, how he simply assumed that Malcolm would be able to save Halt.

Horace was nodding. "That could be it. If they've had to stop, it only makes sense that he should keep tabs on us. He might well assume that if Halt dies, we'll give up and head back home. And obviously, he has no way of knowing that Halt is getting better."

"Don't be too quick with that assumption," Malcolm said from behind him. They turned to face him, and his expression was grave.

"But he must be!" Horace protested. "I could see it myself and I'm certainly no healer. He was much better this morning and yesterday afternoon. Totally lucid."

But Malcolm was shaking his head and Horace stopped his protesting.

"I'm not sure what the poison is yet. But if I'm right, those are the symptoms."

"Of what?" Will asked. His mouth was a tight line.

Malcolm looked at him apologetically. As a healer, he hated times like this, when all he had to offer was bad news.

"It starts with delirium and fever. One minute he's in the present, the next he's in the past. Then he's totally in the past and hallucinating. That's the second stage. That's when you said he mistook you for someone else. Then there's the final stage: clarity and awareness once again and an apparent recovery."

"An *apparent* recovery?" Will repeated. He didn't like the sound of that phrase.

Malcolm shrugged. "I'm afraid so. He's a long way gone. I'm not sure how much time he might have left."

"But . . . you can treat him?" Horace asked. "There is an antidote to this poison, isn't there? You said you know what it is."

"I think I know what it is," Malcolm said. "And there is an antidote."

"Then I don't see the problem," Horace said.

Malcolm took a deep breath. "The poison looks like one of two possible types—both of the genus aracoina," he said. "One is derived from the aracoina plant that grows blue flowers. The other comes from the white-flowered variety. The two cause virtually the same symptoms—the ones I've just described here."

"Then . . . ," Will began, but Malcolm stopped him.

"There are two antidotes. They're quite common. They're effective almost immediately and I have the ingredients for both. But if I treat him for white aracoina and he's been poisoned with the blue variety, it will almost certainly kill him. And vice versa."

Horace and Will stood in stunned silence as Malcolm spoke. Then he continued.

"That's why murdering swine like these Genovesans favor aracoina poison. Even if a healer can prepare an antidote, there's still an even chance that the victim will die."

"And if we don't know which one was used?" Will asked. Malcolm had known the question was coming, and now he had to present this young man he admired so much with a truly terrible dilemma.

"If we don't treat him, he'll certainly die. If it comes down to it,

I'll prepare both remedies and we'll flip a coin and decide which one to use."

Will straightened his slumped shoulders and looked Malcolm in the eye.

"No," he said. "There'll be no coin tossing. If a decision has to be made, I'll make it. I won't have Halt's life decided by tossing a coin. I could never go back and tell Lady Pauline that was how we did it. I want it done by someone who loves him. And that's me."

Malcolm nodded acknowledgment of the statement.

"I hope I'd have your courage in such a moment," he said. Once again, as he had done many months previously, he regarded the Ranger before him and wondered at the strength and depth of character in one so young. Horace stepped closer to his friend and put his big hand on Will's shoulder. Malcolm saw the knuckles whiten with the pressure of his grip as he squeezed, letting Will know he was not alone.

With a sad little smile, Will put his hand up and covered his friend's hand. They didn't need to speak in this moment.

And that night, around midnight, after hours spent staring wordlessly into the dying coals of the fire, Will made his decision.

35

THE SUN HAD RISEN MORE THAN AN HOUR AGO. IT WAS GOING to be a fine day, but the group stood around the low mound of fresh-turned earth with their heads lowered in sorrow. They had no eyes for the fine weather or the promise of a clear day to come.

Head bowed, Will drove a wooden marker into the newly dug earth at the head of the shallow grave, then stepped away to give Horace room to smooth the last few shovelfuls of dirt into place. Horace stood back as well, leaning on the shovel.

"Should someone say a few words?" he asked tentatively. Malcolm looked to Will for an answer, but the young Ranger shook his head.

"I don't think I'm ready for that."

"Perhaps it would be appropriate if we just stand here quietly for a few moments?" Malcolm suggested. The other two exchanged glances and nodded agreement.

"I think that would be best," Will said.

Horace straightened to a position of attention and the three stood, heads bowed, by the grave site. Finally, Will broke the silence.

"All right. Let's go."

They packed their gear, loading it onto the horses. Horace kicked dirt over the fire to extinguish it and they mounted. Will looked for a long moment at the fresh earth that formed a low mound over the grave. Then he turned Tug's head and rode off without another backward glance. The others followed.

They rode slowly, heading north, away from the trail they had been following for days. They left the grave and Tennyson and his followers behind them. Nobody spoke as they topped the first ridge. Then, as they dropped out of sight from anyone who might be watching, Will made a brief hand signal.

"Let's pace it up," he said, and the three of them urged their horses into a canter. A few hundred meters away, where the ground flattened out, and before it rose to yet another low ridgeline, there was a small copse of trees. He headed for it now, swinging slightly to the left, the others following close behind him. As they neared the copse, he glanced back over his shoulder to see if there was anyone in sight behind them yet. But the skyline was empty.

"Hurry!" he called. They had to be under cover by the time the Genovesan spy reached that ridge.

He wheeled Tug to a stop at the edge of the trees and ushered the other two past him. They rode into the shelter of the copse for a few meters, then dismounted. Will, checking once more that there was no sign of a pursuer yet, followed them. He dismounted as well.

"Lead the horses well into the shadows," he said.

Horace led Kicker farther into the trees. At a gesture from Will, Abelard and Tug followed the larger horse.

"I'll take a look at Halt," Malcolm said.

The Ranger lay, asleep still, on his bedroll in the center of the copse. They had brought him here after nightfall, on a litter slung between Abelard and Tug, and made him comfortable. Malcolm stayed by him through the night. Before dawn, he had crept back to the campsite to be on hand for the "funeral," during which he stood, feigning a mournful demeanor, as Will and Horace buried a small log wrapped in a blanket.

"No change," Malcolm called softly now to Will, after his examination of Halt.

Will nodded, satisfied. It had worried him that Halt had been left here unattended for a few hours while they pretended to wake, find the "body" and bury it with all the outward signs of grief they could muster. But Malcolm had to be back at the camp before the watcher returned shortly after dawn, and they had decided it had been a necessary risk.

He waited now, just inside the trees, but far enough back so that he was in deep shadow and would be invisible to anyone watching from a distance. He scanned the horizon to the south eagerly.

"Any sign?" Horace asked softly as he and Malcolm moved to join Will. Horace had donned the cloak Halt had given him, and Malcolm was wearing Halt's own cloak. Every extra bit of concealment would help, and Will had instructed them both to keep their cowls up and pulled well forward.

"No! And for god's sake stop your bellowing!"

Horace couldn't help smiling at Will's irritated reply. It had hardly been a bellow, Horace knew. But he forgave his friend the exaggeration. Will was tensed to fever pitch. This ploy of his had to work if Halt was to have a chance of surviving.

"What exactly do you have in mind?" Malcolm said, being careful to keep his voice down. Will and Horace had discussed Will's plan the night before, but as Malcolm had spent the time keeping a watch over Halt, he wasn't sure of the details.

"I'm hoping he'll come to check that we've really gone," Will said.

"And then you'll rush out and capture him?" Malcolm asked. He sounded doubtful about the wisdom of such a haphazard plan, and Will's vehement reply confirmed his doubts.

"I most certainly will not! I've got no wish to get myself killed. The Genovesans are expert shots. If I charge out at him, he'll have plenty of time to put a bolt through me."

"You're a better shot than he is," Malcolm said. But he was missing a vital point.

"Maybe. But I want to take him alive. He'll just want me dead."

"Couldn't you shoot to wound him?" Malcolm suggested.

Will was shaking his head before he finished speaking. "Too risky. I'd be galloping flat out on Tug. One stumble, one false stride and I could be off target. If I miss by a couple of inches, I could kill the Genovesan. And besides, even if I did manage to wound him, he could still kill me."

"Then . . . what will you do?" Malcolm asked.

"I have to wait until he's not expecting trouble. When he comes looking for us, he'll be fully alert," Will explained. "He'll be looking to make sure that we've really gone. I expect he'll ride to the next ridge. Then, if he can't see any sign of us, I'm hoping he'll head back to Tennyson's camp."

"That sounds reasonable," Malcolm said. But Will could sense that he was still puzzled by the situation, so he explained further.

"Once he heads for home, he'll probably check behind him for the next hour or so. Then he'll relax a little as he's convinced we've really gone. The farther he goes, the more he'll relax. That means I'll have a better chance of taking him by surprise. I'll give him a head start and then swing out and parallel his course until I catch up to him. Then I'll cut back in and get as close as I can before he sees me."

"You'll still have to chase him down."

Will nodded. "Yes. But he'll be tired and he won't be expecting me. I'll have a much better chance of taking him alive if I wait a few hours."

Malcolm nodded, understanding. But there was a worried look on his face.

"Halt may not have a few hours, Will," he said quietly, and the young Ranger sighed.

"I know that, Malcolm. But it won't do him any good if I get myself killed here, will it?"

Suddenly, he held up a hand to cut off any possible reply. Tug had rumbled a low warning sound, barely audible, and he knew the little horse had heard something.

Will nodded to him. "Good boy," he whispered. "I hear it too."

It was the sound of a horse's hooves drumming on the soft ground. The sound grew and Will dropped to a crouch, motioning to the others to do the same.

"Remember," he cautioned them, "if he looks this way, don't move a muscle."

For several seconds, there was nothing, and then the hoofbeats slowed and Will saw movement on the horizon. Slowly, a horse and rider rose above the skyline. Will's lip curled in contempt. The Genovesan might be a dangerous enemy in the alleys and back streets of a town or city, he thought. But his field skills were sadly lacking. If you were going to show yourself above a skyline like that, there was nothing to be gained by doing it slowly.

For it was the Genovesan. Will recognized him easily, noting the dull purple cloak and the crossbow held, loaded and ready, across his saddlebow. The man stood in his stirrups, shielding his eyes with one hand, and searched the ground below him, looking for any sign of the three riders. The terrain here continued for kilometers in a series of undulating low ridges. To the Genovesan, it appeared that Horace, Will and Malcolm had already ridden over the next one to the north and were out of sight. That made sense, as he'd waited some minutes before setting out after them, in case they were delayed.

The Genovesan urged his horse forward now, cresting the ridge and riding down the shallow slope before him. He was no tracker, Will could see. The clumsy hints the Genovesans had left through the drowned forest had told him they knew little of real tracking skills. He watched as the assassin cantered past, about one hundred and fifty meters from where they crouched in concealment, then rode up to the next crest. Again, he repeated the useless maneuver of slowing down before he reached the crest, then exposing himself and his horse completely to look beyond it.

Obviously, he saw no sign of the three riders from that vantage point either. He hesitated for a few minutes, then wheeled his horse to the south and cantered back the way he had come, passing the copse of trees once more.

But, as before, he paid no attention to the spot where the three were hiding. He rode without pausing over the ridge and they heard his hoofbeats slowly fading. Will waited a few minutes, then looked at Tug, standing back among the trees.

"Anything?" he asked. The horse neighed softly and tossed his head. His ears went up, then down again. There was no sound for him to hear. For the first time in perhaps thirty minutes, Will relaxed his tense muscles. He could feel the result of the tension across his shoulders.

"You think he fell for it?" Horace asked.

Will hesitated a second, then nodded. "I think so. Unless he's double-gaming us. But I doubt that's the case. He's not very good in open country. Even you could probably fool him, Horace," he added with a grin.

"Well, thank you very much," Horace said, raising an eyebrow at him. He was beginning to enjoy that expression.

"You're supposed to do that without moving the other eyebrow," Will told him. "Otherwise you just look lopsided and surprised."

Horace sniffed in haughty disbelief. He was convinced he had that action down pretty well now and the Rangers were simply jealous that he'd mastered one of their pet expressions.

"So what's next?" Malcolm interrupted. He knew these two and sensed that this exchange could go on for some time. Will turned to him, his mind back on the present situation.

"I'll wait half an hour or so," he said. "I want him to be completely convinced that we've gone. Then I'll swing in a wide arc, cut back to find his trail and catch up with him before he reaches Tennyson's camp."

"And then you'll capture him," Horace said.

Will nodded at him. "With any luck, yes."

Malcolm shook his head in admiration.

"Just like that," he said. It all sounded so simple.

Will regarded him, a serious expression on his face. "Just like that." Then, realizing that he might be sounding a little boastful, he explained further. "I've got no choice, Malcolm, have I? You need to know which poison was used on the bolt, and he's the only man who can tell us."

"So now we wait?" Horace said, and Will nodded.

"Now we wait."

36

In spite of the long distances they'd traveled in the past few days, Tug was surprisingly fresh. Will cantered him slowly to the spot where the Genovesan had lain, watching the campsite. As he approached, he dismounted and moved forward in a crouch. Close to the highest point, he dropped to his belly and crawled forward to see over the ridge, exposing only a few centimeters of his head as he did so.

There was no sign of the Genovesan, although he found the spot where he had been easily enough. The grass was pushed down in a large circle, like the nest of some big animal. Will could see clear tracks in the grass leading away from the ridge, where the Genovesan had left each evening. He had followed the same path each time and his trail was obvious to Will's trained eye. He had headed southeast—the same direction the Outsiders group had been following. There seemed to be no reason now to think that they might have altered their course.

Will considered the situation briefly. The Genovesan was obviously satisfied that they had left after burying Halt. So there was no reason for him to be laying a false trail and no reason why he might suspect that he was still being followed. But he was no fool, even if his field craft left a lot to be desired. He would probably check his back trail from time to time, at least for the first few hours, and if Will was going to take him alive, he'd have to catch him with his guard down. Accordingly, Will took Tug in a long arc for two kilometers to the east. Then he turned to parallel the assassin's southeasterly course and brought Tug's pace up to a fast canter.

They rode steadily and as they crossed each ridgeline, Will took the same precautions against being sighted, but there was never any sign of the Genovesan.

After an hour and a half, he veered back in to cross the Genovesan's trail. He found it after a few minutes, satisfying himself that the man was continuing on that same course. He rode out to the west this time, then turned so that he was once more paralleling the course.

It was midafternoon when he caught sight of his quarry. He was ambling along, his horse plodding, head down, at a walk. Will smiled. The horse was one they must have stolen from a local farm and it looked in poor condition. It would be no match for Tug's stamina and speed. And now that he was as close as he was, he knew that the last kilometer or so would probably become a race.

Will angled Tug back in, heading to intercept the other rider. The man was slumped in his saddle. Obviously, he was nearly as tired as his horse. By now, he would be confident that there was no pursuit. As he drew closer, Will could see that the man's crossbow was now slung over his shoulder. His thoughts would be focused on the campsite somewhere ahead of him, on the hot food and drink that awaited him there.

"Gently, boy," Will whispered to Tug as he leaned forward over his neck, urging him to more speed. The little horse responded. His hoofbeats thudded dully on the ground, but they were muted by the grass and the damp earth underneath, and Will hoped they could get closer before the Genovesan heard them and realized he was in danger.

As he rode, he slung the longbow over his shoulder and, letting the reins lie across Tug's neck, reached into his jacket for his two strikers.

At first, Tug's movement made it difficult for him to screw the two brass pieces together. He would begin to insert one into the other and a sudden lurch would bring them apart before he had the threaded sections engaged. He paused, and concentrated on matching his body movements exactly to Tug's rhythm. Then, remaining loose and fluid, he tried again and felt the threads engage. After the first few careful turns, he quickened his pace, screwing the two strikers together into one long piece. He hefted it in his right hand, feeling the familiar balance. The strikers were designed to have the same throwing characteristics as his saxe knife. But to use them, he'd have to get to within twenty meters—and that could prove to be difficult.

He saw that the Genovesan was almost at another ridge. A sixth sense warned Will, and he realized that it would be only natural for the man to cast a last look behind him as he reached the crest. He brought Tug to a sliding halt, slipped out of the saddle and pulled sideways on the reins as he dropped to the ground. Tug, trained to respond to a wide variety of signals from his rider, reacted instantly. He came to his knees, then rolled over on one side in the grass, lying motionless as Will placed an arm over his neck. They lay unmoving, concealed partly by the grass and partly by their own lack of movement. From a distance, the gray horse and his cloaked rider would resemble nothing more threatening than a large rock surrounded by low bushes. From beneath his cowl, Will saw the Genovesan rein in at the top of the ridge. He heaved a sigh of relief that he had foreseen this moment.

The rider turned, easing his stiff muscles up out of his saddle, and cast a quick glance over the land behind him. But it was a cursory glance only. He had done the same thing from time to time over the past four hours. He had seen no sign of pursuit then and expected to see no sign of it now. As Halt had so often told Will during his training, *ninety percent of the time, people see only what they expect to see.* The Genovesan expected to see empty grassland behind him, and that was what he saw.

After a minute or two, he turned back to the southeast and rode down from the crest. Will waited. The oldest trick in the book was to appear to ride away and then suddenly return to look once more. But the Genovesan seemed satisfied that the land behind him was empty of any threat, and he didn't reappear.

Will tapped Tug on the shoulder, and as the horse rolled upright and came to his feet, he stepped astride him so that they came up together. With the sound of Tug's hoofbeats now screened by the ridge between him and the Genovesan, he took the opportunity to urge the horse into a gallop. When they came over the crest, he would expect to be only a few hundred meters from the other rider.

This time, he didn't pause at the crest. It was time to commit. They had been traveling for almost four hours, and logic told him they must be close to the Genovesan's goal. They crested the rise at a full gallop and Will gave a small cry of surprise.

Tug's ears went up at the sound, but Will hurriedly reassured him.

"Keep going!" he said. The little horse's ears went down again and he maintained his gallop, never missing a beat.

Before them, the landscape had changed. The series of undulating ridges now gave way to a long, gradual slope leading down until it opened out into a wide, long valley. Tennyson's camp was visible, some three kilometers away. The numbers had grown from the twelve or fifteen people who had been with him originally. Now, he estimated, there must be a hundred people gathered there.

But Will's more immediate problem was the Genovesan, now less than two hundred meters ahead of him. He couldn't believe his luck. The assassin hadn't heard the thudding of Tug's hooves on the grass. He continued at a slow walk, his horse plodding heavily.

Then Will saw the man's head jerk up and turn toward them as, inevitably, he heard them. Will was close enough to hear his sudden shout of surprise and saw him put his heels into his horse's ribs, rousing it to a lumbering canter, then a weary gallop. It was a tactical mistake, Will thought. The shock of seeing him had startled the man into an error. Armed with a crossbow, he would have been better to dismount and face his onrushing pursuer.

But then, he wasn't aware that Will needed to take him alive. Perhaps he wasn't ready to face the Ranger's phenomenal accuracy and speed once more. He must be aware that only luck had saved him in their previous encounter.

Will saw the pale oval of the Genovesan's face as he glanced over his shoulder. Tug was closing the range rapidly now, and the man was kicking desperately with his heels to spur his own horse on. But the lumbering farm horse never had a chance to outrun the fleet-footed Ranger horse, and Tug was gaining with each stride.

The Genovesan struggled now to unsling his crossbow. As he saw what the man was doing, Will shoved the joined strikers through his belt and unslung his own longbow. The Genovesan's hand went to his quiver, selecting a bolt and placing it in the groove of the cross-bow. Will's throat constricted and his mouth went dry as he realized he was about to face one of the man's deadly poisoned bolts. Under normal circumstances, he would have shot first. All the advantages were on his side. The other man had to twist in the saddle to get off a shot, whereas Will could shoot straight over Tug's ears. At this distance, he could pick him off easily.

But he needed the man alive.

The Genovesan had finally managed to load the bolt. He turned awkwardly, fighting against the jolting, uneven gait of his horse, to bring the crossbow to bear. He was twisting around to his right, so Will guided Tug with his knees, veering him to the left, forcing the Genovesan to twist farther, making it more difficult for him to take aim.

The assassin realized what he was doing and swung suddenly the other way, twisting around to his own left for a clearer shot. But as soon as he did, Will zigzagged again, taking Tug back to the right. The maneuver was successful. The Genovesan found that his target was again out of sight. And Tug had closed the range by another twenty meters in the process.

The Genovesan twisted right again. This time, Will kept galloping steadily, without swerving. But now he had an arrow nocked and rode with the reins dropped on Tug's neck, guiding the horse with knee signals. He couldn't risk killing the Genovesan, but his quarry didn't know that. The assassin would get one chance for a shot. There wouldn't be time for him to reload, even if he could manage the task on horseback.

When he came to shoot, Will planned to spoil his aim. He was confident that he could loose several arrows in rapid succession, putting them close enough to the Genovesan's head to make him flinch. He remembered the duel with the man's compatriot. These men were primarily assassins, used to shooting from cover at a helpless target, someone who was unaware of their presence. They weren't used to open combat, facing an enemy who shot back—and who shot with deadly accuracy.

He was closer now. Tug's gait was smooth and controlled, unlike the farm horse, who was clumsy and tired and had the Genovesan bouncing unevenly in the saddle.

Here it came! The crossbow leveled and he saw the Genovesan's hand begin to tighten around the trigger lever. Will's hands moved in a blur, drawing, releasing and flicking a new arrow out of the quiver and onto the string in such rapid succession that he had three arrows on their way in the seconds before the Genovesan released.

As his hand tightened on the crossbow's trigger, the assassin suddenly became aware of the danger. Something hissed viciously past his head, seemingly only a few centimeters away. And he was aware that two more shots were on the way, a fraction of a second behind the first. It would have taken far more steady nerves than he possessed to hold a cool, deliberate aim—even if he weren't being jolted and jounced by the galloping horse. He ducked, shouting an involuntary curse, and his hand spasmed, jerking hard on the trigger lever and sending the bolt arcing high into the air, so that it fell harmlessly into the long grass nearly a hundred meters away.

The danger was past. Will tossed the longbow aside. There was no time to re-sling it, and he could recover it later. He drew the strikers from his belt and urged Tug to one last burst of speed. The assassin, seeing him only forty meters away, drummed frantically with his heels on his horse's ribs. The exhausted animal had slowed to a trot while his rider had been preoccupied, and now he needed speed again. The horse responded as much as it could, but Tug was eating up the distance between them now. Too late, the Genovesan began to reach for one of the many daggers he carried. But Will's right arm went up and then came forward in a smooth, powerful throw.

The strikers glinted in the sunlight as they spun end over end. For a second, the other rider didn't see them, didn't register the danger. Then he saw the spinning metal and ducked low over his horse's neck.

The man had reflexes like a cat, Will thought. The strikers spun harmlessly over his head and disappeared into the long grass. Will cursed. He'd never find them again. He dragged his saxe from its scabbard.

"Go get him, Tug," he said, and he felt the response from his horse as he accelerated once more, now moving as fast as Will had ever felt him move.

He saw a glint of steel in the Genovesan's hand and recognized it as one of the long-bladed daggers the assassins carried. He held the saxe ready, and drove Tug forward. The Genovesan started to turn his horse to meet the charge, but he was too late. He struck once, aiming for Tug, but Will leaned forward over his horse's neck and deflected the thin blade with his saxe.

Then Tug's shoulder smashed at full speed into the exhausted, off-balance farm horse and sent him crashing over, so that he hit the ground on his side and slid for several meters along the slick surface of the grass. The violent movement trapped the Genovesan's right leg under the animal's body. The horse's hooves flailed weakly in the air, but it made no attempt to rise. It was finished.

Instantly, Will was out of the saddle. He ran toward the trapped assassin. The Genovesan had lost his dagger in the collision and was scrabbling frantically under his purple cloak to draw another. Without a second's hesitation, Will stepped in and slammed the heavy brass-shod hilt of his saxe into the side of the man's head. Then, without waiting to see if the first blow had been successful, he repeated the action, a little harder.

The man's eyes rolled up in his head. He let out a weak groan and fell back, his right leg still trapped under the fallen horse. Will stepped back to regain his breath. The second strike had probably been unnecessary, he realized. But he had enjoyed it.

37

MALCOLM WAS WORRIED. THE VENOM HAD BEEN IN HALT'S system for several days now, and at any time, he could go into the final stages. He was peaceful for the moment, and his temperature was normal. But if he became agitated and feverish again, tossing and turning and calling out, that would signal that the end was only a few hours away. Will was racing against time to bring back the Genovesan before Halt reached that stage. Their best guess was that Tennyson's camp would be about four hours away. Four hours there and four hours back.

In one hour, Halt could be dead.

He glanced over to the tall young warrior, sitting hunched over his knees, staring into space. He wished there was some way to help Horace, some encouragement he could offer. But Horace knew the situation as well as he did. And Malcolm wasn't in the habit of offering false hope and soothing words at a time like this. False hope was worse than the small hope they did have.

Halt gave a low moan and turned on his side. Instantly, Malcolm was alert, watching him like a hawk. Had he simply stirred in his sleep? Or would this be the beginning of the end? For a few seconds, Halt lay still and his anxiety began to abate. Then he muttered again, louder this time, and began to thrash about, trying to throw the blankets off. Malcolm hurried to his side, dropping to his knees and putting his hand on the bearded Ranger's forehead. It was hot to the touch—far too hot to be normal. Halt's eyes were screwed shut now but he continued to cry out. At first, they were just inarticulate sounds. Then he suddenly cried a warning.

"Will! Take your time! Don't rush the shot!"

Malcolm heard Horace's quick footsteps as the young man moved to stand behind him.

"Is he all right?" Horace asked. Under the circumstances, it was a ridiculous question. Halt was anything but all right, and Malcolm drew breath to give a cutting reply. Then he stopped. It was a natural reaction on Horace's part.

"No," he said. "He's in trouble. Hand me my medicine satchel, please, Horace."

The satchel was actually within easy reach, but he knew it would be better for the young man to think he was helping. Horace passed the leather case to Malcolm, who searched quickly through it, his practiced fingers going quickly to the vial he needed. It contained a light brown liquid, and he used his teeth to remove the stopper.

"Hold his jaw open," he said briefly. Horace knelt on Halt's other side and forced the Ranger's mouth open. Halt struggled against him, trying to toss his head from side to side to avoid his touch. But he was weakened by the ordeal of the past few days and Horace was too strong for him. Malcolm leaned forward and allowed a few drops of the brown liquid to fall onto Halt's tongue. Again, the Ranger reacted, arching his back and trying to break free.

"Hold his mouth shut until he swallows," Malcolm said tersely. Horace obliged, clamping his big hands over the Ranger's mouth and closing it. Halt tossed and moaned. But after some time, they saw his throat move and Malcolm knew he had swallowed the draft.

"All right," he said. "You can let go."

Horace relinquished his iron grip on Halt's jaw. The Ranger spluttered and coughed and tried to rise. But now Horace had his hands on his shoulders, holding him down. After a minute or so, his movements gradually began to weaken. His voice died away to a mumble and he slept fitfully.

Malcolm signaled for Horace to relax. There was perspiration on the young warrior's forehead and the healer knew it was from more than just exhaustion. It was nervous perspiration, brought on by his fear for Halt and his uncertainty. Powerful emotions, Malcolm knew, and capable of taking a heavy physical toll.

"Malcolm," Horace said. "What's happening?"

He had recognized that this was a new phase in Halt's suffering. Malcolm had told them that Halt would go through various phases, although he hadn't described this, the final phase, in any detail. But Horace knew that any change in behavior or condition could only be bad news now. Halt was deteriorating, and Horace wanted to know how bad the situation was.

Malcolm looked up and met his worried gaze.

"I'm not going to lie to you, Horace. He's calmer now because of the drug I just gave him. That'll wear off in an hour or so and he'll start to thrash around again. Each time he does, it'll be worse. He'll drive the poison further and further through his system and that'll be the end."

"How long can you keep giving him the drug?" Horace asked. "Will could be back here at any time."

Malcolm shrugged. "Maybe twice more. Maybe three times. But he's weak, Horace, and it's a powerful drug. If I give it to him too often, it could kill him just as easily as the poison."

"Isn't there anything you can do?" Horace said, feeling tears stinging his eyes. He felt so . . . helpless, so useless, standing by and watching Halt sink deeper and deeper. If the Ranger were in a battle, surrounded by enemies, Horace wouldn't hesitate to charge to his aid. He understood that sort of situation and could cope with it.

But this! This terrible waiting and watching, wringing his hands in anguish and unable to accomplish anything. This was worse than any battle he could imagine.

Malcolm said nothing. There was nothing for him to say. He saw the anger in Horace's eyes, saw his face flushing with rage.

"You healers! You're all the same! You have your potions and spells and mumbo jumbo, and in the end, it all comes down to nothing! All you can do is say *wait and see!*"

The accusation was unfair. Malcolm wasn't like the general run of healers, many of whom were mountebanks and charlatans. Malcolm dealt in herbs and drugs and knowledge of the human body and its systems. He was undoubtedly the most skilled and learned healer in Araluen. But sometimes, skill and knowledge simply weren't enough. After all, if healers were infallible, nobody would ever die. Deep down, Horace knew this, and Malcolm, knowing that he knew, took no offense. He understood that the warrior's anger was directed at the situation, at his own feeling of utter helplessness, and not at Malcolm himself.

"I'm sorry, Horace," he said simply. Horace stopped his tirade and released a long breath, his shoulders sagging. He knew his words had been ill considered. And he knew too that Malcolm must feel an even worse sense of helplessness than he did. After all, this was what Malcolm was trained for, and he could do nothing. Horace made a small sideways gesture with his hand.

"No. No," he said. "You've nothing to apologize for. I know you've done your best for him, Malcolm. Nobody could have done better. It's just . . ."

He couldn't finish the sentence. He wasn't even sure what it was he had been going to say. But he realized that his words spelled his acceptance of the fact that Halt would die. There was nothing more they could do for him. If Malcolm couldn't help him, nobody could.

He turned, his hand up to his eyes, hiding the tears there, and walked away. Malcolm started after him, then decided it might be better to leave him. He turned back to Halt and dropped to his knees beside him once more. He frowned in concentration, staring at the Ranger. In another half an hour, the brown liquid would begin to lose effect and Halt would go into another paroxysm. He could ease that, but it would be a temporary solution. The attacks would continue and get worse. It was a downward spiral.

Unless . . .

An idea was forming in his mind. It was a desperate idea, but this was a desperate situation. He breathed deeply several times, closing his eyes and concentrating. He forced his mind to ignore side issues and to focus on the main problem, turning the idea over in his mind, seeking the faults and the dangers and finding many of both.

Then he considered the alternative. He could keep Halt comfortable for a few more hours—maybe two or three—in the hope that Will would return. But he knew what a remote chance that was. Even if Will caught the Genovesan before that, he would travel more slowly on the return journey with a prisoner. In four hours, Halt would probably be dead. Not probably, he amended, almost certainly.

He came to a decision and rose, walking toward the young warrior who was leaning miserably against a tree some meters away. He saw the drooping shoulders, the bowed head, the body language that told him Horace had given up. Then he felt a sudden stab of doubt. Did he have the right to give him this renewed hope—hope that might well prove to be misplaced? If he buoyed Horace's expectations and Halt still died, how could he forgive himself?

Would it be better to simply accept the situation, do what he could for Halt and let nature take its course?

He shook his head, a new resolve forming in his mind. That was not his way. It never would be. If there was the slightest chance to save a patient, then he would take it. He would fight to the very end.

"Horace?" he said softly. The young man turned to him and Malcolm saw the tears that streaked his face.

"There might be something . . . ," he began. He saw the hope in Horace's eyes and held up a hand to forestall him. "It's a very slim chance. And it might not work. It could even kill him," he warned. For a moment, he saw Horace recoil mentally from that outcome, and then the warrior recovered himself.

"What do you have in mind?"

"It's something I've never done before. But it could work. The drug I gave him is a very dangerous drug. As I said, it could kill him, even without the poison. But if I were to give him enough so that he was almost dead, it might save him."

Horace frowned, not understanding. "How can you save him if you almost kill him?" And Malcolm had to admit that, put that way, it seemed like a crazy plan. But he stuck to his guns.

"If I take him right to the edge, everything in his body will slow down. His pulse. His breathing. His entire system. And the effects of the poison will slow down as well. We'll buy him time. Maybe eight hours. Maybe more."

He saw the effect those words had on Horace. In eight hours, Will would almost certainly be back—if he had managed to capture the Genovesan. Suddenly, Horace felt a terrible doubt. What if the Genovesan had killed Will? He pushed the thought aside. He had to believe in something today.

Will would be back. And if Halt were still alive, Malcolm could cure him. Suddenly, there was hope where there had been only black despair.

"How do you do it?" he asked. Malcolm chewed his lip for a second or two, then decided there was no easy way to express what he had in mind.

"I'll give him a massive overdose of the drug. But not quite enough to kill him."

"And how much will that be? Do you know? Have you ever done this before?"

Again, Malcolm hesitated.

"No," he said. "I've never done this before. I don't know of anyone who has. As for how much I should give him, frankly, I'll be guessing. He's weak already. I think I know how much to give him, but I can't be sure."

There was a long silence between them. Then Malcolm continued.

"It's not a decision I want to make, Horace. It should be made by a friend."

Horace met his gaze and nodded, understanding. "It should be made by Will."

Malcolm made a small gesture of agreement. "Yes. But he's not here. And you're Halt's friend too. You may not be as close to him as Will is, but you do love him and I'm asking you to make that decision. I can't make it for you."

Horace heaved a deep sigh and turned away, looking out through the trees to the empty horizon, as if Will might suddenly appear and make this all unnecessary. Still looking away, he said slowly, "Let me ask you this. If this were *your* friend, your closest friend, would you do it then?"

Now it was Malcolm's turn to pause and consider his answer.

"I think so," he said, after several seconds. "I hope I'd have the courage. I'm not sure I would, but I hope I would."

Horace turned back to him with the ghost of a sad smile on his face.

"Thanks for an honest answer. I'm sorry about what I said before. You deserve better than that."

Malcolm waved the apology aside.

"Already forgotten," he said. "But what's your decision?" He indicated Halt, and as he did so, the Ranger began to stir again, muttering in a low voice. The first dose of the drug was beginning to wear off. Malcolm realized that this was an important moment, a window of opportunity.

"The drug's wearing off," he continued. "It's out of his system. That makes it easier for me to figure out the right dosage. I don't have to allow for what I've already given him."

Horace looked from Malcolm to Halt, and came to a decision.

"Do it."

38

DUSK WAS ROLLING IN OVER THE RIDGE WHEN ABELARD RAISED his head and gave a long whinny.

Horace and Malcolm looked at the small horse in surprise. Ranger horses didn't normally make unnecessary noise. They were too well trained. Kicker looked up curiously as well, and then lowered his head and went back to his grazing.

"What's wrong with Abelard?" Malcolm asked.

Horace shrugged. "He must have heard or smelled something." He had been sitting by the fire, staring into the coals as they alternately glowed and dulled in the inconstant wind that gusted through the trees. He rose now, his sword ready in his hand, and walked toward the edge of the copse where they were camped.

As he did so, he heard an answering whinny from some distance away. Then an indistinct shape appeared over the horizon to the south.

"It's Will," he said. "And he's got a prisoner."

The outline of horse and rider had been blurred by the fact that Will was riding with the Genovesan, tied hand and foot, stomach down across the saddlebow in front of him.

He trotted Tug down the slope toward the copse, raising his

hand in greeting as he saw Horace step clear of the trees. In front of him, the Genovesan grunted uncomfortably with each of Tug's jolting strides.

Malcolm had left the campfire to join Horace in the open, and he rubbed his hands in anticipation as he saw that the young warrior was right. Will had a prisoner, and the purple cloak was clear evidence that it was their man.

Will reined in beside them. He looked worn out, Horace realized, although that was no surprise, considering what the young Ranger had been through in the past few days.

"How's Halt?" Will asked.

Horace made a reassuring gesture. "He's okay. It was touch-and-go for a while there. But Malcolm has put him into a deep, deep sleep to slow the poison down." He thought it was better to put it that way than to say *Malcolm had to nearly kill him to slow the poison down.* "He'll be fine now that you're back."

Will's face was drawn with weariness and his eyes were bloodshot. But now that his worry about Halt had been answered, there was an unmistakable air of satisfaction about him.

"Yes, I'm back," he said. "And look who I ran into."

Horace grinned at him. "I hope you ran into him hard."

"As hard as I could."

Horace stepped forward to lift the Genovesan to the ground, but Will waved him back.

"Stand clear," he said. He gripped the collar of the prisoner's cloak and heaved him up and away, nudging Tug to step to the opposite direction as he did so. The assassin slid down from the horse's back like a sack of potatoes. He hit the ground awkwardly, tried to keep his feet and failed, thumping into a heap on the ground.

"Careful!" said Malcolm. "We need him, remember!"

Will snorted derisively at the Genovesan, squirming weakly, trying to regain his feet.

"He's fine," he said. "It'd take more than that to kill him. And we only need him talking, not standing."

At Malcolm's signal, Horace stepped forward and heaved the Genovesan to his feet. The prisoner snarled at him in his own tongue, and Horace regarded him from a very close range. Something in the warrior's eyes seemed to register with the assassin, and he stopped his stream of abuse.

"What's your name?" Malcolm asked him, using the common language. The Genovesan switched his glare to the healer and shrugged contemptuously, saying nothing. It was an insulting action, and it was also a mistake. Horace's open hand slapped hard across the side of his head, jerking it to one side and setting his ears ringing.

"Make no mistake, you vulture," Horace said. "We don't like you. We have no interest in making sure you're comfortable. In fact, the more uncomfortable you are, the better I'm going to like it."

"Your name?" Malcolm repeated.

Horace sensed the man's shoulders beginning to rise again in that same dismissive shrug. His right hand went up and back, this time bunched into a fist.

"Horace!" Malcolm called out. He needed the man conscious to answer his questions. Horace kept his fist raised. The Genovesan's eyes were riveted on it. He'd felt the casual power behind the young man's slap. A punch would be a lot worse, he knew.

"He can still talk with a broken nose," Horace said. But now the Genovesan seemed to decide there was no point in taking more punishment for the sake of concealing his name.

"*Sono Bacari.*"

Again, he shrugged. It seemed to be a favorite action with the man and he could imbue it with enormous contempt, Horace noted. It was as if he were saying, "So my name is Bacari, so what? I only tell you because I choose to." The arrogant attitude antagonized Horace even further. He lowered his fist, and when he saw Bacari smile to himself, he suddenly kicked the man's legs from underneath him, sending him sprawling heavily on the ground again, the fall driving the wind out of him. Horace placed the flat of his foot on the man's chest and pinned him down.

"Speak the common tongue," he ordered.

Horace glanced at Will, who had dismounted and was leaning wearily against Tug's side, watching with a suspicion of a smile on his face. Like Horace, he felt not one ounce of compassion toward the Genovesan. And he knew it would be important for the man to understand that they would not spare him any pain in finding out the information they were seeking.

"If he doesn't behave, kick him in the ribs," Will said.

Horace nodded. "With pleasure." He leaned down again to the man, who had regained his breath. "Now let's try it again. In the common tongue. Your name?"

There was a moment's hesitation as the man, glaring in fury, met Horace's eyes. Then he muttered, "My name is Bacari."

Horace straightened up and glanced at Malcolm. "All right. He's all yours."

The healer nodded, and gestured toward the campfire and the unconscious form beside it.

"Bring him over here, will you, Horace," he asked. He walked to the campfire and sat down cross-legged. Horace simply reached down, grabbed Bacari by the scruff of his neck and dragged him across the ground to a spot facing Malcolm. He jerked him upright into a sitting position and stood over him, his arms folded. Bacari was very aware of his threatening presence.

"Just give us a little room, please," Malcolm asked in a mild tone. Horace stepped back a few paces, although he remained alert, watching the Genovesan keenly.

"Now, Bacari." Malcolm's tone was calm and conversational. "You shot our friend here with one of your bolts." He indicated Halt, lying a few meters away, his chest barely moving as he breathed. Bacari seemed to register the Ranger's presence for the first time, and his eyes widened. After all, he had seen them bury their companion. Or he had thought as much.

"Still alive?" he said, surprised. "He should have been dead two days ago!"

"Sorry to disappoint you," Horace said sardonically.

Malcolm gave him a warning glance and then continued. "You used a poison on the tip of your bolt."

Bacari shrugged again. "Maybe I did," he said carelessly.

Malcolm shook his head. "Certainly you did. You poisoned the tip of your crossbow with aracoina."

That definitely took Bacari by surprise. His eyes widened, and before he could stop himself he replied, "How can you know that?" He realized it was too late to recover, that he had given away a vital piece of information.

Malcolm smiled at him. But the smile went no further than his lips.

"I know many things," he said.

Bacari recovered from his initial surprise and pushed out his bottom lip in an insolent, careless expression.

"Then you know the antidote," he said, his former dismissive manner having returned. "Why not give it to him?"

Malcolm leaned forward to make full eye contact.

"I know there are two antidotes," he said. Again Bacari gave an involuntary start of surprise as he spoke, and although he recovered quickly, Malcolm had noticed the reaction. "And I know the wrong one will kill him."

"*Che sarà, sarà,*" Bacari replied.

"What did he say?" Horace demanded instantly, taking a step forward. But Malcolm gestured him back again.

"He said, 'What will be, will be.' He's obviously a philosopher." Then he turned his gaze back to the Genovesan. "Speak the common tongue. Last warning, or my big friend will slice your ears off and cram them down your murdering throat."

It was the mild, conversational tone in which the brutal words were delivered that made the threat more frightening—that and the unblinking stare that Malcolm now fixed on the assassin. He saw that the message had gone home. Bacari's eyes dropped from his.

"All right. I speak," he said softly. Malcolm nodded several times.

"Good. So long as we understand each other." He noticed that the man's quiver still hung by his belt. Will had secured his hands behind his back with thumb cuffs so that the quiver and its contents were well beyond his reach. He had seen no reason to waste more time unbuckling it and discarding it. Malcolm leaned across to Bacari, reaching out for the quiver. Initially, Bacari tried to withdraw, thinking another blow might be coming. Then he relaxed as Malcolm carefully withdrew one of the bolts and inspected the point.

Malcolm's brows knotted in a frown as he saw the discolored, gummy substance coating the first few centimeters of the steel tip.

"Yes," he said softly, the disgust obvious in his voice. "This is poisoned, all right. Now all we need to know is, which variety did you use? The blue flower or the white?"

Bacari broke Malcolm's gaze. He glanced at the still figure a few meters away and then allowed his eyes to roam, taking in the threatening form of Horace and the exhausted young Ranger standing back some distance, watching in silence. He sensed the expectancy in the two young men, read the tension in the air as they awaited his answer. In spite of their threats, he instinctively knew that these three would not kill him in cold blood. They might beat him, and he could stand that. In the heat of battle, he knew either of the younger men would kill him without hesitation. But here, with his hands tied behind his back and his feet hobbled? Never.

If the situation were reversed, he would kill them without a second's thought. He possessed the cold-blooded cruelty necessary to perform such an act. And because he had it himself, he could see that it was missing in them.

Sure of himself now, he looked back to Malcolm and allowed the inner smile to break through to the surface.

"I forget," he said.

39

BACARI HEARD THE SUDDEN RUSH OF FEET AND TURNED TOO late. The younger Ranger was upon him before he could make any attempt at evasion. He felt hands grip the front of his jacket and lift him to his feet. The young face was thrust close to his. Gray with fatigue, eyes red-rimmed, Will found renewed energy in the sudden burst of hatred he felt for this sneering killer.

Malcolm started to scramble to his feet to stop him, but he was too late.

"You forget? You *forget?*" Will's voice rose to a shout as he shook the Genovesan like a rat.

He shoved him away violently. Bacari, his hands and feet securely tied, staggered, stumbled and fell, grunting with pain as he landed awkwardly on his side. Then the hands were upon him again and he was dragged to his feet once more.

"Then you'd better remember!" Will shouted, and sent him staggering and falling again with another shove. This time, Bacari fell close to the fire so that his left side was actually in the outer embers. He cried out in pain as he felt the glowing coals burn through his sleeve and begin to sear into the flesh.

"Will!" It was Malcolm, attempting to intervene, but Will shook him off. He grabbed the Genovesan by the feet and heaved him clear of the fire. As he reached for his feet, Bacari tried to kick out at him, but Will easily avoided the clumsy attempt. He lashed out in reply, the tip of his boot catching Bacari in the thigh, bringing another grunt of pain from the Genovesan.

"Stop it, Will!" Malcolm shouted. He could see that the situation was escalating. Will, exhausted physically and emotionally, wasn't thinking clearly. He was on the brink of making a terrible mistake.

As Malcolm had the thought, he saw the Ranger's hand drop to the hilt of his saxe knife. With his left hand, Will pulled the struggling assassin to his feet once more, holding him so that their faces were only centimeters apart. Now Bacari recognized that blind rage as well and realized that he had pushed the matter too far. This gray-cloaked stranger was quite capable of killing him. He had miscalculated badly. He had forced him into this killing fury.

But still, he realized that his only hope for survival lay in not telling them what they wanted to know. So long as he held the key to their friend's survival, they couldn't kill him.

He felt the tip of the saxe knife now against his throat. The face, so close to his, was distorted with grief and rage.

"Start remembering! White or blue? Which one? Tell us. TELL US!"

Then Bacari saw a large hand descend onto the Ranger's shoulder. Horace gently but firmly pulled Will back from the edge of the killing madness that had overcome him.

"Will! Take it easy! There's a better way."

Will turned, his eyes brimming now with tears of frustration and fear—fear for Halt, lying so silently, while this . . . this creature knew the secret that could save him.

"Horace?" he said, his voice breaking as he appealed to his friend for help. Will had done all he possibly could and it had come to nothing. Bone weary, totally exhausted, he had found the strength to trail this man for hour after hour. He had fought him, defeated him and captured him. He had brought him back here. And now Bacari sneered at them and refused to tell them which poison he had used. It was too much. Will could think of nothing further to do, no further avenue to explore.

But Horace could. He met his friend's desperate gaze and nodded reassuringly. Then, gently, he disengaged Will's hands from Bacari's jerkin. Dumbly, Will complied and stepped back. Then Horace smiled at Bacari. He turned him around and reached down to seize the cuff of his right sleeve in both hands. With a quick jerk, he tore the material for about fifteen centimeters, exposing the flesh of the man's inside forearm and the veins there.

Bacari, his hands still fastened behind his back, twisted desperately to see what Horace was doing. His face was contorted now in a worried frown. Horace wasn't raging or ranting at him. He was calm and controlled. That worried the Genovesan more than Will's shouting.

Horace reached for the quiver still hanging from Bacari's belt. There were four or five bolts left in it. He withdrew one and inspected the tip. The gummy substance that Malcolm had indicated before could be seen on the sharpened iron point of this bolt as well. Horace held the bolt before Bacari's eyes, letting him see the poison, so there could be no mistake.

At that moment, Bacari realized what Horace had in mind. He started to struggle desperately, trying to loosen his bonds. But the thumb cuffs held him fast, and Horace's grip on his right arm was like a vise. The young warrior put the razor-sharp tip of the bolt against Bacari's inner forearm, then deliberately pressed it into the flesh, penetrating deeply so that hot blood sprang from the wound and ran down Bacari's hands. Bacari screamed in pain and fear as

Horace dragged the sharpened iron through the flesh of his arm, opening a deep, long cut. Now, Bacari could feel the blood pumping out in a regular stream. Horace had found a vein with the bolt. That meant the poison would penetrate the Genovesan's bloodstream and system much faster than it had done via the glancing scratch on Halt's arm.

"No! No!" the assassin screamed, trying to break free. But he knew it was already too late. The poison was in him, already beginning to spread, and he knew what was in store. He had seen his victims die before, many times. He stopped struggling and his knees sagged, but Horace held him firmly, keeping him standing. The young warrior tossed the crossbow bolt aside and looked around at his two friends, seeing the shock on their faces as they realized what he had done. Then he saw the expression on Will's face change to one of satisfied approval.

Malcolm was a different matter. He was a healer, dedicated to saving life, and Horace's action went against all his basic principles. He could never bring himself to intentionally put a life in danger the way Horace had done.

"Malcolm," Horace was saying, "the more the victim moves about and exerts himself, the faster the poison will spread through his system. Is that right?"

Wordless, Malcolm nodded confirmation.

"Good," Horace said. He let go of Bacari's arm and tore the already ripped sleeve free. Then, working quickly, he wrapped it firmly around the bleeding wound in the Genovesan's arm.

"Can't have you bleeding to death before the poison kills you," he said. He finished tying the makeshift bandage and released his grip on the Genovesan. Bacari, horrified at what had happened to him, sank slowly to his knees, head bowed. He looked to Malcolm, saw his only possible source of survival, and pleaded with the healer.

"Please! I beg you! Don't let him do this."

Malcolm shrugged unhappily. The matter was out of his hands. Horace stooped swiftly and removed the ankle cuffs that secured Bacari. Then the assassin felt that powerful grip under his arm again as he was hauled to his feet.

"Up you come, my murdering friend. Can't have you sitting around all day. We're going to walk. We're going to run. We're going to get that poison just racing through you!"

And so saying, he began to propel Bacari before him, forcing the Genovesan into an awkward, shambling trot. They crossed the little copse, leaving the shelter of the trees. Horace pointed to the southern ridge.

"What do you say we go admire the view from up there?" he said. "Sound like a plan? Then let's go!"

With Horace holding the prisoner firmly by the elbow, they began to trot up the slope. Then he increased the pace so that they were running. Bacari slipped and fell half a dozen times, but on each occasion, Horace would drag him to his feet and get him running once more. Will and Malcolm could hear Horace's sarcastic exhortations as he drove Bacari to greater and greater efforts.

"Come on, my old Genovesan runner! Up you come!"

"On your feet, poison peddler!"

"Move it along! We have to keep that poison spreading!"

Gradually, the voice faded away as the two figures ran awkwardly up the slope, one half dragging the other. Malcolm met Will's eyes. Will could see the disapproval there.

"Can you stop him?" the healer asked.

Will looked coldly at him. "Perhaps I could. But why would I?"

Malcolm shook his head and turned away. Will moved to him and touched his shoulder, turning the healer back to face him again.

"Malcolm, I think I understand. I know you find it hard to condone this. But it has to be done."

The little man shook his head unhappily. "It goes against everything I've ever done and believed, Will. The idea of deliberately infecting a healthy body, of putting poison into it . . . it's just wrong for me!"

"Perhaps it is," Will conceded. "But it's Halt's only chance. You know that creature was never going to tell us which poison he used. No matter how much we threatened him, he didn't believe we'd follow through on the threats. And he was probably right. I couldn't put a knife to his throat and simply kill him if he refused to answer."

"So this is different?" Malcolm asked, and Will nodded.

"Of course it is. This way, the choice is up to him. If he tells us which poison he used, you can counteract it. You've said yourself the antidote will be effective almost immediately. This way, we're not killing him. We're here to save him. And if he dies, it will be his choice."

Malcolm lowered his eyes. There was a long silence between them.

"You're right," he said at length. "I don't like it, but I can see there is a difference. And it's necessary."

They heard the sound of thudding footsteps coming back down the hill, and then Horace led a white-faced, shuffling Bacari into the clearing among the trees. There was an unmistakable expression of grim satisfaction on Horace's face.

"Guess what?" he said. "Our friend has his memory back."

The poison was derived from the white aracoina. Bacari babbled the information to Malcolm, his eyes wide with fear. Malcolm nodded and hurried to fetch his medical kit. He rummaged inside it and produced half a dozen small containers of liquids and sacks of powder. Hastily, he began measuring and mixing, and within five minutes he had a thin yellow liquid prepared. He took the bowl containing the liquid and moved to Halt's side.

"No," Will said, gesturing to the bowl. "Not Halt. Give it to Bacari first."

At first, Malcolm was surprised by the statement. Then he saw the reasoning behind it. There was still the chance that the Genovesan had deceived them about the poison. If he saw that he was about to be given the wrong antidote, the antidote that could kill him, he would have to tell them. But the killer looked quickly at Will as he heard the words and stepped forward, trying to twist so that his wounded arm, still tied behind his back, was closer to the healer.

"Yes! Yes!" he said. "Give it to me now!"

Horace had been right. The fact that he had penetrated a vein with the poison meant that it was working far more quickly on the Genovesan than it had on Halt. Already, Bacari could feel the heat in his injured arm, the burning pain of the poison. And he could feel it moving up the arm as well. His pulse was starting to race—another side effect of the poison—and he knew that would force the venom around his system even more quickly.

Malcolm looked at him, glanced at Will and nodded. Halt was safe for the time being, and it would take only minutes to administer the antidote to Bacari. He gestured to the man's arm.

"Untie him, please, Will," he said. "I need to get at that arm."

Will reached behind the Genovesan and undid the thumb cuffs. As he did so, he dropped his hand warningly to the hilt of his saxe knife.

"Remember, we don't need you alive any longer. Be very careful in all your movements."

Bacari nodded and dropped eagerly beside where Malcolm was

kneeling. He stretched out his arm for treatment, gasping in alarm as Malcolm removed the bandage and he could see the banded, discolored flesh of his inside forearm. With the pressure of the constricting bandage removed, the arm was swollen badly. Malcolm took the injured arm, studied it for a moment, and then turned it so that the inner part faced upward. He had a small, very sharp blade in his free hand.

"I'm going to have to cut, you understand?" he said. "I'm cutting into a vein to administer the antidote."

"Yes! Yes!" the Genovesan said, his words stumbling over each other. "Cut the vein. I know this! Just hurry!"

Malcolm glanced up at him, then back down to the arm. Deftly he found a vein and cut into it with the small blade. Blood welled up immediately, and he nodded to a small square of linen that he had placed ready on the ground beside him.

"Wipe the blood away, please, Will."

Will dropped to his knees to do so. As he cleared the wound, and in the seconds he had before blood welled up again, Malcolm quickly inserted a thin hollow tube into the cut vein. There was a bell-shaped end to the tube and he poured some of the yellow liquid into it, watching it as it ran down the inside, tapping the tube until the liquid coalesced into a single mass, without air bubbles in it.

He continued to hold the tube upright until the liquid ran down to the end that was inserted in Bacari's arm. Then, leaning forward, he put his lips to the bell-shaped opening and blew gently, forcing the antidote into the man's vein, where the blood flow would distribute it around his system. Deftly, Malcolm placed a linen pad over the small incision he had made in the man's arm, then bound it firmly in place with a bandage.

Bacari's shoulders sagged in relief and he looked up at the healer, bowing his head several times in gratitude.

"Thank you. Thank you," he said.

Malcolm shook his head contemptuously. "I'm not doing it for you. I'm doing it because I can't stand by and watch another human being die." He looked at Will. "You can tie this animal up again if you like."

"I'll do that," Horace said, stepping forward and picking up the thumb cuffs from where Will had dropped them. "You give Malcolm a hand with Halt."

Malcolm started to demur. He didn't really need any help. Then he saw the anxious look on Will's face and knew he would feel better if he were doing something to speed his mentor's recovery. He nodded briefly.

"Good idea. Bring my kit, would you?"

Kneeling beside Halt, he cleaned the end of the thin tube with a colorless, strong-smelling liquid he took from his satchel. Then he took Halt's arm from under the blankets and removed the bandage, exposing the sight of the shallow wound. He used more of the pungent liquid to clean his small blade, then went to work administering the antidote to Halt. Throughout the process, there was no sound or reaction from the Ranger, even when the blade cut into his arm. Will noticed that Malcolm used considerably more of the antidote liquid than he had used on Bacari.

"Poison's been in him longer than in Bacari," Malcolm said, sensing his curiosity. "He'll need more of the antidote." When he was done, Malcolm bandaged Halt's arm again. He looked up at Will, saw the anxiety in the young man's eyes and smiled reassuringly.

"He'll be fine in a few hours," he said. "All I have to do now is give him something to bring him awake again. The faster his system is working, the sooner the antidote will take effect."

He prepared another compound and poured a little between Halt's lips. As the liquid trickled back into his throat, Halt swallowed reflexively and Malcolm nodded approval. He cleaned his in-strument and rose to his feet, groaning slightly with the effort.

"I'm getting too old for this outdoor lark," he said. "I need a camp with a few armchairs around the fire."

Will hadn't moved. He was still on his knees beside Halt, leaning forward slightly, his eyes fixed on the bearded Ranger's face, looking for any sign of recovery. Malcolm touched his shoulder gently.

"Come on, Will," he said. "It'll be a few hours before there's any improvement. For now, you need food and rest. I don't want Halt to recover only to find you've collapsed."

Reluctantly, Will stood and followed Malcolm. Now that the healer mentioned it, he was ravenous, he realized. And bone tired. His Ranger training told him that it was always wise to rest and re-cuperate when the chance arose. But there was one task left to be done, he realized.

"Malcolm," he called, and the little healer turned, his eyebrows raised in a question. Before he could say anything, Will continued. "Thank you. Thank you so much."

Malcolm grinned and made a dismissing gesture with his hand. "It's what I do."

40

BACARI MADE HIS MOVE SHORTLY BEFORE DAWN. HE KNEW IT
as the time when people's spirits were at their lowest ebb—when a
sentry would become drowsy and careless. The first hint of gray in
the eastern sky, the first sign of the predawn light signaling the im-
pending end of the dark hours, would give a false sense of relaxation
and security. When the light came, the hours of danger were over.

That was the way people's minds worked—even trained warriors like the tall, broad-shouldered one who was now on watch.

The assassin had listened carefully as Malcolm and Horace had
discussed their security arrangements for the night.

"We'll take alternate watches," Horace had said. "Will's exhausted
and he needs a proper night's rest to get his strength back."

The healer had agreed immediately. Will had been under immense strain—both physically and emotionally—and he could use
a full night's sleep without interruption. Worn out as he was, he had
refused to go to sleep before he saw signs that Halt was recovering.
Halt's breathing had become deep and even, and there was color
back in his face instead of the gray pallor that they had seen in the
past few days. And his arm, when Malcolm inspected it, was almost
back to normal. There was no swelling, and none of the ominous-

looking discoloration that had surrounded the graze. The wound itself was almost healed over now as well.

Bacari lay, apparently sleeping, watching through slitted eyes as the night wore on. He could feel his own strength returning as the antidote counteracted the poison in his body. In the small hours of the morning, Malcolm woke Horace to take the last watch. Bacari waited an hour as the young warrior sat hunched, a little way from the campfire. From time to time, he heard him stifle a yawn. Horace was weary as well. The past few days hadn't exactly been a rest cure for him, and he'd gone without a lot of sleep. Now, in his second spell of guard duty for the night, it was beginning to catch up with him. He shifted position and breathed deeply. Then he blinked rapidly, clearing his eyes, forcing them wide open.

Within a few minutes, his shoulders had sagged and his eyelids began to droop again. He stood up and patrolled around the camp for some minutes, then returned to sit again.

Eventually, inevitably, he began to doze. He wasn't fully asleep and any small noise would rouse him instantly. But Bacari made no noise at all.

Horace had refastened his thumb and ankle cuffs after Malcolm had administered the antidote. Slowly, carefully, Bacari stretched his bound hands down behind his back until he was touching the heel of his drawn-up right boot. He twisted the heel and there was a faint click as a small sharp blade shot out of a recess there. Gently, he began to saw the rawhide thong between the two cuffs up and down along the razor edge. The blade was short and several times the rawhide slipped away from it. Once, he gritted his teeth as he accidentally cut himself. But after half a minute's silent, steady work, the thong parted and his hands were free.

He waited several minutes before his next move, making sure that he had made no sound or movement to alert Horace. But the broad-shouldered figure remained still, head hunched forward and shoulders rising rhythmically with his breathing.

Bacari brought his hands around to the front and drew his knees up under his chin so that he could reach the ankle cuffs that bound him. He felt around in the dark until he found the release knot and twisted it. Instantly, the pressure on his ankles faded as the two loops widened. He slipped the twin loops over his feet and then carefully stripped the severed cuffs from his wrists as well. Now he was free.

But still he waited, allowing circulation to return to his limbs, mentally rehearsing his next sequence of actions.

He would kill Horace first. He had the means at his disposal. Then he would take the warrior's dagger—Bacari was no hand with a sword—and hamstring the two smaller horses. He would mount the larger horse and make his escape.

Later, at a time of his choosing, he would return to finish off the other two. Or not. Bacari was a pragmatist. He would enjoy having revenge on Will and Malcolm, but if, by doing so, he would disadvantage or endanger himself, he would forgo the pleasure. He was, after all, a professional, and there was no profit in simply killing them for the sake of a little revenge. On the other hand, if Tennyson were willing to offer a bonus of some kind . . .

While he had been turning this over in his mind, he had been preparing for his attack on Horace. His cloak was fastened at the neck by a drawstring. Carefully, he undid the knot at one end and slipped it out of the sewn fold that it was threaded through. The drawstring was in reality a thin cord, and it measured some fifty centimeters in length. He wound the cord around each of his hands several times, leaving a long loop between them. Then, catlike, he rose into a crouch and stole across the campsite toward the dozing figure of Horace.

Horace came awake in panic as he felt something whip over his

head and then tighten inexorably around his throat, dragging him
back away from the fire, cutting off his air and strangling any attempt
he made to call out. He felt a knee in his back as Bacari used it to
gain extra purchase, straining backward on the garrote and pulling
Horace's head back so that he was off balance and unable to struggle
effectively.

Too late, Horace realized what was happening and tried to force
his fingers under the cord, between it and his neck. But it was already
biting too deep and set too securely, and there was no way he could
relieve the dreadful pressure.

He looked desperately at the three sleeping figures around the
campfire. Will was exhausted, he knew. There was little chance that
he would hear any sound. Malcolm wasn't attuned to this sort of life.
He couldn't expect help from that quarter either. And Halt, of
course, was still sleeping off the effects of the poison.

Even the horses were too far away to notice anything amiss. They
had wandered farther into the copse of trees, looking for grass. Besides, Ranger horses were trained to warn of danger and movement
coming from without, not within.

He tried to call out but could manage only a small awkward
croak. The minute he did so, the noose around his neck tightened
even further and he started to black out as his body and brain were
starved of oxygen.

His struggles, already ineffectual, weakened further, and as Bacari
felt it happen, he increased his pressure. Horace felt he was looking
down a long tunnel now. He could see the campsite as if he were
looking through a circular hole, where the outer edges were black
and impenetrable. His lungs cried out for air and he plucked feebly
at the cord around his neck. Too late, he thought to thrash out with
his legs to make some sort of noise. But he was too weak to accomplish anything more than a feeble movement.

Horrified, he realized he was dying. The horror was mixed with a senseless fury as he realized it was Bacari who would kill him. It was galling to think that the assassin would triumph over him after all.

"Will!"

The shout rang through the trees. For a moment, Bacari was taken by surprise and the pressure on Horace's windpipe relaxed. Horace gasped and shuddered, managing to drag in one short breath before the noose tightened again. Who had called? It was a familiar voice. He tried to place it, then, as he blacked out, he realized who it had been.

It was Halt.

Years of training and experience had asserted themselves with Halt. Something had alerted him. Some slight noise, perhaps. Or maybe it was something less definable: some sixth sense of danger, developed over the years, that sent a warning to his brain that all was not well. He raised himself on one elbow and saw the dim figures struggling, just outside the circle of firelight. He tried to stand, realized he was too weak to help and forced all his remaining strength into one agonized shout to his apprentice.

Then fell back, defeated by the effort.

Exhausted, depleted, even in the deepest sleep, Will's own training came to the fore. The call penetrated through the fog of sleep, and before he was fully awake, he rolled out of the blankets, springing to his feet, his saxe knife sliding free of the scabbard at his side.

He too saw the figures on the ground, and he started toward them. But now Bacari released his grip on the garrote and shoved Horace's limp body aside, reaching down to pluck the broad-bladed dagger from Horace's scabbard as he did so.

Dagger forward, held low in a classic knife-fighter's stance, he moved toward Will. He assessed the situation quickly. Malcolm was no danger. So far, the healer hadn't even stirred. Horace was dead or unconscious, Bacari wasn't sure which. But either way, he would take no hand in this fight.

There was only Will, facing him with that large knife he wore at his side. Whereas Bacari was armed with Horace's broad-bladed dagger. The Genovesan smiled. He was an expert knife fighter. Will's weapon might be a little longer, but the Genovesan could see from his stance that the Ranger was no expert at knife fighting, and his knife skills would be no match for Bacari's own lightning sweeps, thrusts and reverse slashes—techniques that he had practiced for years and perfected in the cutthroat, crowded towns of Genovese.

He shuffled forward, watching the Ranger's eyes. There was a light of uncertainty in them. Roused suddenly from sleep, Will was still slightly confused and unready for combat. His system would be flooding with adrenaline, his pulse racing. This was why Bacari had waited, breathing deeply, before he had launched his attack on Horace. He wanted to make sure that he was ready. That his nerves were settled and his reactions sharp.

Will, for his part, backed away. He saw the confidence in Bacari's eyes and realized he was facing an expert. The assassin had trained and practiced with the dagger for years, just as Will had trained with the bow. And he knew his own limitations in this sort of fight.

The thought remained unfinished as Bacari suddenly slid forward with amazing speed. He feinted high with the dagger, and as Will went to parry the knife, he flicked it to his other hand and slashed low, opening a tear in Will's jacket, just scraping the skin as Will leapt desperately back out of reach.

Will felt warm blood trickling down his ribs. His reactions and speed had saved him that time. Just.

But the switch of hands had nearly caught him. Bacari was in-credibly fast. It was like trying to parry a striking snake with his saxe—a snake that could switch direction in a heartbeat. He could try a throw, of course. But he had seen the Genovesan's speed and knew he would probably be able to avoid a thrown saxe knife.

Bacari slid forward again, this time slashing with the knife in his left hand, and again Will was forced to leap back to avoid him. The movement gave Bacari time to switch back to his right hand and he attacked once more, thrusting first, then describing a bewildering series of high and low slashes and thrusts, lightning fast and per-fectly controlled, so that he never left himself exposed to a return strike from Will.

Will remembered the last time he had faced this man, on the grassland, knowing that he couldn't afford to kill him. Then as that thought came, a strange sense of resolve followed it.

Bacari was before him now, on the balls of his feet, poised and ready to strike again. He began a dazzling succession of movements, switching the knife from one hand to the other, tossing and catching it like a juggler, forcing Will's attention to switch constantly from left to right, distracting him from the moment when the final attack would come.

Will switched the saxe to his left hand. The moment he did, Bacari tossed the dagger back to his right. And laughed.

"You're not very good at this," he said.

"I used to watch a man who—" Will began, and then, without warning or hesitating in his speech, he threw the saxe left-handed, an underarm spinning throw.

It was an old trick Halt had taught him years ago. *When you're overmatched, deception and distraction are your best friends. Begin to speak. Say anything. Your opponent will expect you to finish the statement, but act before you do. Chances are, you'll catch him napping.*

But Bacari knew the trick too. He had used it himself, many times. And now he simply stepped to one side and the saxe went spinning past him. He laughed.

He was still laughing when Will's throwing knife, drawn and thrown the moment the saxe had left his hand, buried itself in his heart. He looked down and saw it for a fraction of a second before his sight went black and his legs collapsed underneath him.

"I don't need you alive anymore," Will said coldly.

41

THE SMALL RED DEER BENT ITS HEAD TO THE GRASS TO EAT. Then some instinct warned it and the head came up again, the large ears twitching to catch any faint sound, the nose quivering for any scent of danger. Its senses told it that danger lay to the left, downwind, and it began to turn its head in that direction.

It was the last move it would make. The arrow came out of nowhere, hissing through the air and burying its razor-sharp broad head in the animal's heart. With a low grunt of surprise, it tried to gather its hind legs under it to spring away. But there was no strength left in them, and the little animal buckled to the grass.

Will rose from concealment, pushing back the cowl of his cloak. After so long on the road, they were short of food. The deer would give them fresh meat and strips to dry over the fire as well. He felt a faint sense of regret at having to kill the beautiful animal, but knew it was necessary.

Quickly, he field-dressed the deer where it lay. He whistled and Tug appeared from a clump of trees a hundred meters away, trotting toward him. He looked at the deer, which they had been stalking for more than two hours.

It's not very big. Is that the best you could do?

"No sense killing more meat than we need," Will told him. But he could see the little horse was unconvinced. He tied the deer's carcass behind the saddle and mounted up for the ride back to their camp in the trees.

Two days had passed since his final confrontation with Bacari. In that time, he had been amazed by the speed of Halt's recovery. The gray-bearded Ranger was still weak, of course. That was a result of the aftereffects of the strain the poison had placed upon his body and the fact that for several days he had eaten little but a few mouthfuls of broth.

But the fever, the disorientation, the morbid swelling and discoloration of his arm were all long gone. He was his old self again, and chafing to be back on the road.

In this matter, Malcolm had objected.

"You need rest. Complete rest for at least four days. Otherwise, you're likely to have a relapse," he told Halt in a firm tone that brooked no argument.

Of course, Will knew, Halt would have argued in any other situation, regardless of Malcolm's tone of voice. But he seemed to be deferring to Malcolm's judgment, at least for the time being.

There was another problem that had been weighing on Will's mind. He felt he should escort Malcolm back to Grimsdell. The healer's work was finished here, and Will knew he had other responsibilities back in the dark forest that he called home. The road to Macindaw was an uncertain one, through wild, potentially dangerous territory, and Will felt an obligation to see Malcolm safely home. After all, he thought, the little healer had no weapons skills and his field craft was virtually nonexistent. But to do so would only delay their pursuit of Tennyson even longer.

It was Malcolm who solved the problem when Will had tentatively raised the subject with him.

"I'm coming with you," he said simply.

That possibility hadn't occurred to Will. He stopped, a little surprised. Then he saw several problems with the idea.

"But Malcolm, it's going to be dangerous . . ."

The healer's lip curled. "Oh deary, deary me," he said in a high-pitched, exaggerated voice. "I'm so frightened. Perhaps I should throw my apron over my head and burst into tears."

Will made a placating gesture, realizing that his remark had been taken as insulting.

"That's not what I meant," he began, and Malcolm seized on his words.

"Oh? So you mean it's *not* going to be dangerous? Then there's no problem if I come along, is there?"

"No. I meant . . . I mean, I'm not questioning your courage . . ."

"I'm glad to hear it," Malcolm said coldly. "Exactly what *are* you questioning then?"

"Look, it's just . . ." Will paused, aware that he should choose his words carefully. He hadn't seen this acerbic side of Malcolm's nature before. He didn't want to make him angry again. Malcolm gestured for him to continue. "I mean, we'll probably have to fight them, and you're not . . ." Malcolm's brows drew together. Will had always thought of the little man as birdlike. Now, with those drawn brows, balding head and beaked nose, he looked positively vulturine.

"What, precisely, am I not?" he asked. Will was beginning to wish he had never begun this conversation, but it was too late now to go back.

"I mean to say . . . you're not a warrior, are you?" It was weak, he knew. But Malcolm could hardly dispute the fact.

"So you're worried that I'll be a burden to you?" Malcolm asked. "You'll have to look after me when the fighting starts?"

"No!" Will said. But he said it too quickly. In fact, that was exactly what he was worried about. Malcolm said nothing for a few seconds, simply raising one eyebrow in disbelief. Will found himself wishing that people would stop using that facial expression. It was becoming overdone.

"May I remind you," Malcolm said finally, "that I have been known to reduce a big, brave, famous Ranger to a state of near-gibbering terror?"

"Well, that's a bit rich," Will said hotly. "I certainly wasn't gibbering!"

"You weren't far from it," Malcolm pointed out, and Will's mind flashed back to that night in Grimsdell Wood, where voices spoke to him out of the dark, threatening and warning him. And where a gigantic figure suddenly towered over him in the mist. He had to admit Malcolm was right. He hadn't been far from it.

"Look, Will," Malcolm continued, in a more conciliatory tone, "I'm not a warrior, that's true. But I've survived in a hostile world for quite a few years. I have methods of my own. And there's another point. There's Halt."

He saw that got Will's attention. The young Ranger's head came up, a worried look on his face, as if he suddenly feared that Malcolm had been hiding something about Halt's condition.

"Halt? What about him? He's all right now, isn't he?"

Malcolm raised his hand to allay Will's concern.

"He's fine. He's doing very well. But he is weak still. And from what I've seen of him, he's going to want to start out after this Tennyson person much sooner than he should. Am I right?"

Will hesitated. He didn't want to be disloyal to Halt, but he sensed that Malcolm was spot-on.

"Yes. Probably," he admitted.

Malcolm nodded several times. "Just so. Well, he's a patient of mine. And I feel a sense of responsibility to him. I'm not going to ride off and let him undo all my good work. I need to be with you to keep an eye on him."

Will considered what he had said for some time. The more he thought about it, the more it made sense. Finally, he nodded.

"All right," he said. Then he smiled. "I'll be glad to have you along."

Malcolm smiled in return. "I promise you, Will, I can look after myself. And who knows? I might even surprise you and make myself useful."

For the past few days, when he wasn't checking on Halt, Malcolm had taken himself away from the campsite and built a small fire. He busied himself mixing and boiling potions and drying them out in the sun and over hot rocks to form a brownish powdery residue. As he worked, an acrid smell rose from the chemicals. Whenever Will asked him what he was doing, the little man had smiled enigmatically.

"Just making myself useful, that's all," he would reply.

From time to time, the others would be startled by the sound of small explosions from the fireplace where Malcolm worked. The first time this happened, they rushed to see if he was all right. He waved them away cheerfully.

"Nothing to worry about," he said to them. "I'm just working with a new compound based on iodine powder. It's a little volatile and I have to get the mixture just right."

Eventually, they had become used to these interruptions in their day, and the explosions grew less and less frequent as Malcolm apparently refined his formula.

Now, riding back to the camp, Will heard a more familiar sound and he frowned slightly.

It was the deep-throated *thrum* of a powerful longbow being released. And not just any longbow. He followed the sound, diverting slightly from the path to the copse of trees where they had sited their camp. Again he heard the thrumming sound, followed a few seconds later by a solid SMACK!

There was a slight depression in the ground, lined by alder trees, and the sound seemed to be coming from that direction. He rode toward it and, as he crested the slight rise above the depression, saw Halt. He had his massive longbow in his hand, and as Will watched, he nocked an arrow, drew and released almost immediately, without even seeming to take aim. Will followed the black streak of the arrow through the air and heard it smack into a small pine log, standing upright, about eighty meters away. There were three other arrows jutting from the soft wood, grouped so closely together that a man's hand could have covered them all.

"You're dropping the bow hand as you release," he called, although Halt certainly wasn't.

His mentor looked around, saw him and replied pithily, "I believe your grandmother needs lessons in sucking eggs."

He turned back to his practice and dispatched another three arrows in the blink of an eye, all of them thudding into that same small section of pine log.

"Not bad," Will was forced to concede.

Halt raised an eyebrow. "Not bad? You should do so well." He gestured at the deer slung behind Tug's saddle. "Been hunting?"

Will nodded. "We need meat."

Halt snorted softly. "Won't get much off that. Couldn't you find something bigger? It's barely the size of a large squirrel."

Will frowned and glanced back at the carcass behind him.

"It's big enough," he said. "Why shoot anything bigger?"

Halt considered that, leaning on his bow and nodding several times. Then he asked, "Did you see anything bigger?"

"Well, no. I didn't," Will admitted. "But there's plenty of meat here for four people."

Halt smiled. "Three people and Horace?"

Will pursed his lips thoughtfully. Halt had a definite point, he realized. "I hadn't thought of that." And, of course, Tug chose that moment to toss his head and shake his mane. *I told you so.*

Everyone seemed to be conspiring to belittle his efforts, so he decided to change the subject. He nodded toward the pine log, now bristling with arrows.

"Any reason for all this practice?" he asked.

Halt shrugged. "Wanted to make sure I had the strength to draw my bow," he said. "Apparently, I do."

Halt's bow was one of the heaviest Will had seen. Years of practice had built up the bearded Ranger's arm and back muscles to the point where he could draw it without any seeming effort. Yet Will had seen strong men who, lacking the correct technique and specific muscle development, were unable to bring it past half draw. Seeing the speed and accuracy with which Halt had been sending his shafts thudding into the log, Will realized that Halt was right. His strength was back.

"Are we moving out?" he asked.

Halt nodded. "Tomorrow at first light. Time we saw what Tennyson is up to."

"Malcolm thinks you need another two days' rest," Will said.

Halt's eyebrows lowered into a glare. He and Malcolm had already had words on this matter. In fact, it was the reason why Halt had come out here to test himself. He had been worried that perhaps Malcolm was right.

"Malcolm doesn't know everything," he said shortly.

Will couldn't help grinning. "And you do?"

"Of course I do," Halt replied. "That's a well-known fact."

42

Tennyson looked around the campsite and nodded contentedly. For several days, converts to the Outsiders cult had been coming into the camp. Now that they were gathered, he was ready to move in and whip them into a state of religious frenzy so that they would be willing to hand over their gold and valuables to him—just as they had done in Hibernia. It was a task in which he excelled.

The numbers were smaller here, of course. But they would be enough to provide him with enough booty for a fresh start somewhere else. Hibernia and Araluen were becoming increasingly dangerous for him, and he planned to escape to a new location. He hadn't told his followers that he was planning to take the valuables they collected and abscond with them. They all assumed that he would begin rebuilding the Outsiders cult here in northern Araluen. And he was content to let them continue thinking that. He felt no loyalty toward the people who followed him.

As he had that thought, he frowned, wondering what had become of the Genovesan Bacari. It had been days now since the mercenary had reported in. He knew that the leader of his pursuers had been fatally injured in the confrontation in the drowned forest. Bacari had seen him wounded by a poisoned bolt, and he was definite in his assurances that there was no way the cloaked stranger could survive that wound. That was good news. The other two were little more than boys, and Tennyson was confident that without their leader, they would soon become discouraged, give up on the pursuit and return to wherever it was they had come from. The fact that there had been no sign of them for the past few days seemed to confirm the idea. He knew they had been close on his heels for weeks. Now they had simply disappeared.

Perhaps Bacari had killed them—and been killed himself in a final confrontation with them. That was a possibility. More likely, he thought, the Genovesan had simply slipped away and left the country. After all, he had seen two of his compatriots killed, and mercenaries like him had only one loyalty—to money. It was unlikely that he would continue to fight for Tennyson when he knew he was outnumbered and outmatched. But he had served his purpose. He had killed the leader of Tennyson's pursuers and, one way or another, caused the other two to abandon their pursuit. And this way, there was no need for Tennyson to pay him the final installment of the fee he had been promised.

All in all, he thought, it had turned out well. The last of the local converts had arrived at the camp that morning. Tomorrow, he would break camp here and move them to the cave complex that had been picked out for the purpose. He would inflame them and excite them, as he had done with so many simple country folk before, and persuade them to contribute their gold and jewels to build another altar to Alseiass. Then, when the time was right, he would quietly slip away with it.

With the last of the Genovesans dead, Halt expressed his doubt that Tennyson would send anyone else back to spy on them or monitor their progress. In fact, he hoped that the preacher would assume they had given up the chase.

"After all," he told them while they were preparing to leave the campsite, "Bacari will have told him that he hit me with a poisoned bolt. And since Tennyson knows nothing about Malcolm here, he probably thinks that I'm dead."

"Horace and I could still be following him," Will pointed out.

Halt looked doubtful. "Possibly. But he knows you're both young. And he doesn't know you as well as I do. Chances are, he will have seen me as the real threat."

"I don't know whether to be insulted by that or not," Horace said. Halt grinned easily at him.

"As I said, he doesn't know you as well as I do. He's an arrogant man and he'll probably think you're too young to offer any threat to him. But just in case," he said, looking at Will, "you'd better take the point."

Will nodded. It was never wise to assume too much. He touched Tug's ribs with his heels and galloped ahead to scout the way. He reined in when he was about four hundred meters ahead, and maintained that distance.

Malcolm, who was riding double with Horace, watched the distant figure as he scouted the land ahead of them, quartering back and forth to make sure there was no one waiting in ambush on either side of the trail they were following. Will reminded the healer of a hound, questing for a scent.

"He's a remarkable young man," he said to Halt, and he saw the small glow of pride in the bearded Ranger's eyes as he turned in his saddle to reply.

"The best," he said briefly.

"You've known him how long?" Malcolm asked.

"Since he was a small boy. I first noticed him when he slipped into Master Chubb's kitchen to steal some pies."

"Master Chubb?" Malcolm asked.

Halt grinned at the memory of that day. "He's the chef at Castle Redmont. A formidable man, wouldn't you say, Horace?"

Horace grinned in his turn. "He's deadly with his wooden ladle," he said. "Fast and accurate. And very painful. I once suggested that he give ladle-whacking lessons to Battleschool students."

"You were joking, of course?" Malcolm said.

Horace looked thoughtful before he replied. "You know, not entirely."

"So," Malcolm said, turning back to Halt, "what did you have to say to Will when you caught him stealing these pies—and apparently risking life and limb to do so?"

"Oh, I didn't let on that I was there. We Rangers can be very unobtrusive when we choose," he said with mock modesty. "I remained out of sight and watched him. I thought then that he had potential to be a Ranger."

Malcolm nodded. But an anomaly in the sequence of the story had Horace frowning thoughtfully.

"Why?" he asked Halt.

Halt looked quickly at him. Something in Horace's tone set off alarms in his mind. Horace lately had a tendency to ask awkward questions, he thought. He answered carefully.

"Why? Because he was excellent at moving from cover to cover and remaining unseen. Chubb came into the room three times and never noticed him. So I thought, if he could manage that without formal training, he'd make a good Ranger."

"No," said Horace deliberately, "that wasn't what I meant. I meant, why did you remain unseen? Why were you hiding in the kitchen in the first place?"

"I *told* you," Halt said with an edge to his voice, "I was watching Will to see if he might have the potential to be a Ranger. So I didn't want him to see that I was watching."

"That's not what you said," Horace replied. A little furrow had formed between his eyebrows.

"Yes. It is." Halt's answers were becoming shorter and shorter. Malcolm leaned back behind Horace's broad form to hide a smile. Halt's tone indicated that he no longer wanted to discuss this matter. But Horace wasn't inclined to give up.

"No. You said, when Malcolm asked, that this was the *first time* you'd noticed Will. So you couldn't have gone to the kitchen to see what he was going to get up to. You hadn't noticed him before that day. That's what you said," he added, driving his point home.

"That's true. You did say that," Malcolm chipped in helpfully, and was rewarded with a glare from Halt.

"Does it matter?" Halt asked.

Horace shrugged. "Not really, I suppose. I just wondered why you'd gone to the kitchen and why you took the trouble to remain unseen. Were you hiding from Master Chubb yourself? And Will just turned up by coincidence?"

"And why would I be hiding from Master Chubb in his own kitchen?" Halt challenged. Again, Horace shrugged innocently.

"Well, there was a tray of freshly made pies airing on the windowsill, wasn't there? And you're quite fond of pies, aren't you, Halt?"

Halt drew himself up very straight in the saddle. "Are you accusing me of sneaking into that kitchen to steal the pies for myself? Is that it?"

His voice and body language simply reeked of injured dignity.

"Of course not, Halt!" Horace hurried to assure him, and Halt's stiff-shouldered form relaxed a little.

"I just thought I'd give you the opportunity to confess," Horace added. This time, Malcolm couldn't conceal his sudden explosion of laughter. Halt gave them both a withering glance.

"You know, Horace," he said at length, "you used to be a most agreeable young man. Whatever happened to you?"

Horace turned a wide grin on him. "I've spent too much time around you, I suppose," he said.

And Halt had to admit that was probably true.

Later that day, they reached the spot where Will had fought with Bacari. Will signaled for them to stop before they crested the final ridge, then he and Halt crept forward to survey the ground ahead.

The campsite that he had seen previously was now deserted.

"They've moved on," Will said, and Halt rested his weight on his elbows, chewing a blade of grass thoughtfully.

"Wherever it is they're going," he agreed. "How many would you say there were?"

Will considered his answer for a few seconds before replying.

"It was quite a big camp," he said. "I'd say up to a hundred people."

They rose and walked back down the slight slope to where Horace and Malcolm were preparing a quick meal of cold meat, fruit and bread.

"Is there time to make coffee?" Horace asked.

Halt nodded. "There's *always* time for coffee." He sat down by the small fire that Horace had built and glanced at Malcolm. He liked the healer and knew he had a good, analytical head on his shoulders.

"Tennyson's party has joined up with a larger group," he said. "What would you make of that?"

Malcolm paused thoughtfully. "From what you've told me about his methods, I'd say the bulk of them are probably converts to his 'religion'—people who've been living in this area."

"That's what I thought. He usually has twenty or so in his inner circle—the ones who know the whole religion is a fake. They run things for him. They collect the money. But the bulk of his followers are gullible country folk who actually believe his brand of nonsense."

"But where would they have come from, Halt?" Horace asked. "I thought you and Crowley destroyed the Outsiders movement in Araluen."

Halt shook his head. "We did our best. We got rid of the hierarchy. But you can never stamp these cults out entirely. They'll move into remote areas like this and recruit the locals. He's probably had agents in this area for the past six months or so—just the way he was doing in Selsey."

"And it would have been a simple matter to send a messenger ahead to arrange that rendezvous point in the valley," Will put in.

"Exactly. And now he's gathering his people together for another push. They'll keep recruiting, and then when they have the numbers, they'll move on to the next area—just as they did in Hibernia." Halt shook his head angrily. "They're like vermin! You stamp them out in one place and they rise up again in another."

Malcolm nodded. "It's interesting, isn't it, how people are so ready to believe these charlatans? You realize you'll have to do more than just stamp this group out, don't you?"

Halt looked up at him. He had a good idea what the balding little healer was talking about.

"How's that?" he asked.

Malcolm pursed his lips and leaned forward, idly poking a stick into the glowing coals of the fire.

"If people believe in him, if they've accepted the line of claptrap he's peddling, it won't be enough to take him prisoner and put him on trial. Or even kill him, if that's what you had in mind."

Halt nodded wearily. "I know," he said. "A public trial would give him the forum he needs. And if he dies, he'll become a martyr. Either way, another person will step up to take his place and build on the doubt and uncertainty that he's raised in people's minds. It'll be one long repeating cycle."

"Exactly," Malcolm agreed. "So there's only one course for you to follow. You have to discredit him. You have to prove to these followers of his that he is a cheat and a liar and a thief."

"We managed to do it in Clonmel," Horace said.

"We caught him unawares there, with the legend of the Sunrise Warrior. And we tricked him into pinning everything on trial by combat. He won't fall for that again. This time, we'll have to do something new. Something he's not expecting."

"Like what?" Will asked, and Halt gave that tired smile again.

"When I think of it, you'll be the first to know."

43

THE ABANDONED CAMP TOLD THEM LITTLE THAT THEY DIDN'T already know. They walked through the areas of flattened grass where tents had been pitched, inspected the blackened circles left by a score of small cook fires and examined the small items that had been discarded or forgotten—a shoe here with a broken strap and holes in the underside that were past repairing, a rusted cook pot, a broken knife. And, of course, food scraps and garbage that had been hastily buried and dug up once more by foxes after the people had left.

"A hundred people is rather a large handful for the four of us to take on," Malcolm pointed out. "Do you have any ideas about how we're going to handle that task?"

"Simple," Halt told him. "We'll surround them."

And he said it with such a straight face that, for a moment, Malcolm actually thought he was serious.

There was one item of interest to be found, and that was the direction Tennyson and his newly augmented band of followers had taken when they broke camp and departed. After several weeks of traveling consistently to the southeast, Tennyson now swung to the left, heading due east. The small party gathered around Halt as he unfolded his chart of the area. He indicated a range of hills marked on the map, a day's journey away.

"Looks as if he's heading for these hills—as we thought."

Horace, craning to read the map over his shoulder, read the notation on the map where Halt was pointing. "Caves," he said.

Halt looked up and nodded. "Those old sandstone cliffs and hills will be honeycombed with them, according to what it says here. I'd wager this is Tennyson's destination."

"Yes," Malcolm agreed. "If he's planning to set up a headquarters and add to his band of followers, a nice cave complex would be as good a place as any."

"Well, standing here isn't going to get us any closer to him," Halt said. "We've given him too much of a lead already."

He strode back to where Abelard waited for him and mounted quickly. Then he sat impatiently while the others followed his example. Will noticed him fidgeting with his reins as he watched Malcolm make two unsuccessful attempts to mount behind Horace.

"For god's sake, Horace," Halt finally cried out. "Can't you just haul him up behind you?"

"Take it easy," Will said softly.

Halt looked at him quickly, then gave him a shamefaced smile. "Sorry," he said. "It's just that after all these delays, I'm anxious to catch up with him."

But it was that very eagerness to close with Tennyson that eventually let him down. Halt was pushing himself too hard under normal circumstances. He would have had no trouble keeping up to the pace he was setting, but he wasn't fully recovered from the effects of the poison, or the days lying close to death in his blankets.

That evening, when they camped, he slid from the saddle and stood, head bowed and exhausted. When Will went to unsaddle and water Abelard, Halt offered only token resistance.

Will and Horace took care of the minor chores, gathering fire-wood, building the fire and preparing the meal. Horace even set out Halt's bedroll and blankets for him, laying them out on a small pile of leafy branches that he gathered together. Halt reacted with surprise when he saw it.

"Thanks, Horace," he said, touched by the young warrior's concern for him.

Horace shrugged. "Think nothing of it."

They noticed that when the meal was done, and after the obligatory cups of coffee, Halt didn't linger around the campfire talking, as he usually did. He took himself off to his bedroll and slept soundly.

"The sleep of the exhausted," Malcolm said wryly, eyeing the still figure.

"Is he all right?" Will asked anxiously.

"He's fine, so far as the poison is concerned. But he's working himself too hard. He doesn't have the strength to keep this pace up. See if you can get him to ease up a little." He knew that if the suggestion came from Will, there was more chance that Halt might take heed. Will wasn't so sure.

"I'll try," he said.

But the following morning, refreshed by a long night's sleep, Halt wasn't in any mood to take things easily. He fussed and fretted while they had breakfast and packed up their camp. Then he mounted Abelard and set out at a brisk pace.

By eleven that morning, he was swaying in the saddle, his face gray with fatigue, his shoulders slumped. Will rode up beside him, leaned over and seized Abelard's reins, bringing the little horse to a stop. Halt shook himself out of the exhausted daze that had claimed him and looked around in surprise.

"What are you doing?" he asked. "Let go!" He tried to pull the reins out of Will's grip, but the young Ranger held firm. Abelard neighed in consternation, sensing that all wasn't well with his master.

"Halt, you have to slow down," Will told him.

"Slow down? Don't talk such nonsense! I'm fine. Now give me back those reins." Halt tried again to pull them from Will's grasp but realized with some surprise that he couldn't break his former apprentice's grip. Abelard, sensing the tension between them, neighed nervously. Then he shook his mane and turned his head so that he could look Halt in the eye. That was something else that surprised Halt. Normally, if someone had grabbed hold of his reins, Abelard would have reacted violently against them. Instead, in this confrontation, he seemed to be taking Will's side.

That, more than anything else, made Halt feel that perhaps Will was right. Perhaps he hadn't recovered as fully as he thought. Time was that he would have shaken off the effects of the poisoning in a matter of a few hours. But maybe that period was behind him. For the first time, Halt had a sense of his own limitations.

At Malcolm's urging, Horace brought Kicker up alongside Abelard, on the other side of Tug and Will.

"He's right," he said. "You're pushing too hard. If you keep this up, you'll have a relapse."

"And that will lose more time than if you simply take a little time to recover now," Malcolm put in. Halt glared from one to the other.

"What is this?" he asked. "Are you all conspiring against me? Even my horse?"

It was the last three words that made Will smile. "We figured you mightn't listen to a healer, a Ranger or a knight of the realm," he said. "But if your horse agreed with them, you'd have no choice but to pay attention."

In spite of himself, Halt couldn't suppress the faintest hint of a smile. He tried to hide it, but the corners of his mouth twitched defiantly. He realized, when he considered the position honestly, that his friends weren't urging him to rest in order to annoy him. They were doing so because they cared about him and were worried about him. And he realized that he respected their judgment enough to admit that perhaps they might be right and he might be wrong. And there were very few people who could bring Halt to admit that.

"Halt, you need to rest," Will said. "If you'll just stop being stubborn and admit it, we'll make better time in the long run. Stay here for a day, get your strength back. Horace and I can push on ahead and scout the situation. If you're right, Tennyson will have set up at these caves. So there's no rush anymore to catch up with him."

Will's tone was reasonable, not argumentative, and he saw from Halt's body language that he was on the brink of giving in. Seeing that he needed just one more mental shove, Will provided it, invoking the ultimate authority in the bearded Ranger's world.

"You know Lady Pauline would agree with me," he said.

Halt's head jerked up at the name. "Pauline? What does she have to do with this situation?"

Will held his gaze steadily. "If you continue the way you are, I'll have to go back and face her and tell her I failed in the task she set me."

Halt opened his mouth to reply, but words failed him. He closed his mouth again, realizing how foolish he must look. Will seized the opportunity to continue.

"And if you continue like this and run yourself into the ground, I'm not going to have the nerve to face her."

Halt considered that statement and slowly nodded. He could understand Will's sentiments there.

"No," he said thoughtfully, "I shouldn't imagine you would." Then, to Malcolm's surprise, Halt slowly dismounted.

"Well," he said mildly, "perhaps I should rest up for a day or so. I wouldn't want to overdo things." He looked around, saw a small grove of trees a few meters away from the track they had been following and nodded toward them. "I suppose that's as good a place to camp as any."

Will and Horace exchanged relieved glances. Before Halt could change his mind, they dismounted and began to set up camp. Halt, now that he had given in to their concerns, decided he might as well take advantage of the situation. He found a fallen tree and sat down by it, resting his back against it and letting out a small sigh.

"I'll start getting my strength back straight away," he told them, a satisfied smile on his face.

Horace shook his head as he and Will began to gather stones for a fireplace.

"Even when he gives in, he has to have the last word, doesn't he?" he said.

Will smiled in reply. "Every time." But he felt a sense of relief that Halt was willing to stop pushing himself to the limit.

Malcolm, on the other hand, was intrigued to learn more about the person whose name could bring Halt to such a state of meek compliance. He sidled up to Will as the young man was unstrapping his camping equipment from Tug's saddle.

"This Lady Pauline," he began, "she must be a fearful person. She sounds like a terrible sorceress." His face was deadpan, but Will sensed the underlying amusement and replied in kind.

"She's very slim and beautiful. But she has amazing power. Some time ago, she persuaded Halt to have a haircut for their wedding."

Malcolm, who had noticed Halt's decidedly slapdash hair styling, raised his eyebrows.

"A sorceress indeed."

44

THERE WERE STILL SOME HOURS OF DAYLIGHT LEFT FOR TRAVEL. So after a quick meal, Will and Horace remounted and pushed on after the Outsiders.

Sensing that in the days to come he would have a need for concealment, Horace was now eager to experiment with the camouflage cloak that Halt had given him. From time to time, when they were passing small clumps of trees or bushes, Horace would rein in Kicker beside them, pull his cowl forward, wrap the cloak around himself and attempt to sit without any movement.

"Can you see me now?" he would ask.

Sighing, Will would pretend to search for him, thinking that his friend, the foremost knight in the Kingdom of Araluen, a warrior who would be feared and respected on any battlefield, was behaving like an overgrown child with a new toy.

"I can just make you out," he would say through gritted teeth.

Somewhere around the eighth or ninth time that the grinning Horace asked the same question, Will's patience finally gave out.

"Horace," he said wearily, "you're sitting on top of a great big brown battlehorse. It's nearly two meters high and three meters long and it weighs a quarter of a ton. Of course I can see you."

Horace looked crestfallen. "But if Kicker weren't here? Could you see me then?"

"A little hard to answer, Horace," Will said. "Because Kicker *is* there and it's hard to ignore him. He sort of draws the eye, and that goes against the whole concept of camouflage and concealment, you see."

"Couldn't you use your imagination?"

"You want me to imagine Kicker isn't here?" Will asked him.

"That's right," Horace replied, determined not to be put off by the sarcasm in Will's voice. "If he wasn't here, could you see me then?"

There was a long silence between them.

"Let's push on for a few more hours before we stop for the night," Will said. He thought the wisest course was to ignore Horace's question. Horace shrugged agreeably.

"Suits me," he said. Then he added as an afterthought, "Are you sure you won't lose track of me? I could just disappear in the dark . . ."

"I'll do my best," Will said.

Just for a moment, he wished his friend *would* disappear.

That night they had a cold camp and rose at dawn to continue. They were drawing closer to their quarry now—assuming that the cave complex was Tennyson's planned destination. Horace abandoned his light-hearted attempts at concealment and became far more businesslike in his approach.

It occured to Will, as it had to Halt in recent times, that Horace might well have been engaging in a subtle piece of leg-pulling with all his "Can you see me now?" antics. Horace had years of leg-pulling and practical jokes to make up for, and Will had the uncomfortable suspicion that the tall warrior had been secretly chuckling to himself the day before.

The ground began to rise now as they found themselves heading for the line of hills. The trees were fewer and farther between, and they moved carefully, conscious that there could be hidden watchers observing their approach.

But there was no sign that they had been seen, and eventually the ground leveled out into a plateau, leading to the foot of the hills proper. The trees grew more thickly there and the two friends reined in, concealed by the shadows of a large grove, surveying the open ground that remained before them. Just a few hundred meters distant, the hills rose into the sky, steep and forbidding, a natural barrier. There was no sign of Tennyson or any of his followers.

"Nobody here," Horace muttered.

"Nobody we can see," Will amended. He was peering closely at the base of the hills. The sun was sinking in the west, and even though it threw direct light on the hills, the irregular folds of the sandstone created patches of light and shade, and several darker patches could well have marked the entrance to caves. Or they could have been just deeper shadows.

Will had a sudden concern that Tennyson hadn't stopped here after all. That he had continued, maybe climbing the hills through some as-yet-unseen pass, and was now heading away on the far side of the ranges.

Yet, reason told him, the Outsiders leader could have done that at any time in the past few weeks. He had headed specifically for this range, where, according to the map, there was a large number of caves. If he'd wanted to simply disappear into the east, he could have done so without the difficulty of having to find a way over the hills.

And now that he could see them, Will realized they were closer to cliffs than hills and that finding a way across them would be difficult indeed.

Horace nudged him with his elbow. "Smell that?"

Will raised his head and sniffed the air experimentally. He caught the very slightest scent of wood smoke on the air. It was faint, but it was definitely there.

"They're here all right. They're starting to get dinner ready," Horace said.

"But where?" Will asked, scanning the cliff faces once more. Then Horace touched his arm and pointed.

"Look," he said. "There's a tree growing at an angle from the face of the cliff—about ten meters up." He waited until Will nodded that he could see it. Then he held his hand out at arm's length, squinting with one eye closed, and held up first one finger, then two, vertically.

Then he folded the second finger down again. "To the left of the tree, about one and a half fingers, there's a cleft. In the rock."

Will mimicked the action of holding the fingers up and sighting down them. It was a simple but effective way of providing directions, and he soon saw the cleft Horace had spotted.

A thin gray ribbon of smoke issued from it. The faint breeze grabbed it almost immediately, and dissipated it. But it was there. And so, he realized, was Tennyson.

"They're in the caves," he said, and Horace nodded.

"We're going to have to get closer to take a look," Will said, scanning the ground in front of them. There was plenty of low cover, but not enough to conceal Tug and Kicker. "We'll have to leave the horses here and push forward."

"You're planning to go into the caves?" Horace said, his voice very level. Will glanced at him. Since they had been small children,

Horace had disliked confined spaces. It was one of the reasons that he never wore a full face helmet, preferring the simple cone-shaped cap. When they were younger, Will had used the fact to escape him on numerous occasions.

"I'll need you to keep an eye on things outside," he said, and he saw Horace's shoulders slump in relief.

"You're sure?" he asked. "I'll come with you if you really need me."

Will reached over and squeezed his shoulder. "I appreciate the offer," he said. "But it'll be easier for me to move around inside without being seen."

"All right then," Horace said. "I can't say I'm disappointed."

"Besides," Will couldn't resist saying, "with your newfound camouflage skills, I'd probably lose you in there."

45

They waited until late afternoon. Will knew the light was more uncertain and deceptive at that time. Then, leaving Tug and Kicker in the grove of trees, they stole forward. Horace was wearing the camouflage cloak, and Will gave him some last-minute instructions.

"Keep the cowl up so your face is shaded," he said. "When we stop, lie perfectly still, keeping the cloak around you. Halt's old saying used to be *trust the cloak*. It'll conceal you."

"What about my legs and feet?" Horace asked. As he was a good deal taller than Halt, more of his legs were exposed below the cloak. Will shook his head in a dismissive gesture.

"Don't worry about them. The cloak will conceal your body and people don't expect to see disembodied legs lying around. They see what they expect to see."

Horace grinned. "Is that more of Halt's wisdom?"

Will grinned in return, nodding.

"One other thing," Will reminded him. It was something the tall warrior had heard before, but it always bore repeating. "If we're moving and someone appears, just freeze. Stand perfectly still. It's the movement—"

"—that attracts attention and gets you seen." Horace finished the statement. "I know."

"So long as you do. The temptation to try to hide is almost irresistible in that situation."

They moved forward, Will taking the lead and slipping silently and almost invisibly through the uncertain light. He dropped behind an outcrop of rocks some thirty meters away from the trees and signaled Horace to follow. He watched the warrior for a few meters, then turned his attention to the hills ahead. Tennyson didn't seem to have any guards in place. But that didn't mean they weren't concealed somewhere. A part of his mind was impressed with the progress that Horace was making with his silent movement. He still made a certain amount of noise, of course. It took years of training to achieve the level of silence with which a Ranger could move. But he was surprisingly quiet, and Will doubted that any casual listener in the vicinity would have realized that someone was moving through the grass. Horace slowly lowered himself into cover beside him. Will glanced at the face inside the folds of the cowl. He could feel the tension in Horace's body. The young warrior was concentrating fiercely on moving with minimal noise and visibility. Too fiercely, in fact.

"Relax a little. There's a tendency to make more noise if you're all tensed up," Will told him in a lowered voice. "You're doing fine. You're definitely getting the hang of this."

He saw the brief flash of Horace's teeth, bared in a grin of pleasure.

"Think I'd make a Ranger?" he asked.

Will snorted derisively. "Don't get ahead of yourself," he said. Then he gestured toward the hills ahead of them. "Come on."

Moving carefully, in short increments, it took them more than half an hour to reach the base of the hills. There, they found a jumble of rocks—sandstone mainly—which had fallen from higher up the slopes. There was plenty of cover and they settled in a cleft between two boulders, looking around to spot the entrance to one of the caves.

"See anything?" Will asked.

Horace shook his head. "No. But I can still smell that smoke."

They both looked up to the spot where they had seen smoke issuing from a cleft in the rocks. Now they could see nothing. But Horace was right. The smell of wood smoke was still strong on the evening air.

Will surveyed the rocks and open ground around them. There was no sign of any human habitation. Finally, he leaned closer to Horace and whispered, "You stay here and keep an eye on things. I'll see if I can find a way in."

Horace nodded. He settled himself between two large boulders, placing himself so that he had a good field of vision yet stayed relatively concealed himself. His hand went to the sword at his side but he left it undrawn. If he needed it, he could have it out and ready in a heartbeat. Yet if he drew it now, the gleaming blade might reflect the dull light and give his position away.

Will ghosted forward until he reached the base of the cliffs. Flattening himself against the almost sheer rock, he edged along laterally. A large buttress of sandstone jutted out and he slid around it, disappearing from view for a few seconds. Then he reappeared, signaling to Horace, pointing to the rock face on the other side of the outcrop. His meaning was clear. He had found an opening. He was going inside.

Horace waved that he understood and Will disappeared again, walking soft-footed around the sandstone outcrop.

The opening was well concealed, all but invisible until you were almost upon it. It was barely a body width wide, nothing more than a slit in the rock, but on closer inspection, Will saw that it ran deeper.

He turned sideways and slipped through the cleft. His quiver snagged momentarily on the rough rock at his back and he had to wriggle it free. Then he continued.

Horace would have loved this, he thought. It was pitch dark, and the narrow, constricting passage twisted like a snake so that the walls seemed to bear down upon him. He fought back a moment of panic, understanding for the first time in his life how such a place could unnerve his friend. He inched forward, beginning to fear that this was a false trail and the narrow gap would eventually peter out, leading nowhere. Then, rounding a final right angle, he found himself in a larger open space—about the size of a bedchamber. The ceiling of the cave was high, and light came through several clefts high in the wall. It was the last light of day and only faint, yet after the total darkness of the passage he had just traversed, it was a welcome change.

He hesitated at the entrance, taking stock of his surroundings. There was no sign of anyone here, and the light was too dim for him to inspect the sandy floor for footprints. He toyed with the idea of lighting a torch, but decided against it. The darkness was his protection, his friend, his shield. In these stygian conditions, the sudden bright flare of a flint on steel might well be noticeable for hundreds of meters.

He stepped out into the open space. His eyes were of little use in this dimness, so he reached out around him with his other senses: his hearing, his sense of smell and that peculiar sixth sense that he had been trained to develop and listen to—an instinctive awareness of the space around him and the possible presence of other people in it that had alerted him so many times in the past to potential danger.

The air was surprisingly fresh. He had expected it to be dank and earthy here inside the rocks. But then, of course, the clefts that provided light would also ensure that the cave was well ventilated. He turned around, slowly, describing a full circle. His eyes were closed as he sought to concentrate on his other senses.

He heard voices.

Many voices, in a low rising and falling pattern that could be only one thing. Chanting. They came from the far wall of the cavern and he crossed quickly to it, feeling his way along until his fingers discovered another cleft. This one was lower, barely a meter and a half in height. He bent and slipped through it, once again in darkness, reaching ahead and upward and crabbing forward in a half crouch. Gradually, the ceiling became higher and he could walk upright— his outstretched hand above him touching only empty air.

This tunnel ran relatively straight, without the twists and turns of the first. And after the first few meters, it widened out into a comfortable thoroughfare.

At least, he assumed it did. He stayed touching the wall of rock and stretched his hand out into the darkness, searching for the far wall. He encountered nothing.

The muffled sound of chanting, which had continued as he progressed through the darkness, gradually became stronger and louder, then suddenly stopped. Instinctively, he stopped as well. Had he made some noise? Had he alerted the chanters? Did they suddenly realize that he was here?

Then a single voice began to speak. He couldn't make out the words; they were muffled and distorted by the rock. But he could hear the timbre and pitch and cadence of the voice. It was the voice of a trained speaker, an orator accustomed to swaying his listeners to his own point of view.

He'd heard the voice before. It was Tennyson.

He sighed with relief.

"So you're here after all," he said softly into the darkness.

He edged forward again and the voice became more distinct. Now he was able to make out individual words. One in particular he heard repeated over and over: *Alseiass.*

Alseiass, the false Golden God of the Outsiders.

Now Tennyson seemed to be asking the crowd questions. His voice would rise in an interrogative tone and there would be a pause and then an answering roar from the crowd. And although Tennyson's questions weren't yet decipherable, the answering roar from the crowd definitely was.

"Alseiass!" they cried in answer to his every question.

The tunnel Will was following veered slightly to the right, and as he rounded an elbow in the wall, he saw something ahead.

A glimmer of light.

He moved forward more quickly, his soft boots making no sound on the sand underfoot. Ten more meters and the light was stronger with each pace.

Then he reached the opening. And before him, in the light of fifty or more torches, he saw the man they had been pursuing for the past month. White robed, burly and with long, gray hair, he stood on a natural rock platform in the massive cavern that had opened out from the narrow tunnel. Around him were grouped about twenty followers, also dressed in white. And beyond them were close to a hundred people—men, women and children, mostly dressed in rough homespun country clothing, all listening with rapt attention to the words that came from the prophet's mouth. And as Will watched, he heard, and this time understood, the question that the fake prophet was posing to his new followers.

"Who will lead us out of the darkness? Who will take us to a new golden age of friendship and prosperity? Tell me his name."

And the reply came from more than a hundred voices, young and old.

"Alseiass!"

Will shook his head sadly. The same old rigmarole. The same old mumbo jumbo. But people were just as willing to buy it here as they had been in Hibernia. People were gullible, he thought, particularly when they were told they could buy their way to happiness.

"You know, my friends, that times were bad before Alseiass came among you."

There was a murmur of agreement from the crowd.

"Your animals were dying or disappearing. Your homesteads were burned and leveled. Isn't that true?"

The crowd called out their confirmation of his words. So, thought Will, the Outsiders have had their armed brigands operating in this area as well—no doubt long before Tennyson arrived.

"But since you have taken Alseiass as your god, have these attacks stopped?"

"Yes!" cried the crowd. Some embellished the shout with cries of "Bless Alseiass!" and "Praise the Golden God!"

"And is it time we gave thanks to Alseiass? Is it time we built him the golden, jeweled altar that he desires—an altar that you can worship at for generations to come?"

"Yes!" cried the crowd. This time, at the prospect of donating gold and other valuables, there was a little less enthusiasm. But the white robes around Tennyson added their voices to the cry.

Except, Will thought to himself, that altar will be covered with a thin veneer of gold, and when you move on, the rest of it will go with you.

But Tennyson's congregation didn't seem aware of that fact. Spurred on by the white robes, and by Tennyson himself, they continued to raise their voices until the massive cavern rang with their cries of praise for Alseiass and his priest, Tennyson.

Time to leave, Will thought. He'd seen all this before.

46

"The entrance is hard to find," Will said. "That's why they don't need guards outside."

He sketched with a pointed stick in the dirt beside the fireplace. Halt, Horace and Malcolm were gathered around him, watching carefully as he explained the layout of Tennyson's new headquarters.

"That first entry tunnel leads to this: a cavern about the size of a small room. High ceilinged, well lit and ventilated. But completely bare."

"So, even if someone finds that entrance, they can still get this far and think this is all there is to it?" Malcolm put in.

Will nodded. "That's why there are no guards. The entrance to the second tunnel is well hidden—and it's barely more than waist high."

"More fun for me," Horace said heavily.

Will flashed him a smile. "It's not so bad. It stays low for a few meters and then it widens out and the ceiling gets higher. Plenty of room in this tunnel, once you're past the first few meters."

"It's those first few meters that are the problem," Horace said. He looked at Malcolm hopefully. "Don't you have a potion that will cure my hatred of confined spaces?"

Malcolm shook his head. "Sadly, no. But it's a very understandable affliction. I think the cure for it is to face the fear and overcome it."

Horace nodded gloomily. "How did I know you were going to say that? What good is a healer if he can't give you a potion for the really important things?"

Halt gestured to the map drawn in the dirt, signaling for Will to get back to his briefing.

Will nodded and continued. "The tunnel veers to the right here—that's where I saw their lights—and opens out into the cathedral."

"The cathedral?" Halt said sardonically. "Are you getting carried away with Tennyson's religious fervor, Will?"

Will grinned. "It seemed like a good name for it, Halt. It's easily the size of a small cathedral. I can call it the Great Hall if you'd rather," he added. Halt didn't answer. Will hadn't expected him to.

"And how many people in all?" Halt asked.

"Counting twenty of Tennyson's white robes . . ."

"His white robes? Who are they?" Malcolm interrupted.

"They're his bullyboys and collectors," Will explained. "His henchmen, if you like, the ones who are in on the secret." Malcolm signaled his understanding and indicated for Will to proceed. "Counting them, there's close to one hundred and twenty, I'd say. Plus there's obviously one of the bandit gangs operating in the area."

Halt chewed on a twig for a few seconds. "The outlaws can wait," he said. "Our first priority is to discredit Tennyson in front of these new converts and then to take care of him and his henchmen."

"How do you propose doing that?" Malcolm asked. He looked at the three determined faces before him.

There were only three of them. And Will had said at least twenty of Tennyson's henchmen were still with him.

"There will probably be violence involved," Halt said with deceptive mildness in his voice.

"Three against twenty?" Malcolm queried, pushing the matter.

Halt shrugged. "Few, if any, of those twenty will be trained warriors. They'll mostly be thugs, used to killing from behind and terrorizing unarmed farmers. It's amazing how those people melt away when they face people who know one end of a weapon from the other."

Malcolm wasn't completely convinced. But then, he thought, he'd seen Will and Horace in action at the storming of Castle Macindaw, where the two of them had forced their way to the top of the walls and held out against the garrison until their own men could scale the ladders and join them. Maybe they could handle twenty roughnecks.

Horace, watching him, saw the doubt in his eyes. "There's an old saying, Malcolm," he said. "*One riot, one Ranger.* Do you understand?"

"I assume it means that in the event of a riot or disturbance, all it takes is one Ranger to restore order?" Malcolm said.

Horace nodded. "Exactly. Well, looking around, I see we have twice as many Rangers as we need here. So I imagine I'll be able to have a little vacation while they take care of matters."

Halt and Will both snorted disdainfully and he smiled at them. "I'll be happy to sit back and watch you both do all the work," he added.

"In other words, it'll be business as usual?" Will asked.

Horace looked a little hurt. He'd left himself open for that, he realized. Then he became more serious.

"Halt, I've been thinking . . ." He paused, looking expectantly at the two Rangers. "Aren't you going to say *always a dangerous thing?*" he asked.

Halt and Will exchanged a glance, then shook their heads. "No. You're expecting it. It's no fun when you're expecting it," Will told him.

Horace shrugged, disappointed. He'd had a snappy comeback ready for them. Now he'd have to save it for another time.

"Oh, well, anyway, it occurred to me that you want to discredit Tennyson, not just take him prisoner and march him off to Castle Araluen, right?"

Halt nodded. "That's important. We have to destroy his myth. What do you have in mind?"

"Well, I thought it might help if he was confronted by the spirit of King Ferris."

Halt considered the idea. Tennyson had never realized that on the first occasion when "Ferris" had challenged and defied him, he was actually facing Halt, disguised as his twin brother. And on other occasions when he had seen the Ranger, his features had been obscured by the deep cowl he wore.

"Not a bad idea, Horace," he said. "Tennyson deals in hocus-pocus and trickery. If we serve up some of the same, it might throw him off balance. And he might just be surprised into some sort of damning admission."

He fingered his beard, which had grown back in the weeks that had passed since Horace had shaved it to resemble his twin's.

"Pity," he said. "I was just getting used to having my beard back in its usual condition."

"Scruffy," Will said before he could stop himself. Halt turned a withering gaze on him.

"I prefer to think *luxuriant*," he said with considerable dignity.

Will hurried to agree. "Of course. That's the word I was looking for. I don't know why I ever said *scruffy*."

And he managed to say it with such a straight face that Halt couldn't help knowing that, inside, Will was holding his sides with laughter.

47

THE FOLLOWING DAY, BEFORE THEY BROKE CAMP AND SET OUT, Malcolm insisted on giving Halt a complete physical examination.

"Let's make sure you're up to all this exertion," he said. "Take off your shirt and sit down here." He indicated a fallen log that was close to the fireplace.

"Of course I'm up to it," Halt told him briskly. But then he realized he'd met his match when it came to stubbornness. The healer stepped back and drew himself to his full height. Because he was a little shorter than Halt, who wasn't the tallest person in the Kingdom, this, of itself, didn't amount to a great deal. But his air of authority added immensely to his stature.

"Look here," he said severely, "your former apprentice dragged me across league after league of wild country, on a half-mad horse in the middle of the night, to come here and save your miserable, ungrateful hide. Which I did, without complaint or hesitation.

"Now I intend to finish the job I started—and not let *you* finish the job the Genovesan started. So I intend to give you a complete check-over now to make sure you're fit again—and up to the relatively minor task of confronting a hundred-odd enemies with just two people to back you up. Is that perfectly all right with you?"

When he put it that way, Halt had to admit that he had a point. And he knew he owed the birdlike man his life. Still, it went against the grain for Halt to submit meekly to anyone's orders—as King Duncan had discovered on several occasions. He threw out one last challenge.

"And if it's not all right with me?" he said belligerently. But Malcolm matched his attitude, stepping forward so that his face was only a few centimeters from the Ranger's.

"Then I'll ask Will to report the fact to this Lady Pauline I've heard so much about," he said. He was rewarded by a quick flicker of doubt in Halt's eyes.

"And I'll do it," Will called from the other side of the campsite, where he had been sitting quietly for several minutes enjoying the clash of wills between these two stubborn men.

"Well, I suppose you might as well . . . ," Halt said, and stripping off his shirt, he straddled the log. Malcolm began his examination, peering into his throat and eyes and ears, tapping him on the inside of the elbows with a soft wood mallet, placing a hollow tube with a bell-shaped end against his back and chest and putting his ear to the other end.

"What's that for?" Horace asked. He had moved closer as Malcolm went to work and now stood a few paces away, watching with interest, in spite of Halt's growing irritation.

"It's none of your business," the Ranger growled warningly. But Horace was not to be deterred.

"What can you hear?" he asked Malcolm. The healer hid a smile as he answered.

"His heart and lungs."

Horace made a small moue of interest. "Really? What do they sound like?"

"It's none of his business what my heart and lungs sound like," Halt began.

But Malcolm was already beckoning Horace forward. "Have a listen for yourself."

Halt reflected on how difficult it was to retain dignity and authority when someone else was poking and probing and tapping and you were sitting, half dressed, on a log. He glared at Horace but the young warrior ignored him. Stepping forward eagerly, Horace held the end of the tube in his ear, bending to put the large end against Halt's back. His eyes widened as he listened.

"That's amazing!" he said. "Is that *boompa boompa boompa* sound his heartbeat?"

"Yes," Malcolm said, smiling. Like most people, he enjoyed showing off his expertise in his chosen field. "It's very strong and regular."

"I'll say it is!" Horace was impressed both by Malcolm's medical knowledge and the sheer volume of Halt's heartbeat when it was amplified by the tube. "You're like a regular bass drum in there, Halt."

"How kind of you to say so," Halt said, a sour expression on his face. But Horace was still eager to quiz Malcolm further.

"And what about that great, rushing, *hoooooooosh-hoooooosh* sound? It's vaguely like a draft horse breaking wind."

"That's his lungs. His breathing," Malcolm replied. "Again, quite healthy—although that's an original description of the sound, I must say. Haven't seen that in any of my medical texts."

"Let me have another listen!" Horace said, and he bent once more toward Halt's back. But the angry Ranger twisted around on the log to confront him.

"Get away from me! Listen to your own heart and lungs if you must!"

Horace shrugged apologetically, showing him the straight listening tube. "That's a little difficult, Halt. I'd have to twist my head right around behind my back to do that."

Halt smiled evilly at him.

"I'm sure I could manage that for you," he said.

Horace regarded him for a moment, trying to ascertain if he were joking. He decided that he wasn't totally sure, so he stepped away, handing the tube to Malcolm. "Might be best if you continue," he said.

Malcolm took the tube back and continued with his examination. Fifteen minutes later, he announced that he was satisfied.

"You're strong as a horse," he told Halt.

The Ranger glared back at him. "And you're stubborn as a mule."

Malcolm shrugged. "People do say that," he replied without taking offense.

Horace, who had withdrawn to watch the rest of the examination, now stood and moved forward as Halt pulled his shirt over his head again. The Ranger looked up at him, still less than pleased with him.

"What do you want?" he asked belligerently. "My heart and lungs have been put away for the day, I'm afraid." But Horace pointed to Halt's face.

"The beard," he said. "If you decide to impersonate Ferris again, you'll need a shave."

"Which I can attend to myself," Halt told him. "But if you want to make yourself useful while I'm doing so, get a few strips of leather and plait a headband like the one Ferris wore."

Horace nodded and, while Halt fetched hot water and trimmed his regrowing beard back to a semblance of Ferris's more subdued version, Horace found some leather thongs in his pack and plaited them together, creating a reasonable facsimile of the simple royal crown of Clonmel.

Halt was rinsing the lather from his face when he noticed Malcolm carefully packing a small box with a dozen irregular-shaped balls of what appeared to be dried brown mud.

"Are they more of those whizbangs you were playing with?" he asked.

The healer nodded. He didn't look up from his task, and Halt, stepping closer, could see that he had the box packed with bundles of cut grass, which he used to keep the mud balls separated. The tip of Malcolm's tongue protruded through his teeth as he concentrated on his work.

"What do they do, exactly?" Halt asked.

The final ball packed carefully in the grass, Malcolm looked up. "If I throw one on the ground," he explained, "it will create a loud bang and a thick cloud of yellow-brown smoke. They're very volatile. That's why I need to pack them so carefully."

"And what do you plan on doing with them?" Halt asked.

"I thought they might come in handy if you need a diversion. They won't actually injure anyone . . ." He hesitated, then amended that thought. "Well, aside from setting their ears ringing. They're just noise and smoke makers."

Halt grunted thoughtfully but said nothing more. He was beginning to see a possible use for the noisemakers.

Finally, with their preparations complete, they struck camp and moved forward, closer to the range of cliffs where Tennyson had gone to ground—literally. They left the horses well back in the grove of trees that Horace and Will had discovered the previous day, then crept forward to observe the caves.

"Now what?" Malcolm asked.

"We wait and watch," Halt told him. Malcolm took the hint and settled down, finding himself a comfortable vantage point from which to watch the comings and goings at the cliffs.

Not that there was much to see. A group of four men left the cave in the late morning, returning several hours later burdened down by the carcass of a deer.

"Hunting party," Horace said.

Both Halt and Will looked at him sarcastically.

"You think?" Will asked. "Maybe they found the deer and brought him back to repair him."

"I was only *saying* . . . ," Horace began. But Halt silenced him.

"Then don't," he said.

Horace muttered to himself. One of the trials involved in traveling with Rangers was times like these. Halt and Will seemed to have boundless reserves of patience, never finding it necessary to lighten the passing hours with idle chatter. Horace didn't think there was any harm in making the occasional remark, even if it wasn't absolutely necessary. Or enlightening. It was just . . . making conversation, that was all.

"And stop muttering," Halt said. Scowling, Horace obeyed.

In the early afternoon, half a dozen people, four men and two women, emerged from the caves, blinking in the sunlight and shading their eyes with their hands. They didn't seem to have any real purpose in emerging.

"What are they up to?" Will asked softly.

Horace was about to reply, "Probably getting fresh air" when he remembered Halt's curt orders from several hours back. He clamped his jaw shut and said nothing.

"Probably just getting a breath of fresh air," Halt said.

Horace glared at him. It wasn't fair, he thought.

The small group stayed outside in the sunshine for half an hour, then retreated once more inside the cave. Horace, who had been watching the upper reaches of the cliff, noticed a small ribbon of smoke trickling out of the cleft in the rock once more. He mentioned it to Halt.

"Hmm . . . well spotted. Could be starting to get the evening meal together." He turned to Will. "When you were in Tennyson's camp, what was his schedule for prayer meetings?"

"Morning and late afternoon," Will replied promptly. "After the second one, they'd usually have dinner."

"So, assuming he hasn't changed his schedule, they might be getting ready for a little bit of hymn-singing and 'hand over your money' any time now."

Will nodded. "That'd be my guess."

Halt looked at his three companions.

"Let's get ready to join them, shall we? I'd hate to miss the sermon."

48

Will led the way, slipping around the rock buttress and into the narrow entrance to the cave system. The others waited for him outside the entrance. After several minutes, he reappeared, beckoning them forward.

"The first chamber is empty," he reported. "I can hear them in the inner chamber. Sounds like they're chanting."

Halt waved him forward. "Lead the way."

Will disappeared into the narrow slit in the rock face once more. Halt followed, giving him a few seconds to get ahead, then Horace started after him. Before he entered the cave, Malcolm laid a hand on his arm to stop him.

"Horace," he said, "this might help if you feel a little panicky."

He handed the warrior a small canvas packet. Horace opened it and looked at the contents, puzzled. It appeared to be a small pile of rotten bark, covered in some kind of greenish fungus. He sniffed it experimentally. It was decidedly earthy to smell.

"It's moss, mixed with a kind of fungus," Malcolm explained. "It occurs naturally on trees throughout the north. But it glows in the dark. It'll give you a little light. Just enough for you to get your bearings, but not enough to be seen farther down the tunnel. Just unwrap it if you need it."

"Thanks, Malcolm," Horace told him, and turning sideways, he squeezed his way through the narrow entry to the tunnel. He was a good deal larger than Halt and Will, and it took a little effort for him to force his way through. He had to draw in his chest and hold his breath, but finally, he made it.

For the first few meters, there was enough light from the entrance to keep him oriented. But after the tunnel began to twist and turn, it became darker, and he felt the old familiar sense of panic as he imagined the blackness around him squeezing in on him. In his mind, the darkness was a solid thing, like the rock itself, and he began to fantasize that it was crushing him, holding him in a gradually tightening vise so that he couldn't breathe. His heart began to race as he stared around him, seeing nothing. His chest was tightening, and then he realized that, in his nervousness, he had actually neglected to breathe. He drew in a deep shuddering breath.

From a few meters away, he heard Malcolm's soft whisper. "Open the packet."

Remarkable, Horace thought. The panic had been so complete that he had forgotten the packet Malcolm had given him only a few minutes before. He felt for the cover and flipped it open.

A soft, green light glowed from the center of the packet. It was dim, but after the total, impenetrable blackness, it was more than enough to let him see the rough walls of rock only a few centimeters from his face. Instantly, his breathing eased and he felt his heart rate relax a little. He still wasn't happy about being in a confined space, but it was infinitely better than being in a totally dark, confined space.

"What's that?" Halt's voice said out of the darkness ahead of him.

Then Horace could make out the dim shape of the Ranger's face reflected in the green light. He was only a meter or so away.

"Malcolm gave it to me," he explained. He heard Malcolm close up on the other side of him.

"It's not bright enough to be seen past the next bend in the tunnel," the healer said.

"You're probably right," Halt agreed. "Regular bundle of tricks, aren't you?" But he knew of Horace's aversion to confined, dark spaces and realized the small green, glowing bundle wasn't posing any risk. "All right, Horace. I'll go ahead. If you hear me click my fingers, it means I can see you coming. Cover it up as soon as you hear it."

And with that, he melted away into the darkness again. Horace gave him a few seconds' start and followed on. In spite of his best efforts, his footsteps grated in the sand underfoot and his belt and scabbard tended to scrape against the rocks at his back. When they reached the first chamber, he decided, he'd take them off and carry them. There would be less chance of their snagging that way. He rounded another outcrop in the rock and realized he could see a dim gray light ahead. He covered the glowing bark and put the package away inside his jacket. The light grew stronger until he emerged into the chamber Will had described.

Shafts of light from the late afternoon sun struck through the clefts set high in the walls of the chamber. Horace breathed in deeply. The smaller of the two caverns wasn't the sort of place he would choose to spend time in. But it was a lot less constricting and challenging than the narrow, black tunnel he had just passed through.

Will and Halt had moved to the inner wall of the chamber and were crouched, listening. As Malcolm emerged from the tunnel in his turn, he and Horace moved across to stand beside the Rangers. Horace could see the small, low-level entrance to the next part of the tunnel. He set his jaw in a tight line. He wasn't going to like going through there, luminous bark or no luminous bark. Will glanced up, saw his pale face and grinned encouragingly.

"All right so far?" he asked.

Horace tried to grin in return, but he knew it was a feeble effort. "Loving it."

Then Halt hushed them both with an impatient gesture, bending closer to the mouth of the second tunnel.

"Listen," he said, and they all gathered more closely around him. They could hear the faintest suggestion of a voice carrying down the tunnel. It was too faint to discern words, but they could hear the rise and fall of the cadence of the speech. Then the sound stopped and a fraction of a second later, a louder sound could be heard. This time it was recognizable. It was the sound of a large group of voices, responding to that first lone voice. They still couldn't make out the words—the echo created by the twists and turns in the tunnel and the muffling effect of the solid rock itself saw to that. But the enthusiasm and energy behind the response was unmistakable.

"Fanatics," Halt said. "Don't you just love 'em?" He glanced up at Will and jerked his head toward the tunnel.

"See what they're up to," he said. Will nodded briefly. He crouched and disappeared into the black mouth of the tunnel.

Horace unconsciously felt inside his jacket for the package of luminous bark. Then, remembering his previous thought, he unbuckled his sword, wrapping the belt itself around the scabbard. Halt glanced up at him, saw the action and nodded.

"Good idea," he said. He unslung his quiver from over his shoulder. For a second or two, he debated whether to unstring his bow. It would be easier to carry that way and less cumbersome in the confined space of the tunnel. But the thought of emerging unarmed at the far end was not one that held any appeal.

It was ten minutes before Will's face reappeared at the entrance. He grinned up at them.

"All clear," he said. Then he scrambled out and stood erect. "There's no guard in the tunnel or at the entrance," he told them. "Tennyson has an altar at the far end of the cavern and all the faithful are in a half circle, facing him."

"And not the tunnel?" Halt said, a satisfied note in his voice.

Will nodded. "We'll come out behind them, and at a forty-five-degree angle to the way they're facing. Nobody will be looking in our direction. Even Tennyson will find it hard to see us. His end of the cavern is lit up by candles, torches and a large fire. We'll be more or less in darkness. And there are plenty of rocks to provide cover for us."

The voices were discernible again as Tennyson began another sequence of question and answer with the crowd. It was all too familiar to Horace, Halt and Will. They'd heard it before. Malcolm, whom they had apprised about Tennyson's operating methods, could guess pretty accurately what was being said in the cavern. As Halt had said, it would be a version of *praise Alseiass and hand over your money*. Although, the healer thought with a wry smile, perhaps a little less blatant.

"All right," Halt said. "Let's get going. Lead the way again, Will. And Horace, the minute you see light at the end of the tunnel, cover up that moss of yours."

Horace nodded. Halt bent and disappeared into the low entrance. The tall warrior took several deep breaths, preparing himself. He felt a light touch on his arm.

"I'll be right behind you," Malcolm said. "Let me know if you're in trouble."

The healer had personal knowledge of Horace's courage, and he knew this fear of dark, confined spaces had nothing to do with phys-

ical bravery. It was something locked deep in Horace's mind—
perhaps some incident in early childhood that he had long forgotten.
Knowing this, he recognized the real courage that Horace was showing in overcoming his fear.

"I'll be fine," the young warrior said, his face set in tight lines.
Then he relaxed and grinned ruefully. "Well, maybe not fine," he admitted. "But I'll manage."

Holding his sword in one hand, he reached into his jacket for the
canvas packet and then ducked down and shuffled forward into the
tunnel.

After the brief period in the dim light of the cavern, the darkness
of the tunnel seemed overwhelming once more. He reached up with
his scabbarded sword, tracing the roofline above him. Then, as it
receded out of reach, he stood slowly erect. Once again, he felt the
terrifying sensation of blindness, the feeling that his world had been
reduced to his own personal space, with nothing beyond it. The fear
that his eyes no longer functioned. His heart began thumping more
rapidly once again, and he flipped back the cover on the luminous moss, seeing that wonderful little glow of light nestled in the
palm of his hand. Behind him, he heard Malcolm shuffling along the
tunnel.

Calmed by the little light source, Horace continued down the
tunnel, moving with greater assurance now that the darkness wasn't
total. He glanced up several times, but the dim glow from the moss
wasn't sufficient to reach the ceiling high above him. It was swallowed by the blackness. Rounding another twist in the tunnel, he
became aware of a dim gray light ahead. Quickly, he covered the
moss and made his way around one last corner of rock. Light
seemed to pour in from the large cavern as he approached the end of
the tunnel, where Will and Halt crouched, surveying the scene before them.

As Will had told them, the cavern was the size of a small cathedral, with a high, soaring roof that disappeared into the darkness above it. The far end of the high cavern was a blaze of light, where torches and candles were set in brackets. In the middle of the floor was a vast fireplace, and the leaping flames from this cast shadows on the walls. Beyond the fire, and lit by what appeared to be scores of torches and candles, was an altar. It was the usual Outsiders' altar, built in gold and silver and decorated with precious gems. Yet if this one ran true to form, the gold was a thin veneer over wood and the silver and gems were fake. The real items would be safely stowed in Tennyson's packs.

Tennyson was in full flight, arms thrown wide, as he delivered an impassioned appeal to the assembly.

"Alseiass loves you!" he intoned. "Alseiass wants to bring light and joy and happiness into your lives."

"Praise Alseiass!" the congregation cried.

"You say the words!" Tennyson told them. "But are your hearts sincere? For Alseiass hears prayers only from those who believe. Do you truly believe?"

"Yes!" the crowd replied.

Malcolm, his mouth close to Horace's ear, whispered, "More to the point, do people really fall for this claptrap?"

Horace nodded. "It never ceases to amaze me how gullible people can be."

"There's danger in this land!" Tennyson continued. His voice now was full of foreboding. "Danger and death and destruction. Who can save you from this danger?"

"Alseiass!" the crowd roared. Tennyson threw his head back now and looked up above them all, into the dark recesses of the ceiling of the cavern.

"Show us a sign!" he asked. "Show us a sign, Golden Alseiass, god of light, that you hear the voices of these people before you!"

Malcolm eased forward a little to get a better view. He had spent years devising signs and manifestations in the depths of Grimsdell Wood—signs such as the one Tennyson was now asking for from his nonexistent god.

"This ought to be good," he said.

49

Watching the fake preacher, Will noticed that, as he called for Alseiass to show a sign to the congregation, he glanced up at the jumble of rocks at the rear of the cavern—to a spot some twenty meters from the tunnel entrance where Will and the others crouched, concealed by the shadows.

Following the direction of his eyes now, Will saw a flicker of movement. Then there was the dull gleam of reflected light among the rocks and he made out the figure of a man there, hidden by the rocks from the worshippers below him.

He nudged Halt and pointed. As the older Ranger looked, a sudden ball of light seemed to sweep across the cavern's walls behind the altar where Tennyson was standing. There was a quick, collective gasp of surprise from those among the crowd who had noticed it, then a low buzz of excited conversation.

Then the flash of light traveled across the cavern again, this time in the opposite direction. As it reached a spot behind Tennyson, it described three flashing circles, then darted away again and disappeared. This time, alerted, more of the crowd saw it and there was a louder reaction. Tennyson let it die down a little and then raised his voice to speak over the excited muttering.

"Alseiass is the god of light and enlightenment!" he intoned. "His light of mercy can be seen even in the darkest reaches of the earth. Do you see his light?"

Led by the white robes, the crowd took up the cry again. "Praise to Alseiass! Praise the god of light!"

Halt beckoned Will closer and put his mouth near Will's ear to speak.

"He's got a helper up there with a mirror and a lantern," he whispered. "He's reflecting the lantern light on the walls."

Will shook his head. "Pretty basic trick," he commented.

"It's working. They can all 'see the light.'" He gestured to the pile of rocks where the man was sheltered. "Get up there and take care of him. Quietly."

Will started to move away, then he hesitated and turned back. "You want me to knock him out?"

Halt answered brusquely, wondering what the delay was about. "No. I want you to invite him to dinner. Of course I want you to knock him out! Use your strikers."

Will shrugged unhappily. "I don't have them. Lend me yours?"

Halt couldn't believe his ears. He hissed angrily at Will, alarming Horace and Malcolm, who were sure he would be overheard.

"What do you mean *you don't have them?* They're part of your kit, for god's sake!" He couldn't believe that Will, a fully qualified Ranger, could be so undisciplined as to forget his strikers. Young people, he thought, shaking his head. What was the world coming to?

"I lost them," Will said. He didn't add that he had lost them trying to capture Bacari alive, to save Halt's life. But he thought the older Ranger was being unduly harsh under the circumstances.

"You lost them? You *lost* them?" Halt repeated. "D'you think we issue valuable equipment so you can just lose it?"

Will shook his head. "No. But I . . ."

He didn't get any further. Horace interrupted their discussion, an incredulous look on his face.

"Will you two stop blithering on?" he demanded in a fierce whisper. "Any minute now, someone will hear you and the fat will really be in the fire!"

Halt glared at him for a moment and then realized he was right. He thrust his hand into an inside pocket and retrieved one of his own strikers, which he shoved into Will's hand.

"Here. Take this! And don't lose it!"

On the altar, Tennyson was again exhorting the crowd to call upon Alseiass to show them another sign. There was a quick flash of light across the cave, followed by more cries of surprise and wonder. Watching carefully, Halt could see Will's dark shape climbing the rock pile, seeming to flow upward across the jumble of boulders like a giant spider. He reached the spot where Tennyson's helper crouched with his lantern and mirror and paused, concealed from the man, a meter or so below his hiding place.

"Show us your light again, Alseiass!" Tennyson cried. "Let these people know they are worthy of you!"

Halt saw the crouching figure at the lantern move slightly, preparing to send another flash of light across the cavern. Then Will rose behind him. The young Ranger's arm went up, then down as he crashed the brass striker into the man's head, behind the ear. Tennyson's disciple slumped forward without a sound. Will turned to Halt and gave him a thumbs-up. Halt waved acknowledgment and then gestured for Will to remain where he was. It was a good tactical position, with a clear overview of the cavern but concealed from those below him.

"Alseiass!" Tennyson called, a little louder and with a slight edge to his voice. "Let us see your light!"

Hidden among the rocks, Will raised the polished metal mirror the man had been using as a reflector and pointed to it, looking interrogatively at Halt. Did the senior Ranger want him to send light flashing across the cavern? the gesture said. Halt shook his head. He had another idea in mind, and this seemed to be a perfect opportunity to put it into effect.

"Alseiass! We need to see your light!" Tennyson called. It was more of a command than a prayer, Halt thought. The people in the congregation were beginning to look restless.

Halt leaned close to Malcolm and indicated a large boulder a few meters away on their left.

"I'm going to move over to that boulder," he said. "When I call out to Tennyson, lob one of your mud balls in front of me." Malcolm nodded his understanding. He crouched, gingerly set the wooden case down and opened the lid. Halt slid through the shadows to the boulder he had indicated. Malcolm took one of the balls out of the case, closed the lid and stood upright again. He made eye contact with Halt and the Ranger nodded to him. Malcolm saw Halt discard his cloak and don the leather circlet that Horace had made up—a replica of the simple crown of Clonmel. Using his fingers, he roughly combed his hair to either side, parting it in the middle and holding it in place with the leather loop.

Malcolm readied the ball for an underarm toss. At that moment, Tennyson chose to implore Alseiass once more.

"Alseiass! Show us a sign, we beg you!"

Halt took a deep breath, then shouted in a voice that rang through the cavern, waking the echoes.

"Tennyson! Tennyson! You are a fake and a liar!"

Heads turned, seeking the source of the words. As they did, Malcolm tossed the ball underarm, lobbing it high in the air to land on the spot just in front of Halt. The sand covering the cavern floor was relatively soft. But the ball came down from a considerable height and, as Malcolm had pointed out, it was extremely volatile.

There was a loud BANG! followed by a giant cloud of yellow-brown smoke. A trickle of sand and pebbles, loosened by the vibrations set up by the explosion, slithered down from the ceiling of the cave.

Then Halt stepped forward, passing through the cloud, and people gasped as he appeared to materialize out of the smoke.

"Tennyson! Your god is false. And you are a liar!"

Tennyson was completely startled by this turn of events. He peered through the smoky interior of the cavern to see the slight figure standing at the rear of the cave. He took in the hair, parted in the middle, held back from the face by the simple leather circlet, and the neatly trimmed beard. Suddenly, with a rush of fear, he knew who this was.

"You!" he cried before he could stop himself. "But you're dead! I k—" He stopped just a little too late.

"You killed me?" said the figure. "Yes, you did. But I've come back. And I want my revenge."

"No!" Tennyson cried, holding up one hand as if to ward off the apparition before him. Taken by surprise, he was completely un-nerved by the sight of the man he had believed to be dead. He *knew* to be dead.

"Say my name, Tennyson. Say my name and I may spare you," Halt demanded.

"It can't be you!" Tennyson shouted. But the doubt was obvious in his voice. Aside from one brief meeting, he had never seen Halt at close quarters, and then the Ranger's hair and beard had been long and unkempt. But he knew Ferris when he saw him, and the voice, with its distinctive Hibernian accent, was instantly recognizable.

And he knew Ferris was dead. The Genovesan assassin had assured him of the fact. He had shot Ferris from behind, with a poisoned crossbow bolt. There was no possibility that the King could have survived. Yet here he was, calling for revenge. And there was only one way that could have happened. Ferris had returned from beyond the grave.

Halt moved forward, forcing his way through the assembled worshippers. They moved back from him, clearing a path as they sensed Tennyson's uncertainty and fear.

"Say my name!" Halt demanded. As he advanced, Tennyson drew back a few paces. He glanced desperately at one of his white robes, a heavily built thug armed with a spiked mace.

"Stop him!" he cried, his voice breaking in fear.

His henchman started forward, the mace rising in his right hand. Then his face contorted with pain as his right leg collapsed underneath him. The weapon dropped from his hand as he fell awkwardly to the sand, clutching at the arrow that had suddenly appeared in his thigh.

"Good boy, Will," Halt muttered to himself. The people around him whispered fearfully and drew back farther. In the dim light of the cavern, none of them had seen the arrow in flight. And only a few of them could see it now. All they knew was that the white robe had suddenly been struck down in agony. Tennyson saw the arrow and now he knew a new fear. The next one could well be aimed at him. And he knew that those mysterious cloaked archers who had dogged his steps from Dun Kilty and through Celtica very rarely missed their target.

"Ferris?" he said uncertainly. "Please . . . I didn't . . ."

Whatever he was about to say, he didn't get the chance to finish. Halt stopped and threw his arms wide.

"You want to stop me, Tennyson? Then ask Alseiass to do it. I'm a ghost. He's a god. Surely he outranks me." His voice was heavy with sarcasm. "So come on! Let's ask Alseiass to stop me in my tracks. Ask him to smite me with lightning! Go ahead!"

Tennyson could do no such thing, of course. He hesitated, looking to his white robes. But they weren't eager to come forward, having seen their companion struck down by an arrow out of the darkness. In addition, those who had followed Tennyson from Hibernia had seen Ferris before, and surely this was him, standing before them in the cavern, challenging Tennyson.

"You won't ask him?" Halt said. "Well, I'll do it for you! Come on, Alseiass! You're a fake and a fraud and you don't exist! Prove me wrong and strike me down!"

A frightened ripple ran through the crowd, and those nearest Halt shrank back farther, half fearful that Alseiass might in fact strike him with a bolt of lightning. But, as nothing happened, as there was no answer to his blasphemous challenge, they began to look suspiciously toward the prophet who had come among them preaching the word of Alseiass.

They began to mutter among themselves. The atmosphere in the cavern was suddenly thick with suspicion. Sensing that the moment was right, Halt addressed them directly now, turning his back on the heavyset figure at the altar.

"If Alseiass is real, let him strike me now! Let him show his power. Tennyson has told you that Alseiass can protect you from the bandits who are attacking your homes and villages. How can he do that if he can't even answer a simple challenge like this?" He looked up at the roof of the cavern. "Come on, Alseiass! Let's hear from you! Strike me down! Flash your light at me! Do something! Anything!"

An expectant hush fell over the people in the cavern. They waited, but nothing happened. Finally, Halt shook his head and looked around the people watching him. He dropped the thick

Hibernian brogue he had been using and spoke in his normal voice.

"People of Araluen, you've seen for yourself that this so-called god has no real power. That's because he isn't a real god. He's a fake. And that man," he said, jerking a thumb in Tennyson's direction, "is a fraud and a thief and a murderer. He murdered the King of Hibernia, King Ferris, who, coincidentally, looks a lot like me. You heard him call me Ferris. You saw how terrified he was when he thought that I was Ferris, back from the grave. Why would he feel that way if he hadn't been the one who killed Ferris?"

Tennyson, who had been cowering before what he believed to be a ghost, slowly drew himself up, leaning forward to look more closely, realizing finally that he had been tricked. He could see that Halt's words were reaching the people gathered in the cavern, slowly turning them against him.

"He's told you that he's here to protect you from the bandits who are raiding in this area. He hasn't told you that those bandits are actually working hand in glove with him. And he's asked you for gold and jewelry to build his altar, hasn't he?"

He looked at the faces around him. Heads nodded in confirmation. Then the confusion and doubt on their faces slowly began to give way to suspicion and anger.

"Take a closer look at that altar and you'll find it's plain wood, coated with a thin layer of gold. And the jewels are fake. The real gold and jewels are in Tennyson's saddlebags, ready for the day when he and his friends slip away with them."

"He's lying!" Tennyson suddenly found his voice. The stranger had admitted that he was no ghost, and Tennyson's confidence began to return. He knew he could sway a mob when it came to a contest of words. After all, this person was a nobody, a nonentity.

"He's lying! Alseiass has protected you! You know that! Now this stranger comes among you and blasphemes the god and accuses me. You know me. You know Alseiass. But who is he? A stranger. A wanderer. A vagabond!"

"A King's Ranger," Halt interrupted, and there was a further buzz of interest from the crowd.

He reached into his shirt and pulled out the silver oakleaf on its chain, showing it to the people closest to him. They craned forward to look and then confirmed the fact to those farther away.

Tennyson watched the reaction, puzzled. But this wasn't Hibernia, where Rangers were unknown and had no status. This was Araluen, where everyone knew of the Ranger Corps. In Araluen, some people might be nervous around Rangers. But everyone respected them and knew they were the principal protectors of the King's peace.

"My name is Halt," Halt continued, raising his voice. If the news that he was a Ranger had caused a stir, the name Halt had a more far-reaching effect. Halt was famous throughout the Kingdom. He was a legend. Those who had pulled back from him when he first challenged Alseiass now began to crowd in to get a closer look at him.

Halt decided to up the ante a little. He pointed to the jumble of rocks where Will was concealed.

"And up there is another Ranger you may have heard of. Will Treaty."

Heads turned and Will rose slowly from his position in the rocks. They could see the well-known Ranger cloak and cowl and the unmistakable longbow, favored weapon of the Ranger Corps. He pushed the cowl back now so they could see his face in the dim light.

If people had shown interest at Halt's name, it was redoubled when he mentioned Will. They weren't all that far from Macindaw, where Will had defeated a Scotti invasion. Halt might be a national legend, but Will Treaty was a local hero.

"We've been trailing this man," Halt indicated Tennyson once more, "for months. He murdered King Ferris, King of Clonmel. He stole from the people of Hibernia and he fled to Picta. Now he's here to steal from you—he and his cohorts who were here before him. Chances are they've already killed friends and neighbors of yours."

Again, there was an angry reaction from the crowd. People had been killed by the bandit group that worked in parallel with the Outsiders cult. Now those present began to realize who had really been responsible.

"You've been tricked," Halt told them after the angry muttering had died down. "And we're here to take Tennyson and his gang into custody. But first, I wanted to prove to you that Tennyson is a fraud and that Alseiass, the god he pretends to worship, is a fake. If you choose to stand by him, well and good. But if not, I'll give you this chance to leave now. Turn your back on him and get out."

50

For a moment there was silence in the vast cavern. Then one of the crowd called out.

"What about our gold?"

There was a chorus of assent from the others. They might be prepared to walk away from the false religion they had embraced. But their gold and jewels were another matter. Halt held his hands up for silence.

"You'll have a chance to get it back," he told them. "But right now you have to make a decision. You've been fooled by this man. But stupidity isn't a crime. Go now and there'll be no further consequences. Stay and we'll consider you part of his gang."

He pointed to the tunnel leading out of the cavern. There was another long pause, and then two people began to make their way toward it. They were followed by three more. Then another man on his own. And slowly, the trickle of people leaving the cavern became a flood.

Tennyson, watching, couldn't believe his luck. The stranger was letting them go. And in doing so, he was giving Tennyson and his men an advantage. Against a hundred or so angry country people, they would have stood no chance. But now he had twenty men and they were faced by only three—four if you counted the small monk-like figure he could now make out at the rear of the cavern. He gestured to his men to wait. And he backed up a few paces to the wall behind him. There was another exit he knew about, but the secret was shared by only a few of his followers. The access to it was high above him, where a tunnel led off from a ledge on the wall.

Once the local people had left, he would order his men to attack. In the confusion, he'd climb quickly to the ledge, go through the tunnel and emerge at the top of the cliffs, free to move on and start again. He'd have to abandon most of the loot they had taken from the local countryside. But he'd stashed a bag of gold and a selection of the more valuable jewels in the tunnel, against such an eventuality as this one. It would be enough for him to escape and start up again somewhere else, far away from here. Perhaps this time he'd head for Gallica. There was no real law and order in that disorganized country. A man could do very well for himself there, he thought.

The last of the local people were making their way out of the cavern now. Halt watched them go. He'd wanted to get them out of the way. He knew Tennyson wouldn't go quietly, and with the cave full of people, it would be difficult to tell friend from foe. Besides, as he had said, these people were fools, not criminals, and he didn't want to see any of them injured or killed. Now, he thought, it might be time to pare down the odds even further. He looked at the row of white robes facing him. They were all armed, he saw. A few had swords or maces. Most carried clubs and daggers. There might be a few real fighters among them, he thought, but the majority would be nothing more than thugs. He was confident that he, Horace and Will could handle them relatively easily.

"My argument isn't with any of you either," he said. "I want Tennyson, that's all. Any of you who choose to leave now can go freely."

He saw a few of the white robes exchanging uncertain glances. They'd be Araluens, he thought, people who knew that tangling with two Rangers might not be the best idea in the world. Tennyson's Hibernian followers stood fast.

But before any of his followers could desert him, Tennyson's voice rose in a high-pitched screech.

"Do you think he'll just let you go?" he challenged them. "He'll hunt you down once you're out of here. There's only one thing to do. We've got them outnumbered! An old man and two boys! Kill them! Kill them!"

And as his voice reached a peak of urgency, the tension broke and the white robes surged forward in a bunch, weapons raised.

Quickly, Halt retreated before their first rush, drawing his saxe to deflect a dagger thrust, then slashing the razor edge across his attacker's forearm. The man yelled in pain and dropped out of the fight, nursing his bloodied arm. But there were others behind him and Halt continued to back away. He had drawn his smaller knife now as well. He blocked a man's sword cut with his saxe, stepped in and rammed the short knife home. Halt saw the man's eyes glaze as his knees slowly gave way. But there was no time to see any more. Another attacker was pressing him, and there were two more on his right. He turned to face the new attack.

Then there was space around him as Horace leapt to his aid, his sword flashing in the uncertain light of candles and fire like a giant blazing wheel of light. He cut down three attackers in the space of a few seconds. A fourth staggered away, clutching at the shaft of an arrow that protruded from his chest. Will again, Halt thought.

The white robes drew back to take stock. They had lost nearly a quarter of their number in that first mad rush. Clubs and daggers were no match for Horace's sword, and even those among them with swords had no real weapon skill. And the Ranger with the two knives was as fast as a striking snake.

Then one, bolder or angrier than the others, stepped forward, waving at them to follow.

"Come on! There's only . . ."

A deafening BANG! drowned out his words and a vast cloud of yellow-brown smoke billowed up right before him. He staggered back in panic. Another loud detonation and another dense cloud of smoke followed as Malcolm hurled a second mud ball at the group of men. They fell back, crying out in fear.

Then the first man stopped, shaking his head. The explosion had happened right at his feet, barely a meter away. Yet, apart from a ringing in his ears and the sour smell of the smoke, he was uninjured. The missiles, whatever they were, were harmless.

"They can't hurt you!" he yelled. "They're just noise and smoke! Come on!"

He led the way forward, but only a few of the others went with him. The rest huddled uncertainly, disoriented by the deafening explosions and the whirling smoke.

Perched on the rocks, Will stood ready to pick off any of the white robes who might pose a threat to Halt and Horace. His instincts cried out for him to scramble down the rocks and join them, but reason told him he would be more use to them up here.

Besides, he could see that the bulk of the white robes were no longer interested in the fight. They were cowed, huddled together in a group, backing slowly away from Halt and Horace. Something rattled against the boulder beside him, then a thin trickle of sand fell from the ceiling of the cavern, lost in the darkness above him. He had noticed this happening with each of the explosions. The mud balls might be harmless, but the noise set up vibrations in the cavern and sent loose rocks and sand falling from the walls and roof.

There was a louder noise of falling rocks now, and a small cascade tumbled down from the roof in the center of the cavern, falling close to the group of dispirited white robes. Will hoped that Malcolm would be a little more circumspect with the explosive balls. The roof seemed to be decidedly unstable. Too much vibration and they could be in trouble. It wouldn't take a lot to . . .

Where was Tennyson?

The thought struck him out of nowhere. He looked wildly around the cavern. He wasn't with the small group left facing Halt and Horace. He'd been by the altar when Will had last seen him, when he called on his followers to attack. But he . . .

There! There was a robed figure climbing the far wall, behind the altar. He was nearly six meters from the floor of the cave already. Above Tennyson, Will saw a ledge and the black mouth of another tunnel just a few meters away from the desperately climbing figure. There was no doubt that he was heading for it.

And there was no doubt in Will's mind that the tunnel was an alternative route out of the cavern. In a few more minutes, Tennyson would reach it and he'd be gone.

He nocked an arrow, drew and shot. But the uncertain, flickering firelight, coupled with the roiling brown smoke that filled the cavern, made it almost impossible to shoot accurately. The arrow struck sparks off the rock half a meter above Tennyson and screeched off into the darkness. Galvanized by the sight and sound of it, Tennyson quickly moved sideways, into the cover of a vertical buttress that protruded from the wall. Will could see only occasional glimpses of him as he continued to climb—not enough to get away an accurate shot. When he reached the ledge, Will would have a second to aim and shoot again. But the flickering light and clouds of smoke would make an accurate shot almost impossible. And if he missed, Tennyson would escape.

He hesitated. Then he was bounding down the rocks to the floor of the cavern, racing across the cleared ground to the boulder where Malcolm was perched, his padded box of mud balls at his feet. Will scrambled up beside him. He had time to register that now there were only three attackers facing Halt and Horace, and as he did so, he saw the three men throw down their weapons and call for quarter.

But across the cavern, Tennyson was escaping.

He reached down and grabbed the box of explosive mud balls from Malcolm, glancing into it to see how many there were.

Malcolm had started with a dozen and had used three. Like Will, he had noticed the effect the noise vibrations were having on the cavern and decided it was too risky to continue with them. Besides, Horace and Halt were taking care of things quite admirably, he thought. Now he watched, aghast, as Will seized the box containing nine more mud balls and drew his arm back.

"Will! Don't!" he cried. "You'll bring down the . . ."

He got no further. The young Ranger brought his arm forward and sent the box spinning across the cavern. Instinctively, Malcolm fell into a crouch and covered his ears with his hands. The violent movement involved in throwing the box could be enough to rattle the mud balls together and detonate them.

But the box, spinning slowly, sailed across the vast cavern, reaching almost halfway to the altar before it sank to hit the sandy floor. It skipped, bouncing into the air again, then toppled and hit the ground again, this time on one corner.

In the instant before the cavern filled with the massive eruption of noise and smoke, Will saw Tennyson emerge onto the ledge lead-ing to the escape tunnel. The false prophet glanced back once at the scene on the cavern floor.

Then the earth shook beneath their feet and thunder filled the cavern. Rocks and earth fell from the ceiling in ever-increasing amounts. Small landslides started in the jumbled rocks that lined the sides of the cave, rapidly growing in size and violence. A gigantic pil-lar of brownish yellow smoke shot up. Just before it obscured the far wall, Will saw a massive rock shaken loose from the wall above the ledge where Tennyson stood. It hit beside him, barely a meter away. Instinctively, the preacher recoiled, stepping back onto empty air and toppling slowly off the ledge. He smashed against the jagged rocks at the base of the wall and Will had one final glimpse of his broken, lifeless body.

Then he was hidden from sight by the billowing masses of brown smoke.

Rocks were falling faster and in increasingly greater numbers now, and the sand trickle had become a dozen cascades in differ-ent parts of the cavern. There was no doubt. The walls and roof were coming down and they had only seconds to get clear. Will grabbed Malcolm's arm and dragged him down from the perch on the boulder.

"Come on!" he yelled.

Malcolm was frozen momentarily. He stared at the falling rubble and tumbling showers of sand. "Are you mad?" he asked, and Will shoved him roughly toward the tunnel entrance.

"Yes! Now get the hell out of here!" Will yelled, and finally, the healer started toward the exit. Satisfied that he was moving, Will ran back to where Halt and Horace still stood, facing the defeated white robes, barring their way to the tunnel. Tennyson's followers, already subdued and demoralized, were now totally disoriented as well by the terrifying sequence of events they had just witnessed.

"Come on!" Will shouted. He grabbed Horace's arm, dragging him along with him. "Halt! We've got to get out now!"

Horace was moving with him, but Halt hesitated.

"Tennyson?" he queried, but Will beckoned him urgently.

"He's finished! I saw him fall. Come *on*, Halt!"

Still Halt lingered. But then an entire section of roof gave way and came crashing down in a cloud of dust and sand, adding to the masses of brown smoke, and his decision was made. He turned and ran for the tunnel entrance.

In a fatal mistake, the surviving white robes ran in the opposite direction, disappearing into the swirling dust and smoke.

Will, with Horace in tow, reached the tunnel entrance. For a moment, the tall warrior balked at the dark hole, but Will dragged him forward.

"I'm with you!" he said, and he felt Horace's resistance disappear as he followed his friend into the stygian darkness of the tunnel. A shadow filled the entrance as Halt came behind them.

For Horace, the tunnel was even worse than before. The whole space echoed with the thunder of falling rocks and crashing landslides. He could feel the terrifying vibrations in the ground under his feet and in the walls as he brushed against them. And now the tunnel was filling with clouds of choking dust. He couldn't see the dust in the total darkness, but it rasped in his throat and nose and set him coughing helplessly. The darkness, the noise, the choking dust—they were all parts of his worst dreams, and he was close to losing control. But Will's grip was firm on his arm and he fought back the panic, following his friend.

He felt the downward pressure on his arm and realized they

must be close to the low exit from this tunnel. He crouched, following Will, felt something bump against him from behind and after a moment of searing terror realized it was Halt.

Then the three comrades staggered, coughing violently, into the smaller cavern and the blessed relief of the dim gray light that came through the ventilation slits high in the wall. Dust billowed from the aperture they had just come through, and they moved away from it as the dust clouds began to fill the smaller cavern. Malcolm was waiting for them at the entrance to the second tunnel, gesturing feverishly for them to join him.

"Come on!" he yelled. "The whole cave system is unstable. It could all collapse at any moment!"

As if on cue, a section of the inner wall fell away and slid, crumbling into small pieces, to the floor. More dust exploded into the air.

Then it was into the darkness once more and the twisting, turning, narrow tunnel, with the sound of the earth collapsing behind them and Will's steady grip on Horace's arm to lead him. For a moment, Horace had the horrifying thought that the tunnel itself might collapse and he would be buried here inside it. But he forced it away, knowing that if he gave in to the sickening sense of panic, his limbs would freeze and he would never move from this spot.

Then the blackness around him was not quite so black and he realized he could make out the dim figure of Will, leading him, outlined against the dull gray light that came from the entrance to the tunnel.

With a moan of relief, Horace staggered out of the tunnel. Malcolm, waiting just outside, grabbed his arm and hurried him away. Will waited to make sure that Halt had followed them and when his mentor emerged from the cloud of dust, the two Rangers ran side by side, coughing and eyes streaming, till they were well clear of the cave entrance.

Wearily, the four turned to view the narrow cleft in the rock face. Dust poured from it. Then there was a huge rumble in the earth and the dust became a massive billowing cloud that jetted in a solid stream from the narrow cleft, vomiting from the high-level vents, forced out by the collapsing cave system behind it.

Halt wiped one hand across his dirt-stained face.

"Well," he said, "looks as if the Outsiders cult has finally gone underground."

Then he sank wearily to the ground. Slowly the others joined him and they sat in silence, watching the dust as it continued to billow from the tunnel. Halt rubbed his knee, aching from where he'd knocked it against a rock outcrop in their headlong, blind dash through the tunnel.

"I really am getting too old for this sort of thing."

51

They were heading north again, back to Grimsdell Wood.

It was only fair, Will thought, that they escort Malcolm home. He had been prepared to do this on his own, but Halt had announced that they would all make the trip.

"You can see Malcolm back to his forest," he said. "Horace and I have some business at Castle Macindaw." Will looked curiously at him for a few moments, not understanding. Then Halt explained.

"The outlaw band that's been working with Tennyson is still at large," he said. "They'll need to be rounded up. We'll arrange for a patrol from Macindaw to take care of it. Harrison can lead them. He's probably itching for something to do."

Harrison was the newly appointed Ranger to Norgate Fief, Will remembered. The appointment had been announced at the Gathering. He shook his head. It seemed so long since the Gathering. So much had happened in the intervening time.

They had found the horses Tennyson and his men had appropriated, grazing in a meadow close by the ruined cavern system. They took the quietest for Malcolm. As was often the case, the quietest horse was also the biggest, and the little healer perched on top of it, his legs not reaching around the barrel of the horse's body, but sticking straight out.

Before they left, Halt had addressed the ex-converts to the Outsiders cult, lecturing them on the need to be more suspicious of religious leaders who offered to solve all their problems in return for their gold. The people hung their heads and shuffled their feet in embarrassment, and he finally dismissed them to return to their farms.

"Looks like they've learned their lesson," Horace said.

Halt snorted dismissively. "Right until the next charlatan arrives and promises them heaven on earth."

Malcolm smiled at his cynicism. "You don't have a great deal of respect for your fellow man's common sense, do you?"

Halt shook his head. "I've been around too long. Greed and fear will always win out over common sense."

Malcolm nodded his agreement. His own experience bore out the truth of Halt's words. "I'm afraid you're right."

"How long before they're all back here, do you think?" Will asked. Horace looked at him, not understanding.

"What would they come back here for?"

Will grinned at him. "Their gold," he said. "It's buried under that cliff there, remember? I wager they'll be back here digging for it within a week."

Horace laughed, understanding. "That should keep them busy for the next ten years or so."

So they rode north, and several days later, they saw the solid bulk of Castle Macindaw before them, crouching astride the entry route from Picta, barring the way to the fierce northern tribes. Halt turned in his saddle to face Malcolm.

"In all the excitement," he said, "I may have forgotten something important. Thank you for saving my life," he said simply.

Malcolm smiled. "It was my pleasure," he said. "I always enjoy rubbing shoulders with legends."

But Halt wasn't going to let Malcolm pass it off so casually.

"Nonetheless, if you ever need help in any form, send for me. I'll come. You have my word on it."

Malcolm grew serious. He met Halt's steady gaze and nodded once.

"I'll remember it," he said.

The two men clasped hands in farewell. They held the grip for long seconds. Then Malcolm released Halt's hand and turned to Horace, the smile creeping back onto his face.

"As for you, Horace, try to stay out of trouble, won't you? And don't eat poor Xander out of house and home."

Xander was the steward at Macindaw, and he guarded the castle lord's supplies more keenly than a miser would hoard his gold. Horace grinned in return and shook hands.

"Thanks for everything, Malcolm. If it hadn't been for you, Will and I would never be able to face Lady Pauline again."

"I'm going to have to meet this remarkable woman one of these days," he said. "Come on then, Will. There are people waiting to see you again."

And as Halt and Horace continued north, Will and the little healer angled their horses off to the east and the dark line on the horizon that marked the beginning of Grimsdell Wood.

As they rode in under the dark canopy once more, Will marveled at Malcolm's sure sense of direction. Once they were surrounded by the tangle of trees and foliage, with no sign of the sun, Will rapidly lost his orientation. But Malcolm pressed on, and in a surprisingly short space of time, they emerged into the clearing where his thatched cottage stood.

First to greet them was a black and white shape who slipped

across the clearing toward them, heavy tail sweeping back and forth. Tug whinnied a short greeting, and Will swung down from the saddle to fondle the dog's head and the soft fur under her chin and neck. She closed her eyes blissfully at his touch. A massive shadow fell over him and he glanced up.

"Hello, Trobar," he said. "You're taking good care of her. She looks wonderful."

Indeed, Shadow was sleek and glossy, and her long coat was obviously groomed regularly. Trobar smiled at the compliment to his best friend.

"We'come, Wi' Trea'y," he said, his words distorted by the deformation of his mouth and palate. Will stood and Trobar enveloped him in a bone-crushing hug. Malcolm smiled at the contrast between the slightly built Ranger and the massive Trobar.

Then more familiar faces emerged shyly from the trees around the clearing and Will greeted them all, noticing their smiles as he remembered names and events that had taken place on his previous visit. Under Trobar's direction, a table was set up in the middle of the clearing and food was prepared. An impromptu feast ensued and lasted until long after sunset. Will looked around at these happy, welcoming people. They had been rejected by the world outside because of their infirmities or the fact that their bodies were deformed. Because they were *different*, he thought. But really, that was a falsehood. These people were no different from anyone else.

Eventually, exhausted by the feast and the days of travel, he took himself off to bed in the spare room in Malcolm's cabin. As he drifted off to sleep, he could hear the distant hooting of an owl somewhere in the forest and the soft whisper of the wind in the trees.

He bade farewell to Malcolm early the following morning, before too many of the inhabitants of Healer's Clearing were up and moving.

"You know how much I owe you," he said. "I want to thank you not just for what you did, but for the way you did it."

Malcolm frowned, not quite understanding, so Will elaborated.

"I arrived here unannounced, asking for help for a friend miles away. You didn't ask questions. You didn't hesitate. You packed your things and came with me."

The frown disappeared. "We're friends," Malcolm said simply. "That's what friends do for each other."

"Just remember what Halt said. If you ever need help . . ."

"I'll send for the two of you." Malcolm embraced Will quickly. "Good luck, Will. Travel safely. I'd say stay out of trouble, but I doubt you'll ever do that."

Will stepped back. He always felt awkward at farewells. He turned toward Tug, saddled and ready to go. But a voice stopped him.

"Wi' Trea'y!"

It was Trobar, standing on the far side of the clearing. He was beckoning to Will. Malcolm smiled at some secret knowledge.

"I think Trobar has something to show you," he said. Will started across the clearing toward the giant. Something was amiss, he thought, then realized what it was. There was no sign of Shadow, who usually never let Trobar out of her sight.

As Will drew closer, Trobar turned and led him in under the trees. A few meters inside the tree line, a low hut stood. Will realized this was where Trobar slept. Off to one side was a smaller structure, barely a meter high, with a large opening facing them. Trobar gestured toward it and Will went down on his knees to peer inside.

Shadow's blue and brown eyes looked back at him, and he saw the slow wag of her tail. Then he saw other movement as well and made out four small black and white shapes tumbling around her, climbing over her, fastening their needle-sharp teeth on any loose part of her flesh they could find.

"Puppies!" he said in delight. "She's had puppies!"

Trobar grinned at him and reached one giant hand into the kennel. Gently pushing the others aside, he took hold of one and lifted her, yipping in excitement, out of the kennel. Shadow watched him carefully as he held the little ball of black and white fluff out to Will.

"Pi' o' the li'er," he said, and for a moment Will frowned, trying to decipher the words. Then he had it. When he had left Shadow with Trobar, he had told the giant, "If she ever has pups, I want the pick of the litter."

"Pick of the litter?" he translated now, and Trobar beamed, holding the squirming little shape out to him.

"For you, Wi' Trea'y."

He took the pup, who immediately fastened her teeth on the ball of his thumb, growling and yipping alternately. He studied her. She was still covered in soft puppy fur, and her tail, which would later become a bushy, slow-sweeping extension of her body, was now a narrow, whip-shaped affair, with a white tip at the end. She glared up at him and he laughed in delight as he saw that she had inherited her mother's eyes—one blue, one brown. The blue eye had a peculiar, manic look to it. He smoothed the fur on her head and she stopped worrying at his thumb. The whip tail went back and forth in pleasure.

"She's beautiful!" he said. "Thanks, Trobar. Thank you so much." He grinned down at the struggling little pup. "I wonder what I should call her," he mused.

"Eb'ny," Trobar said firmly. "Her na' i' Eb'ny."

Again Will frowned as he tried to interpret the word. Then he had it.

"Ebony," he said, and Trobar grinned confirmation. "That's a good name. I like it."

Then Trobar, still grinning, said, "Be'er tha' Bla'hy."

"Better than Blackie?" Will asked, referring to the original name he had come up with for Shadow. Trobar had been scathing about it when he renamed the dog.

Trobar nodded vigorously.

"I suppose I'll never live that down, will I?" Will asked.

"Ne'er," Trobar replied with great conviction. He smiled down at the pup, then put a massive hand on Will's shoulder.

"Ne'er," he repeated. Will raised an eyebrow at him.

"I got it the first time," he said.

52

WILL FOUND THE OTHERS WAITING FOR HIM ON THE ROAD south of Macindaw.

As the young Ranger rode up to join them, Horace couldn't help smiling when he saw the small black and white bundle perched on Will's saddlebow. He knew how much it had torn Will's heart to give Shadow away to Trobar all those months ago.

"From Trobar?" he asked, and Will nodded, grinning.

"Who else?" he said. Then he added, "Her name is Ebony."

"Good name," Halt said. "Did you pick it?"

Will shook his head. "Trobar's choice."

Horace nodded sagely. "That figures."

Will considered glaring at him but decided it wasn't worth the effort. For the first time in months, they were free of any pressing obligation.

"What do we do now?" he asked.

It was Halt who replied. "We go home." And there was a wealth of contentment in his voice as he said it.

So they turned their horses south and rode at an easy pace for home. There was no need to hurry, there were no emergencies waiting to be dealt with, so they took their time, enjoying each other's company. Horace would be heading back to Castle Araluen and they didn't know when they would see him again. So they made the most of their time together, with Halt as often as not sitting back and watching and listening to the conversation between his two young friends. They were a good pair, he thought, just as he and Crowley had been in their younger days, when the Ranger Corps had fallen on bad times and needed to be reinvigorated. He was glad to think that Will had a friend like Horace. He had a vague memory that in his delirium, he had told an imaginary Crowley that these two young men might well hold the future of Araluen in their hands. If he had said that, he thought, he had been right.

The atmosphere around the campfire each evening was lightened by the puppy. She seemed to attach herself to Tug, crouching in front of the shaggy horse, her chin on her paws and her rump high in the air, tail waving as she challenged him with a fierce growl. If Tug made the slightest move toward her, she would dart away, sidestepping and twisting furiously as she ran in a circle to escape. Then she would return to crouch before him and challenge once again, her manic blue eye fixed on the animal that towered over her.

Tug, for his part, treated the little pup with good-humored tolerance. On one occasion, Horace was convinced that he saw the horse raise an eyebrow at Ebony. The others didn't believe him, but he knew he was right.

Occasionally, she would growl and crouch in front of Abelard as well. But they noticed that she never tried it with Kicker. Small and pugnacious she might be, but border shepherds were never stupid, and she sensed that, while the smaller horses would tolerate her approaches, the battlehorse was likely to unthinkingly kick her into the middle of next week.

His name was "Kicker," after all.

On one occasion, she crouched before Tug, snarling and yipping and making little forward darting movements at the horse, who eyed her with an air of amusement. Slowly, Tug lowered his head until his muzzle was a few centimeters away from the tiny black and white face. Then he suddenly snorted, and the dog, caught by surprise, was bowled over backward in shock, scrambling to her feet and shaking herself to make sure everything was still in place and still working.

Don't annoy me, little dog, Tug seemed to say. *I know your mother.*

Later that night, making the rounds of the camp before turning in, Will found Tug lying quietly under a tree, his legs folded up beneath him. Nestled between his front upper legs was a small furry shape, its sides rising and falling as it breathed. Tug looked up as Will approached.

She's had a long day. She's tired.

All too soon, they reached the junction in the highway where Horace would branch off for Castle Araluen. They camped there, the two young men talking long into the night. As they went to turn in, Will dropped a hand on Horace's well-muscled shoulder.

"I wish we could get you assigned to Redmont," he said. "I'm sure Crowley could arrange it."

Horace allowed a smile to touch the corner of his mouth. "I'll come visit," he said. "But you know, there are some things I like about life at Castle Araluen."

Will looked at him, his head tilted a little to one side as he considered the statement.

"Like Evanlyn?"

"Maybe," Horace said, trying to sound casual. But he couldn't keep the smile from widening into a grin as he said it.

Will smiled in return. He'd long suspected that there was something special growing between Horace and the princess.

"Good for you," he said.

In the morning, they went their separate ways, and for once, as he rode away after a farewell, Will did look back as he reached the crest of a hill. He saw Horace turned in his saddle looking back at him, and they waved, then turned and rode on.

The two Rangers were spotted long before they reached Castle Redmont, and by the time they rode in under the portcullis, their horses' hooves clattering on the flagstones, a sizable crowd had gathered to greet them.

In the forefront, of course, was the bulky form of Baron Arald. But as Halt and Will swung wearily down from their saddles, the Baron grinned at them and stepped aside, bowing as he ushered two other people forward.

Both tall. Both elegant. Both clad in the white gowns that marked them as King's Couriers.

Halt stood, unmoving, as his wife approached. Normally, he was a person who avoided public display. But he felt his heart rise into his throat as he saw her now—the woman he had loved all his life. He remembered how close to death he had been as he lay on his bedroll in the north, fighting a losing battle against the Genovesan poison. He had come so close to leaving her behind. Casting aside his usual reticence, he stepped forward to meet her, swept her into his arms and kissed her for a long, long time.

"Ooooooooooooh!" went the assembled crowd.

Will, watching in no little surprise, felt a gentle hand on his arm and looked up slightly to meet Alyss's smiling eyes.

"Looks like a good idea," she said, inclining her head toward Halt and Lady Pauline. Will had to agree. He stepped forward, embraced her and kissed her. His head swam a little as she responded enthusiastically.

"Ooooooooooooh!" went the crowd again.

Finally, the two couples separated and stood back, hands joined, looking deep into each other's eyes. Baron Arald approached and cleared his throat.

"My friends! An occasion such as this deserves a speech to mark it . . ."

"Ohhhhhhhhhhh," sighed the crowd, this time with a disappointed inflection. The Baron smiled beatifically.

"But perhaps not," he concluded, and the disappointed sigh turned into a giant "Aahhhhhh" of relief. Arald might like the sound of his own voice, Will thought. But he knew how to work a crowd.

"Instead," the Baron continued, "I'll announce a welcome-home feast in the hall tonight."

And now the crowd broke out in cheers.

"Who's this?" Alyss asked, noticing a little bundle squirming in the open neck of Will's jacket.

"This is Ebony." He took the puppy out of his jacket and Alyss patted her head gently.

"Careful! She'll nip you," Will warned, but Alyss rolled her eyes at him.

"Of course she won't," she said. "She's a lady."

And true to Alyss's words, Ebony allowed herself to be patted without her usual growling and yipping and nipping. Will raised his eyebrows in surprise.

"You just have to know how to treat a lady," Alyss told him, smiling. He nodded acknowledgment and set the little dog down on the cobbles. For a moment, she stood there, feet braced, studying the scene around her. Her world was suddenly filled with a forest of legs and feet and massive beings. Her tail went down and she scuttled into the sanctuary between Tug's front hooves. Once there, the tail went up and she decided it was safe to yip at the world once more.

Tug rolled his head to one side to look down at her. Then he looked up at Will and Alyss.

You go ahead and enjoy yourselves. I'll keep an eye on her.

Baron Arald loved a good banquet. And the best ones were those when Master Chubb, the Head Chef at Castle Redmont, and Jenny, his former pupil, competed with each other to create the finest dishes. Which was why he suggested that they share the catering responsibilities for Halt and Will's welcome-home feast.

The food was magnificent, and honors were declared even between the Head Chef and his protégée. Both of them fussed over the head table, where the guests of honor sat, both offering increasingly wonderful tidbits to the two Rangers.

A succession of well-wishers filed past the table, welcoming Halt and his former apprentice home. People in Redmont were inordinately proud of their two famous Rangers. Sir Rodney, the Battlemaster, was one of the first. He immediately asked Halt for a report on Horace, his own former apprentice. He glowed with pleasure when Halt assured him that Horace had performed magnificently on their mission.

Gilan arrived halfway through the meal and was a welcome addition. He'd been the temporary Ranger for Redmont in their absence and been called away to attend to a band of highway thieves. Knowing the fief's Rangers had been sent on a mission, the thieves had begun to bother travelers on Redmont's roads. They were surprised to find that Halt's place had been taken by Gilan, an equally skilled and possibly even more energetic nemesis. Gilan had tracked them down to their lair and then led a cavalry patrol to arrest them.

It was noticeable that once Gilan joined their table, young Jenny concentrated less on offering choice food items to Halt and Will and more on presenting them to the tall, handsome Ranger.

As was always the case, Halt and Will said little about the details of their mission. They gave a brief outline to the Baron, who nodded his approval of their actions. Their final report would go to Crowley and then to the King. But people were accustomed to the usual Ranger reluctance to be in the spotlight. They were simply glad to see them home safe.

One person, of course, heard the full story of the mission from Halt's lips. Later that night, when the dining hall at Redmont was almost empty and the last guests were noisily heading for their beds, Lady Pauline beckoned to Will and drew him aside to speak privately to him. Her normally grave expression was more serious than ever, and Will realized that she had worried about her husband the whole time he had been gone.

"Halt told me what happened up there in the north, Will. He said he would have died if it hadn't been for you and Horace."

Will shifted his feet a little uncomfortably.

"The real credit should go to Malcolm, my lady," he said, and then as she raised a finger to remind him, he corrected himself. "Pauline, I mean. After all, he was the one who cured Halt."

"But you were the one who rode day and night to fetch him. And you were the one who captured that assassin so that Malcolm could discover which poison had been used. I know where the thanks are due, Will. And I thank you with all my heart."

But Will was shaking his head. He had been bothered by something ever since they had discovered that terribly infected wound on Halt's arm. It had been at the back of his mind all that time, and only now could he put it into words.

"My lady . . . Pauline, before we left, you asked me to look after him," he said, and she nodded.

"I remember."

"Well, I didn't do a very good job of it. I should have realized something was wrong. I should have looked at that wound sooner. I knew he'd been hit but I just let it go. He was behaving strangely. The signals were all there and I should have seen them. But I just wasn't thinking. I should have done something sooner. I should have . . ."

"Pauline," Will continued, trying to compose himself, "I came within an inch of failing you. I came within an inch of letting Halt down."

So young to feel so much responsibility, Pauline thought fondly. She knew that she and Halt would probably never have children. This young man would be their son, she thought. And she couldn't have asked for a finer one.

She touched one gentle hand to his cheek.

"But you didn't, don't you see? You didn't let him down," she said, and took his hand. "And I know you never will."

COMING SPRING 2011!

RANGER'S APPRENTICE

BOOK 10: THE EMPEROR OF NIHON-JA